MAD MONKTON

AND OTHER STORIES

WILKIE COLLINS was born in London in 1824, the elder son of a successful painter, William Collins. He left school at 17, and after an unhappy spell as a clerk in a tea broker's office, during which he wrote his first, unpublished novel, he entered Lincoln's Inn as a law student in 1846. He considered a career as a painter, but after the publication, in 1848, of his life of his father, and a novel, *Antonina*, in 1850, his future as a writer was assured. His meeting with Dickens in 1851 was perhaps the turning-point of his career. The two became collaborators, and lifelong friends. Collins contributed to Dickens's magazines *Household Words* and *All the Year Round*, and his two best-known novels, *The Woman in White* and *The Moonstone*, were first published in *All the Year Round*. Collins's private life was as complex and turbulent as his novels. He never married, but lived with a widow, Mrs Caroline Graves, from 1858 until his death. He also had three children by a younger woman, Martha Rudd, whom he kept in a separate establishment. Collins suffered from 'rheumatic gout', a form of arthritis which made him an invalid in his later years, and he became addicted to the laudanum he took to ease the pain of the illness. He died in 1889.

NORMAN PAGE is Emeritus Professor of Modern English Literature, University of Nottingham. His publications include *Wilkie Collins: The Critical Heritage* (1974) and an edition of Collins's *Man and Wife* (1995) in the Oxford World's Classics series. He is currently editing *The Oxford Reader's Companion to Thomas Hardy*.

OXFORD WORLD'S CLASSICS

For almost 100 years Oxford World's Classics have brought readers closer to the world's great literature. Now with over 700 titles—from the 4,000-year-old myths of Mesopotamia to the twentieth century's greatest novels—the series makes available lesser-known as well as celebrated writing.

The pocket-sized hardbacks of the early years contained introductions by Virginia Woolf, T. S. Eliot, Graham Greene, and other literary figures which enriched the experience of reading. Today the series is recognized for its fine scholarship and reliability in texts that span world literature, drama and poetry, religion, philosophy and politics. Each edition includes perceptive commentary and essential background information to meet the changing needs of readers.

OXFORD WORLD'S CLASSICS

WILKIE COLLINS

Mad Monkton
and Other Stories

Edited with an Introduction and Notes by
NORMAN PAGE
with the assistance of KAMAL AL–SOLAYLEE

OXFORD
UNIVERSITY PRESS

OXFORD
UNIVERSITY PRESS

Great Clarendon Street, Oxford OX2 6DP

Oxford University Press is a department of the University of Oxford.
It furthers the University's objective of excellence in research, scholarship,
and education by publishing worldwide in

Oxford New York

Athens Auckland Bangkok Bogotá Buenos Aires Calcutta
Cape Town Chennai Dar es Salaam Delhi Florence Hong Kong Istanbul
Karachi Kuala Lumpur Madrid Melbourne Mexico City Mumbai
Nairobi Paris São Paulo Singapore Taipei Tokyo Toronto Warsaw

with associated companies in Berlin Ibadan

Oxford is a registered trade mark of Oxford University Press
in the UK and in certain other countries

Published in the United States
by Oxford University Press Inc., New York

Introduction, Note on the Text, Select Bibliography, and Explanatory Notes
© Norman Page 1994
Chronology © Catherine Peters 1993

British Library Cataloguing in Publication Data

Data available

Library of Congress Cataloging in Publication Data

Collins, Wilkie, 1824–1889.
Mad Monkton and other stories / Wilkie Collins;
edited with an introduction by Norman Page,
with the assistance of Kamal Al-Solaylee.
p. cm.—(Oxford world's classics)
Includes bibliographical references.
I. Page, Norman. II. Title. III. Series.
PR4492.P34 1994 823'.8—dc20 93–10772

ISBN 0-19-283772-9

3 5 7 9 10 8 6 4 2

Printed in Great Britain by
Cox & Wyman Ltd.
Reading, Berkshire

CONTENTS

INTRODUCTION

[Since this Introduction includes references to the plots of some of the stories, readers may prefer to turn to it after reading the stories themselves.]

IT is no exaggeration to say that Wilkie Collins's status among mid-Victorian novelists has undergone a quiet revolution in the past twenty years. In 1969 the *New Cambridge Bibliography of English Literature* placed his contemporary Charles Reade in the company of Dickens, Thackeray, George Eliot, and Trollope, but consigned Collins to the small-print muster-roll of practitioners of 'minor fiction', along with Surtees, Sala, Mrs Gatty, Thomas Adolphus Trollope, and others considerably less well known. If it seemed a faintly odd discrimination at the time, it now seems inexplicable, or at least indefensible, for in barely a generation the whirligig of time has reversed their roles. Reade's work is out of print, but the number of Collins titles available in modern editions is constantly increasing, so that the present-day reader has access not only to the familiar novels of the 1860s but to earlier and later books from *Basil* (1852) to *Blind Love* (1890). Moreover, while there has been virtually no substantial biographical or critical attention paid to Reade, Collins has been the subject of a major critical biography and several full-length critical studies, as well as extended attention in other books and articles. Almost exactly a century after his death, it is now becoming possible to see his achievement as a whole and to assess the true extent of his originality and his influence. At the same time he has become for readers not merely the author of two or three classic novels whose other work has sunk without trace but a prolific writer and expert story-teller who, once launched on a narrative, is almost incapable of failing to hold his audience's attention.

Collins published not only more than twenty novels but travel books, biography, drama, a large number of essays and sketches, and numerous short stories, some of these last almost long enough to count as novellas. His stories are interesting both in their own right and as constituting small-scale explorations of themes, situations, and characters, and even small-scale experiments in techniques, that recur in his full-length fiction. Many of them also undertake another kind of experiment in exploiting, playing variations on, and even subverting sub-genres that were either established or newly emerging: for example, the Gothic tale of terror, the ghost story, and the detective story. In Collins's hands, these popular varieties of narrative can assume a subtlety that has led some anthologists and editors astray. The very titles of, for instance, 'The Dead Hand' and 'John Jago's Ghost' are calculated to deceive, and there is at least one collection of Collins's ghost stories containing items that are nothing of the kind—and that may even be described as anti-ghost stories. Even an apparently simple title like 'Mad Monkton' conceals a problem that the narrative itself will implicitly pose and ultimately decline to solve: when all is said and done, *is* Monkton mad? For Collins is a master of the open ending, the final teasing or unsettling ambiguity, as in 'The Ostler'. A Collins ending often leaves the reader in the position of having to take sides, or to declare for belief or unbelief, rather than settling the matter on his or her behalf.

Introducing an anthology of Victorian short stories in which most of the examples chosen belong to the last quarter of the century, Harold Orel has noted that both technological and educational factors conspired to help create the popular magazines that published these stories and the readership that ensured their prosperity. These factors include 'the development, after mid-century, of hot-metal composing machines that reduced costs spectacularly from those required by hand-labourers working with the screw-press, a technique that had dominated the printing industry for hundreds of years. The linotype and the autoplate multiplied production of sheets in a truly wondrous fashion. In turn, the revolution in technology (it cannot be called less) made possible the lowering of prices for mass-circulation periodicals specializing in fiction both long and short.'[1] Simultaneously, of course, the spread of literacy created a new audience for the cheap popular magazine. The beginning of Collins's career (his earliest known story appeared in 1843) coincides closely with the onset of this revolutionary phase in the development of popular literature and its mass audience. The first story included in this selection appeared in Dickens's *Household Words*—which cost twopence a week, less than a copy of *The Times*—in 1852, that magazine having come into existence only two years earlier.

Collins's career was to extend over some forty years, and the stories in this volume belong both to his earlier and to his later periods. It is worth noting that that career begins very early in the history of the English short story, as distinct both from American and Continental models and from the interpolated tale as used (for instance) by Dickens in *Pickwick Papers*. More specifically, Collins made his mark very early as a pioneer of the English detective story and scored a number of firsts even before the genre was recognized as having a distinct identity. While *The Moonstone* (1868) has repeatedly been nominated as the first English detective novel, it is worth recalling that Collins was already introducing important elements of the genre into his stories of the previous decade. A recent historian of Victorian fiction has suggested that in writing such stories of the 1850s as 'A Stolen Letter' and 'The Biter Bit', which deal with investigations conducted by professional or amateur detectives, Collins could have turned not only to the writings of Poe, much of whose best work had appeared in the 1840s (and who had died in 1849), but to such English models as De Quincey's 'The Avenger' (1836) and a series that ran in *Chambers's Journal* from 1849 to 1852 under the title 'Recollections of a Police-Officer'.[2] But by 1852 Collins's own career was launched, so that he must be regarded as belonging to the first wave of English writers to exploit this genre

[1] Harold Orel (ed.), *Victorian Short Stories: An Anthology* (London, 1987), pp. vi–vii.
[2] Alan Horsman, *The Victorian Novel* (Oxford, 1990), 213.

extensively and even as being—despite competition from
Dickens and others—the most important of them all.

As already noted, 'A Terribly Strange Bed' was the first of
Collins's contributions to *Household Words* (24 April 1852),
his acquaintance with Dickens having been formed in the
previous year. It has become the best known and most
widely anthologized of all Collins's stories, with slightly
unfortunate results for his reputation as a practitioner of
this form, since it is uncharacteristically lacking in complex-
ity. It does, however, establish what was to become a favourite pattern of setting the main narrative within a frame
—a more than usually appropriate metaphor in this instance, since the initial narrator is an artist. Confronted
with the task of painting the portrait of a sitter who seems
unable to relax, he is relieved when the sitter begins to tell
the story of an adventure that befell him in France many
years earlier. Engrossed in his story-telling, the sitter loses
his self-consciousness and the artist is able to produce a
good likeness. The story thus draws attention both to the
narrative act and to the power of narrative art.

The story depends for its effectiveness almost entirely on
the rapid and economical narrative: there is virtually no
development of character or analysis of motive, and relatively little description, though the narrator's horrified real-
ization that the bed is designed to kill him is graphically
depicted, and the narrative as a whole gains much from the
use of the first-person method. As elsewhere in Collins's
fiction, the tradition of Gothic horror tales has been transformed and domesticated, with the ensuing paradox that
appalling wickedness and ingenious crimes are shown to
exist in commonplace, even banal present-day settings. At
one point this becomes explicit: as he discovers the true
nature of the bed, the narrator reflects that it is 'in the
nineteenth century, and in the civilised capital of France'
that he has stumbled upon 'such a machine for secret murder by suffocation, as might have existed in the worst days
of the Inquisition, in the lonely Inns among the Hartz
Mountains, in the mysterious tribunals of Westphalia!' Related to this is the unconscious irony with which the nar-

rator, grappling with insomnia, reflects that 'unless I found out some method of diverting my mind, I felt certain that I was in the condition to imagine all sorts of horror, to rack my brain with foreboding of every possible and impossible danger': no flights of imagination are necessary, for the 'horror' is right there in the third-rate bedroom. But this is Paris, not the Hartz Mountains; and equally characteristically, what at first appears to be inexplicable and uncanny turns out to have a rational explanation—the 'terribly strange bed' is no more than a piece of ingenious machinery designed for a specialized purpose.

Collins said that the idea for the story was given him by an artist friend, W. S. Herrick. The French setting may owe something to Poe as well as to the French writer Eugène Sue, whose *Les Mystères de Paris* had appeared a decade earlier. Joseph Conrad's 'The Inn of the Two Witches' (1913) has some strikingly similar features, though Conrad (not always a reliable guide to his own career) denied any knowledge of Collins's story. When Collins decided to follow Dickens's lucrative example and give readings from his own work in America, he prepared a version of this story and gave a trial reading at the Olympic Theatre in London on 28 June 1873. This was extensively but not always sympathetically reviewed, some pointing out, not unfairly, that Collins lacked Dickens's vocal and dramatic powers and would be well advised to adopt a less histrionic style of reading. Later one member of the audience recalled that Collins 'seemed to think that the word "bedstead" was full of tragic meaning, and we heard again this "*bedstead*" repeated till it became almost comic . . .'.[3] In the event Collins chose different material for the American readings.

Robert Ashley has described 'A Terribly Strange Bed' as 'the most exciting short story Collins ever wrote and a first-rate story by any standard, Victorian or modern'.[4] There is surely some exaggeration here, for by the standard of psychological realism that we might apply to, say, a short

3   Percy Fitzgerald, *Memories of Charles Dickens* (London, 1913), 261.
4   Robert Ashley, *Wilkie Collins* (London, 1952), 49.

story by D. H. Lawrence or Katherine Mansfield, the tale can hardly be taken seriously. More to the point, it is considerably less subtle and suggestive than some of Collins's own later stories. As an example of pure narrative, however, it has pace and power, and the cool, almost scientific detachment of Collins's always lucid prose increases the effect.

'A Stolen Letter' was also written for *Household Words*, though it was designed to be accommodated in a more elaborate format than 'A Terribly Strange Bed'. It provides in fact a good example of Collins's knack of establishing a personal tone and style, and even of effecting important innovations, within the strict requirements of a collectively authored set of tales. Originally forming one instalment of 'The Seven Poor Travellers', which constituted the 1854 Extra Christmas Number of the magazine, it has been variously described as 'the first English . . . detective story' and as having 'a presumptive claim to recognition as the first *British* detective story'.[5] Such claims ignore the precedents of Dickens's *Bleak House* (1852–3) and Collins's own *Hide and Seek* (1854), unless the centrality or even protagonist status of the detective is insisted upon as a qualification. Whereas Dickens's Bucket is a professional, however, the sleuthing in Collins's story, as in his novel of the same year, is conducted by an eccentric amateur—the forerunner of a long line. The story indeed embodies ingredients that recur in the exploits of Sherlock Holmes, whose career does not begin until more than thirty years later: the bizarre boy-assistant, for instance, looks forward to the Baker Street Irregulars. The force of 'English' and 'British' in relation to 'A Stolen Letter' is to recognize the likely influence and certain primacy of Poe's 'The Purloined Letter'.

The vigorous and idiosyncratic manner of the narrator-protagonist is established at the outset: the down-at-heel but strong-minded ex-attorney 'absolutely decline[s] to tell

---

[5] R. V. Andrew, 'A Wilkie Collins Check-list', *English Studies in Africa*, 3 (1960), 79; Robert Ashley, 'Wilkie Collins and the Detective Story', *Nineteenth Century Fiction*, 6 (1951), 49.

you a story' but is prepared to 'make a statement' (Collins again drawing attention to the narrative act of his surrogate). He quickly creates a sense of audience ('you man in the corner there') and produces a brisk crisp narrative that relates 'a shocking secret' and includes forgery, an incriminating letter, blackmail, young lovers whose marriage is threatened, plotting and counter-plotting, spying, a cryptic memorandum to be deciphered, a surreptitious search against the clock, and a practical joke at the expense of the villain— all this in fourteen columns of Dickens's magazine. Dickens himself may conceivably have had Collins's narrator in mind a few years later in creating a figure of the same profession and with a similar rhetorical style, the Jaggers of *Great Expectations*.

'Mad Monkton', one of Collins's longest tales, illustrates a characteristic that has been referred to earlier: his gift for appropriating and then subverting the established conventions of a popular form of fiction. Superficially a Gothic tale of an ancient family living in a mouldering abbey, a family curse, a haunting, a ghastly quest, and a tragic outcome, it has a subtlety and ultimately an ambiguity that are not the usual attributes of the tale of terror. For, although we are told in the opening lines that Alfred Monkton's family 'had suffered for generations past from the horrible affliction of hereditary insanity', we find ourselves compelled to question the bold assertion of the title.

The narrator, Monkton's friend and companion in his strange adventures, is a rationalist and a sceptic who sees Monkton's behaviour as proceeding from a disordered mind. But it would be rash to accept the narrator's authority too eagerly, and by the end even he is prepared to concede that Monkton's dark imaginings have received some support from events, though he is disposed to invoke 'coincidence' as an explanation. Even quite early in the story, however, Collins drops hints that may lead the reader to question the ready assumption of Monkton's insanity. While his preoccupation with the family curse that he is seeking to elude is put down to monomania, the narrator is forced to admit that he 'talks like a sensible well-educated man' on all other topics and is 'the gentlest and most temperate of human beings'; it is even necessary to grant that 'Mad as his conduct looks to us, he may have some sensible reason for it that we cannot imagine'. Monkton himself squarely confronts the issue, telling his friend: ' "If you hear the fools at Naples talk about my being mad, don't trouble yourself to contradict them: the scandal is so contemptible that it must end by contradicting itself." '

The narrator, bluffly describing himself as 'a derider of all ghost stories' who looks at the situation from 'a practical point of view', presents throughout the case for the opposition: if not the result of madness, then Monkton's convictions—that he constantly sees the ghost of his unburied uncle, and that the family curse will destroy him if he does not find the corpse and bury it in the family vault—are ascribed to delusion or 'hypochondria'. But the implication that a good dose of salts will set things right becomes less and less convincing, since in a curious way Monkton's obsessions receive authentication. He *does* begin to see his uncle's ghost (not the malevolent phantom of the classic ghost story, but a pathetic figure demanding decent burial) before the news of his death in Italy has reached England; the body *is* found to be lying unburied; and the curse *does*, in a final twist of the plot and a thrilling climax, prove inescapable. Repeatedly the narrator's common sense is shown to be misleading and inadequate in dealing with the strangeness of life. He insists on the stubbornness of his friend's monomania: 'Whenever his dead uncle formed the subject of conversation, he still persisted—on the strength of the old prophecy, and under the influence of the apparition which he saw, or thought he saw, always—in asserting that the corpse of Stephen Monkton, wherever it was, lay yet unburied. On every other topic he deferred to me with the utmost readiness and docility; on this, he maintained his strange opinion with an obstinacy which set reason and persuasion alike at defiance.' But the arguments of 'reason and persuasion' are themselves erroneous, and events prove Monkton right in this respect. In the closing pages of the story the narratorial scepticism is still unshaken, though he

is prepared to grant that there have been 'strange coincidences':

When I reflected on the hereditary taint in his mental organisation
on that first childish fright of Stephen Monkton from which he had
never recovered, on the perilously secluded life that he had led at
the Abbey, and on his firm persuasion of the reality of the apparition by which he believed himself to be constantly followed, I
confess I despaired of shaking his superstitious faith in every word
and line of the old family prophecy. If the series of striking coincidences which appeared to attest its truth had made a strong and
lasting impression on *me* (and this was assuredly the case), how
could I wonder that they had produced the effect of absolute
conviction on *his* mind, constituted as it was? If I argued with him,
and he answered me, how could I rejoin? If he said, 'The prophecy
points at the last of the family: *I* am the last of the family. The
prophecy mentions an empty place in Wincot vault: there is such
an empty place there at this moment. On the faith of the prophecy
I told you that Stephen Monkton's body was unburied, and you
found that it was unburied'—if he said this, of what use would it
be for me to reply, 'These are only strange coincidences, after all?'

The reader, however, may find this too easy and too question-
begging a stance, and Collins's art in this story lies in creating an area of uncertainty in which, without necessarily giving
full credence to the kind of experience enacted, we may find
it difficult to dismiss it with the comforting label of 'coincidence' or the more desperate one of 'madness'.

 The horrific scene in which the narrator discovers, in-
itially through olfactory evidence, the decomposing corpse
in an outhouse of the mouldering convent—a scene that is,
by an audacious stroke, immediately followed by the comic
interview with the snuff-taking monk—is surely one of the
most truly shocking in all Victorian fiction. Putrefaction—
even human putrefaction—would not have been an unfamiliar experience to most Victorians, but writers were not
notably eager to make dramatic use of it. It was for other
reasons, however, that Dickens declined the story when it
was offered to *Household Words*: editorial caution led him to
be nervous about upsetting readers whose own families
might be afflicted by 'hereditary insanity', and he lost the

chance of publishing one of Collins's most powerful tales. At the same time Dickens recognized Collins's gifts, writing to his sub-editor, W. H. Wills: 'I think there are many things, both in the inventive and descriptive way, that he could do for us if he would like to work in our direction. And I particularly wish him to understand this, and to have every possible assurance conveyed to him that I think so, and that I should particularly like to have his aid.'[6]

Like 'Mad Monkton', 'The Ostler' is a story of monomania with an artfully inconclusive conclusion, and as in many of Collins's stories its central narrative, involving violence, terror, and the uncanny, is set within a deliberately commonplace frame. Encountering in the stable of an inn the strange and pathetic figure of the ostler, tormented by his ghastly and ever-recurring dreams, the narrator asks the landlord to recount the ostler's history. Years earlier, spending the night unexpectedly at a remote inn (that favourite locale), Isaac Scatchard has had a dream, or seen an apparition (exactly which remains unclear): a woman with a knife has tried to murder him in his bed. On reaching home, he describes his experience to his mother, who writes down his description of the woman and tells him that this has happened not only on his birthday but at the exact hour of his birth.

Seven years later Isaac meets by chance a mysterious woman whom he prevents from committing suicide, and is teased by the feeling that he has seen her before. When his mother meets her she tells Isaac that she is 'the woman of the dream', but Isaac ignores the warning and marries her. Like Stephen Blackpool's wife in Dickens's *Hard Times* (published in the previous year and in the same magazine), she turns out to be a drunkard; visiting her home, his mother notices that the woman cuts the bread with 'the knife of the dream'. Isaac's wife soon leaves him, but returns at the precise date and hour of his birth to re-enact his earlier experience by standing over his bed with the knife in her hand. He seizes the knife and she disappears, but he

[6] *The Letters of Charles Dickens*, ed. Walter Dexter (London, 1938), ii. 447.

remains in permanent dread of her return: 'Had he escaped the mortal peril which his dream foretold? or had he only received a second warning?' This ambiguity leaves the story open-ended: Isaac may, thanks to the dream-warning, have escaped 'mortal peril' once and for all—in which case the anxiety that torments him is pathetically causeless—or he may be waiting for a fate that is ineluctable, though he cannot know when the blow will fall.

There are motifs here that Collins had used before and would use again. The prophetic dream, for instance, is an important element in both *Basil* (1852) and *Armadale* (1866). The chance meeting with a mysterious woman, always a potent stimulus to Collins's imagination, recurs most famously in *The Woman in White* (1860), though Collins had used it earlier, and crucially, in *Basil*; the parallel with *Basil* is particularly close, Basil's sister being replaced by Isaac's mother and the chance meeting on an omnibus being moved to a chemist's shop. Catherine Peters has suggested that Collins's preoccupation with mysterious or sinister women encountered by chance conceals 'a barely suppressed anxiety [on Collins's part] about the dangers of marriage'.[7]

In an expanded form, with a more conclusive ending that sacrificed artistic boldness to audience satisfaction, and retitled 'The Dream-Woman', this story became part of Collins's repertoire for his public readings in America in 1873–4, and it was expanded again for volume publication. As Peters points out, to have the woman murder her husband turned 'a story in which the uncanny and irrational predominate . . . into a piece of low-grade sensation'.[8] The original version, given in this volume, has the deft economy of narrative and the unsettling sense of the inexplicable that are leading characteristics of Collins's shorter fiction at its best.

'The Diary of Anne Rodway' opens in a very different vein: the diarist is a poor seamstress or 'Plain Needlewoman' who

[7] Catherine Peters, *The King of Inventors: A Life of Wilkie Collins* (London, 1991), 155.

[8] Ibid. 361.

has no family and whose lover has emigrated to America in the vain hope of finding success. Her friend and fellow lodger is in a similar plight, her only relative being a brother in Assam of whom she has heard nothing for years. (Both cases, incidentally, underline the large-scale phenomenon of mid-century working-class emigration, put to good novelistic use earlier in the decade in *David Copperfield*.) The diary employs an artless style that nevertheless permits some unconscious ironies and revelations: for example, the sketch of the fashionable clergyman ('a very clever gentleman who fills the church to crowding') in the opening paragraph. Into this muted, realistic portrayal of life at the level of bare subsistence, mystery intervenes. Mary is brought home unconscious after a street accident, and dies. Natural causes are blamed (it turns out that at the time of her death she is weak with hunger and overwork), but she is inexplicably found to be clutching a fragment torn from a gentleman's cravat.

Against all expectations, Anne turns into a resourceful amateur detective (possibly the first woman detective in English fiction),[9] and what has begun as a slightly sentimental and pathetic account of sisterly affection between poor working girls becomes Collins's first attempt at a murder mystery as Anne embarks on the quest for Mary's killer. The story is thus a very early example of the use of the murder-victim's friend as self-appointed sleuth and also of Collins's sympathy, later evident in his full-length fiction, with the woman's point of view, especially when confronted by an oppressive male enjoying superior social and economic power. Dickens was delighted to secure the story for *Household Words*, praised its 'genuine form and beauty', declared—perhaps hyperbolically, but certainly flatteringly—that he knew 'no one else who could have done it', and confessed that in reading the second instalment on the train he had 'cried as much as you could possibly desire'.[10] It is, however, less its pathos than its presentation of a young

[9] Ashley, 'Wilkie Collins and the Detective Story', 50.
[10] *Letters of Charles Dickens*, ii. 792.

women's courage in taking on a hostile, cruel, and exploitative male world that will commend it to modern readers.

'The Lady of Glenwith Grange' is a particularly good illustration of Collins's general tendency to anticipate in his short stories elements that would reappear more prominently in his—and sometimes not only his—longer fictions. As Robert Ashley has said, its 'sinister house' looks forward to the Satis House of *Great Expectations* while its 'double identity plot . . . antedates the double identity plots of both *A Tale of Two Cities* and *The Woman in White*'.[11] As for the relationship between Ida and her sister Rosamond, this surely represents a first sketch for that between Marian Halcombe and her half-sister Laura Fairlie in *The Woman in White*: a relationship part sisterly, part maternal. (Ida has 'refused two good offers of marriage' and 'seemed bent on remaining single all her life'.) Just as Ida watches the 'growth of her sister's liking for the baron [Franval] with an apprehension and sorrow which she tried fruitlessly to conceal' and comes to realize that 'she must bid farewell to the brighter and happier part of her life on the day when she went to live under the same roof with her sister's husband', Marian in the novel of five years later writes that 'before another month is over our heads, she will be his Laura instead of mine! His Laura! I am as little able to realize the idea which these two words convey . . . as if writing of her marriage were to be writing of her death.' Both characters —Ida to a limited extent, Marian much more strikingly— exemplify Collins's rapport with the deepest feelings of an unusual (and even, by the accepted notions of the day, an unfeminine) woman.

As for the alleged Baron Franval (actually an impostor and a criminal impersonating the real aristocrat), he is very much in the line of villains in the sensation novel, though that genre had hardly come into existence and was certainly not identified by that label when the story was written. His foreign origins and title and his harsh treatment of Rosamond make him the prototype of the two villains in *The*

---

[11] Ashley, *Wilkie Collins*, 49.

Woman in White, Count Fosco and Sir Percival Glyde re-
spectively. Towards the end, the story moves towards another nascent genre, that of the detective story, as the secret
agent of the French police, suspecting the 'Baron', plots his
unmasking and discovers the clue that will lead to his arrest:
a clue whose discovery involves cutting away his nightgown
as he sleeps. All in all, 'The Lady of Glenwith Grange' may
be regarded as a sensation novel in miniature written half a
decade before that variety of fiction is generally regarded as
having come into existence—though it is only fair to add
that, even earlier in the decade, Collins's second novel,
Basil, had already incorporated a number of features of the
form.

'The Dead Hand' again draws on the stock situation of a
traveller compelled by circumstances to take shelter overnight in an unpromising hostelry (a tradition still potent in
Hitchcock's *Psycho*). Collins, however, now gives a double
twist to the well-worn device. His setting is not some lonely
inn in the Carpathians or Apennines, or even in the Paris of
'A Terribly Strange Bed', but, with an entirely deliberate
stroke of the prosaic, Doncaster during race-week. In this
banal situation there unfolds what bears all the signs of
being a tale of the uncanny: sharing a room with a corpse
faute de mieux in the crowded town, the traveller finds it
coming to life. Then realism again reasserts itself, for the
setting is after all not the distant past but 'this present
nineteenth century', as the opening words of the story
declare, and a medical explanation is forthcoming. (The melancholy and reclusive doctor, incidentally, is a first sketch
for one of Collins's most memorable characters, Ezra Jen-
nings in *The Moonstone*.)

This is not quite the end of the marvels, however, for
though the supernatural has been banished a terrific coincidence takes its place: the 'dead' man, now fully restored
to life, is the half-brother of the traveller (Collins's preoccupation with illegitimacy here rearing its head) as well as the
former lover of the woman he is to marry. The message
seems to be that, while modern scientific rationalism may
have removed the supernatural, extraordinary happenings

can still give actual existence a quality that is hardly less strange and unpredictable. The view is one that would have been whole-heartedly endorsed by Dickens, whose influence may have been felt on this as on other points.

'The Biter Bit' has been described as 'the first humorous or satirical detective story'.[12] A slightly different view might be that, written towards the close of the decade that had witnessed the emergence of the detective as a character-type in English fiction, it comically subverts the genre by recounting a 'crime' that turns out to be insignificant—virtually, indeed, a joke—investigated by a detective who is hopelessly incompetent. Conducted through a series of letters, the narrative presents different points of view and contrasts the ironically named Sharpin (the new-style detective who 'has not served his time among the rank and file of the force') with the experienced older men who have 'mounted up, step by step, to the places we now fill'. The arrogant newcomer, who considers himself 'an uncommonly sharp man', is told at the end that he is 'not quite sharp enough for our purpose'.

The crime itself shows Collins using what was later to become a favourite ploy of detective fiction, the least likely criminal; and as in the much later 'Who Killed Zebedee?'—and in many a story by Agatha Christie and the like—the field of suspects is restricted to the occupants of a single house. This relatively slight story does, however, offer a vivid close-up of lower-middle-class urban life. The stationer's shop that is the principal setting recalls the establishment run by the mild-mannered Snagsby in Dickens's *Bleak House*, another *petit bourgeois* who finds himself caught up in lurid melodrama—except that in 'The Biter Bit' the melodrama is spurious. There is also a strong sense of a London that is rapidly expanding and of neighbourhoods taking on an identity that reflects the city's social structure: for example, a girl from a 'genteel villa-residence in the neighbourhood of the Regent's Park' makes a runaway match, honeymoons at Richmond, and settles in a brand-

[12] Ashley, 'Wilkie Collins and the Detective Story', 50.

new suburb at 14 Babylon Terrace. Collins was always to
have a strong feeling for urban and suburban locales, especially for the mushrooming new residential areas, and in his
full-length novels from *Basil* onwards likes to demonstrate
that in the modern age wickedness and crime, plots and
mysteries, are to be found not in castles and abbeys but
behind the neat, newly-painted front doors of middle-class
dwellings.

With 'John Jago's Ghost' this selection leaps from the
1850s to the 1870s, a chronological gap accounted for by
Collins's marked neglect of the short story form during the
1860s, when he was producing the novels upon which his
reputation and influence as a sensation novelist were to
depend. This story was in fact written during his tour of the
United States in 1873 and makes interesting use of an
American setting. The narrator-protagonist is a young London barrister who, having nearly killed himself through
overwork, is ordered rest and a sea-voyage by his doctor and
takes the opportunity to visit American relatives whom he
has never seen. Anticipating what was to become a favourite
situation of detective and adventure fiction, the holiday and
rest-cure turn into a period of excitement, mystery, and
suspense that includes quarrels, violence, an apparent murder, a trial, alleged confessions, two near-executions, and a
successful love-affair. As usual, the narrative moves forward
at a brisk pace, the hero finding himself on the very first
evening in an 'atmosphere of smouldering hostilities': the
farm is no pastoral retreat from the busy legal chambers he
has left behind but a hotbed of ill will, suspicion, and
secrets. Before he has been there for more than a few hours
he seems to have plunged into an atmosphere of mystery
and menace, and a nocturnal meeting between the lively
heroine and the dour farm-manager draws on some of the
stock ingredients of sensation fiction:

They had met. I saw the two shadowy figures slowly pacing backwards and forwards in the moonlight, the woman a little in advance of the man. What was he saying to her? Why was he so
anxious that not a word of it should be heard? Our presentiments
are sometimes, in certain rare cases, the faithful prophecy of the

future. A vague distrust of that moonlight-meeting stealthily took a hold on my mind. 'Will mischief come of it?' I asked myself, as I closed the door and entered the house.

Yet in the event the story turns its back on sensation and refuses to redeem the promise of its title or titles. For both the title used for American magazine publication, 'The Dead Alive', and that given to its simultaneous appearance in an English magazine and preferred when the story was collected, 'John Jago's Ghost', are confidence tricks played on the reader in their promise of a supernatural tale. After a quarrel Jago disappears and is believed to have been murdered; there is plenty of circumstantial evidence, including the remains of bones, ambiguously animal or human, in a lime-kiln, but no body. A trial follows, and a double death-sentence, narrowly averted when the 'dead' man reappears in his own good time. Human cunning and malice, not murder, has been responsible for his disappearance, and human motives, rather than the supernatural, explain his reappearance.

The American heroine is not only brave and resourceful but has a self-confidence and directness that distinguish her from most of her contemporary English counterparts and clearly win Collins's approval. Uninhibited by the constraints of the English class-system and the roles it prescribes for middle-class women, she can speak freely of her feelings and where necessary show initiative and decisiveness in her actions. As she tells the hero at one point, ' "In America, the women take care of themselves" '.

Catherine Peters has pointed out that the plot of 'John Jago's Ghost' is based on an actual American case but at the same time has 'a curious similarity' to certain elements in *The Mystery of Edwin Drood*.[13] In his half-written last novel, barely three years old when Collins wrote his story, Dickens seems to have intended to make use of the destructive properties of quicklime (though Collins's handling of the motif is much more detailed and graphic) and of a central situation in which a man, supposedly dead, reappears (an

---

[13] Peters, *King of Inventors*, 364.

idea he had used earlier in *Our Mutual Friend*). One of the seventeen possible titles for his new novel that Dickens jotted down on 20 August 1869 was 'Dead? Or Alive?', a rejected idea taken up afresh in one of Collins's own titles. And John Jago's name is, of course, strongly reminiscent of that of Dickens's villain, John Jasper.

In 'The Clergyman's Confession', a late story with a strong vein of pathos and sentiment, the main narrative is set within a frame and at the same time acts as a frame to another narrative. The initial narrator recounts a story told to him by his brother, now dead, and entrusted to him as 'a secret as long as I live'. The brother has by chance encountered a young and pretty Frenchwoman with a mysterious past (yet another instance of Collins's predilection for such encounters); she is also 'an incurable fatalist, and a firm believer in the ghostly reality of apparitions from the dead'. She tells him that she is hopelessly in love with a man who has abandoned her but whose return is hinted at. Although the brother falls in love with her, he comes to realize that her unrequited passion for the other man will prevent her from ever marrying him, and he gives her up and promises his dying mother that he will enter the Church. The woman, who has 'forebodings' that she will 'die young, and die miserably', promises him that if this happens he will 'hear of it'. Superstitions and premonitions aside, the story has up to this point been scrupulously realistic, its main setting a shabby lodging-house in a London back street not far from the mist-covered river.

Later the brother, now a clergyman, takes a pupil into his home who, by a large coincidence, turns out to be his 'unknown rival'. The man leaves suddenly with a comic excuse of 'Business in London' that soon turns sinister, for his business is the murder of the woman who loves him. The final part of the story, with the woman's ghostly return (at first as 'a pillar of white mist'), has urgency and power, and what concludes as a ghost story, and involves Collins's favourite theme of an inescapable destiny revealed to the victim beforehand, gains added force from being set in the contemporary world of the railway train and the electric telegraph.

In 'The Captain's Last Love' Collins abandons his customary urban settings in favour of a Pacific island in which
the sensations are provided by an earthquake and an erupt-
ing volcano. Beginning as a sea-story, however, it turns into
a love-story with some decidedly familiar elements, including an initial mystery—a sailor who hates the sight of the sea
and who declares he will never marry—and, as the retro-
spective narrative gets into its stride, a fateful meeting with
a Miranda-like figure (her father is a priest or wizard, her
mother is dead, and she has never left the island or seen any
other human than her parents). At one point the Captain's
experience in this remote region is linked with that of other
characters in stories set nearer home:

A man, passing a woman in the street, acts on the impulse to turn
and follow her, and in that one thoughtless moment shapes the
destiny of his future life. The Captain had acted on a similar
impulse, when he took the first canoe he found on the beach, and
shaped his reckless course for the tabooed island.

Catherine Peters has shown that this late story was salvaged
from a novel with a Polynesian setting written more than
thirty years earlier and submitted to a publisher in January
1845, though in the event never published. As Peters points
out, 'Early western accounts of Tahiti stressed the shocking
promiscuity of the women before they learnt Christian
ideas of marriage'[14]—precisely the kind of information that
Collins would have relished—and the story included some
(by the standards of the day) daring references to the reception given to the white men, who for 'twelve delightful
hours' are 'fed by the male people, and fondled by the
female people' before being 'torn from the flesh-pots and
the arms of their new friends'. In its final phases, however,
it takes on a more sombre, dramatic, and even tragic complexion.

The last story in this volume, 'Who Killed Zebedee?', is
also Collins's last detective story and belongs to the final
decade of his life. A dying man who has been a policeman

[14] Ibid. 65, 382.

in his youth makes a confession concerning an unsolved crime that has many of the ingredients of the classic whodunit. A man is found stabbed in his bed and his wife accuses herself of the apparently motiveless crime, revealing that she is a sleep-walker who has read of a similar incident in a book before falling asleep. Clearly, however, the real murderer must be sought elsewhere, though he or she will be among the occupants of the lodging-house where the crime has taken place. There is a too-obvious villain, graphically described, and a false trail laid by the real criminal; also a weapon of unknown origin and bearing a puzzlingly incomplete inscription. The ambitious young policeman, keen to further his career by solving the mystery, ends by destroying evidence and quitting the force.

There is obviously a good deal here that anticipates the development of the detective story over the next half century. At the same time, there is a strong sense of the profession of detective and the techniques of detection having made considerable strides since Collins's own stories of the 1850s: for example, 'Our last resource was to have the knife photographed, with the inscribed side uppermost, and to send copies to every police station in the kingdom.'

As these comments on individual items have suggested, Collins's stories not only share some of the distinctive strengths of his full-length novels but can anticipate or rework specific themes, character-types, plot-situations, and techniques in those works. In the stories of the 1850s, he is often breaking genuinely fresh ground and making an important contribution to the development of a new fictional subgenre. He may not have been the first to recognize the literary possibilities of the new profession of detective that was defined in the 1840s, but he has a serious claim to have initiated what were later to become leading features of the detective story. It is, as Ashley says, striking that he should 'have to his credit so many firsts: the first dog detective [in 'My Lady's Money', a late story not included in this selection], the first lady detective, the first application of epistolary narrative to detective fiction, the first humorous detective story, the first *British* detective story, and the first full-length detective novel in English'.[15]

In the short stories no less than in the novels, 'secret' and 'mystery' are keywords. But in an age that had, not without profound stress and strain, learned to accommodate itself to a scientific world-view, secrets could be uncovered and mysteries solved by those with the necessary talents. The detective, one of the innumerable brand-new products of the increasing specialization of nineteenth-century occupational roles, thus becomes (like the doctor and the lawyer) a secular priest, magician, or guru, one of society's power-figures, and a prime candidate for fictional appropriation. Though the Detective Department had been established in 1842 (it was to be reorganized as the CID in 1878), the first literary reference recorded by the *OED* is in the following year, when an allusion in *Chambers's Journal* hinted unconsciously at the literary possibilities of the new race of policeman: 'Intelligent men have been recently selected to form a body called the "detective police" . . . at times the detective policeman attires himself in the dress of ordinary individuals.' The adjective was adopted as a noun in 1850, the *OED*'s citation now coming appropriately enough from an article in *Household Words* by Dickens: 'To each division of the Force is attached two officers, who are denominated "detectives".' In the 1850s, therefore, the word still bore the gloss of freshness upon it, and Collins's readers must have had a distinct sense of the topical and the innovative in his stories of crime and detection. The term 'detective story' was not to become current until 1883, near the end of Collins's life, but this marked the conclusion, not the beginning, of a process to which Collins had made a major contribution a full generation earlier.

As with the Gothic novel, where barely half a dozen years seem to have elapsed between *The Mysteries of Udolpho* and the origins of *Northanger Abbey*, influential models quickly turned into objects of parody. By the mid-1860s, Mary Elizabeth Braddon could write to the journalist and

[15] Ashley, 'Wilkie Collins and the Detective Story', 60.

editor Edmund Yates (a friend of both Dickens and Collins):

The Balzac-morbid-anatomy school is my especial delight, but it seems you want the downright sensational: floppings at the end of chapters, and bits of paper hidden in secret drawers, bank-notes and title-deeds under the carpet, and a part of the body putrefying in a coal-scuttle. By the bye, what a splendid novel, *à la* Wilkie Collins, one might write on a protracted search for the missing members of a murdered man, dividing the tale not into *books* but *bits*! 'BIT THE FIRST: The leg in the gray stocking found at Deptford.' 'BIT THE SECOND: The white hand and the onyx ring with half an initial letter (unknown) and crest, skull with a coronet, found in an Alpine *crevasse*!'

Seriously, though, you want a sensational fiction . . . I cannot promise you anything new, when . . . everything on this earth seems to have been done, and done, and done again! . . . I will give the kaleidoscope (which I cannot spell) another turn, and will do my very best with the bits of old glass and pins and rubbish.[16]

Such good-humoured ridicule constitutes an oblique tribute to the power and currency of the 'sensation' mode of fiction; and it is clear that it is primarily Collins's example that Braddon has in mind—indeed, she may have been drawing her examples, consciously or otherwise, from specific stories. The traditional view has been that the sensation novel is a product of the 1860s with *The Woman in White* conveniently ushering in the new decade, but it is now clear that Collins's work, not least in his short stories, in the previous decade had already established some of the leading features of the new form. The stories in this collection exemplify the ways in which he took over elements from established forms, notably the Gothic tale of terror and the ghost story, transformed them from remote and exotic to familiar and contemporary settings, and devised the prototypes of what was to turn into one of the most popular varieties of modern fiction, the detective story. He worked, of course, without the benefit of relatively clear generic concepts that hindsight affords, and it would have

[16] Quoted in Robert Lee Woolf, *Sensational Victorian: The Life and Fiction of Mary Elizabeth Braddon* (New York, 1979), 137.

been surprising if he had not at times blended elements from different sub-genres, so that (for instance) 'The Dead Hand' starts like a tale of terror but ends as something quite different. It may be, however, that something more creative than conceptual confusion is in question, and that Collins's critical and sceptical mind is eager to question and even subvert the forms in which he is working.

But he was also, of course, a professional author mindful of his audience, and the stimulus to his experiments, and to the writing of the stories themselves (as later of his serialized fiction), was the growth of the popular magazine and the mass readership it created: that 'all-influencing periodical literature of the present day', as he calls it in 'The Lady of Glenwith Grange', 'whose sphere is already almost without limit, whose readers, even in our time, may be numbered by millions'. As so often in the Victorian age, there is a heady sense of entirely new conditions, propitious to experiment and innovation, emerging.

Those last phrases in the quotation from Collins's story have shifted the ground of discussion from the historical significance of his work, which is considerable, to his unfading power over an audience, which is undeniable. As with many great entertainers, his art has a deceptively simple look: beside the firework displays and electrical storms of Dickensian rhetoric, Collins's plain prose can seem flat and humdrum. If Dickens, as Ruskin said, has the manner of one who speaks in 'a circle of stage fire', Collins often seems to speak from the witness box or the columns of a popular newspaper reporting police-court proceedings. Lacking (like practically everyone else) Dickens's supreme creative powers and poetic impulse to remake the language, Collins was nevertheless the more inclined of the two to take risks and challenge conventions in his work no less than in his private life, and the small scale of the stories does not prevent them from being at times profoundly original. Ultimately, however, his claim to greatness must rest on his narrative gifts. Long as they are, his best novels retain the power to seize and hold the reader's attention; his short stories display different aspects of his art and technique, a

pared-down economy of language and a rapid, almost ellipt-
ical narration of events, but in their own way possess a
comparable power.

NOTE ON THE TEXT

THERE is no collected edition of Collins's short stories, and no edition of his works includes all his short fiction. Most of his stories appeared during his lifetime in a variety of periodicals on both sides of the Atlantic, and many of them were subsequently collected by him for volume publication, though a number of stories remain uncollected. Before republication Collins sometimes revised the stories, on occasion drastically, and in these instances the original version has been given in this selection. He was also in the habit of retitling his stories, and here again the original title has usually been preferred. Details of original publication and (where appropriate) republication, and of changes of title, are given for each story in the Explanatory Notes.

Obvious misprints in the original texts have been silently corrected, and where necessary spelling and punctuation have been modernized (e.g. 'choking' for 'choaking', 'picnic' for 'pic-nic').

SELECT BIBLIOGRAPHY

(The place of publication is London unless otherwise stated.)

Editions of Collins's Short Stories

(Details of magazine publication of the stories included in this selection are given, where appropriate, in the Explanatory Notes.)

After Dark, 2 vols. (1856).
The Queen of Hearts, 3 vols. (1859).
Miss or Mrs? And Other Stories in Outline (1873).
The Frozen Deep and Other Tales, 2 vols. (1874).
Little Novels, 3 vols. (1887).

Modern editions and selections include the following:
Tales of Terror and the Supernatural, ed. Herbert Van Thal (New York, 1972).
Little Novels (New York, 1977).
The Biter Bit and Other Stories (Gloucester, 1982).
The Yellow Mask and Other Stories (Gloucester, 1987).
My Lady's Money (Gloucester, 1990).
No Thoroughfare and Other Stories (Gloucester, 1990).
The Best Supernatural Stories of Wilkie Collins, ed. Peter Haining (1990).

Bibliographies

Andrew, R. V., 'A Wilkie Collins Check-list', *English Studies in Africa*, 3 (1960), 79–98.

Ashley, Robert, 'Wilkie Collins', in George H. Ford (ed.), *Victorian Fiction: A Second Guide to Research* (New York, 1978).

Beetz, Kirk H., *Wilkie Collins: An Annotated Bibliography, 1889–1976* (1976).

Lohrli, Anne (ed.), *Household Words* (Toronto, 1973).

Wolff, Robert L., 'Wilkie Collins', in *Nineteenth Century Fiction: A Bibliographical Catalogue* (New York, 1981–6), i. 254–72.

Biography and Criticism

Ashley, Robert, *Wilkie Collins* (1952).

—— 'Wilkie Collins and the Detective Story', *Nineteenth Century Fiction*, 6 (1951), 47–60.

Collins, Philip, *Dickens and Crime* (1964).

Hughes, Winnifred, *The Maniac in the Cellar* (Princeton, NJ, 1980).

Lonoff, Sue, *Wilkie Collins and His Victorian Readers* (New York, 1982).

Marshall, William H., *Wilkie Collins* (New York, 1970).

Page, Norman (ed.), *Wilkie Collins: The Critical Heritage* (1974).

Peters, Catherine, *The King of Inventors: A Life of Wilkie Collins* (1991).

Rance, Nicholas, *Wilkie Collins and Other Sensation Novelists* (1991).

Robinson, Kenneth, *Wilkie Collins* (1974).

A CHRONOLOGY OF WILKIE COLLINS

Age

1824 (8 Jan.) Born at 11 New Cavendish Street, St Marylebone, London, elder son of William Collins, RA (1788–1847), artist, and Harriet Collins, née Geddes (1790–1868).

1826 (Spring) Family moves to Pond Street, Hampstead.   2

1828 (25 Jan.) Brother, Charles Allston Collins, born.   4

1829 (Autumn) Family moves to Hampstead Square.   5

1830 Family moves to Porchester Terrace, Bayswater.   6

1835 (13 Jan.) Starts school, the Maida Hill Academy.   11

1836 (19 Sept.–15 Aug. 1838) Family visits France and Italy.   12–14

1838 (Aug.) Family moves to 20 Avenue Road, Regent's Park. Attends Mr Cole's boarding school, Highbury Place, until Dec. 1840.   14–16

1840 (Summer) Family moves to 85 Oxford Terrace, Bayswater.   16

1841 (Jan.) Apprenticed to Antrobus & Co., tea merchants, Strand.   17

1842 (June–July) Trip to Highlands of Scotland, and Shetland, with William Collins.   18

1843 (Aug.) First signed publication 'The Last Stage Coachman' in the *Illuminated Magazine*.   19

1844 Writes his first (unpublished) novel, 'Iolani; or Tahiti as it was; a Romance'.   20

1845 (Jan.) 'Iolani' submitted to Chapman & Hall, rejected (8 Mar.).   21

1846 (17 May) Admitted student of Lincoln's Inn.   22

1847 (17 Feb.) Death of William Collins.   23

1848 (Summer) Family move to 38 Blandford Square. (Nov.) First book, *Memoirs of the Life of William Collins, Esq., R.A.* published.   24

1849 Exhibits a painting at the Royal Academy summer exhibition.   25

1850 (27 Feb.) First published novel, *Antonina*. (Summer) Family move to 17 Hanover Terrace.   26

1851 (Jan.) Travel book on Cornwall, *Rambles Beyond Railways* published.   27

(Mar.) Meets Dickens for the first time.

(May) Acts with Dickens in Bulwer-Lytton's *Not So Bad as We Seem*.

1852   (Jan.) *Mr Wray's Cash Box* published, with frontispiece by Millais.   28

(24 Apr.) 'A Terribly Strange Bed', first contribution to *Household Words*.

Tours provinces with Dickens's theatrical company.

(16 Nov.) *Basil* published.

1853   (Oct.–Dec.) Tours Switzerland and Italy with Dickens and Augustus Egg.   29

1854   (5 June) *Hide and Seek* published.   30

1855   (16 June) First play, *The Lighthouse*, performed by Dickens's theatrical company at Tavistock House.   31

1856   (Feb.) *After Dark*, a collection of short stories, published.   32

(Mar.) *A Rogue's Life* serialized in *Household Words*. (Oct.) Joins staff of *Household Words* and begins collaboration with Dickens in *The Wreck of the Golden Mary* (Dec.)

1857   (Jan.–June) *The Dead Secret* serialized in *Household Words*, published in volume form (June).   33

(6 Jan.) *The Frozen Deep* performed by Dickens's theatrical company at Tavistock House.

(Aug.) *The Lighthouse* performed at the Olympic Theatre.

(Sep.) Tours Cumberland, Lancashire, and Yorkshire with Dickens, their account appearing as *The Lazy Tour of Two Idle Apprentices* in *Household Words* (Oct.).

Collaborates with Dickens on *The Perils of Certain English Prisoners*.

1858   (Oct.) *The Red Vial* produced at the Olympic Theatre; a failure.   34

1859   From this year no longer living with his mother; lives for the rest of his life (with one interlude) with Mrs Caroline Graves. (Jan.–Feb.) living at 124 Albany Street; (May–Dec.) Living at 2a Cavendish Street.   35

(Oct.) *The Queen of Hearts*, a collection of short stories, published.

(26 Nov.–25 Aug. 1860) *The Woman in White* serialized in *All the Year Round*.

(Dec.) Moves to 12 Harley Street.

1860 (Aug.) *The Woman in White* published in volume form: a best-seller in Britain and the United States, and rapidly translated into most European languages.   36

1861 (Jan.) Resigns from *All the Year Round*.   37

1862 (15 Mar.–17 Jan. 1863) *No Name* serialized in *All the Year Round*, published in volume form (31 Dec.).   38

1863 *My Miscellanies*, a collection of journalism from *Household Words* and *All the Year Round* published.   39

1864 (Nov.–June 1866) *Armadale* serialized in *The Cornhill*.   40

(Dec.) Moves to 9 Melcombe Place, Dorset Square.

1866 (May) *Armadale* published in two volumes.   42

(Oct.) *The Frozen Deep* produced at the Olympic Theatre.

1867 (Sept.) Moves to 90 Gloucester Place, Portman Square.   43

Collaborates with Dickens on *No Thoroughfare*, published as Christmas Number of *All the Year Round*; dramatic version performed at the Adelphi Theatre (Christmas Eve).

1868 (4 Jan.–8 Aug.) *The Moonstone* serialized in *All the Year Round*; published in three volumes (July).   44

(19 Mar.) Mother, Harriet Collins, dies.

Collins forms liaison with Martha Rudd ('Mrs Dawson').

(4 Oct.) Caroline Graves marries Joseph Charles Clow.

1869 (Mar.) *Black and White*, written in collaboration with Charles Fechter, produced at the Adelphi Theatre.   45

(4 July) Daughter, Marian Dawson, born to Collins and Martha Rudd, at 33 Bolsover Street, Portland Place.

1870 (June) *Man and Wife* published in volume form.   46

(9 June) Dickens dies.

(Aug.) Dramatic version of *The Woman in White* tried out in Leicester.

*Mad Monkton
and Other Stories*

A TERRIBLY STRANGE BED

THE most difficult likeness I ever had to take, not even excepting my first attempt in the art of Portrait-painting, was a likeness of a gentleman named Faulkner. As far as drawing and colouring went, I had no particular fault to find with my picture; it was the *expression* of the sitter which I had failed in rendering—a failure quite as much his fault as mine. Mr Faulkner, like many other persons by whom I have been employed, took it into his head that he must assume an expression, because he was sitting for his likeness; and, in consequence, contrived to look as unlike himself as possible, while I was painting him. I had tried to divert his attention from his own face, by talking with him on all sorts of topics. We had both travelled a great deal, and felt interested alike in many subjects connected with our wanderings over the same countries. Occasionally, while we were discussing our travelling experiences, the unlucky set-look left his countenance, and I began to work to some purpose; but it was always disastrously sure to return again, before I had made any great progress—or, in other words, just at the very time when I was most anxious that it should not re-appear. The obstacle thus thrown in the way of the satisfactory completion of my portrait, was the more to be deplored, because Mr Faulkner's natural expression was a very remarkable one. I am not an author, so I cannot describe it. I ultimately succeeded in painting it, however; and this was the way in which I achieved my success:—

On the morning when my sitter was coming to me for the fourth time, I was looking at his portrait in no very agreeable mood—looking at it, in fact, with the disheartening conviction that the picture would be a perfect failure, unless the expression in the face represented were thoroughly altered and improved from nature. The only method of accomplishing this successfully, was to make Mr Faulkner, somehow, insensibly forget that he was sitting for his picture. What topic could I lead him to talk on, which would entirely engross his attention while I was at work on his likeness?—I was still puzzling my brains to no purpose on this subject when Mr Faulkner entered my studio; and, shortly afterwards, an accidental circumstance gained for me the very object which my own ingenuity had proved unequal to compass.

While I was 'setting' my palette, my sitter amused himself by turning over some portfolios. He happened to select one for special notice, which contained several sketches that I had made in the streets of Paris. He turned over the first five views rapidly enough; but when he came to the sixth, I saw his face flush directly; and observed that he took the drawing out of the portfolio, carried it to the window, and remained silently absorbed in the contemplation of it for full five minutes. After that, he turned round to me; and asked very anxiously, if I had any objection to part with that sketch.

It was the least interesting drawing of the series—merely a view in one of the streets running by the backs of the houses in the Palais Royal. Some four or five of these houses were comprised in the view, which was of no particular use to me in any way; and which was too valueless, as a work of Art, for me to think of *selling* it to my kind patron. I begged his acceptance of it, at once. He thanked me quite warmly; and then, seeing that I looked a little surprised at the odd selection he had made from my sketches, laughingly asked me if I could guess why he had been so anxious to become possessed of the view which I had given him?

'Probably'—I answered—'there is some remarkable historical association connected with that street at the back of the Palais Royal, of which I am ignorant.'

'No'—said Mr Faulkner—'at least, none that *I* know of. The only association connected with the place in *my* mind, is a purely personal association. Look at this house in your drawing—the house with the water-pipe running down it from top to bottom. I once passed a night there—a night I shall never forget to the day of my death. I have had some awkward travelling adventures in my time; but *that* adventure——! Well, well! suppose we begin the sitting. I make but a bad return for your kindness in giving me the sketch, by thus wasting your time in mere talk.'

He had not long occupied the sitter's chair (looking pale and thoughtful), when he returned—involuntarily, as it seemed—to the subject of the house in the back street. Without, I hope, showing any undue curiosity, I contrived to let him see that I felt a deep interest in everything he now said. After two or three preliminary hesitations, he at last, to my great joy, fairly started on the narrative of his adventure. In the interest of his subject he soon completely forgot that he was sitting for his portrait—the very expression that I wanted, came over his face—my picture proceeded towards completion, in the right direction, and to the best purpose. At every fresh touch, I felt more and more certain that I was now getting the better of my grand difficulty; and I enjoyed the additional gratification of having my work lightened by the recital of a true story, which possessed, in my estimation, all the excitement of the most exciting romance.

This, as nearly as I can recollect, is, word for word, how Mr Faulkner told me the story:—

Shortly before the period when gambling-houses were suppressed by the French Government, I happened to be staying at Paris with an English friend. We were both young men then, and lived, I am afraid, a very dissipated life, in the very dissipated city of our sojourn. One night, we were idling about the neighbourhood of the Palais Royal, doubtful to what amusement we should next betake ourselves. My friend proposed a visit to Frascati's; but his suggestion was not to my taste. I knew Frascati's, as the French saying is, by heart; had lost and won plenty of five-franc pieces there, 'merely for the fun of the thing,' until it was 'fun' no longer; and was thoroughly tired, in fact, of all the ghastly respectabilities of such a social anomaly as a respectable gambling-house. 'For Heaven's sake'—said I to my friend—'let us go somewhere where we can see a little genuine, blackguard, poverty-stricken gaming, with no false gingerbread glitter

thrown over it at all. Let us get away from fashionable
Frascati's, to a house where they don't mind letting in a
man with a ragged coat, or a man with no coat, ragged, or
otherwise.'—'Very well,' said my friend, 'we needn't go out
of the Palais Royal to find the sort of company you want.
Here's the place, just before us; as blackguard a place, by all
report, as you could possibly wish to see.' In another minute
we arrived at the door, and entered the house, the back of
which you have drawn in your sketch.

When we got upstairs, and had left our hats and sticks
with the doorkeeper, we were admitted into the chief gambling-room. We did not find many people assembled there.
But, few as the men were who looked up at us on our
entrance, they were all types—miserable types—of their
respective classes. We had come to see blackguards; but
these men were something worse. There is a comic side,
more or less appreciable, in all blackguardism—here, there
was nothing but tragedy; mute, weird tragedy. The quiet in
the room was horrible. The thin, haggard, long-haired
young man, whose sunken eyes fiercely watched the turning
up of the cards, never spoke; the flabby, fat-faced, pimply
player, who pricked his piece of paste-board perseveringly, to register how often black won, and how often red—
never spoke; the dirty, wrinkled old man, with the vulture
eyes, and the darned great coat, who had lost his last *sous*,
and still looked on desperately, after he could play no
longer—never spoke. Even the voice of the croupier sounded
as if it were strangely dulled and thickened in the atmosphere of the room. I had entered the place to laugh; I felt
that if I stood quietly looking on much longer, I should
be more likely to weep. So, to excite myself out of the
depression of spirits which was fast stealing over me, I
unfortunately went to the table, and began to play. Still
more unfortunately, as the event will show, I won—won
prodigiously; won incredibly; won at such a rate, that the
regular players at the table crowded round me; and staring
at my stakes with hungry, superstitious eyes, whispered to
one another, that the English stranger was going to break
the bank.

The game was *Rouge et Noir*.* I had played at it in every city in Europe, without, however, the care or the wish to study the Theory of Chances—that philosopher's stone of all gamblers! And a gambler, in the strict sense of the word, I had never been. I was heart-whole from the corroding passion for play. My gaming was a mere idle amusement. I never resorted to it by necessity, because I never knew what it was to want money. I never practised it so incessantly as to lose more than I could afford, or to gain more than I could coolly pocket without being thrown off my balance by my good luck. In short, I had hitherto frequented gambling-tables—just as I frequented ball-rooms and opera-houses—because they amused me, and because I had nothing better to do with my leisure hours.

But, on this occasion, it was very different—now, for the first time in my life, I felt what the passion for play really was. My success first bewildered, and then, in the most literal meaning of the word, intoxicated me. Incredible as it may appear, it is nevertheless true, that I only lost, when I attempted to estimate chances, and played according to previous calculation. If I left everything to luck, and staked without any care or consideration, I was sure to win—to win in the face of every recognised probability in favour of the bank. At first, some of the men present ventured their money safely enough on my colour; but I speedily increased my stakes to sums which they dared not risk. One after another they left off playing, and breathlessly looked on at my game. Still, time after time, I staked higher and higher; and still won. The excitement in the room rose to fever pitch. The silence was interrupted, by a deep, muttered chorus of oaths and exclamations in different languages, every time the gold was shovelled across to my side of the table—even the imperturbable croupier dashed his rake on the floor in a (French) fury of astonishment at my success. But one man present preserved his self-possession; and that man was my friend. He came to my side, and whispering in English, begged me to leave the place, satisfied with what I had already gained. I must do him the justice to say, that he repeated his warnings and entreaties several times; and only left me and went away, after I had rejected his advice (I was to all intents and purposes gambling-drunk) in terms which rendered it impossible for him to address me again that night.

Shortly after he had gone, a hoarse voice behind me cried:—'Permit me, my dear sir!—permit me to restore to their proper place two Napoleons which you have dropped. Wonderful luck, sir!—I pledge you my word of honour as an old soldier, in the course of my long experience in this sort of thing, I never saw such luck as yours!—never! Go on, sir—*Sacré mille bombes!* Go on boldly, and break the bank!'

I turned round and saw, nodding and smiling at me with inveterate civility, a tall man, dressed in a frogged and braided surtout. If I had been in my senses, I should have considered him, personally, as being rather a suspicious specimen of an old soldier. He had goggling bloodshot eyes, mangy mustachios, and a broken nose. His voice betrayed a barrack-room intonation of the worst order, and he had the dirtiest pair of hands I ever saw—even in France. These little personal peculiarities exercised, however, no repelling influence on me. In the mad excitement, the reckless triumph of that moment, I was ready to 'fraternise' with anybody who encouraged me in my game. I accepted the old soldier's offered pinch of snuff; clapped him on the back, and swore he was the honestest fellow in the world; the most glorious relic of the Grand Army that I had ever met with. 'Go on!' cried my military friend, snapping his fingers in ecstasy,—'Go on, and win! Break the bank— *Mille tonnerres!* my gallant English comrade, break the bank!'

And I *did* go on—went on at such a rate, that in another quarter of an hour the croupier called out: 'Gentlemen! the bank has discontinued for tonight.' All the notes, and all the gold in that 'bank,' now lay in a heap under my hands; the whole floating capital of the gambling-house was waiting to pour into my pockets!

'Tie up the money in your pocket-handkerchief, my worthy sir,' said the old soldier, as I wildly plunged my hands into my heap of gold. 'Tie it up, as we used to tie up a bit of dinner in the Grand Army; your winnings are too heavy for any breeches pockets that ever were sewn. There! that's it!—shovel them in, notes and all! *Credié!* what luck! —Stop! another Napoleon on the floor! *Ah! sacré petit polisson de Napoleon!* have I found thee at last? Now then, sir —two tight double knots each way with your honourable permission, and the money's safe. Feel it! feel it, fortunate sir! hard and round as a cannon ball—*Ah, bah!* if they had only fired such cannon balls at us, at Austerlitz*—*nom d'une pipe!* if they only had! And now, as an ancient grenadier, as an ex-brave of the French army, what remains for me to do? I ask what? Simply this: to entreat my valued English friend to drink a bottle of champagne with me, and toast the goddess Fortune in foaming goblets before we part!'

Excellent ex-brave! Convivial ancient grenadier! Champagne by all means! An English cheer for an old soldier! Hurrah! Hurrah! Another English cheer for the goddess Fortune! Hurrah! Hurrah! Hurrah!

'Bravo! the Englishman; the amiable, gracious Englishman, in whose veins circulates the vivacious blood of France! Another glass? *Ah, bah!*—the bottle is empty! Never mind! *Vive le vin!* I, the old soldier, order another bottle, and half-a-pound of *bon-bons* with it!'

No, no, ex-brave; never—ancient grenadier! *Your* bottle last time; *my* bottle this. Behold it! Toast away! The French Army!—the great Napoleon!—the present company! the croupier! the honest croupier's wife and daughters—if he has any! the Ladies generally! Everybody in the world!

By the time the second bottle of champagne was emptied, I felt as if I had been drinking liquid fire—my brain seemed all a-flame. No excess in wine had ever had this effect on me before in my life. Was it the result of a stimulant acting upon my system when I was in a highly-excited state? Was my stomach in a particularly disordered condition? Or was the champagne particularly strong?

'Ex-brave of the French Army!' cried I, in a mad state of exhilaration. '*I* am on fire! how are *you*? You have set me on fire! Do you hear; my hero of Austerlitz? Let us have a third bottle of champagne to put the flame out!' The old soldier wagged his head, rolled his goggle-eyes, until I expected to see them slip out of their sockets; placed his dirty forefinger by the side of his broken nose; solemnly ejaculated 'Coffee!' and immediately ran off into an inner room.

The word pronounced by the eccentric veteran, seemed to have a magical effect on the rest of the company present. With one accord they all rose to depart. Probably they had expected to profit by my intoxication; but finding that my new friend was benevolently bent on preventing me from getting dead drunk, had now abandoned all hope of thriving pleasantly on my winnings. Whatever their motive might be, at any rate they went away in a body. When the old soldier returned, and sat down again opposite to me at the table, we had the room to ourselves. I could see the croupier, in a sort of vestibule which opened out of it, eating his supper in solitude. The silence was now deeper than ever.

A sudden change, too, had come over the 'ex-brave.' He assumed a portentously solemn look; and when he spoke to me again, his speech was ornamented by no oaths, enforced by no finger-snapping, enlivened by no apostrophes, or exclamations.

'Listen, my dear sir,' said he, in mysteriously confidential tones—'listen to an old soldier's advice. I have been to the mistress of the house (a very charming woman, with a genius for cookery!) to impress on her the necessity of making us some particularly strong and good coffee. You must drink this coffee in order to get rid of your little amiable exaltation of spirits, before you think of going home—you *must*, my good and gracious friend! With all that money to take home tonight, it is a sacred duty to yourself to have your wits about you. You are known to be a winner to an enormous extent, by several gentlemen present to-night, who, in a certain point of view, are very worthy and excellent fellows; but they are mortal men, my dear sir, and they have their amiable weaknesses! Need I say more? Ah, no, no! you understand me! Now, this is what you must do—send for a cabriolet when you feel quite well again—draw up all the windows when you get into it—and tell the driver to take you home only through the large and well-lighted thoroughfares. Do this; and you and your money will be safe. Do this; and tomorrow you will thank an old soldier for giving you a word of honest advice.'

Just as the ex-brave ended his oration in very lachrymose tones, the coffee came in, ready poured out in two cups. My attentive friend handed me one of the cups, with a bow. I was parched with thirst, and drank it off at a draught. Almost instantly afterwards, I was seized with a fit of giddiness, and felt more completely intoxicated than ever. The room whirled round and round furiously; the old soldier seemed to be regularly bobbing up and down before me, like the piston of a steam-engine. I was half deafened by a violent singing in my ears; a feeling of utter bewilderment, helplessness, idiotcy, overcame me. I rose from my chair, holding on by the table to keep my balance; and stammered out, that I felt dreadfully unwell—so unwell, that I did not know how I was to get home.

'My dear friend,' answered the old soldier; and even his voice seemed to be bobbing up and down, as he spoke—'My dear friend, it would be madness to go home, in *your* state. You would be sure to lose your money; you might be robbed and murdered with the greatest ease. *I* am going to sleep here: do *you* sleep here, too—they make up capital beds in this house—take one; sleep off the effects of the wine, and go home safely with your winnings, tomorrow—tomorrow, in broad daylight.'

I had no power of thinking, no feeling of any kind, but the feeling that I must lie down somewhere, immediately, and fall off into a cool, refreshing, comfortable sleep. So I agreed eagerly to the proposal about the bed, and took the offered arms of the old soldier and the croupier—the latter having been summoned to show the way. They led me along some passages and up a short flight of stairs into the bed-room which I was to occupy. The ex-brave shook me warmly by the hand; proposed that we should breakfast together the next morning; and then, followed by the croupier, left me for the night.

I ran to the wash-hand-stand; drank some of the water in my jug; poured the rest out, and plunged my face into it—then sat down in a chair, and tried to compose myself. I soon felt better. The change for my lungs, from the fetid atmosphere of the gambling-room to the cool air of the apartment I now occupied; the almost equally refreshing change for my eyes, from the glaring gas-lights of the 'Salon' to the dim, quiet flicker of one bed-room candle; aided wonderfully the restorative effects of cold water. The giddiness left me, and I began to feel a little like a reasonable being again. My first thought was of the risk of sleeping all night in a gambling-house; my second, of the still greater risk of trying to get out after the house was closed, and of going home alone at night, through the streets of Paris, with a large sum of money about me. I had slept in worse places than this, in the course of my travels; so I determined to lock, bolt, and barricade my door.

Accordingly, I secured myself against all intrusion; looked under the bed, and into the cupboard; tried the fastening of the window; and then, satisfied that I had taken every proper precaution, pulled off my upper clothing, put my light, which was a dim one, on the hearth among a feathery litter of wood ashes: and got into bed, with the handkerchief full of money under my pillow.

I soon felt, not only that I could not go to sleep, but that I could not even close my eyes. I was wide awake, and in a high fever. Every nerve in my body trembled—every one of my senses seemed to be preternaturally sharpened. I tossed, and rolled, and tried every kind of position, and perseveringly sought out the cold corners of the bed, and all to no purpose. Now, I thrust my arms over the clothes; now, I poked them under the clothes; now, I violently shot my legs straight out, down to the bottom of the bed; now, I convulsively coiled them up as near my chin as they would go; now, I shook out my crumpled pillow, changed it to the cool side, patted it flat, and lay down quietly on my back; now, I fiercely doubled it in two, set it up on end, thrust it against the board of the bed, and tried a sitting posture. Every effort was in vain; I groaned with vexation, as I felt that I was in for a sleepless night.

What could I do? I had no book to read. And yet, unless I found out some method of diverting my mind, I felt certain that I was in the condition to imagine all sorts of horrors; to rack my brains with forebodings of every possible and impossible danger; in short, to pass the night in suffering all conceivable varieties of nervous terror. I raised myself on my elbow, and looked about the room—which was brightened by a lovely moonlight pouring straight through the window—to see if it contained any pictures or ornaments, that I could at all clearly distinguish. While my eyes wandered from wall to wall, a remembrance of Le Maistre's delightful little book, 'Voyage autour de Ma Chambre,'* occurred to me. I resolved to imitate the French author, and find occupation and amusement enough to relieve the tedium of my wakefulness, by making a mental inventory of every article of furniture I could see, and by following up to their sources the multitude of associations which even a chair, a table, or a wash-hand-stand, may be made to call forth.

In the nervous unsettled state of my mind at that moment, I found it much easier to make my proposed inventory, than to make my proposed reflections, and soon gave up all hope of thinking in Le Maistre's fanciful track—or, indeed, thinking at all. I looked about the room at the different articles of furniture, and did nothing more. There was, first, the bed I was lying in—a four-post bed, of all things in the world to meet with in Paris!—yes, a thorough clumsy British four-poster, with the regular top lined with chintz—the regular fringed valance all round—the regular stifling, unwholesome curtains, which I remembered having mechanically drawn back against the posts, without particularly noticing the bed when I first got into the room. Then, there was the marble-topped wash-hand-stand, from which the water I had spilt, in my hurry to pour it out, was still dripping, slowly and more slowly, on to the brick floor. Then, two small chairs, with my coat, waistcoat, and trousers flung on them. Then, a large elbow chair covered with dirty-white dimity: with my cravat and shirt-collar thrown over the back. Then, a chest of drawers, with two of the brass handles off, and a tawdry, broken china inkstand placed on it by way of ornament for the top. Then, the dressing-table, adorned by a very small looking-glass, and a very large pincushion. Then, the window—an unusually large window. Then, a dark old picture, which the feeble candle dimly showed me. It was the picture of a fellow in a high Spanish hat, crowned with a plume of towering feathers. A swarthy sinister ruffian, looking upward; shading his eyes with his hand, and looking intently upward—it might be at some tall gallows at which he was going to be hanged. At any rate he had the appearance of thoroughly deserving it.

This picture put a kind of constraint upon me to look upward too—at the top of the bed. It was a gloomy and not an interesting object, and I looked back at the picture. I counted the feathers in the man's hat; they stood out in relief; three, white; two, green. I observed the crown of his hat, which was of a conical shape, according to the fashion supposed to have been favoured by Guido Fawkes.* I wondered what he was looking up at. It couldn't be at the stars; such a desperado was neither astrologer nor astronomer. It must be at the high gallows, and he was going to be hanged presently. Would the executioner come into possession of his conical crowned hat, and plume of feathers? I counted the feathers again; three, white; two, green.

While I still lingered over this very improving and intellectual employment, my thoughts insensibly began to wander. The moonlight shining into the room reminded me of a certain moonlight night in England—the night after a picnic party in a Welsh valley. Every incident of the drive homeward through lovely scenery, which the moonlight made lovelier than ever, came back to my remembrance, though I had never given the picnic a thought for years; though, if I had *tried* to recollect it, I could certainly have recalled little or nothing of that scene long past. Of all the wonderful faculties that help to tell us we are immortal, which speaks the sublime truth more eloquently than memory? Here was I, in a strange house of the most suspicious character, in a situation of uncertainty, and even of peril, which might seem to make the cool exercise of my recollection almost

out of the question; nevertheless remembering, quite involuntarily, places, people, conversations, minute circumstances of every kind, which I had thought forgotten for ever,
which I could not possibly have recalled at will, even under
the most favourable auspices. And what cause had produced in a moment the whole of this strange, complicated,
mysterious effect? Nothing but some rays of moonlight
shining in at my bedroom window.

I was still thinking of the picnic; of our merriment on the
drive home; of the sentimental young lady who *would* quote
Childe Harold,* because it was moonlight. I was absorbed
by these past scenes and past amusements, when, in an
instant, the thread on which my memories hung, snapped
asunder; my attention immediately came back to present
things, more vividly than ever, and I found myself, I neither
knew why nor wherefore, looking hard at the picture again.

Looking for what? Good God, the man had pulled his hat
down on his brows!—No! The hat itself was gone! Where
was the conical crown? Where the feathers; three, white;
two, green? Not there! In place of the hat and feathers, what
dusky object was it that now hid his forehead—his eyes—his
shading hand? Was the bed moving?

I turned on my back, and looked up. Was I mad? drunk?
dreaming? giddy again? or was the top of the bed really
moving down—sinking slowly, regularly, silently, horribly,
right down throughout the whole of its length and
breadth—right down upon Me, as I lay underneath?

My blood seemed to stand still; a deadly, paralysing coldness stole all over me, as I turned my head round on the
pillow, and determined to test whether the bed top was
really moving, or not, by keeping my eye on the man in the
picture. The next look in that direction was enough. The
dull, black, frowsy outline of the valance above me was
within an inch of being parallel with his waist. I still looked
breathlessly. And steadily, and slowly—very slowly—I saw
the figure, and the line of frame below the figure, vanish, as
the valance moved down before it.

I am, constitutionally, anything but timid. I have been, on
more than one occasion, in peril of my life, and have not lost

my self-possession for an instant; but, when the conviction first settled on my mind that the bed-top was really moving, was steadily and continuously sinking down upon me, I looked up for one awful minute, or more, shuddering, help-less, panic-stricken, beneath the hideous machinery for murder, which was advancing closer and closer to suffocate me where I lay.

Then the instinct of self-preservation came, and nerved me to save my life, while there was yet time. I got out of bed very quietly, and quickly dressed myself again in my upper clothing. The candle, fully spent, went out. I sat down in the arm-chair that stood near, and watched the bed-top slowly descending. I was literally spell-bound by it. If I had heard footsteps behind me, I could not have turned round; if a means of escape had been miraculously provided for me, I could not have moved to take advantage of it. The whole life in me, was, at that moment, concentrated in my eyes.

It descended—the whole canopy, with the fringe round it, came down—down—close down; so close that there was not room now to squeeze my finger between the bed-top and the bed. I felt at the sides, and discovered that what had appeared to me, from beneath, to be the ordinary light canopy of a four-post bed was in reality a thick, broad mattress, the substance of which was concealed by the valance and its fringe. I looked up, and saw the four posts rising hideously bare. In the middle of the bed-top was a huge wooden screw that had evidently worked it down through a hole in the ceiling, just as ordinary presses are worked down on the substance selected for compression. The frightful apparatus moved without making the faintest noise. There had been no creaking as it came down; there was now not the faintest sound from the room above. Amid a dead and awful silence I beheld before me—in the nine-teenth century, and in the civilised capital of France—such a machine for secret murder by suffocation, as might have existed in the worst days of the Inquisition, in the lonely Inns among the Hartz Mountains, in the mysterious tribu-nals of Westphalia! Still, as I looked on it, I could not move; I could hardly breathe; but I began to recover the power of thinking; and, in a moment, I discovered the murderous conspiracy framed against me, in all its horror.

My cup of coffee had been drugged, and drugged too strongly. I had been saved from being smothered, by having taken an over-dose of some narcotic. How I had chafed and fretted at the fever-fit which had preserved my life by keeping me awake! How recklessly I had confided myself to the two wretches who had led me into this room, determined, for the sake of my winnings, to kill me in my sleep, by the surest and most horrible contrivance for secretly accomplishing my destruction! How many men, winners like me, had slept, as I had proposed to sleep, in that bed; and never been seen or heard of more! I shuddered as I thought of it.

But, erelong, all thought was again suspended by the sight of the murderous canopy moving once more. After it had remained on the bed—as nearly as I could guess—about ten minutes, it began to move up again. The villains, who worked it from above, evidently believed that their purpose was now accomplished. Slowly and silently, as it had descended, that horrible bed-top rose towards its former place. When it reached the upper extremities of the four posts, it reached the ceiling too. Neither hole nor screw could be seen— the bed became, in appearance, an ordinary bed again, the canopy, an ordinary canopy, even to the most suspicious eyes.

Now, for the first time, I was able to move, to rise from my chair, to consider of how I should escape. If I betrayed, by the smallest noise, that the attempt to suffocate me had failed, I was certain to be murdered. Had I made any noise already? I listened intently, looking towards the door. No! no footsteps in the passage outside; no sound of a tread, light or heavy, in the room above—absolute silence everywhere. Besides locking and bolting my door, I had moved an old wooden chest against it, which I had found under the bed. To remove this chest (my blood ran cold, as I thought what its contents *might* be!) without making some disturbance, was impossible; and, moreover, to think of escaping through the house, now barred-up for the night, was sheer insanity. Only one chance was left me— the window. I stole to it on tiptoe.

My bedroom was on the first floor, above an *entresol*,* and looked into the back street, which you have sketched in your view. I raised my hand to open the window, knowing that on that action hung, by the merest hair's-breadth, my chance of safety. They keep vigilant watch in a House of Murder—if any part of the frame cracked, if the hinge creaked, I was, perhaps, a lost man! It must have occupied me at least five minutes, reckoning by time—five *hours*, reckoning by suspense—to open that window. I succeeded in doing it silently, in doing it with all the dexterity of a house-breaker: and then looked down into the street. To leap the distance beneath me, would be almost certain destruction! Next, I looked round at the sides of the house. Down the left side, ran the thick water-pipe which you have drawn—it passed close by the outer edge of the window. The moment I saw the pipe, I knew I was saved; my breath came and went freely for the first time since I had seen the canopy of the bed moving down upon me!

To some men, the means of escape which I had discovered might have seemed difficult and dangerous enough —to *me*, the prospect of slipping down the pipe into the street did not suggest even a thought of peril. I had always been accustomed, by the practice of gymnastics, to keep up my schoolboy powers as a daring and expert climber; and knew that my head, hands, and feet would serve me faithfully in any hazards of ascent or descent. I had already got one leg over the window-sill, when I remembered the handkerchief, filled with money, under my pillow. I could well have afforded to leave it behind me; but I was revengefully determined that the miscreants of the gambling-house should miss their plunder as well as their victim. So I went back to the bed, and tied the heavy handkerchief at my back by my cravat. Just as I had made it tight, and fixed it in a comfortable place, I thought I heard a sound of breathing outside the door. The chill feeling of horror ran through me again as I listened. No! dead silence still in the passage—I had only heard the night air blowing softly into the room.

The next moment I was on the window-sill—and the next, I had a firm grip on the water-pipe with my hands and knees.

I slid down into the street easily and quietly, as I thought I should, and immediately set off, at the top of my speed, to a branch 'Prefecture' of Police, which I knew was situated in the immediate neighbourhood. A 'Sub-Prefect' and several picked men among his subordinates, happened to be up, maturing, I believe, some scheme for discovering the perpetrator of a mysterious murder, which all Paris was talking of just then. When I began my story, in a breathless hurry and in very bad French. I could see that the Sub-Prefect suspected me of being a drunken Englishman, who had robbed somebody, but he soon altered his opinion, as I went on; and before I had anything like concluded, he shoved all the papers before him into a drawer, put on his hat, supplied me with another (for I was bare-headed), ordered a file of soldiers, desired his expert followers to get ready all sorts of tools for breaking open doors and ripping-up brick-flooring, and took my arm, in the most friendly and familiar manner possible, to lead me with him out of the house. I will venture to say, that when the Sub-Prefect was a little boy, and was taken for the first time to the Play, he was not half as much pleased as he was now at the job in prospect for him at the 'Gambling-House'!

Away we went through the streets, the Sub-Prefect cross-examining and congratulating me in the same breath, as we marched at the head of our formidable *posse comitatus*.* Sentinels were placed at the back and front of the gambling-house the moment we got to it; a tremendous battery of knocks was directed against the door; a light appeared at a window; I waited to conceal myself behind the police—then came more knocks, and a cry of 'Open in the name of the law!' At that terrible summons, bolts and locks gave way before an invisible hand, and the moment after, the Sub-Prefect was in the passage, confronting a waiter, half-dressed and ghastly pale. This was the short dialogue which immediately took place.

'We want to see the Englishman who is sleeping in this house?'

'He went away hours ago.'

'He did no such thing. His friend went away; *he* remained. Show us to his bedroom!'

'I swear to you, Monsieur le Sous-Prefet, he is not here! he——'

'I swear to you, Monsieur le Garçon, he is. He slept here—he didn't find your bed comfortable—he came to us to complain of it—here he is, among my men—and here am I, ready to look for a flea or two in his bedstead. Picard! (calling to one of the subordinates, and pointing to the waiter) collar that man, and tie his hands behind him. Now, then, gentlemen, let us walk upstairs!'

Every man and woman in the house was secured—the 'Old Soldier', the first. Then I identified the bed in which I had slept; and then we went into the room above. No object that was at all extraordinary appeared in any part of it. The Sub-Prefect looked round the place, commanded everybody to be silent, stamped twice on the floor, called for a candle, looked attentively at the spot he had stamped on, and ordered the flooring there to be carefully taken up. This was done in no time. Lights were produced, and we saw a deep raftered cavity between the floor of this room and the ceiling of the room beneath. Through this cavity there ran perpendicularly a sort of case of iron, thickly greased; and inside the case, appeared the screw, which communicated with the bed-top below. Extra lengths of screw, freshly oiled—levers covered with felt—all the complete upper works of a heavy press, constructed with infernal ingenuity so as to join the fixtures below—and, when taken to pieces again, to go into the smallest possible compass, were next discovered, and pulled out on the floor. After some little difficulty, the Sub-Prefect succeeded in putting the machinery together, and, leaving his men to work it, descended with me to the bedroom. The smothering canopy was then lowered, but not so noiselessly as I had seen it lowered. When I mentioned this to the Sub-Prefect, his answer, simple as it was, had a terrible significance. 'My men,' said he, 'are working down the bed-top for the first time—the men whose money you won, were in better practice.'

We left the house in the sole possession of two police agents—every one of the inmates being removed to prison on the spot. The Sub-Prefect, after taking down my '*procès-verbal*' in his office, returned with me to my hotel to get my passport. 'Do you think,' I asked, as I gave it to him, 'that any men have really been smothered in that bed, as they tried to smother *me?*'

'I have seen dozens of drowned men laid out at the Morgue,' answered the Sub-Prefect, 'in whose pocket-books were found letters, stating that they had committed suicide in the Seine, because they had lost everything at the gaming-table. Do I know how many of those men entered the same gambling-house that *you* entered? won as *you* won? took that bed as *you* took it? slept in it? were smothered in it? and were privately thrown into the river, with a letter of explanation written by the murderers and placed in their pocket-books? No man can say how many, or how few, have suffered the fate from which you have escaped. The people of the gambling-house kept their bedstead machinery a secret from *us*—even from the police! The dead kept the rest of the secret for them. Good night, or rather good morning, Monsieur Faulkner! Be at my office again at nine o'clock—in the meantime, *au revoir!*'

The rest of my story is soon told. I was examined, and re-examined; the gambling-house was strictly searched all through, from top to bottom; the prisoners were separately interrogated; and two of the less guilty among them made a confession. *I* discovered that the Old Soldier was the master of the gambling-house—*justice* discovered that he had been drummed out of the army, as a vagabond, years ago; that he had been guilty of all sorts of villanies since; that he was in possession of stolen property, which the owners identified; and that he, the croupier, another accomplice, and the woman who had made my cup of coffee, were all in the secret of the bedstead. There appeared some reason to doubt whether the inferior persons attached to the house knew anything of the suffocating machinery; and they received the benefit of that doubt, by being treated simply as thieves and vagabonds. As for the Old Soldier and his two

head-myrmidons, they went to the galleys; the woman who
had drugged my coffee was imprisoned for I forget how
many years; the regular attendants at the gambling-house
were considered 'suspicious,' and placed under 'surveil-
lance;' and I became, for one whole week (which is a long
time), the head 'lion' in Parisian society. My adventure was
dramatised by three illustrious playmakers, but never saw
theatrical daylight; for the censorship forbade the introduction on the stage of a correct copy of the gambling-house
bedstead.

Two good results were produced by my adventure, which
any censorship must have approved. In the first place, it
helped to justify the Government in forthwith carrying out
their determination to put down all gambling-houses; in the
second place, it cured me of ever again trying 'Rouge et
Noir' as an amusement. The sight of a green cloth, with
packs of cards and heaps of money on it, will henceforth be
for ever associated in my mind with the sight of a bed-
canopy descending to suffocate me, in the silence and darkness of the night.'

Just as Mr Faulkner pronounced the last words, he started
in his chair, and assumed a stiff, dignified position, in a
great hurry. 'Bless my soul!' cried he—with a comic look of
astonishment and vexation—'while I have been telling you
what is the real secret of my interest in the sketch you have
so kindly given to me, I have altogether forgotten that I
came here to sit for my portrait. For the last hour, or more,
I must have been the worst model you ever had to paint
from!'

'On the contrary, you have been the best,' said I. 'I have
been painting from your expression; and, while telling your
story, you have unconsciously shown me the natural expression I wanted.'

A STOLEN LETTER

NOW, first of all, I should like to know what you mean by a story? You mean what other people do? And pray what is that? You know, but you can't exactly tell. I thought so! In the course of a pretty long legal experience, I have never yet met with a party out of my late profession, who was capable of giving a correct definition of anything.

To judge by your looks, I suspect you are amused at my talking of any such thing ever having belonged to me as a profession. Ha! ha! Here I am, with my toes out of my boots, without a shirt to my back or a rap in my pocket, except the fourpence I get out of this charity (against the present administration of which I protest—but that's not the point), and yet not two years ago I was an attorney in large practice in a bursting big country town. I had a house in the High Street. Such a giant of a house that you had to get up six steps to knock at the front door. I had a footman to drive tramps like me off all or any one of my six hearth-stoned* steps, if they dared sit down on all or any one of my six hearth-stoned steps;—a footman who would give me into custody now if I tried to shake hands with him in the streets. I decline to answer your questions if you ask me any. How I got into trouble, and dropped down to where I am now, is my secret.

Now, I absolutely decline to tell you a story. But, though I won't tell a story, I am ready to make a statement. A statement is a matter of fact; therefore the exact opposite of a story, which is a matter of fiction. What I am now going to tell you really happened to me.

I served my time—never mind in whose office; and I started in business for myself, in one of our English country towns—I decline stating which. I hadn't a quarter of the capital I ought to have had to begin with; and my friends in the neighbourhood were poor and useless enough, with one exception. That exception was Mr Frank Gatliffe, son of Mr Gatliffe, member for the county, the richest man and the proudest for many a mile round about our parts.—Stop a bit! you man in the corner there; you needn't perk up and look knowing. You won't trace any particulars by the name of Gatliffe. I'm not bound to commit myself or anybody else by mentioning names. I have given you the first that came into my head.

Well! Mr Frank was a staunch friend of mine, and ready to recommend me whenever he got the chance. I had given him a little timely help—for a consideration, of course—in borrowing money at a fair rate of interest: in fact, I had saved him from the Jews. The money was borrowed while Mr Frank was at college. He came back from college, and stopped at home a little while: and then there got spread about all our neighbourhood, a report that he had fallen in love, as the saying is, with his young sister's governess, and that his mind was made up to marry her.—What! you're at it again, my man in the corner! You want to know her name, don't you? What do you think of Smith?

Speaking as a lawyer, I consider Report, in a general way, to be a fool and a liar. But in this case report turned out to be something very different. Mr Frank told me he was really in love, and said upon his honour (an absurd expression which young chaps of his age are always using) he was determined to marry Smith the governess—the sweet darling girl, as *he* called her; but I'm not sentimental, and *I* call her Smith the governess (with an eye, of course, to refreshing the memory of my friend in the corner). Mr Frank's father, being as proud as Lucifer, said 'No' as to marrying the governess, when Mr Frank wanted him to say 'Yes.' He was a man of business, was old Gatliffe, and he took the proper business course. He sent the governess away with a first-rate character and a spanking present; and then he looked about him to get something for Mr Frank to do. While he was looking about, Mr Frank bolted to London after the governess, who had nobody alive belonging to her to go to but an aunt—her father's sister. The aunt refuses to let Mr Frank in without the squire's permission. Mr Frank writes to his father, and says he will marry the girl as soon as he is of age, or shoot himself. Up to town comes the squire, and his wife, and his daughter; and a lot of sentimentality, not in the slightest degree material to the present statement, takes place among them; and the upshot of it is that old Gatliffe is forced into withdrawing the word No, and substituting the word Yes.

I don't believe he would ever have done it, though, but for one lucky peculiarity in the case. The governess's father was a man of good family—pretty nigh as good as Gatliffe's own. He had been in the army; had sold out; set up as a wine-merchant—failed—died: ditto his wife, as to the dying part of it. No relation, in fact, left for the squire to make inquiries about but the father's sister; who had behaved, as old Gatliffe said, like a thorough-bred gentlewoman in shutting the door against Mr Frank in the first instance. So, to cut the matter short, things were at last made up pleasant enough. The time was fixed for the wedding, and an announcement about it—Marriage in High Life and all that—put into the county paper. There was a regular biography, besides, of the governess's father, so as to stop people from talking; a great flourish about his pedigree, and a long account of his services in the army; but not a word, mind ye, of his having turned wine-merchant afterwards. Oh, no—not a word about that! I knew it, though, for Mr Frank told me. He hadn't a bit of pride about him. He introduced me to his future wife one day when I met them out walking, and asked me if I did not think he was a lucky fellow. I don't mind admitting that I did, and that I told him so. Ah! but she was one of my sort, was that governess. Stood, to the best of my recollection, five foot four. Good lissome figure, that looked as if it had never been boxed up in a pair of stays. Eyes that made me feel as if I was under a pretty stiff cross-examination the moment she looked at me. Fine red, fresh, kiss-and-come-again sort of lips. Cheeks and complexion——No, my man in the corner, you wouldn't identify her by her cheeks and complexion, if I drew you a picture of them this very moment. She has had a family of children since the time I'm talking of; and her cheeks are a trifle fatter and her complexion is a shade or two redder now, than when I first met her out walking with Mr Frank.

The marriage was to take place on a Wednesday. I decline mentioning the year or the month. I had started as an attorney on my own account—say six weeks, more or less, and was sitting alone in my office on the Monday morning before the wedding-day, trying to see my way clear before me and not succeeding particularly well, when Mr Frank suddenly bursts in, as white as any ghost that ever was painted, and says he's got the most dreadful case for me to advise on, and not an hour to lose in acting on my advice.

'Is this in the way of business, Mr Frank?' says I, stopping him just as he was beginning to get sentimental. 'Yes or no, Mr Frank?' rapping my new office paper-knife on the table to pull him up short all the sooner.

'My dear fellow'—he was always familiar with me—'it's in the way of business, certainly; but friendship——'

I was obliged to pull him up short again and regularly examine him as if he had been in the witness-box, or he would have kept me talking to no purpose half the day.

'Now, Mr Frank,' said I, 'I can't have any sentimentality mixed up with business matters. You please to stop talking, and let me ask questions. Answer in the fewest words you can use. Nod when nodding will do instead of words.'

I fixed him with my eye for about three seconds, as he sat groaning and wriggling in his chair. When I'd done fixing him, I gave another rap with my paper-knife on to the table to startle him up a bit. Then I went on.

'From what you have been stating up to the present time,' says I, 'I gather that you are in a scrape which is likely to interfere seriously with your marriage on Wednesday?' (He nodded, and I cut in again before he could say a word). 'The scrape affects the young lady you are about to marry, and goes back to the period of a certain transaction in which her late father was engaged some years ago?' (He nods, and I cut in once more.) 'There is a party who turned up after seeing the announcement of your marriage in the paper, who is cognisant of what he oughtn't to know, and who is prepared to use his knowledge of the same, to the prejudice of the young lady and of your marriage, unless he receives a sum of money to quiet him? Very well. Now, first of all, Mr

Frank, state what you have been told by the young lady herself about the transaction of her late father. How did you first come to have any knowledge of it?'

'She was talking to me about her father one day, so tenderly and prettily, that she quite excited my interest about him,' begins Mr Frank; 'and I asked her, among other things, what had occasioned his death. She said she believed it was distress of mind in the first instance; and added that this distress was connected with a shocking secret, which she and her mother had kept from everybody, but which she could not keep from me, because she was determined to begin her married life by having no secrets from her husband.' Here Mr Frank began to get sentimental again; and I pulled him up short once more with the paper-knife.

'She told me,' Mr Frank went on, 'that the great mistake of her father's life was his selling out of the army and taking to the wine trade. He had no talent for business; things went wrong with him from the first. His clerk, it was strongly suspected, cheated him——'

'Stop a bit,' says I, 'What was that suspected clerk's name?'

'Davager,' says he.

'Davager,' says I, making a note of it. 'Go on, Mr Frank.'

'His affairs got more and more entangled,' says Mr Frank; 'he was pressed for money in all directions; bankruptcy, and consequent dishonour (as he considered it) stared him in the face. His mind was so affected by his troubles that both his wife and daughter, towards the last, considered him to be hardly responsible for his own acts. In this state of desperation and misery, he——' Here Mr Frank began to hesitate.

We have two ways in the law, of drawing evidence off nice and clear from an unwilling client or witness. We give him a fright or we treat him to a joke. I treated Mr Frank to a joke.

'Ah!' says I. 'I know what he did. He had a signature to write; and, by the most natural mistake in the world, he wrote another gentleman's name instead of his own—eh?'

'It was to a bill,' says Mr Frank, looking very crestfallen, instead of taking the joke. 'His principal creditor wouldn't wait till he could raise the money, or the greater part of it. But he was resolved, if he sold off everything, to get the amount and repay——'

'Of course!' says I. 'Drop that. The forgery was discovered. When?'

'Before even the first attempt was made to negotiate the bill. He had done the whole thing in the most absurdly and innocently wrong way. The person whose name he had used was a staunch friend of his, and a relation of his wife's: a good man as well as a rich one. He had influence with the chief creditor, and he used it nobly. He had a real affection for the unfortunate man's wife, and he proved it generously.'

'Come to the point,' says I. 'What did he do? In a business way, what did he do?'

'He put the false bill into the fire, drew a bill of his own to replace it, and then—only then—told my dear girl and her mother all that had happened. Can you imagine anything nobler?' asks Mr Frank.

'Speaking in my professional capacity, I can't imagine anything greener!' says I. 'Where was the father? Off, I suppose?'

'Ill in bed,' said Mr Frank, colouring. 'But, he mustered strength enough to write a contrite and grateful letter the same day, promising to prove himself worthy of the noble moderation and forgiveness extended to him, by selling off everything he possessed to repay his money debt. He did sell off everything, down to some old family pictures that were heirlooms; down to the little plate he had; down to the very tables and chairs that furnished his drawing room. Every farthing of the debt was paid; and he was left to begin the world again, with the kindest promises of help from the generous man who had forgiven him. It was too late. His crime of one rash moment—atoned for though it had been —preyed upon his mind. He became possessed with the idea that he had lowered himself for ever in the estimation of his wife and daughter, and——'

'He died,' I cut in. 'Yes, yes, we know that. Let's go back for a minute to the contrite and grateful letter that he wrote.

My experience in the law, Mr Frank, has convinced me that if everybody burnt everybody else's letters, half the Courts of Justice in this country might shut up shop. Do you happen to know whether the letter we are now speaking of contained anything like an avowal or confession of the forgery?'

'Of course it did,' says he. 'Could the writer express his contrition properly without making some such confession?'

'Quite easy, if he had been a lawyer,' says I. 'But never mind that; I'm going to make a guess,—a desperate guess, mind. Should I be altogether in error,' says I, 'if I thought that this letter had been stolen; and that the fingers of Mr Davager, of suspicious commercial celebrity, might possibly be the fingers which took it?' says I.

'That is exactly what I tried to make you understand,' cried Mr Frank.

'How did he communicate that interesting fact to you?'

'He has not ventured into my presence. The scoundrel actually had the audacity—'

'Aha!' says I. 'The young lady herself! Sharp practitioner, Mr Davager.'

'Early this morning, when she was walking alone in the shrubbery' Mr Frank goes on, 'he had the assurance to approach her, and to say that he had been watching his opportunity of getting a private interview for days past. He then showed her—actually showed her—her unfortunate father's letter; put into her hands another letter directed to me; bowed, and walked off; leaving her half dead with astonishment and terror!'

'It was much better for you that you were not,' says I. 'Have you got that other letter?'

He handed it to me. It was so extremely humorous and short, that I remember every word of it at this distance of time. It began in this way:

To Francis Gatliffe, Esq., Jun.—Sir,—I have an extremely curious autograph letter to sell. The price is a Five hundred pound note. The young lady to whom you are to be married on Wednesday will inform you of the nature of the letter, and the genuineness of the autograph. If you refuse to deal, I shall send a copy to the local paper, and shall wait on your highly respected father with the original curiosity, on the afternoon of Tuesday next. Having come down here on family business, I have put up at the family hotel— being to be heard of at the Gatliffe Arms.

Your very obedient servant,
Alfred Davager.

'A clever fellow, that,' says I, putting the letter into my private drawer.

'Clever!' cries Mr Frank, 'he ought to be horsewhipped within an inch of his life. I would have done it myself, but she made me promise, before she told me a word of the matter, to come straight to you.'

'That was one of the wisest promises you ever made,' says I. 'We can't afford to bully this fellow, whatever else we may do with him. Don't think I am saying anything libellous against your excellent father's character when I assert that if he saw the letter he would certainly insist on your marriage being put off, at the very least?'

'Feeling as my father does about my marriage, he would insist on its being dropped altogether, if he saw this letter,' says Mr Frank, with a groan. 'But even that is not the worst of it. The generous, noble girl herself says; that if the letter appears in the paper, with all the unanswerable comments this scoundrel would be sure to add to it, she would rather die than hold me to my engagement—even if my father would let me keep it.' He was a weak young fellow, and ridiculously fond of her. I brought him back to business with another rap of the paper-knife.

'Hold up, Mr Frank,' says I. 'I have a question or two more. Did you think of asking the young lady whether, to the best of her knowledge, this infernal letter was the only written evidence of the forgery now in existence?'

'Yes, I did think directly of asking her that,' says he; 'and she told me she was quite certain that there was no written evidence of the forgery, except that one letter.'

'Will you give Mr Davager his price for it?' says I.

'Yes,' says Mr Frank, as quick as lightning.

'Mr Frank,' says I, 'you came here to get my help and advice in this extremely ticklish business, and you are ready, as I know, without asking, to remunerate me for all and any of my services at the usual professional rate. Now, I've made up my mind to act boldly—desperately, if you like— on the hit or miss—win-all-or-lose-all principle—in dealing with this matter. Here is my proposal. I'm going to try if I can't do Mr Davager out of his letter. If I don't succeed before tomorrow afternoon, you hand him the money, and I charge you nothing for professional services. If I do suc- ceed, I hand you the letter instead of Mr Davager; and you give me the money, instead of giving it to him. It's a precious risk for me, but I'm ready to run it. You must pay your five hundred any way. What do you say to my plan? Is it, Yes—Mr Frank—or, No?'

'Hang your questions!' cries Mr Frank, jumping up; 'you know it's Yes, ten thousand times over. Only you earn the money and——'

'And you will be too glad to give it to me. Very good. Now go home. Comfort the young lady—don't let Mr Davager so much as set eyes on you—keep quiet—leave everything to me—and feel as certain as you please that all the letters in the world can't stop your being married on Wednesday.' With these words I hustled him off out of the office; for I wanted to be left alone to make my mind up about what I should do.

The first thing, of course, was to have a look at the enemy. I wrote to Mr Davager, telling him that I was privately appointed to arrange the little business-matter between himself and 'another party' (no names!) on friendly terms; and begging him to call on me at his earliest convenience. At the very beginning of the case, Mr Davager bothered me. His answer was that it would not be convenient to him to call till between six and seven in the evening. In this way, you see, he contrived to make me lose several precious hours, at a time when minutes almost were of importance. I had nothing for it, but to be patient, and to give certain instructions, before Mr Davager came, to my boy Tom.

There was never such a sharp boy of fourteen before, and there never will be again, as my boy, Tom. A spy to look after Mr Davager was, of course, the first requisite in a case of this kind; and Tom was the smallest, quickest, quietest, sharpest, stealthiest little snake of a chap that ever dogged a gentleman's steps and kept cleverly out of range of a gentleman's eyes. I settled it with the boy that he was not to show at all, when Mr Davager came; and that he was to wait to hear me ring the bell, when Mr Davager left. If I rang twice, he was to show the gentleman out. If I rang once, he was to keep out of the way and follow the gentleman wherever he went, till he got back to the inn. Those were the only preparations I could make to begin with; being obliged to wait, and let myself be guided by what turned up.

About a quarter to seven my gentleman came. In the profession of the law we get somehow quite remarkably mixed up with ugly people, blackguard people, and dirty people. But far away the ugliest and dirtiest blackguard I ever saw in my life was Mr Alfred Davager. He had greasy white hair and a mottled face. He was low in the forehead, fat in the stomach, hoarse in the voice, and weak in the legs. Both his eyes were bloodshot, and one was fixed in his head. He smelt of spirits, and carried a toothpick in his mouth. 'How are you? I've just done dinner,' says he—and he lights a cigar, sits down with his legs crossed, and winks at me.

I tried at first to take the measure of him in a wheedling, confidential way; but it was no good. I asked him in a facetious smiling manner, how he had got hold of the letter. He only told me in answer that he had been in the confidential employment of the writer of it, and that he had always been famous since infancy, for a sharp eye to his own interests. I paid him some compliments; but he was not to be flattered. I tried to make him lose his temper; but he kept it in spite of me. It ended in his driving me to my last resource—I made an attempt to frighten him.

'Before we say a word about the money,' I began, 'let me put a case, Mr Davager. The pull you have on Mr Francis Gatliffe is, that you can hinder his marriage on Wednesday. Now, suppose I have got a magistrate's warrant to apprehend you in my pocket? Suppose I have a constable to execute it in the next room? Suppose I bring you up tomorrow—the day before the marriage—charge you only generally with an attempt to extort money, and apply for a day's remand to complete the case? Suppose, as a suspicious stranger, you can't get bail in this town? Suppose ——'

'Stop a bit,' says Mr Davager; 'Suppose I should not be the greenest fool that ever stood in shoes? Suppose I should not carry the letter about me? Suppose I should have given a certain envelope to a certain friend of mine in a certain place in this town? Suppose the letter should be inside that envelope, directed to old Gatliffe, side by side with a copy of the letter, directed to the editor of the local paper? Suppose my friend should be instructed to open the envelope, and take the letters to their right addresses, if I don't appear to claim them from him this evening? In short, my dear sir, suppose you were born yesterday, and suppose I wasn't?'—says Mr Davager, and winks at me again.

He didn't take me by surprise, for I never expected that he had the letter about him. I made a pretence of being very much taken aback, and of being quite ready to give in. We settled our business about delivering the letter and handing over the money, in no time. I was to draw out a document, which he was to sign. He knew the document was stuff and nonsense just as well as I did; and told me I was only proposing it to swell my client's bill. Sharp as he was, he was wrong there. The document was not to be drawn out to gain money from Mr Frank, but to gain time from Mr Davager. It served me as an excuse to put off the payment of the five hundred pounds till three o'clock on the Tuesday afternoon. The Tuesday morning Mr Davager said he should devote to his amusement, and asked me what sights were to be seen in the neighbourhood of the town. When I had told him, he pitched his toothpick into my grate—yawned—and went out.

I rang the bell once; waited till he had passed the window; and then looked after Tom. There was my jewel of a boy on the opposite side of the street, just setting his top going in the most playful manner possible. Mr Davager walked away up the street, towards the market-place. Tom whipped his top up the street towards the market-place too.

In a quarter of an hour he came back, with all his evidence collected in a beautifully clear and compact state. Mr

Davager had walked to a public-house, just outside the town, in a lane leading to the high road. On a bench outside the public-house there sat a man smoking. He said 'All right?' and gave a letter to Mr Davager, who answered 'All right,' and walked back to the inn. In the hall he ordered hot rum and water, cigars, slippers, and a fire to be lit in his room. After that, he went upstairs, and Tom came away.

I now saw my road clear before me—not very far on, but still clear. I had housed the letter, in all probability for that night, at the Gatliffe Arms. After tipping Tom, I gave him directions to play about the door of the inn, and refresh himself, when he was tired, at the tart-shop opposite— eating as much as he pleased, on the understanding that he crammed all the time with his eye on the window. If Mr Davager went out, or Mr Davager's friend called on him, Tom was to let me know. He was also to take a little note from me to the head chambermaid—an old friend of mine— asking her to step over to my office, on a private matter of business, as soon as her work was done for that night. After settling these little matters, having half an hour to spare, I turned to and did myself a bloater at the office-fire, and had a drop of gin and water hot, and felt comparatively happy.

When the head chambermaid came, it turned out, as good luck would have it, that Mr Davager had offended her. I no sooner mentioned him than she flew into a passion; and when I added, by way of clinching the matter, that I was retained to defend the interests of a very beautiful and deserving young lady (name not referred to, of course) against the most cruel underhand treachery on the part of Mr Davager, the head chambermaid was ready to go any lengths that she could safely to serve my cause. In few words, I discovered that Boots was to call Mr Davager at eight the next morning, and was to take his clothes down- stairs to brush as usual. If Mr D. had not emptied his own pockets overnight, we arranged that Boots was to forget to empty them for him, and was to bring the clothes down- stairs just as he found them. If Mr D.'s pockets were emp- tied, then, of course, it would be necessary to transfer the searching process to Mr D.'s room. Under any circumstances,

I was certain of the head chambermaid; and under any circumstances also, the head chambermaid was certain of Boots.

I waited till Tom came home, looking very puffy and bilious about the face; but as to his intellects, if anything, rather sharper than ever. His report was uncommonly short and pleasant. The inn was shutting up; Mr Davager was going to bed in rather a drunken condition; Mr Davager's friend had never appeared. I sent Tom (properly instructed about keeping our man in view all the next morning) to his shake-down behind the office desk, where I heard him hiccuping half the night, as boys will, when over-excited and too full of tarts.

At half-past seven next morning, I slipped quietly into Boots's pantry. Down came the clothes. No pockets in trousers. Waistcoat pockets empty. Coat pockets with something in them. First, handkerchief; secondly, bunch of keys; thirdly, cigar-case; fourthly, pocket-book. Of course I wasn't such a fool as to expect to find the letter there; but I opened the pocket-book with a certain curiosity, notwithstanding.

Nothing in the two pockets of the book but some old advertisements cut out of newspapers, a lock of hair tied round with a dirty bit of ribbon, a circular letter about a loan society, and some copies of verses not likely to suit any company that was not of an extremely wicked description. On the leaves of the pocket-book, people's addresses scrawled in pencil, and bets jotted down in red ink. On one leaf, by itself, this queer inscription: 'MEM. 5 ALONG. 4 ACROSS.' I understood everything but those words and figures; so of course I copied them out into my own book. Then I waited in the pantry, till Boots had brushed the clothes and had taken them upstairs. His report, when he came down was, that Mr D. had asked if it was a fine morning. Being told that it was, he had ordered breakfast at nine, and a saddle-horse to be at the door at ten, to take him to Grimwith Abbey—one of the sights in our neighbourhood which I had told him of the evening before.

'I'll be here, coming in by the back way at half-past ten,' says I to the head chambermaid. 'To take the responsibility of making Mr Davager's bed off your hands for this morning only. I want to hire Sam for the morning. Put it down in the order-book that he's to be brought round to my office at ten.'

Sam was a pony, and I'd made up my mind that it would be beneficial to Tom's health, after the tarts, if he took a constitutional airing on a nice hard saddle in the direction of Grimwith Abbey.

'Anything else,' says the head chambermaid.

'Only one more favour,' says I. 'Would my boy Tom be very much in the way if he came, from now till ten, to help with the boots and shoes, and stood at his work close by this window which looks out on the staircase?'

'Not a bit,' says the head chambermaid.

'Thank you,' says I; and stepped back to my office directly.

When I had sent Tom off to help with the boots and shoes, I reviewed the whole case exactly as it stood at that time. There were three things Mr Davager might do with the letter. He might give it to his friend again before ten—in which case, Tom would most likely see the said friend on the stairs. He might take it to his friend, or to some other friend, after ten—in which case, Tom was ready to follow him on Sam the pony. And, lastly, he might leave it hidden somewhere in his room at the inn—in which case, I was all ready for him with a search-warrant of my own granting, under favour always of my friend the head chambermaid. So far I had my business arrangements all gathered up nice and compact in my own hands. Only two things bothered me: the terrible shortness of the time at my disposal, in case I failed in my first experiments for getting hold of the letter, and that queer inscription which I had copied out of the pocket-book.

'MEM. 5 ALONG. 4 ACROSS.' It was the measurement, most likely, of something, and he was afraid of forgetting it; therefore, it was something important. Query—something about himself? Say '5' (inches) 'along'—he doesn't wear a wig. Say '5' (feet) 'along'—it can't be coat, waistcoat, trousers, or underclothing. Say '5' (yards) 'along'—it can't be anything about himself, unless he wears round his body the rope that he's sure to be hanged with one of these days. Then it is *not* something about himself. What do I know of that is important to him besides? I know of nothing but the Letter. Can the memorandum be connected with that? Say, yes. What do '5 along' and '4 across' mean then? The measurement of something he carries about with him?—or the measurement of something in his room? I could get pretty satisfactorily to myself as far as that; but I could get no further.

Tom came back to the office, and reported him mounted for his ride. His friend had never appeared. I sent the boy off, with his proper instructions, on Sam's back—wrote an encouraging letter to Mr Frank to keep him quiet—then slipped into the inn by the back way a little before half-past ten. The head chambermaid gave me a signal when the landing was clear. I got into his room without a soul but her seeing me, and locked the door immediately. The case was, to a certain extent, simplified now. Either Mr Davager had ridden out with the letter about him, or he had left it in some safe hiding-place in his room. I suspected it to be in his room, for a reason that will a little astonish you—his trunk, his dressing-case, and all the drawers and cupboards were left open. I knew my customer, and I thought this extraordinary carelessness on his part rather suspicious.

Mr Davager had taken one of the best bedrooms at the Gatliffe Arms. Floor carpeted all over, walls beautifully papered, four-poster, and general furniture first-rate. I searched, to begin with, on the usual plan, examining every thing in every possible way, and taking more than an hour about it. No discovery. Then I pulled out a carpenter's rule which I had brought with me. Was there anything in the room which—either in inches, feet, or yards—answered to '5 along' and '4 across?' Nothing. I put the rule back in my pocket—measurement was no good evidently. Was there anything in the room that would count up to 5 one way and 4 another, seeing that nothing would measure up to it? I had got obstinately persuaded by this time that the letter must be in the room—principally because of the trouble I had had in looking after it. And persuading myself of that, I took it into my head next, just as obstinately, that '5 along' and '4 across' must be the right clue to find the letter by—principally because I hadn't left myself, after all my searching and thinking, even so much as the vestige of another guide to go by. '5 along'—where could I count five along the room, in any part of it?

Not on the paper. The pattern there was pillars of trellis-work and flowers, enclosing a plain green ground—only four pillars along the wall and only two across. The furniture? There were not five chairs, or five separate pieces of any furniture in the room altogether. The fringes that hung from the cornice of the bed? Plenty of them, at any rate! Up I jumped on the counterpane, with my penknife in my hand. Every way that '5 along' and '4 across' could be reckoned on those unlucky fringes, I reckoned on them—probed with my penknife—scratched with my nails—crunched with my fingers. No use; not a sign of a letter; and the time was getting on—oh, Lord! how the time did get on in Mr Davager's room that morning.

I jumped down from the bed, so desperate at my ill-luck that I hardly cared whether anybody heard me or not. Quite a little cloud of dust rose at my feet as they thumped on the carpet. 'Hallo!' thought I; 'my friend the head chamber-maid takes it easy here. Nice state for a carpet to be in, in one of the best bedrooms at the Gatliffe Arms.' Carpet! I had been jumping up on the bed, and staring up at the walls, but I had never so much as given a glance down at the carpet. Think of me pretending to be a lawyer, and not knowing how to look low enough!

The carpet! It had been a stout article in its time; had evidently begun in a drawing-room; then descended to a coffee-room; then gone upstairs altogether to a bedroom. The ground was brown, and the pattern was bunches of leaves and roses speckled over the ground at regular distances. I reckoned up the bunches. Ten along the room—eight across it. When I had stepped out five one way and four the other, and was down on my knees on the centre bunch, as true as I sit on this bench, I could hear my own heart beating so loud that it quite frightened me.

I looked narrowly all over the bunch, and I felt all over it with the ends of my fingers; and nothing came of that. Then

I scraped it over slowly and gently with my nails. My second finger-nail stuck a little at one place. I parted the pile of the carpet over that place, and saw a thin slit, which had been hidden by the pile being smoothed over it—a slit about half an inch long, with a little end of brown thread, exactly the colour of the carpet-ground, sticking out about a quarter of an inch from the middle of it. Just as I laid hold of the thread gently, I heard a footstep outside the door.

It was only the head chambermaid. 'Haven't you done yet?' she whispers.

'Give me two minutes,' says I; 'and don't let anybody come near the door—whatever you do, don't let anybody startle me again by coming near the door.'

I took a little pull at the thread, and heard something rustle. I took a longer pull, and out came a piece of paper, rolled up tight like those candle-lighters that the ladies make. I unrolled it—and, by George! gentlemen all, there was the letter!

The original letter!—I knew it by the colour of the ink. The letter that was worth five hundred pound to me! It was all I could do to keep myself at first from throwing my hat into the air, and hooraying like mad. I had to take a chair and sit quiet in it for a minute or two, before I could cool myself down to my proper business level. I knew that I was safely down again when I found myself pondering how to let Mr Davager know that he had been done by the innocent country attorney, after all.

It was not long before a nice little irritating plan occurred to me. I tore a blank leaf out of my pocket-book, wrote on it with my pencil 'Change for a five hundred pound note,' folded up the paper, tied the thread to it, poked it back into the hiding-place, smoothed over the pile of the carpet, and—as everybody in this place guesses before I can tell them—bolted off to Mr Frank. He, in his turn, bolted off to show the letter to the young lady, who first certified to its genuineness, then dropped it into the fire, and then took the initiative for the first time since her marriage engagement, by flinging her arms round his neck, kissing him with all her might, and going into hysterics in his arms. So at least

Mr Frank told me; but that's not evidence. It is evidence, however, that I saw them married with my own eyes on the Wednesday; and that while they went off in a carriage and four to spend the honeymoon, I went off on my own legs to open a credit at the Town and County Bank with a five hundred pound note in my pocket.

As to Mr Davager, I can tell you nothing about him, except what is derived from hearsay evidence, which is always unsatisfactory evidence, even in a lawyer's mouth.

My boy, Tom, although twice kicked off by Sam the pony, never lost hold of the bridle, and kept his man in sight from first to last. He had nothing particular to report, except that on the way out to the Abbey Mr Davager had stopped at the public-house, had spoken a word or two to his friend of the night before, and had handed him what looked like a bit of paper. This was no doubt a clue to the thread that held the letter, to be used in case of accidents. In every other respect Mr D. had ridden out and ridden in like an ordinary sight-seer. Tom reported him to me as having dismounted at the hotel about two. At half-past, I locked my office door, nailed a card under the knocker with 'not at home till tomorrow' written on it, and retired to a friend's house a mile or so out of the town for the rest of the day.

Mr Davager left the Gatliffe Arms that night with his best clothes on his back and with all the valuable contents of his dressing-case in his pockets. I am not in a condition to state whether he ever went through the form of asking for his bill or not; but I can positively testify that he never paid it, and that the effects left in his bedroom did not pay it either. When I add to these fragments of evidence, that he and I have never met (luckily for me), since I jockeyed* him out of his bank note, I have about fulfilled my implied contract as maker of a statement, with the present company as hearers of a statement.

MAD MONKTON

I

THE Monktons of Wincot Abbey bore a sad character for
want of sociability in our county. They held no friendly
intercourse with their neighbours; and, excepting my father,
and a lady and her daughter living near them, they never
received anyone under their own roof.

Proud as they all certainly were, it was not pride but dread
which kept them thus apart from their neighbours. The
family had suffered for generations past from the horrible
affliction of hereditary insanity, and the members of it
shrank from exposing their calamity to others, as they must
have exposed it if they had mingled with the busy little
world around them. There is a frightful story of a crime
committed in past times by two of the Monktons, near
relatives, from which the first appearance of the insanity was
always supposed to date, but it is needless for me to shock
anyone by repeating it. It is enough to say that at intervals
almost every form of madness appeared in the family;
monomania being the most frequent manifestation of the
affliction among them. I have these particulars, and one or
two yet to be related, from my father.

At the period of my youth but three of the Monktons were
left at the Abbey: Mr and Mrs Monkton, and their only
child, Alfred, heir to the property. The one other member
of this, the elder, branch of the family who was then alive,
was Mr Monkton's younger brother, Stephen. He was an
unmarried man, possessing a fine estate in Scotland; but he
lived almost entirely on the Continent, and bore the reputation of being a shameless profligate. The family at Wincot
held almost as little communication with him as with their
neighbours.

I have already mentioned my father, and a lady and her
daughter, as the only privileged people who were admitted
into Wincot Abbey.

My father had been an old school and college friend of Mr Monkton, and accident had brought them so much together in later life, that their continued intimacy at Wincot was quite intelligible. I am not so well able to account for the friendly terms on which Mrs Elmslie (the lady to whom I have already alluded) lived with the Monktons. Her late husband had been distantly related to Mrs Monkton, and my father was her daughter's guardian. But even these claims to friendship and regard never seemed to me strong enough to explain the intimacy between Mrs Elmslie and the inhabitants of the Abbey. Intimate, however, they certainly were, and one result of the constant interchange of visits between the two families in due time declared itself— Mr Monkton's son and Mrs Elmslie's daughter became attached to each other.

I had no opportunities of seeing much of the young lady; I only remember her at that time as a delicate, gentle, lovable girl, the very opposite in appearance, and apparently in character also, to Alfred Monkton. But perhaps that was one reason why they fell in love with each other. The attachment was soon discovered, and was far from being disapproved by the parents on either side. In all essential points, except that of wealth, the Elmslies were nearly the equals of the Monktons, and want of money in a bride was of no consequence to the heir of Wincot. Alfred, it was well known, would succeed to thirty thousand a year on his father's death.

Thus, though the parents on both sides thought the young people not old enough to be married at once, they saw no reason why Ada and Alfred should not be engaged to each other, with the understanding that they should be united when young Monkton came of age, in two years' time. The person to be consulted in the matter, after the parents, was my father in his capacity of Ada's guardian. He knew that the family misery had shown itself many years ago in Mrs Monkton, who was her husband's cousin. The *illness*, as it was significantly called, had been palliated by careful treatment, and was reported to have passed away. But my father was not to be deceived. He knew where the hereditary taint still lurked; he viewed with horror the bare possibility of its reappearing one day in the children of his friend's only daughter; and he positively refused his consent to the marriage engagement.

The result was that the doors of the Abbey and the doors of Mrs Elmslie's house were closed to him. This suspension of friendly intercourse had lasted but a very short time, when Mrs Monkton died. Her husband, who was fondly attached to her, caught a violent cold while attending her funeral. The cold was neglected, and settled on his lungs. In a few months' time, he followed his wife to the grave, and Alfred was left master of the grand old Abbey, and the fair lands that spread all around it.

At this period Mrs Elmslie had the indelicacy to endeavour a second time to procure my father's consent to the marriage engagement. He refused it again more positively than before. More than a year passed away. The time was approaching fast when Alfred would be of age. I returned from college to spend the long vacation at home, and made some advances towards bettering my acquaintance with young Monkton. They were evaded—certainly with perfect politeness, but still in such a way as to prevent me from offering my friendship to him again. Any mortification I might have felt at this petty repulse, under ordinary circumstances, was dismissed from my mind by the occurrence of a real misfortune in our household. For some months past my father's health had been failing, and, just at the time of which I am now writing, his sons had to mourn the irreparable calamity of his death.

This event (through some informality or error in the late Mr Elmslie's will) left the future of Ada's life entirely at her mother's disposal. The consequence was the immediate ratification of the marriage engagement to which my father had so steadily refused his consent. As soon as the fact was publicly announced, some of Mrs Elmslie's more intimate friends, who were acquainted with the reports affecting the Monkton family, ventured to mingle with their formal congratulations one or two significant references to the late Mrs Monkton, and some searching inquiries as to the disposition of her son.

Mrs Elmslie always met these polite hints with one bold form of answer. She first admitted the existence of those reports about the Monktons which her friends were unwilling to specify distinctly; and then declared that they were infamous calumnies. The hereditary taint had died out of the family generations back. Alfred was the best, the kindest, the sanest of human beings. He loved study and retirement; Ada sympathised with his tastes, and had made her choice unbiased; if any more hints were dropped about sacrificing her by her marriage, those hints would be viewed as so many insults to her mother, whose affection for her it was monstrous to call in question. This way of talking silenced people, but did not convince them. They began to suspect what was indeed the actual truth, that Mrs Elmslie was a selfish, worldly, grasping woman, who wanted to get her daughter well married, and cared nothing for consequences as long as she saw Ada mistress of the greatest establishment in the whole county.

It seemed, however, as if there was some fatality at work to prevent the attainment of Mrs Elmslie's great object in life. Hardly was one obstacle to the ill-omened marriage removed by my father's death, before another succeeded it, in the shape of anxieties and difficulties caused by the delicate state of Ada's health. Doctors were consulted in all directions, and the result of their advice was that the marriage must be deferred, and that Miss Elmslie must leave England for a certain time, to reside in a warmer climate; the South of France, if I remember rightly. Thus it happened that just before Alfred came of age, Ada and her mother departed for the Continent, and the union of the two young people was understood to be indefinitely postponed.

Some curiosity was felt in the neighbourhood as to what Alfred Monkton would do under these circumstances. Would he follow his lady-love? Would he go yachting? Would he throw open the doors of the old Abbey at last, and endeavour to forget the absence of Ada and the postponement of his marriage, in a round of gaieties? He did none of these things. He simply remained at Wincot, living as suspiciously strange and solitary a life as his father had lived before him. Literally, there was now no companion for him at the Abbey but the old priest (the Monktons, I should have mentioned before, were Roman Catholics) who had held the office of tutor to Alfred from his earliest years. He came of age, and there was not even so much as a private dinner-party at Wincot to celebrate the event. Families in the neighbourhood determined to forget the offence which his father's reserve had given them, and invited him to their houses. The invitations were politely declined. Civil visitors called resolutely at the Abbey, and were resolutely bowed away from the doors as soon as they had left their cards. Under this combination of sinister and aggravating circumstances, people in all directions took to shaking their heads mysteriously when the name of Mr Alfred Monkton was mentioned, hinting at the family calamity, and wondering peevishly or sadly, as their tempers inclined them, what he could possibly do to occupy himself month after month in the lonely old house.

The right answer to this question was not easy to find. It was quite useless, for example, to apply to the priest for it. He was a very quiet, polite old gentleman; his replies were always excessively ready and civil, and appeared at the time to convey a reasonable amount of information; but when they were tested by after-reflection, it was universally observed that nothing tangible could be extracted from them. The housekeeper, a weird old woman, with a very abrupt and repelling manner, was too fierce and taciturn to be safely approached. The few indoor servants had all been long enough in the family to have learnt to hold their tongues in public as a regular habit. It was only from the farm servants who supplied the table at the Abbey, that any information could be obtained; and vague enough it was when they came to communicate it.

Some of them had observed the 'young master' walking about the library with heaps of dusty papers in his hands. Others had heard odd noises in the uninhabited parts of the Abbey, had looked up, and had seen him forcing open the old windows, as if to let light and air into rooms supposed

to have been shut closed for years and years; or had discovered him standing on the perilous summit of one of the
crumbling turrets, never ascended before within their
memories, and popularly considered to be inhabited by the
ghosts of the monks who had once possessed the building.
The result of these observations and discoveries, when they
were communicated to others, was of course to impress
every one with a firm belief that 'poor young Monkton was
going the way that the rest of the family had gone before
him': which opinion always appeared to be immensely
strengthened in the popular mind by a conviction—founded
on no particle of evidence—that the priest was at the bottom of all the mischief.

Thus far I have spoken from hearsay evidence mostly.
What I have next to tell will be the result of my own
personal experience.

II

About five months after Alfred Monkton came of age I left
college, and resolved to amuse and instruct myself a little by
travelling abroad.

At the time when I quitted England, young Monkton was
still leading his secluded life at the Abbey, and was, in the
opinion of everybody, sinking rapidly, if he had not already
succumbed, under the hereditary curse of his family. As to
the Elmslies, report said that Ada had benefited by her
sojourn abroad, and that mother and daughter were on their
way back to England to resume their old relations with the
heir of Wincot. Before they returned, I was away on my
travels, and wandered half over Europe, hardly ever planning
whither I should shape my course beforehand. Chance,
which thus led me everywhere, led me at last to Naples.
There I met with an old school friend, who was one of the
attachés at the English embassy; and there began the extraordinary events in connexion with Alfred Monkton which
form the main interest of the story I am now relating.

I was idling away the time one morning with my friend the
attaché, in the garden of the Villa Reale, when we were

passed by a young man, walking alone, who exchanged bows with my friend.

I thought I recognised the dark eager eyes, the colourless cheeks, the strangely vigilant, anxious expression which I remembered in past times as characteristic of Alfred Monkton's face, and was about to question my friend on the subject, when he gave me unasked the information of which I was in search.

'That is Alfred Monkton,' said he; 'he comes from your part of England. You ought to know him.'

'I do know a little of him,' I answered; 'he was engaged to Miss Elmslie when I was last in the neighbourhood of Wincot. Is he married to her yet?'

'No; and he never ought to be. He has gone the way of the rest of the family; or, in plainer words, he has gone mad.'

'Mad! But I ought not to be surprised at hearing that, after the reports about him in England.'

'I speak from no reports; I speak from what he has said and done here before me, and before hundreds of other people. Surely you must have heard of it?'

'Never. I have been out of the way of news from Naples or England for months past.'

'Then I have a very extraordinary story to tell you. You know, of course, that Alfred had an uncle, Stephen Monkton. Well, some time ago, this uncle fought a duel in the Roman states, with a Frenchman, who shot him dead. The seconds and the Frenchman (who was unhurt) took to flight in different directions, as it is supposed. We heard nothing here of the details of the duel till a month after it happened, when one of the French journals published an account of it, taken from papers left by Monkton's second, who died at Paris of consumption. These papers stated the manner in which the duel was fought, and how it terminated, but nothing more. The surviving second and the Frenchman have never been traced from that time to this. All that anybody knows, therefore, of the duel is that Stephen Monkton was shot; an event which nobody can regret, for a greater scoundrel never existed. The exact place where he died, and what was done with his body, are still mysteries not to be penetrated.'

'But what has all this to do with Alfred?'

'Wait a moment, and you will hear. Soon after the news of his uncle's death reached England, what do you think Alfred did? He actually put off his marriage with Miss Elmslie, which was then about to be celebrated, to come out here in search of the burial-place of his wretched scamp of an uncle. And no power on earth will now induce him to return to England and to Miss Elmslie, until he has found the body and can take it back with him to be buried with all the other dead Monktons, in the vault under Wincot Abbey Chapel. He has squandered his money, pestered the police, exposed himself to the ridicule of the men and the indignation of the women for the last three months, in trying to achieve his insane purpose, and is now as far from it as ever. He will not assign to anybody the smallest motive for his conduct. You can't laugh him out of it, or reason him out of it. When we met him just now, I happen to know that he was on his way to the office of the police minister, to send out fresh agents to search and inquire through the Roman states for the place where his uncle was shot. And mind, all this time he professes to be passionately in love with Miss Elmslie, and to be miserable at his separation from her. Just think of that! And then think of his self-imposed absence from her here, to hunt after the remains of a wretch who was a disgrace to the family, and whom he never saw but once or twice in his life. Of all the "Mad Monktons", as they used to call them in England, Alfred is the maddest. He is actually our principal excitement in this dull opera season, though, for my own part, when I think of the poor girl in England, I am a great deal more ready to despise him than to laugh at him.'

'You know the Elmslies, then?'

'Intimately. The other day, my mother wrote to me from England, after having seen Ada. This escapade of Monkton's has outraged all her friends. They have been entreating her to break off the match, which it seems she could do if she liked. Even her mother, sordid and selfish as she is, has been obliged at last, in common decency, to side with the rest of the family; but the good faithful girl won't give Monkton up. She humours his insanity, declares he gave her a good reason, in secret, for going away; says she could always make him happy when they were together in the old Abbey, and can make him still happier when they are married; in short, she loves him dearly, and will therefore believe in him to the last. Nothing shakes her; she has made up her mind to throw away her life on him, and she will do it.'

'I hope not. Mad as his conduct looks to us, he may have some sensible reason for it that we cannot imagine. Does his mind seem at all disordered when he talks on ordinary topics?'

'Not in the least. When you can get him to say anything, which is not often, he talks like a sensible, well-educated man. Keep silence about his precious errand here, and you would fancy him the gentlest and most temperate of human beings. But touch the subject of his vagabond of an uncle, and the Monkton madness comes out directly. The other night a lady asked him, jestingly of course, whether he had ever seen his uncle's ghost. He scowled at her like a perfect fiend, and said that he and his uncle would answer her question together some day, if they came from hell to do it. We laughed at his words, but the lady fainted at his looks, and we had a scene of hysterics and hartshorn* in consequence. Any other man would have been kicked out of the room for nearly frightening a pretty woman to death in that way; but "Mad Monkton", as we have christened him, is a privileged lunatic in Neapolitan society, because he is English, good-looking, and worth thirty thousand a year. He goes out everywhere, under the impression that he may meet with somebody who has been let into the secret of the place where the mysterious duel was fought. If you are introduced to him, he is sure to ask you whether you know anything about it; but beware of following up the subject after you have answered him, unless you want to make sure that he is out of his senses. In that case, only talk of his uncle, and the result will rather more than satisfy you.'

A day or two after this conversation with my friend the attaché, I met Monkton at an evening party.

The moment he heard my name mentioned, his face flushed up; he drew me away into a corner, and referring to his cool reception of my advance, years ago, towards making his acquaintance, asked my pardon for what he termed his inexcusable ingratitude, with an earnestness and an agitation which utterly astonished me. His next proceeding was to question me, as my friend had said he would, about the place of the mysterious duel.

An extraordinary change came over him while he interrogated me on this point. Instead of looking into my face as they had looked hitherto, his eyes wandered away, and fixed themselves intensely, almost fiercely, either on the perfectly empty wall at our side, or on the vacant space between the wall and ourselves—it was impossible to say which. I had come to Naples from Spain by sea, and briefly told him so, as the best way of satisfying him that I could not assist his inquiries. He pursued them no further; and mindful of my friend's warning, I took care to lead the conversation to general topics. He looked back at me directly, and as long as we stood in our corner, his eyes never wandered away again to the empty wall or the vacant space at our side.

Though more ready to listen than to speak, his conversation, when he did talk, had no trace of anything the least like insanity about it. He had evidently read, not generally only, but deeply as well, and could apply his reading with singular felicity to the illustration of almost any subject under discussion, neither obtruding his knowledge absurdly, nor concealing it affectedly. His manner was in itself a standing protest against such a nickname as 'Mad Monkton'. He was so shy, so quiet, so composed and gentle in all his actions, that at times I should have been almost inclined to call him effeminate. We had a long talk together on the first evening of our meeting; we often saw each other afterwards, and never lost a single opportunity of bettering our acquaintance. I felt that he had taken a liking to me; and in spite of what I had heard about his behaviour to Miss Elmslie, in spite of the suspicions which the history of his family and his own conduct had arrayed against him, I began to like 'Mad Monkton' as much as he liked me. We took many a quiet ride together in the country, and sailed often along the shores of the Bay on either side. But for two eccentricities in his conduct, which I could not at all understand, I should soon have felt as much at my ease in his society as if he had been my own brother.

The first of these eccentricities consisted in the reappearance on several occasions of the odd expression in his eyes, which I had first seen when he asked me whether I knew anything about the duel. No matter what we were talking about, or where we happened to be, there were times when he would suddenly look away from my face, now on one side of me, now on the other, but always where there was nothing to see, and always with the same intensity and fierceness in his eyes. This looked so like madness—or hypochondria, at the least—that I felt afraid to ask him about it, and always pretended not to observe him.

The second peculiarity in his conduct was that he never referred, while in my company, to the reports about his errand at Naples, and never once spoke of Miss Elmslie, or of his life at Wincot Abbey. This not only astonished me, but amazed those who had noticed our intimacy, and who had made sure that I must be the depository of all his secrets. But the time was near at hand when this mystery, and some other mysteries of which I had no suspicion at this period, were all to be revealed.

I met him one night at a large ball, given by a Russian nobleman, whose name I could not pronounce then, and cannot remember now. I had wandered away from reception-room, ballroom, and card-room to a small apartment at one extremity of the palace, which was half conservatory, half boudoir, and which had been prettily illuminated for the occasion with Chinese lanthorns. Nobody was in the room when I got there. The view over the Mediterranean, bathed in the bright softness of Italian moonlight, was so lovely, that I remained for a long time at the window, looking out, and listening to the dance music which faintly reached me from the ballroom. My thoughts were far away with the relations I had left in England, when I was startled out of them by hearing my name softly pronounced.

I looked round directly, and saw Monkton standing in the room. A livid paleness overspread his face, and his eyes were turned away from me with the same extraordinary expression in them to which I have already alluded.

'Do you mind leaving the ball early tonight?' he asked, still not looking at me.

'Not at all,' said I. 'Can I do anything for you? Are you ill?'

'No, at least nothing to speak of. Will you come to my rooms?'

'At once, if you like.'

'No, not at once. *I* must go home directly; but don't you come to me for half an hour yet. You have not been at my rooms before, I know; but you will easily find them out, they are close by. There is a card with my address. I *must* speak to you tonight; my life depends on it. Pray come! for God's sake come when the half hour is up!'

I promised to be punctual, and he left me directly.

Most people will be easily able to imagine the state of nervous impatience and vague expectation in which I passed the allotted period of delay, after hearing such words as those Monkton had spoken to me. Before the half hour had quite expired, I began to make my way out through the ballroom.

At the head of the staircase, my friend the attaché met me.

'What! going away already?' said he.

'Yes; and on a very curious expedition. I am going to Monkton's rooms, by his own invitation.'

'You don't mean it! Upon my honour, you're a bold fellow to trust yourself alone with "Mad Monkton" when the moon is at the full.'

'He is ill, poor fellow. Besides, I don't think him half as mad as you do.'

'We won't dispute about that: but mark my words, he has not asked you to go where no visitor has ever been admitted before, without a special purpose. I predict that you will see or hear something tonight which you will remember for the rest of your life.'

We parted. When I knocked at the courtyard gate of the house where Monkton lived, my friend's last words on the palace staircase occurred to me; and though I had laughed at him when he had spoken them, I began to suspect even then that his prediction would be fulfilled.

III

The porter who let me into the house where Monkton lived, directed me to the floor on which his rooms were situated. On getting upstairs, I found his door on the landing ajar. He heard my footsteps, I suppose, for he called to me to come in before I could knock.

I entered, and found him sitting by the table, with some loose letters in his hand, which he was just tying together in a packet. I noticed, as he asked me to sit down, that his expression looked more composed, though the paleness had not yet left his face. He thanked me for coming; repeated that he had something very important to say to me; and then stopped short, apparently too much embarrassed to proceed. I tried to set him at his ease by assuring him that if my assistance or advice could be of any use, I was ready to place myself and my time heartily and unreservedly at his service.

As I said this, I saw his eyes beginning to wander away from my face—to wander slowly, inch by inch as it were, until they stopped at a certain point, with the same fixed stare into vacancy which had so often startled me on former occasions. The whole expression of his face altered as I had never yet seen it alter; he sat before me, looking like a man in a death-trance.

'You are very kind,' he said, slowly and faintly, speaking, not to me, but in the direction in which his eyes were still fixed. 'I know you can help me; but——'

He stopped; his face whitened horribly, and the perspiration broke out all over it. He tried to continue; said a word or two; then stopped again. Seriously alarmed about him, I rose from my chair, with the intention of getting him some water from a jug which I saw standing on a side table.

He sprang up at the same moment. All the suspicions I had ever heard whispered against his sanity flashed over my mind in an instant; and I involuntarily stepped back a pace or two.

'Stop,' he said, seating himself again; 'don't mind me; and don't leave your chair. I want—I wish, if you please, to make a little alteration, before we say anything more. Do you mind sitting in a strong light?'

'Not in the least.'

I had hitherto been seated in the shade of his reading-lamp, the only light in the room.

As I answered him, he rose again; and going into another apartment, returned with a large lamp in his hand; then took two candles from the side table, and two others from the chimney-piece; placed them all, to my amazement, together, so as to stand exactly between us; and then tried to light them. His hand trembled so, that he was obliged to give up the attempt, and allow me to come to his assistance. By his direction I took the shade off the reading-lamp, after I had lit the other lamp and the four candles. When he sat down again, with this concentration of light between us, his better and gentler manner began to return: and while he now addressed me, he spoke without the slightest hesitation.

'It is useless to ask whether you have heard the reports about me,' he said; 'I know that you have. My purpose tonight is to give you some reasonable explanation of the conduct which has produced those reports. My secret has been hitherto confided to one person only; I am now about to trust it to your keeping, with a special object which will appear as I go on. First, however, I must begin by telling you exactly what the great difficulty is which obliges me to be still absent from England. I want your advice and your help; and, to conceal nothing from you, I want also to test your forbearance and your friendly sympathy, before I can venture on thrusting my miserable secret into your keeping. Will you pardon this apparent distrust of your frank and open character—this apparent ingratitude for your kindness towards me ever since we first met?'

I begged him not to speak of these things, but to go on.

'You know,' he proceeded, 'that I am here to recover the body of my Uncle Stephen, and to carry it back with me to our family burial place in England; and you must also be aware that I have not yet succeeded in discovering his remains. Try to pass over for the present whatever may seem extraordinary and incomprehensible in such a purpose as mine is; and read this newspaper article, where the ink-line is traced. It is the only evidence hitherto obtained on the subject of the fatal duel in which my uncle fell; and I want to hear what course of proceeding the perusal of it may suggest to you as likely to be best on my part.'

He handed me an old French newspaper. The substance of what I read there is still so firmly impressed on my memory, that I am certain of being able to repeat correctly, at this distance of time, all the facts which it is necessary for me to communicate to the reader.

The article began, I remember, with editorial remarks on the great curiosity then felt in regard to the fatal duel between the Count St Lo and Mr Stephen Monkton, an English gentleman. The writer proceeded to dwell at great length on the extraordinary secrecy in which the whole affair had been involved from first to last; and to express a hope that the publication of a certain manuscript, to which his introductory observations referred, might lead to the production of fresh evidence from other and better in-formed quarters. The manuscript had been found among the papers of Monsieur Foulon, Mr Monkton's second, who had died at Paris of a rapid decline, shortly after returning to his home in that city from the scene of the duel. The document was unfinished, having been left incomplete at the very place where the reader would most wish to find it continued. No reason could be discovered for this, and no second manuscript bearing on the all-important subject had been found, after the strictest search among the papers left by the deceased.

The document itself then followed.

It purported to be an agreement privately drawn up be-tween Mr Monkton's second, Monsieur Foulon, and the

Count St Lo's second, Monsieur Dalville; and contained a statement of all the arrangements for conducting the duel. The paper was dated 'Naples, February 22nd' and was divided into some seven or eight clauses.

The first clause described the origin and nature of the quarrel—a very disgraceful affair on both sides, worth neither remembering nor repeating. The second clause stated that the challenged man having chosen the pistol as his weapon, and the challenger (an excellent swordsman) having, on his side, thereupon insisted that the duel should be fought in such a manner as to make the first fire decisive in its results, the seconds, seeing that fatal consequences must inevitably follow the hostile meeting, determined, first of all, that the duel should be kept a profound secret from everybody, and that the place where it was to be fought should not be made known beforehand, even to the principals themselves. It was added that this excess of precaution had been rendered absolutely necessary, in consequence of a recent address from the Pope to the ruling powers in Italy, commenting on the scandalous frequency of the practice of duelling, and urgently desiring that the laws against duellists should be enforced for the future with the utmost rigour.

The third clause detailed the manner in which it had been arranged that the duel should be fought.

The pistols having been loaded by the seconds on the ground, the combatants were to be placed thirty paces apart, and were to toss up for the first fire. The man who won was to advance ten paces—marked out for him beforehand—and was then to discharge his pistol. If he missed, or failed to disable his opponent, the latter was free to advance, if he chose, the whole remaining twenty paces before he fired in his turn. This arrangement ensured the decisive termination of the duel at the first discharge of the pistols, and both principals and seconds pledged themselves on either side to abide by it.

The fourth clause stated that the seconds had agreed that the duel should be fought *out* of the Neapolitan States, but left themselves to be guided by circumstances as to the

exact locality in which it should take place. The remaining
clauses, so far as I remember them, were devoted to detail-
ing the different precautions to be adopted for avoiding
discovery. The duellists and their seconds were to leave
Naples in separate parties; were to change carriages several
times; were to meet at a certain town, or, failing that, at a
certain post-house on the high road from Naples to Rome;
were to carry drawing-books, colour-boxes, and camp-
stools, as if they had been artists out on a sketching tour;
and were to proceed to the place of the duel on foot,
employing no guides, for fear of treachery. Such general
arrangements as these, and others for facilitating the flight
of the survivors after the affair was over, formed the conclusion of this extraordinary document, which was signed, in
initials only, by both the seconds.

Just below the initials, appeared the beginning of a narrative, dated 'Paris', and evidently intended to describe the
duel itself with extreme minuteness. The handwriting was
that of the deceased second.

Monsieur Foulon, the gentleman in question, stated his
belief that circumstances might transpire which would render an account by an eye-witness of the hostile meeting
between St Lo and Mr Monkton an important document.
He proposed, therefore, as one of the seconds, to testify that
the duel had been fought in exact accordance with the terms
of the agreement, both the principals conducting themselves like men of gallantry and honour(!). And he further
announced that, in order not to compromise anyone, he
should place the paper containing his testimony in safe
hands, with strict directions that it was on no account to be
opened, except in a case of the last emergency.

After this preamble, Monsieur Foulon related that the
duel had been fought two days after the drawing up of the
agreement, in a locality to which accident had conducted
the duelling party. (The name of the place was not mentioned, nor even the neighbourhood in which it was situated.) The men having been placed according to previous
arrangement, the Count St Lo had won the toss for the first
fire, had advanced his ten paces, and had shot his opponent

in the body. Mr Monkton did not immediately fall, but staggered forward some six or seven paces, discharged his pistol ineffectually at the count, and dropped to the ground a dead man. Monsieur Foulon then stated that he tore a leaf from his pocket-book, wrote on it a brief description of the manner in which Mr Monkton had died, and pinned the paper to his clothes; this proceeding having been rendered necessary by the peculiar nature of the plan organised on the spot for safely disposing of the dead body. What this plan was, or what was done with the corpse, did not appear, for at this important point the narrative abruptly broke off.

A footnote in the newspaper merely stated the manner in which the document had been obtained for publication, and repeated the announcement contained in the editor's introductory remarks, that no continuation had been found by the persons entrusted with the care of Monsieur Foulon's papers. I have now given the whole substance of what I read, and have mentioned all that was then known of Mr Stephen Monkton's death.

When I gave the newspaper back to Alfred, he was too much agitated to speak; but he reminded me by a sign that he was anxiously awaiting to hear what I had to say. My position was a very trying and a very painful one. I could hardly tell what consequences might not follow any want of caution on my part, and could think at first of no safer plan than questioning him carefully before I committed myself either one way or the other.

'Will you excuse me if I ask you a question or two before I give you my advice?' I said.

He nodded impatiently.

'Yes, yes; any questions you like.'

'Were you at any time in the habit of seeing your uncle frequently?'

'I never saw him more than twice in my life; on each occasion, when I was a mere child.'

'Then you could have had no very strong personal regard for him?'

'Regard for him! I should have been ashamed to feel any regard for him. He disgraced us wherever he went.'

'May I ask if any family motive is involved in your anxiety to recover his remains?'

'Family motives may enter into it among others—but why do you ask?'

'Because, having heard that you employ the police to assist your search, I was anxious to know whether you had stimulated their superiors to make them do their best in your service, by giving some strong personal reasons at head-quarters for the very unusual project which has brought you here.'

'I give no reasons. I pay for the work I want done, and in return for my liberality I am treated with the most infamous indifference on all sides. A stranger in the country, and badly acquainted with the language, I can do nothing to help myself. The authorities, both at Rome and in this place, pretend to assist me, pretend to search and inquire as I would have them search and inquire, and do nothing more. I am insulted, laughed at almost to my face.'

'Do you not think it possible—mind, I have no wish to excuse the misconduct of the authorities, and do not share in any such opinion myself—but do you not think it likely that the police may doubt whether you are in earnest?'

'Not in earnest!' he cried, starting up and confronting me fiercely, with wild eyes and quickened breath. 'Not in earn-est! *You* think I'm not in earnest, too. I know you think it, though you tell me you don't. Stop! before we say another word, your own eyes shall convince you. Come here—only for a minute—only for one minute!'

I followed him into his bedroom, which opened out of the sitting-room. At one side of his bed stood a large packing case of plain wood, upwards of seven feet in length.

'Open the lid, and look in,' he said, 'while I hold the candle so that you can see.'

I obeyed his directions, and discovered, to my astonishment, that the packing case contained a leaden coffin, magnifi-cently emblazoned with the arms of the Monkton family, and inscribed in old-fashioned letters with the name of 'Stephen Monkton', his age and the manner of his death being added underneath.

'I keep his coffin ready for him,' whispered Alfred, close at my ear. 'Does that look like earnest?'

It looked more like insanity—so like, that I shrank from answering him.

'Yes! yes! I see you are convinced,' he continued, quickly; 'we may go back into the next room, and may talk without restraint on either side now.'

On returning to our places, I mechanically moved my chair away from the table. My mind was by this time in such a state of confusion and uncertainty about what it would be best for me to say or do next, that I forgot for the moment the position he had assigned to me when we lit the candles. He reminded me of this directly.

'Don't move away,' he said, very earnestly; 'keep on sitting in the light; pray do! I'll soon tell you why I am so particular about that. But first give me your advice; help me in my great distress and suspense. Remember, you promised me you would.'

I made an effort to collect my thoughts, and succeeded. It was useless to treat the affair otherwise than seriously in his presence; it would have been cruel not to have advised him as I best could.

'You know,' I said, 'that two days after the drawing up of the agreement at Naples, the duel was fought out of the Neapolitan States. This fact has of course led you to the conclusion that all inquiries about localities had better be confined to the Roman territory?'

'Certainly: the search, such as it is, has been made there, and there only. If I can believe the police, they and their agents have inquired for the place where the duel was fought (offering a large reward in my name to the person who can discover it), all along the high-road from Naples to Rome. They have also circulated—at least, so they tell me—descriptions of the duellists and their seconds; have left an agent to superintend investigations at the post-house, and another at the town, mentioned as meeting-points in the agreement; and have endeavoured by correspondence with foreign authorities to trace the Count St Lo and Monsieur Dalville to their place or places of refuge. All these efforts, supposing them to have been really made, have hitherto proved utterly fruitless.'

'My impression is,' said I, after a moment's consideration, 'that all inquiries made along the high-road, or anywhere near Rome, are likely to be made in vain. As to the discovery of your uncle's remains, that is, I think, identical with the discovery of the place where he was shot; for those engaged in the duel would certainly not risk detection by carrying a corpse any distance with them in their flight. The place, then, is all that we want to find out. Now, let us consider for a moment. The duelling-party changed carriages; travelled separately, two and two; doubtless took roundabout roads; stopped at the post-house and the town as a blind; walked, perhaps, a considerable distance unguided. Depend upon it, such precautions as these (which we know they must have employed) left them very little time out of the two days—though they might start at sunrise, and not stop at nightfall—for straightforward travelling. My belief therefore is, that the duel was fought somewhere near the Neapolitan frontier; and if I had been the police agent who conducted the search, I should only have pursued it parallel with the frontier, starting from west to east till I got up among the lonely places in the mountains. That is my idea: do you think it worth anything?'

His face flushed all over in an instant. 'I think it an inspiration!' he cried. 'Not a day is to be lost in carrying out our plan. The police are not to be trusted with it. I must start myself, tomorrow morning; and you——'

He stopped; his face grew suddenly pale; he sighed heavily; his eyes wandered once more into the fixed look at vacancy; and the rigid, deathly expression fastened again upon all his features.

'I must tell you my secret before I talk of tomorrow,' he proceeded, faintly. 'If I hesitated any longer at confessing everything, I should be unworthy of your past kindness, unworthy of the help which it is my last hope that you will gladly give me when you have heard all.'

I begged him to wait until he was more composed, until he was better able to speak; but he did not appear to notice what I said. Slowly, and struggling as it seemed against himself, he turned a little away from me; and bending his head over the table, supported it on his hand. The packet of letters with which I had seen him occupied when I came in, lay just beneath his eyes. He looked down on it steadfastly when he next spoke to me.

IV

'You were born, I believe, in our county,' he said; 'perhaps therefore you may have heard at some time of a curious old prophecy about our family, which is still preserved among the traditions of Wincot Abbey?'

'I have heard of such a prophecy,' I answered; 'but I never knew in what terms it was expressed. It professed to predict the extinction of your family, or something of that sort, did it not?'

'No inquiries,' he went on, 'have traced back that prophecy to the time when it was first made; none of our family records tell us anything of its origin. Old servants and old tenants of ours remember to have heard it from their fathers and grandfathers. The monks, whom we succeeded in the Abbey in Henry the Eighth's time, got knowledge of it in some way; for I myself discovered the rhymes in which we know the prophecy to have been preserved from a very remote period, written on a blank leaf of one of the Abbey manuscripts. These are the verses, if verses they deserve to be called:

> When in Wincot vault a place
> Waits for one of Monkton's race;
> When that one forlorn shall lie
> Graveless under open sky,
> Beggared of six feet of earth,
> Though lord of acres from his birth—
> That shall be a certain sign
> Of the end of Monkton's line.
> Dwindling ever faster, faster,
> Dwindling to the last-left master;
> From mortal ken, from light of day,
> Monkton's race shall pass away.'

'The prediction seems almost vague enough to have been uttered by an ancient oracle,' said I, observing that he waited, after repeating the verses, as if expecting me to say something.

'Vague or not, it is being accomplished,' he returned. 'I am now the "Last-left Master"—the last of that elder line of our family at which the prediction points; and the corpse of Stephen Monkton is not in the vaults of Wincot Abbey. Wait, before you exclaim against me! I have more to say about this. Long before the Abbey was ours, when we lived in the ancient manor house near it (the very ruins of which have long since disappeared), the family burying place was in the vault under the Abbey chapel. Whether in those remote times the prediction against us was known and dreaded, or not, this much is certain: every one of the Monktons (whether living at the Abbey or on the smaller estate in Scotland) was buried in Wincot vault, no matter at what risk or what sacrifice. In the fierce fighting days of the olden time, the bodies of my ancestors who fell in foreign places were recovered and brought back to Wincot, though it often cost, not heavy ransom only, but desperate blood-shed as well, to obtain them. This superstition, if you please to call it so, has never died out of the family from that time to the present day; for centuries the succession of the dead in the vault at the Abbey has been unbroken—absolutely unbroken—until now. The place mentioned in the prediction as waiting to be filled, is Stephen Monkton's place; the voice that cries vainly to the earth for shelter is the voice of the dead. As surely as if I saw it, I know that they have left him unburied on the ground where he fell!'

He stopped me before I could utter a word in remonstrance, by slowly rising to his feet, and pointing in the same direction towards which his eyes had wandered a short time since.

'I can guess what you want to ask me,' he exclaimed, sternly and loudly; 'you want to ask me how I can be mad enough to believe in a doggerel prophecy, uttered in an age of superstition to awe the most ignorant hearers. I answer' (at those words his voice sank suddenly to a whisper), 'I answer, because *Stephen Monkton himself stands there at this moment, confirming me in my belief.*'

Whether it was the awe and horror that looked out ghastly from his face as he confronted me, whether it was that I had never hitherto fairly believed in the reports about his madness, and that the conviction of their truth now forced itself upon me on a sudden, I know not; but I felt my blood curdling as he spoke, and I knew in my own heart, as I sat there speechless, that I dare not turn round and look where he was still pointing close at my side.

'I see there,' he went on in the same whispering voice, 'the figure of a dark-complexioned man, standing up with his head uncovered. One of his hands, still clutching a pistol, has fallen to his side; the other presses a bloody handkerchief over his mouth. The spasm of mortal agony convulses his features; but I know them for the features of a swarthy man, who twice frightened me by taking me up in his arms when I was a child, at Wincot Abbey. I asked the nurses at the time who that man was, and they told me it was my uncle, Stephen Monkton. Plainly, as if he stood there living, I see him now at your side, with the death-glare in his great black eyes; and so have I ever seen him since the moment when he was shot; at home and abroad, waking or sleeping, day and night, we are always together wherever I go!'

His whispering tones sank into almost inaudible murmuring as he pronounced these last words. From the direction and expression of his eyes, I suspected that he was speaking to the apparition. If I had beheld it myself at that moment, it would have been, I think, a less horrible sight to witness than to see him, as I saw him now, muttering inarticulately at vacancy. My own nerves were more shaken than I could have thought possible by what had passed. A vague dread of being near him in his present mood came over me, and I moved back a step or two.

He noticed the action instantly.

'Don't go!—pray, pray don't go! Have I alarmed you? Don't you believe me? Do the lights make your eyes ache? I only asked you to sit in the glare of the candles, because I could not bear to see the light that always shines from the phantom there at dusk, shining over you as you sat in the shadow. Don't go—don't leave me yet!'

There was an utter forlornness, an unspeakable misery in his face as he said those words, which gave me back my self-possession by the simple process of first moving me to pity. I resumed my chair, and said that I would stay with him as long as he wished.

'Thank you a thousand times! You are patience and kindness itself,' he said, going back to his former place and resuming his former gentleness of manner. 'Now that I have got over my first confession of the misery that follows me in secret wherever I go, I think I can tell you calmly all that remains to be told. You see, as I said, my uncle Stephen,'— he turned away his head quickly, and looked down at the table as the name passed his lips—'my uncle Stephen came twice to Wincot while I was a child, and on both occasions frightened me dreadfully. He only took me up in his arms, and spoke to me—very kindly, as I afterwards heard, for *him*—but he terrified me, nevertheless. Perhaps I was frightened at his great stature, his swarthy complexion, and his thick black hair and moustache, as other children might have been; perhaps the mere sight of him had some strange influence on me which I could not then understand, and cannot now explain. However it was, I used to dream of him long after he had gone away; and to fancy that he was stealing on me to catch me up in his arms, whenever I was left in the dark. The servants who took care of me found this out, and used to threaten me with my uncle Stephen whenever I was perverse and difficult to manage. As I grew up, I still retained my vague dread and abhorrence of our absent relative. I always listened intently, yet without knowing why, whenever his name was mentioned by my father or my mother—listened with an unaccountable presentiment that something terrible had happened to him, or was about to happen to me. This feeling only changed when I was left alone in the Abbey; and then it seemed to merge into the eager curiosity which had begun to grow on me, rather before that time, about the origin of the ancient prophecy predicting the extinction of our race. Are you following me?'

'I follow every word with the closest attention.'

'You must know, then, that I had first found out some fragments of the old rhyme, in which the prophecy occurs, quoted as a curiosity in an antiquarian book in the library. On the page opposite this quotation, had been pasted a rude old woodcut, representing a dark-haired man, whose face was so strangely like what I remembered of my uncle Stephen, that the portrait absolutely startled me. When I asked my father about this—it was then just before his death—he either knew, or pretended to know, nothing of it; and when I afterwards mentioned the prediction he fretfully changed the subject. It was just the same with our chaplain when I spoke to him. He said the portrait had been done centuries before my uncle was born; and called the prophecy doggerel and nonsense. I used to argue with him on the latter point, asking why we Catholics, who believed that the gift of working miracles had never departed from certain favoured persons, might not just as well believe that the gift of prophecy had never departed either? He would not dispute with me; he would only say that I must not waste time in thinking of such trifles, that I had more imagination than was good for me, and must suppress instead of exciting it. Such advice as this only irritated my curiosity. I determined to work secretly to search through the oldest uninhabited part of the Abbey, and to try if I could not find out from forgotten family records what the portrait was, and when the prophecy had been first written or uttered. Did you ever pass a day alone in the long-deserted chambers of an ancient house?'

'Never; such solitude as that is not at all to my taste.'

'Ah! what a life it was when I began my search. I should like to live it over again! Such tempting suspense, such strange discoveries, such wild fancies, such enthralling terrors, all belonged to that life! Only think of breaking open the door of a room which no living soul had entered before you for nearly a hundred years! think of the first step forward in a region of airless, awful stillness, where the light falls faint and sickly through closed windows and rotting curtains! think of the ghostly creaking of the old floor that cries out on you for treading on it, step as softly as you will! think of arms, helmets, weird tapestries of bygone days, that seem to be moving out on you from the walls as you first walk up to them in the dim light! think of prying into great cabinets and iron-clasped chests, not knowing what horrors may appear when you tear them open! of poring over their contents till twilight stole on you, and darkness grew terrible in the lonely place! of trying to leave it, and not being able to go, as if something held you; of wind wailing at you outside; of shadows darkening round you, and closing you up in obscurity within! Only think of these things, and you may imagine the fascination of suspense and terror in such a life as mine was in those past days!'

(I shrunk from imagining that life: it was bad enough to see its results, as I saw them before me now.)

'Well, my search lasted months and months; then it was suspended a little, then resumed. In whatever direction I pursued it, I always found something to lure me on. Terrible confessions of past crimes, shocking proofs of secret wickedness that had been hidden securely from all eyes but mine, came to light. Sometimes these discoveries were associated with particular parts of the Abbey, which have had a horrible interest of their own for me ever since. Sometimes with certain old portraits in the picture-gallery, which I actually dreaded to look at, after what I had found out. There were periods when the results of this search of mine so horrified me, that I determined to give it up entirely; but I never could persevere in my resolution, the temptation to go on seemed at certain intervals to get too strong for me, and then I yielded to it again and again. At last I found the book that had belonged to the monks, with the whole of the prophecy written in the blank leaf. This first success encouraged me to get back further yet in the family records. I had discovered nothing hitherto of the identity of the mysterious portrait, but the same intuitive conviction which had assured me of its extraordinary resemblance to my uncle Stephen, seemed also to assure me that he must be more closely connected with the prophecy, and must know more of it than anyone else. I had no means of holding any communication with him, no means of satisfying myself whether this strange idea of mine were right or wrong, until the day when my doubts were settled for ever, by the same terrible proof which is now present to me in this very room.'

He paused for a moment and looked at me intently and suspiciously; then asked if I believed all he had said to me so far. My instant reply in the affirmative seemed to satisfy his doubts, and he went on:

'On a fine evening in February, I was standing alone in one of the deserted rooms of the western turret at the Abbey, looking at the sunset. Just before the sun went down, I felt a sensation stealing over me which it is impossible to explain. I saw nothing, heard nothing, knew nothing. This utter self-oblivion came suddenly; it was not fainting for I did not fall to the ground, did not move an inch from my place. If such a thing could be, I should say it was the temporary separation of soul and body, without death: but all description of my situation at that time is impossible. Call my state what you will, trance or catalepsy, I know that I remained standing by the window utterly unconscious—dead, mind and body—until the sun had set. Then I came to my senses again; and then, when I opened my eyes, there was the apparition of Stephen Monkton standing opposite to me, faintly luminous, just as it stands opposite me at this very moment by your side.'

'Was this before the news of the duel reached England?' I asked.

'*Two weeks before* the news of it reached us at Wincot. And even when we heard of the duel, we did not hear of the day on which it was fought. I only found that out when the document which you have read was published in the French newspaper. The date of that document, you will remember, is February 22nd, and it is stated that the duel was fought two days afterwards. I wrote down in my pocket-book, on the evening when I saw the phantom, the day of the month on which it first appeared to me. That day was the 24th of February.'

He paused again, as if expecting me to say something. After the words he had just spoken, what could I say? what could I think?

'Even in the first horror of first seeing the apparition,' he went on, 'the prophecy against our house came to my mind, and with it the conviction that I beheld before me, in that spectral presence, the warning of my own doom. As soon as I recovered a little, I determined, nevertheless, to test the reality of what I saw—to find out whether I was the dupe of my own diseased fancy, or not. I left the turret; the phantom left it with me. I made an excuse to have the drawing-room at the Abbey brilliantly lighted up—the figure was still opposite me. I walked out into the park—it was there in the clear starlight. I went away from home, and travelled many miles to the seaside; still the tall dark man in his death-agony was with me. After this, I strove against the fatality no more. I returned to the Abbey, and tried to resign myself to my misery. But this was not to be. I had a hope that was dearer to me than my own life; I had one treasure belonging to me that I shuddered at the prospect of losing, and when the phantom presence stood a warning obstacle between me and this one treasure, this dearest hope—then my misery grew heavier than I could bear. You must know what I am alluding to; you must have heard often that I was engaged to be married?'

'Yes, often. I have some acquaintance myself with Miss Elmslie.'

'You never can know all she has sacrificed for me—never can imagine what I have felt for years and years past'—his voice trembled, and the tears came into his eyes—'but I dare not trust myself to speak of that: the thought of the old happy days in the Abbey almost breaks my heart now. Let me get back to the other subject. I must tell you that I kept the frightful vision which pursued me, at all times, and in all places, a secret from everybody; knowing the vile reports about my having inherited madness from my family, and fearing that an unfair advantage would be taken of any confession that I might make. Though the phantom always stood opposite to me, and therefore always appeared either before or by the side of any person to whom I spoke, I soon schooled myself to hide from others that I was looking at it, except on rare occasions—when I have perhaps betrayed myself to you. But my self-possession availed me nothing with Ada. The day of our marriage was approaching.'

He stopped and shuddered. I waited in silence till he had controlled himself.

'Think,' he went on, 'think of what I must have suffered at looking always on that hideous vision, whenever I looked on my betrothed wife! Think of my taking her hand, and seeming to take it through the figure of the apparition! Think of the calm angel-face and the tortured spectre-face being always together, whenever my eyes met hers! Think of this, and you will not wonder that I betrayed my secret to her. She eagerly entreated to know the worst—nay more, she insisted on knowing it. At her bidding I told all; and then left her free to break our engagement. The thought of death was in my heart as I spoke the parting words—death by my own act, if life still held out after our separation. She suspected that thought; she knew it, and never left me till her good influence had destroyed it for ever. But for her, I should not have been alive now—but for her, I should never have attempted the project which has brought me here.'

'Do you mean that it was at Miss Elmslie's suggestion that you came to Naples?' I asked in amazement.

'I mean that what she said, suggested the design which has brought me to Naples,' he answered. 'While I believed that the phantom had appeared to me as the fatal messenger of death, there was no comfort, there was misery rather in hearing her say that no power on earth should make her desert me, and that she would live for me, and for me only, through every trial. But it was far different when we afterwards reasoned together about the purpose which the apparition had come to fulfil—far different when she showed me that its mission might be for good, instead of for evil; and that the warning it was sent to give, might be to my profit instead of to my loss. At those words, the new idea which gave the new hope of life came to me in an instant. I believed then, what I believe now, that I have a supernatural warrant for my errand here. In that faith I live; without it I should die. *She* never ridiculed it, never scorned it as insanity. Mark what I say! The spirit that appeared to me in the Abbey, that has never left me since, that stands there now by your side, warns me to escape from the fatality which hangs over our race, and commands me, if I would avoid it, to bury the unburied dead. Mortal loves and mortal interests must bow to that awful bidding. The spectre-presence will never leave me till I have sheltered the corpse that cries to the earth to cover it! I dare not return—I dare not marry till I have filled the place that is empty in Wincot vault.'

His eyes flashed and dilated; his voice deepened; a fanatic ecstasy shone in his expression as he uttered these words. Shocked and grieved as I was, I made no attempt to remonstrate or to reason with him. It would have been useless to have referred to any of the usual commonplaces about optical delusions, or diseased imaginations—worse than useless to have attempted to account by natural causes for any of the extraordinary coincidences and events of which he had spoken. Briefly as he had referred to Miss Elmslie, he had said enough to show that the only hope of the poor girl who loved him best and had known him longest of any one, was in humouring his delusions to the last. How faithfully she still clung to the belief that she could restore him! How resolutely was she sacrificing herself to his morbid fancies, in the hope of a happy future that might never come! Little as I knew of Miss Elmslie, the mere thought of her situation, as I now reflected on it, made me feel sick at heart.

'They call me "Mad Monkton"!' he exclaimed, suddenly breaking the silence between us during the last few minutes. 'Here and in England everybody believes I am out of my senses, except Ada and you. She has been my salvation; and you will be my salvation too. Something told me that, when I first met you walking in the Villa Reale. I struggled against the strong desire that was in me to trust my secret to you; but I could resist it no longer when I saw you tonight at the ball—the phantom seemed to draw me on to you, as you stood alone in the quiet room. Tell me more of that idea of yours about finding the place where the duel was fought. If

I set out tomorrow to seek for it myself, where must I go to first?—where?' He stopped; his strength was evidently becoming exhausted, and his mind was growing confused. 'What am I to do? I can't remember. You know everything —will you not help me? My misery has made me unable to help myself!'

He stopped, murmured something about failing if he went to the frontier alone, and spoke confusedly of delays that might be fatal; then tried to utter the name of 'Ada'; but in pronouncing the first letter his voice faltered, and turning abruptly from me he burst into tears.

My pity for him got the better of my prudence at that moment, and without thinking of responsibilities, I promised at once to do for him whatever he asked. The wild triumph in his expression, as he started up and seized my hand, showed me that I had better have been more cautious; but it was too late now to retract what I had said. The next best thing to do was to try if I could not induce him to compose himself a little, and then to go away and think coolly over the whole affair by myself.

'Yes, yes,' he rejoined, in answer to the few words I now spoke to try and calm him, 'don't be afraid about me. After what you have said, I'll answer for my own coolness and composure under all emergencies. I have been so long used to the apparition that I hardly feel its presence at all except on rare occasions. Besides, I have here, in this little packet of letters, the medicine for every malady of the sick heart. They are Ada's letters; I read them to calm me whenever my misfortune seems to get the better of my endurance. I wanted that half hour to read them in tonight, before you came, to make myself fit to see you; and I shall go through them again after you are gone. So, once more don't be afraid about me. I know I shall succeed with your help; and Ada shall thank you as you deserve to be thanked when we get back to England. If you hear the fools at Naples talk about my being mad, don't trouble yourself to contradict them: the scandal is so contemptible that it must end by contradicting itself.'

I left him, promising to return early the next day.

When I got back to my hotel, I felt that any idea of sleeping after all that I had seen and heard, was out of the question. So I lit my pipe, and sitting by the window—how it refreshed my mind just then to look at the calm moonlight!—tried to think what it would be best to do. In the first place, any appeal to doctors or to Alfred's friends in England was out of the question. I could not persuade myself that his intellect was sufficiently disordered to justify me, under existing circumstances, in disclosing the secret which he had entrusted to my keeping. In the second place, all attempts on my part to induce him to abandon the idea of searching out his uncle's remains would be utterly useless after what I had incautiously said to him. Having settled these two conclusions, the only really great difficulty which remained to perplex me was whether I was justified in aiding him to execute his extraordinary purpose.

Supposing that with my help he found Mr Monkton's body, and took it back with him to England, was it right in me thus to lend myself to promoting the marriage which would most likely follow these events—a marriage which it might be the duty of everyone to prevent at all hazards? This set me thinking about the extent of his madness, or, to speak more mildly and more correctly, of his delusion. Sane he certainly was on ordinary subjects; nay, in all the narrative parts of what he had said to me on this very evening he had spoken clearly and connectedly. As for the story of the apparition, other men, with intellects as clear as the intellects of their neighbours, had fancied themselves pursued by a phantom, and had even written about it in a high strain of philosophical speculation. It was plain that the real hallucination in the case now before me, lay in Monkton's conviction of the truth of the old prophecy, and in his idea that the fancied apparition was a supernatural warning to him to evade its denunciations. And it was equally clear that both delusions had been produced, in the first instance, by the lonely life he had led, acting on a naturally excitable temperament, which was rendered further liable to moral disease by an hereditary taint of insanity.

Was this curable? Miss Elmslie, who knew him far better than I did, seemed by her conduct to think so. Had I any reason or right to determine off-hand that she was mistaken? Supposing I refused to go to the frontier with him, he would then most certainly depart by himself, so commit all sorts of errors, and perhaps to meet with all sorts of accidents; while I, an idle man, with my time entirely at my own disposal, was stopping at Naples, and leaving him to his fate after I had suggested the plan of his expedition, and had encouraged him to confide in me. In this way I kept turning the subject over and over again in my mind—being quite free, let me add, from looking at it in any other than a practical point of view. I firmly believed, as a derider of all ghost stories, that Alfred was deceiving himself in fancying that he had seen the apparition of his uncle, before the news of Mr Monkton's death reached England; and I was on this account therefore uninfluenced by the slightest infection of my unhappy friend's delusions, when I at last fairly decided to accompany him in his extraordinary search. Possibly my harum-scarum fondness for excitement at that time, biased me a little in forming my resolution; but I must add, in common justice to myself, that I also acted from motives of real sympathy for Monkton, and from a sincere wish to allay, if I could, the anxiety of the poor girl who was still so faithfully waiting and hoping for him far away in England.

Certain arrangements preliminary to our departure, which I found myself obliged to make after a second interview with Alfred, betrayed the object of our journey to most of our Neapolitan friends. The astonishment of everybody was of course unbounded, and the nearly universal suspicion that I must be as mad in my way as Monkton himself, showed itself pretty plainly in my presence. Some people actually tried to combat my resolution by telling me what a shameless profligate Stephen Monkton had been—as if I had a strong personal interest in hunting out his remains! Ridicule moved me as little as any arguments of this sort; my mind was made up, and I was as obstinate then as I am now.

In two days' time I had got everything ready, and had ordered the travelling carriage to the door some hours

earlier than we had originally settled. We were jovially
threatened with 'a parting cheer' by all our English acquaintances, and I thought it desirable to avoid this on my
friend's account; for he had been more excited, as it was, by
the preparations for the journey than I at all liked. Accordingly, soon after sunrise, without a soul in the street to stare
at us, we privately left Naples.

Nobody will wonder, I think, that I experienced some
difficulty in realising my own position, and shrank instinct-
ively from looking forward a single day into the future,
when I now found myself starting, in company with 'Mad
Monkton', to hunt for the body of a dead duellist all along
the frontier line of the Roman states!

V

I had settled it in my own mind that we had better make the
town of Fondi, close on the frontier, our headquarters, to
begin with; and I had arranged, with the assistance of the
Embassy, that the leaden coffin should follow us so far,
securely nailed up in its packing case. Besides our passports,
we were well furnished with letters of introduction to the
local authorities at most of the important frontier towns,
and to crown all, we had money enough at our command
(thanks to Monkton's vast fortune) to make sure of the
services of anyone whom we wanted to assist us, all along
our line of search. These various resources ensured us every
facility for action—provided always that we succeeded in
discovering the body of the dead duellist. But, in the very
probable event of our failing to do this, our future prospects
—more especially after the responsibility I had undertaken—were of anything but an agreeable nature to contemplate. I confess I felt uneasy, almost hopeless, as we posted,
in the dazzling Italian sunshine, along the road to Fondi.

We made an easy two days' journey of it; for I had insisted,
on Monkton's account, that we should travel slowly.

On the first day the excessive agitation of my companion
a little alarmed me; he showed, in many ways, more symptoms of a disordered mind than I had yet observed in him.

On the second day, however, he seemed to get accustomed to contemplate calmly the new idea of the search on which we were bent, and, except on one point, he was cheerful and composed enough. Whenever his dead uncle formed the subject of conversation, he still persisted—on the strength of the old prophecy, and under the influence of the apparition which he saw, or thought he saw, always—in asserting that the corpse of Stephen Monkton, wherever it was, lay yet unburied. On every other topic he deferred to me with the utmost readiness and docility; on this, he maintained his strange opinion with an obstinacy which set reason and persuasion alike at defiance.

On the third day we rested at Fondi. The packing case, with the coffin in it, reached us, and was deposited in a safe place under lock and key. We engaged some mules, and found a man to act as guide who knew the country thoroughly. It occurred to me that we had better begin by confiding the real object of our journey only to the most trustworthy people we could find among the better-educated classes. For this reason we followed, in one respect, the example of the duelling-party, by starting, early on the morning of the fourth day, with sketch-books and colour-boxes, as if we were only artists in search of the picturesque.

After travelling some hours in a northerly direction within the Roman frontier, we halted to rest ourselves and our mules at a wild little village, far out of the track of tourists in general.

The only person of the smallest importance in the place was the priest, and to him I addressed my first inquiries, leaving Monkton to await my return with the guide. I spoke Italian quite fluently and correctly enough for my purpose, and was extremely polite and cautious in introducing my business; but, in spite of all the pains I took, I only succeeded in frightening and bewildering the poor priest more and more with every fresh word I said to him. The idea of a duelling-party and a dead man seemed to scare him out of his senses. He bowed, fidgetted, cast his eyes up to heaven, and piteously shrugging his shoulders, told me, with rapid Italian circumlocution, that he had not the faintest idea of

what I was talking about. This was my first failure. I confess
I was weak enough to feel a little dispirited when I joined
Monkton and the guide.

After the heat of the day was over, we resumed our
journey.

About three miles from the village, the road, or rather
cart-track, branched off in two directions. The path to the
right, our guide informed us, led up among the mountains
to a convent about six miles off. If we penetrated beyond the
convent, we should soon reach the Neapolitan frontier. The
path to the left led far inwards on the Roman territory, and
would conduct us to a small town where we could sleep for
the night. Now the Roman territory presented the first and
fittest field for our search, and the convent was always
within reach, supposing we returned to Fondi unsuccessful.
Besides, the path to the left led over the wildest part of the
country we were starting to explore; and I was always for
vanquishing the greatest difficulty first—so we decided
manfully on turning to the left. The expedition in which this
resolution involved us lasted a whole week, and produced
no results. We discovered absolutely nothing, and returned
to our headquarters at Fondi so completely baffled that we
did not know whither to turn our steps next.

I was made much more uneasy by the effect of our failure
on Monkton than by the failure itself. His resolution appeared to break down altogether as soon as we began to
retrace our steps. He became first fretful and capricious,
then silent and desponding. Finally, he sank into a lethargy
of body and mind that seriously alarmed me. On the morning after our return to Fondi, he showed a strange tendency
to sleep incessantly, which made me suspect the existence
of some physical malady in his brain. The whole day he
hardly exchanged a word with me, and seemed to be never
fairly awake. Early the next morning I went into his room,
and found him as silent and lethargic as ever. His servant,
who was with us, informed me that Alfred had once or twice
before exhibited such physical symptoms of mental exhaustion as we were now observing, during his father's lifetime
at Wincot Abbey. This piece of information made me feel

easier, and left my mind free to return to the consideration of the errand which had brought us to Fondi.

I resolved to occupy the time until my companion got better in prosecuting our search by myself. That path to the right hand which led to the convent, had not yet been explored. If I set off to trace it, I need not be away from Monkton more than one night; and I should at least be able on my return to give him the satisfaction of knowing that one more uncertainty regarding the place of the duel had been cleared up. These considerations decided me. I left a message for my friend, in case he asked where I had gone, and set out once more for the village at which we had halted when starting on our first expedition.

Intending to walk to the convent, I parted company with the guide and the mules where the track branched off, leaving them to go back to the village and await my return.

For the first four miles the path gently ascended through an open country, then became abruptly much steeper, and led me deeper and deeper among thickets, and endless woods. By the time my watch informed me that I must have nearly walked my appointed distance, the view was bounded on all sides, and the sky was shut out overhead, by an impervious screen of leaves and branches. I still followed my only guide, the steep path; and in ten minutes, emerging suddenly on a plot of tolerably clear and level ground, I saw the convent before me.

It was a dark, low, sinister-looking place. Not a sign of life or movement was visible anywhere about it. Green stains streaked the once white facade of the chapel in all directions. Moss clustered thick in every crevice of the heavy scowling wall that surrounded the convent. Long lank weeds grew out of the fissures of roof and parapet, and dropping far downward, waved wearily in and out of the barred dormitory windows. The very cross opposite the entrance-gate, with a shocking life-sized figure in wood nailed to it, was so beset at the base with crawling creatures, and looked so slimy, green, and rotten all the way up, that I absolutely shrank from it.

A bell-rope with a broken handle hung by the gate. I approached it—hesitated, I hardly knew why—looked up at the convent again, and then walked round to the back of the building, partly to gain time to consider what I had better do next; partly from an unaccountable curiosity that urged me, strangely to myself, to see all I could of the outside of the place before I attempted to gain admission at the gate.

At the back of the convent I found an outhouse, built on to the wall—a clumsy, decayed building, with the greater part of the roof fallen in, and with a jagged hole in one of its sides, where in all probability a window had once been. Behind the outhouse the trees grew thicker than ever. As I looked towards them, I could not determine whether the ground beyond me rose or fell—whether it was grassy, or earthy, or rocky. I could see nothing but the all-pervading leaves, brambles, ferns, and long grass.

Not a sound broke the oppressive stillness. No bird's note rose from the leafy wilderness around me; no voices spoke in the convent garden behind the scowling wall; no clock struck in the chapel-tower; no dog barked in the ruined outhouse. The dead silence deepened the solitude of the place inexpressibly. I began to feel it weighing on my spirits —the more because woods were never favourite places with me to walk in. The sort of pastoral happiness which poets often represent, when they sing of life in the woods, never, to my mind, has half the charm of life on the mountain or in the plain. When I am in a wood, I miss the boundless loveliness of the sky, and the delicious softness that distance gives to the earthly view beneath. I feel oppressively the change which the free air suffers when it gets imprisoned among leaves; and I am always awed, rather than pleased, by that mysterious still light which shines with such a strange dim lustre in deep places among trees. It may convict me of want of taste and absence of due feeling for the marvellous beauties of vegetation, but I must frankly own that I never penetrate far into a wood without finding that the getting out of it again is the pleasantest part of my walk—the getting out on to the barest down, the wildest hill-side, the bleakest mountain-top—the getting out anywhere so that I can see the sky over me and the view before me as far as my eye can reach.

After such a confession as I have now made, it will appear surprising to no one that I should have felt the strongest possible inclination, while I stood by the ruined outhouse, to retrace my steps at once, and make the best of my way out of the wood. I had indeed actually turned to depart, when the remembrance of the errand which had brought me to the convent suddenly stayed my feet. It seemed doubtful whether I should be admitted into the building if I rang the bell; and more than doubtful, if I were let in, whether the inhabitants would be able to afford me any clue to the information of which I was in search. However, it was my duty to Monkton to leave no means of helping him in his desperate object untried; so I resolved to go round to the front of the convent again, and ring the gate-bell at all hazards.

By the merest chance I looked up as I passed the side of the outhouse where the jagged hole was, and noticed that it was pierced rather high in the wall.

As I stopped to observe this, the closeness of the atmosphere in the wood seemed to be affecting me more unpleasantly than ever.

I waited a minute and untied my cravat.

Closeness?—Surely it was something more than that. The air was even more distasteful to my nostrils than to my lungs. There was some faint, indescribable smell loading it—some smell of which I had never had any previous experience—some smell which I thought (now that my attention was directed to it) grew more and more certainly traceable to its source the nearer I advanced to the outhouse.

By the time I had tried the experiment two or three times, and had made myself sure of this fact, my curiosity became excited. There were plenty of fragments of stone and brick lying about me. I gathered some of them together, and piled them up below the hole, then mounted to the top, and, feeling rather ashamed of what I was doing, peeped into the outhouse.

The sight of horror that met my eyes the instant I looked through the hole, is as present to my memory now as if I had beheld it yesterday. I can hardly write of it at this distance of time without a thrill of the old terror running through me again to the heart.

The first impression conveyed to me, as I looked in, was of a long recumbent object, tinged with a lightish blue colour all over, extended on trestles, and bearing a certain hideous, half-formed resemblance to the human face and figure. I looked again, and felt certain of it. There were prominences of the forehead, nose, and chin, dimly shown as under a veil—there, the round outline of the chest, and the hollow below it—there, the points of the knees, and the stiff, ghastly, upturned feet. I looked again, yet more attentively. My eyes got accustomed to the dim light streaming in through the broken roof; and I satisfied myself, judging by the great length of the body from head to foot, that I was looking at the corpse of a man—a corpse that had apparently once had a sheet spread over it—and that had lain rotting on the trestles under the open sky long enough for the linen to take the livid, light-blue tinge of mildew and decay which now covered it.

How long I remained with my eyes fixed on that dread sight of death, on that tombless, terrible wreck of humanity, poisoning the still air, and seeming even to stain the faint descending light that disclosed it, I know not. I remember a dull, distant sound among the trees, as if the breeze were rising—the slow creeping on of the sound to near the place where I stood—the noiseless, whirling fall of a dead leaf on the corpse below me, through the gap in the outhouse roof —and the effect of awakening my energies, or relaxing the heavy strain on my mind, which even the slight change wrought in the scene I beheld by the falling leaf, produced in me immediately. I descended to the ground, and, sitting down on the heap of stones, wiped away the thick perspiration which covered my face, and which I now became aware of for the first time. It was something more than the hideous spectacle unexpectedly offered to my eyes which had shaken my nerves, as I felt that they were shaken now. Monkton's prediction that, if we succeeded in discovering his uncle's body, we should find it unburied, recurred to me the instant I saw the trestles and their ghastly burden. I felt assured on the instant that I had found the dead man—the old prophecy recurred to my memory—a strange yearning sorrow, a vague foreboding of ill, an inexplicable terror, as I thought of the poor lad who was awaiting my return in the distant town, struck through me with a chill of superstitious dread, robbed me of my judgment and resolution, and left me, when I had at last recovered myself, weak and dizzy, as if I had just suffered under some pang of overpowering physical pain.

I hastened round to the convent gate, and rang impatiently at the bell—waited a little while, and rang again—then heard footsteps.

In the middle of the gate, just opposite my face, there was a small sliding panel, not more than a few inches long; this was presently pushed aside from within. I saw, through a bit of iron grating, two dull, light grey eyes starting vacantly at me, and heard a feeble, husky voice saying:

'What may you please to want?'

'I am a traveller——' I began.

'We live in a miserable place. We have nothing to show travellers here.'

'I don't come to see anything. I have an important question to ask, which I believe someone in this convent will be able to answer. If you are not willing to let me in, at least come out and speak to me here.'

'Are you alone?'

'Quite alone.'

'Are there no women with you?'

'None.'

The gate was slowly unbarred; and an old Capuchin, very infirm, very suspicious, and very dirty, stood before me. I was far too excited and impatient to waste any time in prefatory phrases; so telling the monk at once how I had looked through the hole in the outhouse, and what I had seen inside, I asked him in plain terms who the man had been whose corpse I had beheld, and why the body was left unburied.

The old Capuchin listened to me with watery eyes that twinkled suspiciously. He had a battered tin snuff-box in his hand; and his finger and thumb slowly chased a few scattered grains of snuff round and round the inside of the box all the time I was speaking. When I had done, he shook his head, and said, 'that was certainly an ugly sight in their outhouse; one of the ugliest sights, he felt sure, that ever I had seen in all my life!'

'I don't want to talk of the sight,' I rejoined impatiently; 'I want to know who the man was, how he died, and why he is not decently buried. Can you tell me?'

The monk's finger and thumb having captured three or four grains of snuff at last, he slowly drew them into his nostrils, holding the box open under his nose the while, to prevent the possibility of wasting even one grain, sniffed once or twice, luxuriously—closed the box—then looked at me again, with his eyes watering and twinkling more suspiciously than before.

'Yes,' said the monk, 'that's an ugly sight in our outhouse —a very ugly sight, certainly!'

I never had more difficulty in keeping my temper in my life, than at that moment. I succeeded, however, in repressing a very disrespectful expression on the subject of monks in general, which was on the tip of my tongue, and made another attempt to conquer the old man's exasperating reserve. Fortunately for my chances of succeeding with him, I was a snuff-taker myself; and I had a box full of excellent English snuff in my pocket, which I now produced as a bribe. It was my last resource.

'I thought your box seemed empty just now,' said I; 'will you try a pinch out of mine?'

The offer was accepted with an almost youthful alacrity of gesture. The Capuchin took the largest pinch I ever saw held between any man's finger and thumb, inhaled it slowly, without spilling a single grain—half closed his eyes—and, wagging his head gently, patted me paternally on the back.

'Oh! my son!' said the monk, 'what delectable snuff! Oh, my son and amiable traveller, give the spiritual father who loves you, yet another tiny, tiny pinch!'

'Let me fill your box for you. I shall have plenty left for myself.'

The battered tin snuff-box was given to me before I had done speaking—the paternal hand patted my back more approvingly than ever—the feeble, husky voice grew glib and eloquent in my praise. I had evidently found out the weak side of the old Capuchin; and, on returning him his box, I took instant advantage of the discovery.

'Excuse my troubling you on the subject again,' I said, 'but I have particular reasons for wanting to hear all that you can tell me in explanation of that horrible sight in the outhouse.'

'Come in,' answered the monk.

He drew me inside the gate, closed it, and then leading the way across a grass-grown courtyard, looking out on a weedy kitchen garden, showed me into a long room with a low ceiling, a dirty dresser, a few rudely-carved stall seats, and one or two grim mildewed pictures for ornaments. This was the sacristy.

'There's nobody here, and it's nice and cool,' said the old Capuchin. It was so damp that I actually shivered. 'Would you like to see the church?' said the monk; 'a jewel of a church, if we could only keep it in repair; but we can't. Ah! malediction and misery, we are too poor to keep our church in repair!'

Here he shook his head, and began fumbling with a large bunch of keys.

'Never mind the church now!' said I. 'Can you, or can you not, tell me what I want to know?'

'Everything, from beginning to end—absolutely everything! Why, I answered the gate-bell—I always answer the gate-bell here,' said the Capuchin.

'What, in heaven's name, has the gate-bell to do with the unburied corpse in your outhouse?'

'Listen, son of mine, and you shall know. Some time ago —some months—ah, me, I'm old; I've lost my memory; I don't know how many months—ah! miserable me, what a very old, old monk I am!' Here he comforted himself with another pinch of my snuff.

'Never mind the exact time,' said I. 'I don't care about that.'

'Good,' said the Capuchin. 'Now I can go on. Well, let us say, it is some months ago—we in this convent are all at breakfast—wretched, wretched breakfasts, son of mine, in this convent!—we are at breakfast, and we hear *bang! bang!* twice over. "Guns," says I. "What are they shooting for?" says brother Jeremy. "Game," says brother Vincent. "Aha! game," says brother Jeremy. "If I hear more, I shall send out and discover what it means," says the father superior. We hear no more, and we go on with our wretched breakfasts.'

'Where did the report of firearms come from?' I inquired.

'From down below, beyond the big trees at the back of the convent, where there's some clear ground—nice ground, if it wasn't for the pools and puddles. But, ah, misery! how damp we are in these parts! how very, very damp!'

'Well, what happened after the report of firearms?'

'You shall hear. We are still at breakfast, all silent—for what have we to talk about here? What have we but our devotions, our kitchen garden, and our wretched, wretched bits of breakfasts and dinners? I say we are all silent when there comes suddenly such a ring at the bell as never was heard before—a very devil of a ring—a ring that caught us all with our bits—our wretched, wretched bits!—in our mouths, and stopped us before we could swallow them. "Go, brother of mine!" says the father superior to me—"go, it is your duty—go to the gate." I am brave—a very lion of a Capuchin. I slip out on tip-toe—I wait—I listen—I pull back our little shutter in the gate—I wait, I listen again—I peep through the hole—nothing, absolutely nothing, that I can see. I am brave—I am not to be daunted. What do I do next? I open the gate. Ah! Sacred Mother of Heaven, what do I behold lying along our threshold? A man—dead!—a big man; bigger than you, bigger than me, bigger than anybody in this convent—buttoned up tight in a fine coat, with black eyes, staring, staring up at the sky; and blood soaking through and through the front of his shirt. What do I do? I scream once—I scream twice—and run back to the father superior!'

All the particulars of the fatal duel which I had gleaned from the French newspaper in Monkton's room at Naples, recurred vividly to my memory. The suspicion that I had felt when I looked into the outhouse, became a certainty as I listened to the old monk's last words.

'So far I understand,' said I. 'The corpse I have just seen in the outhouse, is the corpse of the man whom you found dead outside your gate. Now tell me why you have not given the remains a decent burial?'

'Wait—wait—wait,' answered the Capuchin. 'The father superior hears me scream, and comes out; we all run together to the gate; we lift up the big man, and look at him close. Dead! dead as this' (smacking the dresser with his hand). 'We look again, and see a bit of paper pinned to the collar of his coat. Aha! son of mine, you start at that. I thought I should make you start at last.'

I had started indeed. That paper was doubtless the leaf mentioned in the second's unfinished narrative as having been torn out of his pocket-book, and inscribed with the statement of how the dead man had lost his life. If proof positive were wanted to identify the dead body, here was such proof found.

'What do you think was written on the bit of paper?' continued the Capuchin. 'We read, and shudder. This dead man has been killed in a duel—he, the desperate, the miserable, has died in the commission of mortal sin; and the men who saw the killing of him, ask us Capuchins, holy men, servants of Heaven, children of our lord the pope—they ask *us* to give him burial! Oh! but we are outraged when we read that; we groan, we wring our hands, we turn away, we tear our beards, we——'

'Wait one moment,' said I, seeing that the old man was heating himself with his narrative, and was likely, unless I stopped him, to talk more and more fluently to less and less purpose—'wait a moment. Have you preserved the paper that was pinned to the dead man's coat; and can I look at it?'

The Capuchin seemed on the point of giving me an answer, when he suddenly checked himself. I saw his eyes wander away from my face, and at the same moment heard a door softly opened and closed again behind me.

Looking round immediately, I observed another monk in the sacristy—a tall, lean, black-bearded man, in whose presence my old friend with the snuff-box suddenly became quite decorous and devotional to look at. I suspected I was in the presence of the father superior; and I found that I was right the moment he addressed me.

'I am the father superior of this convent,' he said in quiet, clear tones, and looking me straight in the face while he spoke, with coldly attentive eyes. 'I have heard the latter part of your conversation, and I wish to know why you are so particularly anxious to see the piece of paper that was pinned to the dead man's coat?'

The coolness with which he avowed that he had been listening, and the quietly imperative manner in which he put his concluding questions, perplexed and startled me. I hardly knew at first what tone I ought to take in answering him. He observed my hesitation, and attributing it to the wrong cause, signed to the old Capuchin to retire. Humbly stroking his long grey beard, and furtively consoling himself with a private pinch of the 'delectable snuff,' my venerable friend shuffled out of the room, making a profound obeisance at the door just before he disappeared.

'Now,' said the father superior, as coldly as ever; 'I am waiting, sir, for your reply.'

'You shall have it in the fewest possible words,' said I, answering him in his own tone. 'I find, to my disgust and horror, there is an unburied corpse in an outhouse attached to this convent. I believe that corpse to be the body of an English gentleman of rank and fortune, who was killed in a duel. I have come into this neighbourhood, with the nephew and only relation of the slain man, for the express purpose of recovering his remains; and I wish to see the paper found on the body, because I believe that paper will identify it to the satisfaction of the relative to whom I have referred. Do you find my reply sufficiently straightforward? And do you mean to give me permission to look at the paper?'

'I am satisfied with your reply, and see no reason for refusing you a sight of the paper,' said the father superior; 'but I have something to say first. In speaking of the impression produced on you by beholding the corpse, you used the words "disgust" and "horror". This licence of expression in relation to what you have seen in the precincts of a convent, proves to me that you are out of the pale of the Holy Catholic Church. You have no right, therefore, to expect any explanation; but I will give you one, nevertheless, as a favour. The slain man died, unabsolved, in the commission of mortal sin. We infer so much from the paper which we found on his body; and we know, by the evidence of our own eyes and ears, that he was killed on the territories of the church, and in the act of committing direct violation of those special laws against the crime of duelling, the strict enforcement of which the Holy Father himself has urged on the faithful throughout his dominions, by letters signed with his own hand. Inside this convent the ground is consecrated; and we Catholics are not accustomed to bury the outlaws of our religion, the enemies of our Holy Father, and the violators of our most sacred laws, in consecrated ground. Outside this convent, we have no rights and no power; and, if we had both, we should remember that we are monks, not gravediggers, and that the only burial with which *we* can have any concern, is burial with prayers of the church. That is all the explanation I think it necessary to give. Wait for me here, and you shall see the paper.' With those words the father superior left the room as quietly as he had entered it.

I had hardly time to think over this bitter and ungracious explanation, and to feel a little piqued by the language and manner of the person who had given it to me, before the father superior returned with the paper in his hand. He placed it before me on the dresser; and I read, hurriedly traced in pencil, the following lines:

This paper is attached to the body of the late Mr Stephen Monkton, an Englishman of distinction. He has been shot in a duel, conducted with perfect gallantry and honour on both sides. His body is placed at the door of this convent, to receive burial at the hands of its inmates, the survivors of the encounter being obliged to separate and secure their safety by immediate flight. I, the second of the slain man, and the writer of this explanation, certify on my word of honour as a gentleman, that the shot which killed my principal on the instant, was fired fairly, in the strictest accordance with the rules laid down beforehand for the conduct of the duel.

(Signed) 'F'.

'F'. I recognised easily enough as the initial letter of Monsieur Foulon's name, the second of Mr Monkton, who had died of consumption at Paris.

The discovery and the identification were now complete. Nothing remained but to break the news to Alfred, and to get permission to remove the remains in the outhouse. I began almost to doubt the evidence of my own senses, when I reflected that the apparently impracticable object with which we had left Naples was already, by the merest chance, virtually accomplished.

'The evidence of the paper is decisive,' I said, handing it back. 'There can be no doubt that the remains in the outhouse are the remains of which we have been in search. May I inquire if any obstacles will be thrown in our way, should the late Mr Monkton's nephew wish to remove his uncle's body to the family burial-place in England?'

'Where is this nephew?' asked the father superior.

'He is now waiting my return at the town of Fondi.'

'Is he in a position to prove his relationship?'

'Certainly; he has papers with him which will place it beyond a doubt.'

'Let him satisfy the civil authorities of his claim, and he need expect no obstacle to his wishes from anyone here.'

I was in no humour for talking a moment longer with my sour-tempered companion than I could help. The day was wearing on fast; and, whether night overtook me or not, I was resolved never to stop on my return till I got back to Fondi. Accordingly, after telling the father superior that he might expect to hear from me again immediately, I made my bow, and hastened out of the sacristy.

At the convent gate stood my old friend with the tin snuff-box, waiting to let me out.

'Bless you, my son,' said the venerable recluse, giving me a farewell pat on the shoulder; 'come back soon to your spiritual father who loves you; and amiably favour him with another tiny, tiny pinch of the delectable snuff.'

VI

I returned at the top of my speed to the village where I had left the mules, had the animals saddled immediately, and succeeded in getting back to Fondi a little before sunset.

While ascending the stairs of our hotel, I suffered under the most painful uncertainty as to how I should best communicate the news of my discovery to Alfred. If I could not succeed in preparing him properly for my tidings, the results—with such an organisation as his—might be fatal. On opening the door of his room, I felt by no means sure of myself; and when I confronted him, his manner of receiving me took me so much by surprise that, for a moment or two, I lost my self-possession altogether.

Every trace of the lethargy in which he was sunk when I had last seen him, had disappeared. His eyes were bright, his cheeks deeply flushed. As I entered, he started up, and refused my offered hand.

'You have not treated me like a friend,' he said passionately; 'you had no right to continue the search unless I searched with you—you had no right to leave me here alone. I was wrong to trust you: you are no better than all the rest of them.'

I had by this time recovered a little from my first astonishment, and was able to reply before he could say anything more. It was quite useless, in his present state, to reason with him, or to defend myself. I determined to risk everything, and break my news to him at once.

'You will treat me more justly, Monkton, when you know that I have been doing you good service during my absence,' I said. 'Unless I am greatly mistaken, the object for which we have left Naples may be nearer attainment by both of us than——'

The flush left his cheeks almost in an instant. Some expression in my face, or some tone in my voice, of which I was not conscious, had revealed to his nervously-quickened perception more than I had intended that he should know at first. His eyes fixed themselves intently on mine; his hand grasped my arm; and he said to me in an eager whisper:

'Tell me the truth at once. Have you found him?'

It was too late to hesitate. I answered in the affirmative.

'Buried or unburied?'

His voice rose abruptly as he put the question, and his unoccupied hand fastened on my other arm.

'Unburied.'

I had hardly uttered the word before the blood flew back into his cheeks; his eyes flashed again as they looked into mine, and he burst into a fit of triumphant laughter, which shocked and startled me inexpressibly.

'What did I tell you? What do you say to the old prophecy now?' he cried, dropping his hold on my arms, and pacing backwards and forwards in the room. 'Own you were wrong. Own it, as all Naples shall own it, when once I have got him safe in his coffin!'

His laughter grew more and more violent. I tried to quiet him in vain. His servant and the landlord of the inn entered the room; but they only added fuel to the fire, and I made them go out again. As I shut the door on them, I observed lying on a table near at hand, the packet of letters from Miss Elmslie, which my unhappy friend preserved with such care, and read and re-read with such unfailing devotion. Looking towards me just when I passed by the table, the letters caught his eye. The new hope for the future, in connexion with the writer of them, which my news was already awakening in his heart, seemed to overwhelm him in an instant at sight of the treasured memorials that reminded him of his betrothed wife. His laughter ceased, his face changed, he ran to the table, caught the letters up in his hand, looked from them to me for one moment with an altered expression which went to my heart, then sank down on his knees at the table, laid his face on the letters, and burst into tears. I let the new emotion have its way uninterruptedly, and quitted the room, without saying a word. When I returned, after a lapse of some little time, I found him sitting quietly in his chair, reading one of the letters from the packet which rested on his knee.

His look was kindness itself; his gesture almost womanly in its gentleness as he rose to meet me, and anxiously held out his hand.

He was quite calm enough now to hear in detail all that I had to tell him. I suppressed nothing but the particulars of the state in which I had found the corpse. I assumed no right of direction as to the share he was to take in our future proceedings, with the exception of insisting beforehand that he should leave the absolute superintendence of the removal of the body to me, and that he should be satisfied with a sight of M. Foulon's paper, after receiving my assurance that the remains placed in the coffin were really and truly the remains of which we had been in search.

'Your nerves are not so strong as mine.' I said, by way of apology for my apparent dictation; 'and for that reason I must beg leave to assume the leadership in all that we have now to do, until I see the leaden coffin soldered down and safe in your possession. After that, I shall resign all my functions to you.'

'I want words to thank you for your kindness,' he answered. 'No brother could have borne with me more affectionately, or helped me more patiently, than you.'

He stopped, and grew thoughtful, then occupied himself in tying up slowly and carefully the packet of Miss Elmslie's letters, and then looked suddenly towards the vacant wall behind me, with that strange expression the meaning of which I knew so well. Since we had left Naples, I had purposely avoided exciting him by talking on the useless and shocking subject of the apparition by which he believed himself to be perpetually followed. Just now, however, he seemed so calm and collected—so little likely to be violently agitated by any allusion to the dangerous topic—that I ventured to speak out boldly.

'Does the phantom still appear to you,' I asked, 'as it appeared at Naples?'

He looked at me, and smiled.

'Did I not tell you that it followed me everywhere?' His eyes wandered back again to the vacant space, and he went on speaking in that direction, as if he had been continuing the conversation with some third person in the room. 'We shall part,' he said slowly and softly, 'when the empty place is filled in Wincot vault. Then I shall stand with Ada before the altar in the Abbey chapel; and when my eyes meet hers, they will see the tortured face no more.'

Saying this, he leaned his head on his hand, sighed, and began repeating softly to himself the lines of the old prophecy:

> When in Wincot vault a place
> Waits for one of Monkton's race;
> When that one forlorn shall lie
> Graveless under open sky,
> Beggared of six feet of earth,
> Though lord of acres from his birth—
> That shall be a certain sign
> Of the end of Monkton's line.
> Dwindling ever faster, faster,
> Dwindling to the last-left master;
> From mortal ken, from light of day,
> Monkton's race shall pass away.

Fancying that he pronounced the last lines a little incoherently, I tried to make him change the subject. He took no notice of what I said, and went on talking to himself.

'Monkton's race shall pass away!' he repeated; 'but not with *me*. The fatality hangs over *my* head no longer. I shall bury the unburied dead; I shall fill the vacant place in Wincot vault. And then—then the new life, the life with Ada!'—That name seemed to recall him to himself. He drew his travelling desk towards him, placed the packet of letters in it, and then took out a sheet of paper. 'I am going to write to Ada,' he said, turning to me, 'and tell her the good news. Her happiness, when she knows it, will be even greater than mine.'

Worn out by the events of the day, I left him writing, and went to bed. I was, however, either too anxious or too tired to sleep. In this waking condition, my mind naturally occupied itself with the discovery at the convent, and with the events to which that discovery would in all probability lead. As I thought on the future, a depression for which I could not account weighed on my spirits. There was not the slightest reason for the vaguely melancholy forebodings that oppressed me. The remains, to the finding of which my unhappy friend attached so much importance, had been traced; they would certainly be placed at his disposal in a few days; he might take them to England by the first merchant vessel that sailed from Naples; and, the gratification of his strange caprice thus accomplished, there was at least some reason to hope that his mind might recover its tone, and that the new life he would lead at Wincot might result in making him a happy man. Such considerations as these were, in themselves, certainly not calculated to exert any melancholy influence over me; and yet, all through the night, the same inconceivable, unaccountable depression weighed heavily on my spirits—heavily through the hours of darkness—heavily, even when I walked out to breathe the first freshness of the early morning air.

With the day came the all-engrossing business of opening negotiations with the authorities.

Only those who have had to deal with Italian officials can imagine how our patience was tried by everyone with whom we came in contact. We were bandied about from one authority to the other, were stared at, cross-questioned, mystified—not in the least because the case presented any special difficulties or intricacies, but because it was absolutely necessary that every civil dignitary to whom we applied, should assert his own importance by leading us to our object in the most roundabout manner possible. After our first day's experience of official life in Italy, I left the absurd formalities, which we had no choice but to perform, to be accomplished by Alfred alone, and applied myself to considering the really serious question of how the remains in the convent outhouse were to be safely removed.

The best plan that suggested itself to me was to write to a friend at Rome, where I knew that it was a custom to embalm the bodies of high dignitaries of the church, and where, I consequently inferred, such chemical assistance as was needed in our emergency might be obtained. I simply stated in my letter that the removal of the body was imperative, then described the condition in which I had found it, and engaged that no expense on our part should be spared if the right person or persons could be found to help us. Here again more difficulties interposed themselves, and more useless formalities were to be gone through; but, in the end, patience, perseverance, and money triumphed, and two men came expressly from Rome to undertake the duties we required of them.

It is unnecessary that I should shock the reader by entering into any detail in this part of my narrative. When I have said that the progress of decay was so far suspended by chemical means as to allow of the remains being placed in the coffin, and to ensure their being transported to England with perfect safety and convenience, I have said enough. After ten days had been wasted in useless delays and difficulties, I had the satisfaction of seeing the convent outhouse empty at last; passed through a final ceremony of snuff-taking, or rather, of snuff-giving, with the old Capuchin; and ordered the travelling carriages to be ready at the inn door. Hardly a month had elapsed since our departure, when we entered Naples successful in the achievement of a design, which had been ridiculed as wildly impracticable by every friend of ours who had heard of it.

The first object to be accomplished on our return was to obtain the means of carrying the coffin to England—by sea, as a matter of course. All inquiries after a merchant vessel on the point of sailing for any British port, led to the most unsatisfactory results. There was only one way of ensuring the immediate transportation of the remains to England, and that was to hire a vessel. Impatient to return, and resolved not to lose sight of the coffin till he had seen it placed in Wincot vault, Monkton decided immediately on hiring the first ship that could be obtained. The vessel in port which we were informed could soonest be got ready for sea, was a Sicilian brig; and this vessel my friend accordingly engaged. The best dockyard artisans that could be got were set to work, and the smartest captain and crew to be picked up on an emergency in Naples, were chosen to navigate the brig.

Monkton, after again expressing in the warmest terms his gratitude for the services I had rendered him, disclaimed any intention of asking me to accompany him on the voyage to England. Greatly to his surprise and delight, however, I offered of my own accord to take passage in the brig. The strange coincidences I had witnessed, the extraordinary discovery I had hit on, since our first meeting in Naples, had made his one great interest in life my one great interest for the time being, as well. I shared none of his delusions, poor fellow; but it is hardly an exaggeration to say that my eagerness to follow our remarkable adventure to its end, was as great as his anxiety to see the coffin laid in Wincot vault. Curiosity influenced me, I am afraid, almost as strongly as friendship, when I offered myself as the companion of his voyage home.

We set sail for England on a calm and lovely afternoon.

For the first time since I had known him, Monkton seemed to be in high spirits. He talked and jested on all sorts of subjects, and laughed at me for allowing my cheerfulness to be affected by the dread of sea-sickness. I had really no such fear; it was my excuse to my friend for a return of that unaccountable depression under which I had suffered at Fondi. Everything was in our favour; everybody on board the brig was in good spirits. The captain was delighted with the vessel; the crew, Italians and Maltese, were in high glee at the prospect of making a short voyage on high wages in a well-provisioned ship. I alone felt heavy at heart. There was no valid reason that I could assign to myself for the melancholy that oppressed me, and yet I struggled against it in vain.

Late on our first night at sea, I made a discovery which was by no means calculated to restore my spirits to their usual equilibrium. Monkton was in the cabin, on the floor of which had been placed the packing-case containing the coffin; and I was on deck. The wind had fallen almost to a calm, and I was lazily watching the sails of the brig as they flapped from time to time against the masts, when the captain approached, and, drawing me out of hearing of the man at the helm, whispered in my ear—

'There's something wrong among the men forward. Did you observe how suddenly they all became silent just before sunset?'

I had observed it, and told him so.

'There's a Maltese boy on board,' pursued the captain, 'who is a smart lad enough, but a bad one to deal with. I have found out that he has been telling the men there is a dead body inside that packing case of your friend's in the cabin.'

My heart sank as he spoke. Knowing the superstitious irrationality of sailors—of foreign sailors especially—I had taken care to spread a report on board the brig, before the coffin was shipped, that the packing-case contained a valuable marble statue which Mr Monkton prized highly, and was unwilling to trust out of his own sight. How could this Maltese boy have discovered that the pretended statue was a human corpse? As I pondered over the question, my suspicions fixed themselves on Monkton's servant, who spoke Italian fluently, and whom I knew to be an incorrigible gossip. The man denied it when I charged him with betraying us, but I have never believed his denial to this day.

'The little imp won't say where he picked up this notion of his about the dead body,' continued the captain. 'It's not my place to pry into secrets; but I advise you to call the crew aft, and contradict the boy, whether he speaks the truth or not. The men are a parcel of fools, who believe in ghosts, and all the rest of it. Some of them say they would never have signed our articles if they had known they were going to sail with a dead man; others only grumble; but I'm afraid we shall have some trouble with them all, in case of rough weather, unless the boy is contradicted by you or the other gentleman. The men say that if either you or your friend tell them on your words of honour that the Maltese is a liar, they will hand him up to be rope's-ended accordingly; but that if you won't, they have made up their minds to believe the boy.'

Here the captain paused, and awaited my answer. I could give him none. I felt hopeless under our desperate emergency. To get the boy punished by giving my word of honour to support a direct falsehood, was not to be thought of even for a moment. What other means of extrication from this miserable dilemma remained? None that I could think of. I thanked the captain for his attention to our interests, told him I would take time to consider what course I should pursue, and begged that he would say nothing to my friend about the discovery he had made. He promised to be silent, sulkily enough, and walked away from me.

We had expected the breeze to spring up with the morning, but no breeze came. As it wore on towards noon, the atmosphere became insufferably sultry, and the sea looked as smooth as glass. I saw the captain's eye turn often and anxiously to windward. Far away in that direction, and alone in the blue heaven, I observed a little black cloud, and asked if it would bring us any wind.

'More than we want,' the captain replied, shortly; and then, to my astonishment, ordered the crew aloft to take in sail. The execution of this manœuvre showed but too plainly the temper of the men; they did their work sulkily and slowly, grumbling and murmuring among themselves. The captain's manner, as he urged them on with oaths and threats, convinced me we were in danger. I looked again to windward. The one little cloud had enlarged to a great bank of murky vapour, and the sea at the horizon had changed in colour.

'The squall will be on us before we know where we are,' said the captain. 'Go below; you will be only in the way here.'

I descended to the cabin, and prepared Monkton for what was coming. He was still questioning me about what I had observed on deck, when the storm burst on us. We felt the little brig strain for an instant as if she would part in two, then she seemed to be swinging round with us, then to be quite still for a moment, trembling in every timber. Last, came a shock which hurled us from our seats, a deafening crash, and a flood of water pouring into the cabin. We clambered, half-drowned, to the deck. The brig had, in the nautical phrase, 'breached to',* and she now lay on her beam ends.*

Before I could make out anything distinctly in the horrible confusion, except the one tremendous certainty that we were entirely at the mercy of the sea, I heard a voice from the fore part of the ship which stilled the clamouring and shouting of the rest of the crew in an instant. The words were in Italian, but I understood their fatal meaning only too easily. We had sprung a leak, and the sea was pouring into the ship's hold like the race of a mill-stream. The captain did not lose his presence of mind in this fresh emergency. He called for his axe to cut away the foremast, and ordering some of the crew to help him, directed the others to rig out the pumps.

The words had hardly passed his lips, before the men broke into open mutiny. With a savage look at me, their ringleader declared that the passengers might do as they pleased, but that he and his messmates were determined to take the boat, and leave the accursed ship, and *the dead man in her*, to go to the bottom together. As he spoke there was a shout among the sailors, and I observed some of them pointing derisively behind me. Looking round, I saw Monkton, who had hitherto kept close at my side, making his way back to the cabin. I followed him directly, but the water and confusion on deck, and the impossibility, from the position of the brig, of moving the feet without the slow assistance of the hands, so impeded my progress that it was impossible for me to overtake him. When I had got below, he was crouched upon the coffin, with the water on the cabin floor whirling and splashing about him, as the ship heaved and plunged. I saw a warning brightness in his eyes, a warning flush on his cheek as I approached and said to him:

'There is nothing left for it, Alfred, but to bow to our misfortune, and do the best we can to save our lives.'

'Save yours,' he cried, waving his hand to me, 'for *you* have a future before you. Mine is gone when this coffin goes to the bottom. If the ship sinks, I shall know that the fatality is accomplished, and shall sink with her.'

I saw that he was in no state to be reasoned with or persuaded, and raised myself again to the deck. The men were cutting away all obstacles, so as to launch the long boat, placed amidships, over the depressed bulwark of the brig, as she lay on her side; and the captain, after having made a last vain exertion to restore his authority, was looking on at them in silence. The violence of the squall seemed already to be spending itself, and I asked whether there was really no chance for us if we remained by the ship. The captain answered that there might have been the best chance if the men had obeyed his orders, but that now there was none. Knowing that I could place no dependence on the presence of mind of Monkton's servant, I confided to the captain, in the fewest and plainest words, the condition of my unhappy friend, and asked if I might depend on his help. He nodded his head, and we descended together to the cabin. Even at this day, it costs me pain to write of the terrible necessity to which the strength and obstinacy of Monkton's delusion reduced us, in the last resort. We were compelled to secure his hands, and drag him by main force to the deck. The men were on the point of launching the boat, and refused at first to receive us into it.

'You cowards!' cried the captain, 'have we got the dead man with us this time? Isn't he going to the bottom along with the brig? Who are you afraid of when we get into the boat?'

This sort of appeal produced the desired effect; the men became ashamed of themselves, and retracted their refusal.

Just as we pushed off from the sinking ship, Alfred made an effort to break from me, but I held him firm and he never repeated the attempt. He sat by me, with drooping head, still and silent, while the sailors rowed away from the vessel: still and silent, when with one accord they paused at a little distance off, and we all waited and watched to see the brig sink: still and silent, even when that sinking happened, when the labouring hull plunged slowly into a hollow of the sea—hesitated, as it seemed, for one moment—rose a little again—then sank to rise no more.

Sank with her dead freight: sank, and snatched for ever from our power the corpse which we had discovered almost by a miracle—those jealously-preserved remains on the safe keeping of which rested so strangely the hopes and the love-destinies of two living beings! As the last signs of the ship disappeared in the depths of the waters, I felt Monkton trembling all over as he sat close at my side, and heard him repeating to himself, sadly, and many times over, the name of 'Ada'.

I tried to turn his thoughts to another subject, but it was useless. He pointed over the sea to where the brig had once been, and where nothing was left to look at but the rolling waves.

'The empty place will now remain empty for ever in Wincot vault.'

As he said those words, he fixed his eyes for a moment sadly and earnestly on my face, then looked away, leant his check upon his hand, and spoke no more.

We were sighted long before nightfall by a trading-vessel, were taken on board, and landed at Cartagena in Spain. Alfred never held up his head, and never once spoke to me of his own accord, the whole time we were at sea in the merchantman. I observed, however, with alarm, that he talked often and incoherently to himself—constantly muttering the lines of the old prophecy—constantly referring to the fatal place that was empty in Wincot vault—constantly repeating in broken accents, which it affected me inexpressibly to hear, the name of the poor girl who was awaiting his return to England. Nor were these the only causes for the apprehension that I now felt on his account. Towards the end of our voyage he began to suffer from alternations of fever fits and shivering fits, which I ignorantly imagined to be attacks of ague. I was soon undeceived. We had hardly been a day on shore before he became so much worse that I secured the best medical assistance Cartagena could afford. For a day or two the doctors differed, as usual, about the nature of his complaint, but ere long alarming symptoms displayed themselves. The medical men declared that his life was in danger, and told me that his disease was brain fever.

Shocked and grieved as I was, I hardly knew how to act at
first under the fresh responsibility now laid upon me. Ultimately, I decided on writing to the old priest who had been
Alfred's tutor, and who, as I knew, still resided at Wincot
Abbey. I told this gentleman all that had happened, begged
him to break my melancholy news as gently as possible to
Miss Elmslie, and assured him of my resolution to remain
with Monkton to the last.

After I had despatched my letter, and had sent to Gibraltar
to secure the best English medical advice that could be
obtained, I felt that I had done my best, and that nothing
remained but to wait and hope.

Many a sad and anxious hour did I pass by my poor
friend's bedside. Many a time did I doubt whether I had
done right in giving any encouragement to his delusion. The
reasons for doing so which had suggested themselves to me,
after my first interview with him, seemed, however, on reflection, to be valid reasons still. The only way of hastening
his return to England and to Miss Elmslie, who was pining
for that return, was the way I had taken. It was not my fault
that a disaster which no man could foresee, had overthrown
all his projects and all mine. But now that the calamity had
happened, and was irretrievable, how, in the event of his
physical recovery, was his moral malady to be combated?

When I reflected on the hereditary taint in his mental
organisation, on that first childish fright of Stephen Monkton from which he had never recovered, on the perilously
secluded life that he had led at the Abbey, and on his firm
persuasion of the reality of the apparition by which he
believed himself to be constantly followed, I confess I despaired of shaking his superstitious faith in every word and
line of the old family prophecy. If the series of striking
coincidences which appeared to attest its truth had made a
strong and lasting impression on *me* (and this was assuredly
the case), how could I wonder that they had produced the
effect of absolute conviction on *his* mind, constituted as it
was? If I argued with him, and he answered me, how could
I rejoin? If he said, 'The prophecy points at the last of the
family: *I* am the last of the family. The prophecy mentions

an empty place in Wincot vault: there is such an empty place there at this moment. On the faith of the prophecy I told you that Stephen Monkton's body was unburied, and you found that it was unburied'—if he said this, of what use would it be for me to reply, 'These are only strange coincidences, after all'?

The more I thought of the task that lay before me, if he recovered, the more I felt inclined to despond. The oftener the English physician who attended on him said to me, 'He may get the better of the fever, but he has a fixed idea, which never leaves him night or day, which has unsettled his reason, and which will end in killing him, unless you or some of his friends can remove it,'—the oftener I heard this, the more acutely I felt my own powerlessness, the more I shrank from every idea that was connected with the hopeless future.

I had only expected to receive my answer from Wincot in the shape of a letter. It was consequently a great surprise, as well as a great relief, to be informed one day that two gentlemen wished to speak with me, and to find that of these two gentlemen the first was the old priest, and the second a male relative of Mrs Elmslie.

Just before their arrival the fever-symptoms had disappeared, and Alfred had been pronounced out of danger. Both the priest and his companion were eager to know when the sufferer would be strong enough to travel. They had come to Cartagena expressly to take him home with them, and felt far more hopeful than I did of the restorative effects of his native air. After all the questions connected with the first important point of the journey to England had been asked and answered, I ventured to make some inquiries after Miss Elmslie. Her relative informed me that she was suffering both in body and in mind from excess of anxiety on Alfred's account. They had been obliged to deceive her as to the dangerous nature of his illness, in order to deter her from accompanying the priest and her relation on their mission in Spain.

Slowly and imperfectly, as the weeks wore on, Alfred regained something of his former physical strength, but no alteration appeared in his illness as it affected his mind.

From the very first day of his advance towards recovery, it had been discovered that the brain fever had exercised the strangest influence over his faculties of memory. All recollection of recent events was gone from him. Everything connected with Naples, with me, with his journey to Italy, had dropped in some mysterious manner entirely out of his remembrance. So completely had all late circumstances passed from his memory, that, though he recognised the old priest and his own servant easily on the first days of his convalescence, he never recognised me, but regarded me with such a wistful, doubting expression, that I felt inexpressibly pained when I approached his bedside. All his questions were about Miss Elmslie and Wincot Abbey; and all his talk referred to the period when his father was yet alive.

The doctors augured good rather than ill from this loss of memory of recent incidents, saying that it would turn out to be temporary, and that it answered the first great healing purpose of keeping his mind at ease. I tried to believe them —tried to feel as sanguine, when the day came for his departure, as the old friends felt who were taking him home. But the effort was too much for me. A foreboding that I should never see him again, oppressed my heart, and the tears came into my eyes as I saw the worn figure of my poor friend half-helped, half-lifted into the travelling carriage, and borne away gently on the road towards home.

He had never recognised me, and the doctors had begged that I would give him, for some time to come, as few opportunities as possible of doing so. But for this request I should have accompanied him to England. As it was, nothing better remained for me to do than to change the scene, and recruit as I best could my energies of body and mind, depressed of late by much watching and anxiety. The famous cities of Spain were not new to me, but I visited them again, and revived old impressions of the Alhambra and Madrid. Once or twice I thought of making a pilgrimage to the East, but late events had sobered and altered me. That yearning unsatisfied feeling which we call 'home-sickness', began to prey upon my heart, and I resolved to return to England.

I went back by way of Paris, having settled with the priest that he should write to me at my banker's there, as soon as he could after Alfred had returned to Wincot. If I had gone to the East, the letter would have been forwarded to me. I wrote to prevent this; and, on my arrival at Paris, stopped at the banker's before I went to my hotel.

The moment the letter was put into my hands, the black border on the envelope told me the worst. He was dead.

There was but one consolation—he had died calmly, almost happily, without once referring to those fatal chances which had wrought the fulfilment of the ancient prophecy. 'My beloved pupil,' the old priest wrote, 'seemed to rally a little the first few days after his return, but he gained no real strength, and soon suffered a slight relapse of fever. After this he sank gradually and gently day by day, and so departed from us on the last dread journey. Miss Elmslie (who knows that I am writing this) desires me to express her deep and lasting gratitude for all your kindness to Alfred. She told me when we brought him back, that she had waited for him as his promised wife, and that she would nurse him now as a wife should; and she never left him. His face was turned towards her, his hand was clasped in hers, when he died. It will console you to know that he never mentioned events at Naples, or the shipwreck that followed them, from the day of his return to the day of his death.'

Three days after reading the letter I was at Wincot, and heard all the details of Alfred's last moments from the priest. I felt a shock which it would not be very easy for me to analyse or explain, when I heard that he had been buried, at his own desire, in the fatal Abbey vault.

The priest took me down to see the place—a grim, cold, subterranean building, with a low roof, supported on heavy Saxon arches. Narrow niches, with the ends only of coffins visible within them, ran down each side of the vault. The nails and silver ornaments flashed here and there as my companion moved past them with a lamp in his hand. At the lower end of the place he stopped, pointed to a niche, and said: 'He lies there, between his father and mother.' I looked a little further on, and saw what appeared at first like a long dark tunnel. 'That is only an empty niche,' said the priest, following me. 'If the body of Mr Stephen Monkton had been brought to Wincot, his coffin would have been placed there.'

A chill came over me, and a sense of dread which I am ashamed of having felt now, but which I could not combat then. The blessed light of day was pouring down gaily at the other end of the vault through the open door. I turned my back on the empty niche, and hurried into the sunlight and the fresh air.

As I walked across the grass glade leading down to the vault, I heard the rustle of a woman's dress behind me, and, turning round, saw a young lady advancing, clad in deep mourning. Her sweet, sad face, her manner as she held out her hand, told me who it was in an instant.

'I heard that you were here,' she said, 'and I wished'—her voice faltered a little. My heart ached as I saw how her lip trembled, but before I could say anything, she recovered herself, and went on—'I wished to take your hand, and thank you for your brotherly kindness to Alfred; and I wanted to tell you that I am sure, in all you did, you acted tenderly and considerately for the best. Perhaps you may be soon going away from home again, and we may not meet any more. I shall never, never forget that you were kind to him when he wanted a friend, and that you have the greatest claim of any one on earth to be gratefully remembered in my thoughts as long as I live.'

The inexpressible tenderness of her voice, trembling a little all the while she spoke, the pale beauty of her face, the artless candour in her sad, quiet eyes, so affected me that I could not trust myself to answer her at first, except by gesture. Before I recovered my voice, she had given me her hand once more and had left me.

I never saw her again. The chances and changes of life kept us apart. When I last heard of her, years and years ago, she was faithful to the memory of the dead, and was Ada Elmslie still, for Alfred Monkton's sake.

THE OSTLER

I FIND an old man, fast asleep, in one of the stalls of the stable. It is midday, and rather a strange time for an ostler to devote to sleep. Something curious, too, about the man's face. A withered woe-begone face. The eyebrows painfully contracted; the mouth fast set, and drawn down at the corners; the hollow cheeks sadly, and, as I cannot help fancying, prematurely wrinkled; the scanty, grizzled hair, telling weakly its own tale of some past sorrow or suffering. How fast he draws his breath, too, for a man asleep! He is talking in his sleep.

'Wake up!' I hear him say, in a quick whisper through his fast-clenched teeth. 'Wake up there! Murder! O Lord help me! Lord help me, alone in this place!'

He stops, and sighs again—moves one lean arm slowly, till it rests over his throat—shudders a little, and turns on his straw—the arm leaves his throat—the hand stretches itself out, and clutches at the side towards which he has turned, as if he fancies himself to be grasping at the edge of something. Is he waking? No—there is the whisper again; he is still talking in his sleep.

'Light grey eyes,' he says now, 'and a droop in the left eyelid. Yes! yes!—flaxen hair with a gold-yellow streak in it—all right, mother—fair, white arms with a down on them—little lady's hand, with a reddish look under the finger-nails—and the knife—always the cursed knife—first on one side, then on the other. Aha! you she-devil, where's the knife? Never mind, mother—too late now. I've promised to marry, and marry I must. Murder! wake up there! for God's sake, wake up!'

At the last words his voice rises, and he grows so restless on a sudden, that I draw back quietly to the door. I see him shudder on the straw—his withered face grows distorted— he throws up both his hands with a quick, hysterical gasp; they strike against the bottom of the manger under which he lies; the blow awakens him; I have just time to slip through the door, before his eyes are fairly open and his senses are his own again.

What I have seen and heard has so startled and shocked me, that I feel my heart beating fast, as I softly and quickly retrace my steps across the inn-yard. The discomposure that is going on within me, apparently shows itself in my face; for, as I get back to the covered way leading to the Inn stairs, the landlord, who is just coming out of the house to ring some bell in the yard, stops astonished, and asks what is the matter with me? I tell him what I have just seen.

'Aha!' says the landlord, with an air of relief. 'I understand now. Poor old chap! He was only dreaming his old dream over again. There's the queerest story—of a dreadful kind, too, mind you—connected with him and his dream, that ever was told.'

I entreat the landlord to tell me the story. After a little hesitation, he complies with my request.

Some years ago, there lived in the suburbs of a large seaport town, on the west coast of England, a man in humble circumstances, by name Isaac Scatchard. His means of subsistence were derived from any employment that he could get, as an ostler; and, occasionally, when times went well with him, from temporary engagements in service, as stable-helper in private houses. Though a faithful, steady, and honest man, he got on badly in his calling. His ill-luck was proverbial among his neighbours. He was always missing good opportunities, by no fault of his own; and always living longest in service with amiable people who were not punctual payers of wages. 'Unlucky Isaac' was his nickname in his own neighbourhood—and no one could say that he did not richly deserve it.

With far more than one man's fair share of adversity to endure, Isaac had but one consolation to support him—and that was of the dreariest and most negative kind. He had no wife and children to increase his anxieties and add to the bitterness of his various failures in life. It might have been from mere insensibility, or it might have been from generous unwillingness to involve another in his own unlucky destiny—but the fact undoubtedly was, that he arrived at the middle term of life without marrying; and, what is much more remarkable, without once exposing himself, from eighteen to eight and thirty, to the genial imputation of ever having had a sweetheart. When he was out of service, he lived alone with his widowed mother. Mrs Scatchard was a woman above the average in her lowly station, as to capacities and manners. She had seen better days, as the phrase is; but she never referred to them in the presence of curious visitors; and, though perfectly polite to every one who approached her, never cultivated any intimacies among her neighbours. She contrived to provide, hardly enough, for her simple wants, by doing rough work for the tailors; and always managed to keep a decent home for her son to return to, whenever his ill-luck drove him out helpless into the world.

One bleak autumn, when Isaac was getting on fast towards forty, and when he was, as usual, out of place, through no fault of his own, he set forth from his mother's cottage on a long walk inland to a gentleman's seat, where he had heard that a stable-helper was required. It wanted then but two days of his birthday; and Mrs Scatchard, with her usual fondness, made him promise, before he started, that he would be back in time to keep that anniversary with her, in as festive a way as their poor means would allow. It was easy for him to comply with this request, even supposing he slept a night each way on the road. He was to start from home on Monday morning; and, whether he got the new place or not, he was to be back for his birthday dinner on Wednesday at two o'clock.

Arriving at his destination too late on the Monday night to make application for the stable-helper's place, he slept at the village-inn, and, in good time on the Tuesday morning, presented himself at the gentleman's house, to fill the vacant situation. Here, again, his ill-luck pursued him as inexorably as ever. The excellent written testimonials, as to character, which he was able to produce, availed him nothing; his long walk had been taken in vain—only the day before, the stable-helper's place had been given to another man.

Isaac accepted this new disappointment resignedly, and as a matter of course. Naturally slow in capacity, he had the bluntness of sensibility and phlegmatic patience of disposition which frequently distinguish men with sluggishly-working mental powers. He thanked the gentleman's steward, with his usual quiet civility, for granting him an interview, and took his departure with no appearance of unusual depression in his face or manner. Before starting on his homeward walk, he made some enquiries at the inn, and ascertained that he might save a few miles, on his return, by following a new road. Furnished with full instructions, several times repeated, as to the various turnings he was to take, he set forth for his homeward journey, and walked on all day with only one stoppage for bread and cheese. Just as it was getting towards dark, the rain came on and the wind began to rise; and he found himself, to make matters worse, in a part of the country with which he was entirely unacquainted, though he knew himself to be some fifteen miles from home. The first house he found to inquire at was a lonely road-side inn, standing on the outskirts of a thick wood. Solitary as the place looked, it was welcome to a lost man who was also hungry, thirsty, footsore, and wet. The landlord was a civil, respectable-looking man; and the price he asked for a bed was reasonable enough. Isaac, therefore, decided on stopping comfortably at the inn for that night.

He was constitutionally a temperate man. His supper simply consisted of two rashers of bacon, a slice of home-made bread, and a pint of ale. He did not go to bed immediately after this moderate meal, but sat up with the landlord talking about his bad prospects and his long run of ill-luck, and diverging from these topics to the subject of horse-flesh and racing. Nothing was said either by himself, his host, or the few labourers who strayed into the tap-room, which could, in the slightest degree, excite the very small and very dull imaginative faculty which Isaac Scatchard possessed.

At a little after eleven the house was closed. Isaac went round with the landlord and held the candle while the doors and lower-windows were being secured. He noticed with surprise the strength of the bolts, bars, and iron-sheathed shutters.

'You see, we are rather lonely here,' said the landlord. 'We never have had any attempts made to break in yet, but it's always as well to be on the safe side. When nobody is sleeping here, I am the only man in the house. My wife and daughter are timid, and the servant-girl takes after her missuses. Another glass of ale, before you turn in?—No!— Well, how such a sober man as you comes to be out of place is more than I can make out, for one.—Here's where you're to sleep. You're our only lodger tonight, and I think you'll say my missus has done her best to make you comfortable. You're quite sure you won't have another glass of ale?— Very well. Good night.'

It was half-past eleven by the clock in the passage as they went upstairs to the bedroom, the window of which looked on to the wood at the back of the house. Isaac locked the door, set his candle on the chest of drawers, and wearily got ready for bed. The bleak autumn wind was still blowing, and the solemn, monotonous, surging moan of it in the wood was dreary and awful to hear through the night-silence. Isaac felt strangely wakeful, and resolved, as he lay down in bed, to keep the candle a-light until he began to grow sleepy; for there was something unendurably depressing in the bare idea of lying awake in the darkness, listening to the dismal, ceaseless moaning of the wind in the wood.

Sleep stole on him before he was aware of it. His eyes closed, and he fell off insensibly to rest, without having so much as thought of extinguishing the candle.

The first sensation of which he was conscious after sinking into slumber, was a strange shivering that ran through him suddenly from head to foot, and a dreadful sinking pain at the heart, such as he had never felt before. The shivering only disturbed his slumbers—the pain woke him instantly. In one moment he passed from a state of sleep to a state of wakefulness—his eyes wide open—his mental perceptions cleared on a sudden as if by a miracle.

The candle had burnt down nearly to the last morsel of tallow; but the top of the unsnuffed wick had just fallen off, and the light in the little room was, for the moment, fair and full. Between the foot of his bed and the closed door there stood a woman with a knife in her hand, looking at him. He was stricken speechless with terror, but he did not lose the preternatural clearness of his faculties; and he never took his eyes off the woman. She said not one word as they stared each other in the face; but she began to move slowly towards the left-hand side of the bed.

His eyes followed her. She was a fair, fine woman, with yellowish flaxen hair, and light grey eyes, with a droop in the left eyelid. He noticed those things and fixed them on his mind, before she was round at the side of the bed. Speechless, with no expression in her face, with no noise following her footfall,—she came closer and closer—stopped—and slowly raised the knife. He laid his right arm over his throat to save it; but, as he saw the knife coming down, threw his hand across the bed to the right side, and jerked his body over that way, just as the knife descended on the mattress within an inch of his shoulder.

His eyes fixed on her arm and hand, as she slowly drew the knife out of the bed. A white, well-shaped arm, with a pretty down lying lightly over the fair skin. A delicate, lady's hand, with the crowning beauty of a pink flush under and round the finger-nails.

She drew the knife out, and passed back again slowly to the foot of the bed; stopped there for a moment looking at him; then came on—still speechless, still with no expression on the blank, beautiful face, still with no sound following the stealthy footfalls—came on to the right side of the bed where he now lay. As she approached, she raised the knife again, and he drew himself away to the left side. She struck, as before, right into the mattress, with a deliberate, perpendicularly-downward action of the arm. This time his eyes wandered from her to the knife. It was like the large clasp knives which he had often seen labouring men use to cut their bread and bacon with. Her delicate little fingers did not conceal more than two thirds of the handle; he noticed that it was made of buck-horn, clean and shining as the blade was, and looking like new.

For the second time she drew the knife out, concealed it in the wide sleeve of her gown, then stopped by the bedside, watching him. For an instant he saw her standing in that position—then the wick of the spent candle fell over into the socket. The flame diminished to a little blue point, and the room grew dark. A moment, or less, if possible, passed so—and then the wick flamed up, smokily, for the last time. His eyes were still looking eagerly over the right-hand side of the bed when the final flash of light came, but they discerned nothing. The fair woman with the knife was gone.

The conviction that he was alone again, weakened the hold of the terror that had struck him dumb up to this time. The preternatural sharpness which the very intensity of his panic had mysteriously imparted to his faculties, left them suddenly. His brain grew confused—his heart beat wildly—his ears opened for the first time since the appearance of the woman, to a sense of the woeful, ceaseless moaning of the wind among the trees. With the dreadful conviction of the reality of what he had seen, still strong within him, he leapt out of bed, and screaming—'Murder!—Wake up, there, wake up!'—dashed headlong through the darkness to the door.

It was fast locked, exactly as he had left it on going to bed.

His cries on starting up, had alarmed the house. He heard the terrified, confused, exclamations of women; he saw the master of the house approaching along the passage, with his burning rush-candle in one hand and his gun in the other.

'What is it?' asked the landlord, breathlessly.

Isaac could only answer in a whisper: 'A woman, with a knife in her hand,' he gasped out. 'In my room—a fair, yellow-haired woman; she jobbed at me with the knife, twice over.'

The landlord's pale cheeks grew paler. He looked at Isaac eagerly by the flickering light of his candle; and his face began to get red again—his voice altered, too, as well as his complexion.

'She seems to have missed you twice,' he said.

'I dodged the knife as it came down,' Isaac went on, in the same scared whisper. 'It struck the bed each time.'

The landlord took his candle into the bedroom immediately. In less than a minute he came out again into the passage in a violent passion.

'The devil fly away with you and your woman with the knife! What do you mean by coming into a man's place and frightening his family out of their wits about a dream?'

'I'll leave your house,' said Isaac, faintly. 'Better out on the road, in rain and dark, on my way home, than back again in that room after what I've seen in it. Lend me a light to get on my clothes by, and tell me what I'm to pay.'

'Pay!' cried the landlord, leading the way with his light sulkily into the bedroom. 'You'll find your score on the slate when you go downstairs. I wouldn't have taken you in for all the money you've got about you, if I'd known your dreaming, screeching ways beforehand. Look at the bed. Where's the cut of a knife in it? Look at the window—is the lock bursted? Look at the door (which I heard you fasten myself)—is it broke in? A murdering woman with a knife in my house! You ought to be ashamed of yourself!'

Isaac answered not a word. He huddled on his clothes; and then they went down stairs together.

'Nigh on twenty minutes past two!' said the landlord, as they passed the clock. 'A nice time in the morning to frighten honest people out of their wits!'

Isaac paid his bill, and the landlord let him out at the front door, asking, with a grin of contempt, as he undid the strong fastenings, whether 'the murdering woman got in that way?' They parted without a word on either side. The rain had ceased; but the night was dark, and the wind bleaker than ever. Little did the darkness, or the cold, or the uncertainty about his way home, matter to Isaac. If he had been turned out into a wilderness in a thunder-storm, it would have been a relief, after what he had suffered in the bedroom of the inn.

What was the fair woman with the knife? The creature of a dream, or that other creature from the unknown world called among men by the name of ghost? He could make nothing of the mystery—had made nothing of it, even when it was midday on Wednesday, and when he stood, at last, after many times missing his road, once more on the door-step of home.

His mother came out eagerly to receive him. His face told her in a moment that something was wrong.

'I've lost the place; but that's my luck. I dreamed an ill dream last night, mother—or, may be, I saw a ghost. Take it either way, it scared me out of my senses, and I'm not my own man again yet.'

'Isaac! your face frightens me. Come in to the fire. Come in, and tell mother all about it.'

He was as anxious to tell as she was to hear; for it had been his hope, all the way home, that his mother, with her quicker capacity and superior knowledge, might be able to throw some light on the mystery which he could not clear up for himself. His memory of the dream was still mechanically vivid, though his thoughts were entirely confused by it.

His mother's face grew paler and paler as he went on. She never interrupted him by so much as a single word; but when he had done, she moved her chair close to his, put her arm round his neck, and said to him:

'Isaac, you dreamed your ill dream on this Wednesday morning. What time was it when you saw the fair woman with the knife in her hand?'

Isaac reflected on what the landlord had said when they passed by the clock on his leaving the inn—allowed as nearly as he could for the time that must have elapsed between the unlocking of his bedroom door and the paying of his bill just before going away, and answered:

'Somewhere about two o'clock in the morning.'

His mother suddenly quitted her hold of his neck, and struck her hands together with a gesture of despair.

'This Wednesday is your birthday Isaac; and two o'clock in the morning was the time when you were born!'

Isaac's capacities were not quick enough to catch the infection of his mother's superstitious dread. He was amazed and a little startled also, when she suddenly rose from her chair, opened her old writing-desk, took out pen and ink and paper, and then said to him:

'Your memory is but a poor one, Isaac, and now I'm an old woman, mine's not much better. I want all about this dream of yours to be as well known to both of us, years hence, as it is now. Tell me over again all you told me a minute ago, when you spoke of what the woman with the knife looked like.'

Isaac obeyed, and marvelled much as he saw his mother carefully set down on paper the very words that he was saying. 'Light grey eyes,' she wrote, as they came to the descriptive part, 'with a droop in the left eyelid. Flaxen hair, with a gold-yellow streak in it. White arms, with a down on them. Little lady's hand, with a reddish look about the finger-nails. Clasp knife with a buck-horn handle, that seemed as good as new.' To these particulars, Mrs Scatchard added the year, month, day of the week, and time in the morning, when the woman of the dream appeared to her son. She then locked up the paper carefully in her writing-desk.

Neither on that day, nor on any day after, could her son induce her to return to the matter of the dream. She obstinately kept her thoughts about it to herself, and even refused to refer again to the paper in her writing-desk. Ere long, Isaac grew weary of attempting to make her break her resolute silence; and time, which sooner or later, wears out all things, gradually wore out the impression produced on him by the dream. He began by thinking of it carelessly, and he ended by not thinking of it at all. This result was the more easily brought about by the advent of some important changes for the better in his prospects, which commenced not long after his terrible night's experience at the inn. He reaped at last the reward of his long and patient suffering under adversity, by getting an excellent place, keeping it for seven years, and leaving it, on the death of his master, not only with an excellent character, but also with a comfortable annuity bequeathed to him as a reward for saving his mistress's life in a carriage accident. Thus it happened that Isaac Scatchard returned to his old mother, seven years after the time of the dream at the inn, with an annual sum of money at his disposal, sufficient to keep them both in ease and independence for the rest of their lives.

The mother, whose health had been bad of late years, profited so much by the care bestowed on her and by freedom from money anxieties, that when Isaac's next birthday came round, she was able to sit up comfortably at table and dine with him.

On that day, as the evening drew on, Mrs Scatchard discovered that a bottle of tonic medicine—which she was accustomed to take, and in which she had fancied that a dose or more was still left—happened to be empty. Isaac immediately volunteered to go to the chemist's, and get it filled again. It was as rainy and bleak an autumn night as on the memorable past occasion when he lost his way and slept at the roadside inn.

On going into the chemist's shop, he was passed hurriedly by a poorly-dressed woman coming out of it. The glimpse he had of her face struck him, and he looked back after her as she descended the door-steps.

'You're noticing that woman?' said the chemist's apprentice behind the counter. 'It's my opinion there's something wrong with her. She's been asking for laudanum to put to a bad tooth. Master's out for half an hour; and I told her I wasn't allowed to sell poison to strangers in his absence. She laughed in a queer way, and said she would come back in half an hour. If she expects master to serve her, I think she'll be disappointed. It's a case of suicide, sir, if ever there was one yet.'

These words added immeasurably to the sudden interest in the woman which Isaac had felt at the first sight of her face. After he had got the medicine-bottle filled, he looked about anxiously for her, as soon as he was out in the street. She was walking slowly up and down on the opposite side of the road. With his heart, very much to his own surprise, beating fast, Isaac crossed over and spoke to her.

He asked if she was in any distress. She pointed to her torn shawl, her scanty dress, her crushed, dirty bonnet—then moved under a lamp so as to let the light fall on her stern, pale, but still most beautiful face.

'I look like a comfortable, happy woman—don't I?' she said with a bitter laugh.

She spoke with a purity of intonation which Isaac had never heard before from other than ladies' lips. Her slightest actions seemed to have the easy negligent grace of a thorough-bred woman. Her skin, for all its poverty-stricken paleness, was as delicate as if her life had been passed in the enjoyment of every social comfort that wealth can purchase. Even her small, finely-shaped hands, gloveless as they were, had not lost their whiteness.

Little by little, in answer to his question, the sad story of the woman came out. There is no need to relate it here; it is told over and over again in Police Reports and paragraphs about Attempted Suicides.

'My name is Rebecca Murdoch,' said the woman, as she ended. 'I have ninepence left, and I thought of spending it at the chemist's over the way in securing a passage to the other world. Whatever it is, it can't be worse to me than this—so why should I stop here?'

Besides the natural compassion and sadness moved in his heart by what he heard, Isaac felt within him some mysterious influence at work all the time the woman was speaking, which utterly confused his ideas and almost deprived him of his powers of speech. All that he could say in answer to her last reckless words was, that he would prevent her from attempting her own life, if he followed her about all night to do it. His rough, trembling earnestness seemed to impress her.

'I won't occasion you that trouble,' she answered, when he repeated his threat. 'You have given me a fancy for living by speaking kindly to me. No need for the mockery of protestations and promises. You may believe me without them. Come to Fuller's Meadow tomorrow at twelve, and you will find me alive, to answer for myself. No!—no money. My ninepence will do to get me as good a night's lodging as I want.'

She nodded and left him. He made no attempt to follow—he felt no suspicion that she was deceiving him.

'It's strange, but I can't help believing her,' he said to himself—and walked away, bewildered, towards home.

On entering the house his mind was still so completely absorbed by its new subject of interest, that he took no notice of what his mother was doing when he came in with the bottle of medicine. She had opened her old writing-desk in his absence, and was now reading a paper attentively that lay inside it. On every birthday of Isaac's since she had written down the particulars of his dream from his own lips, she had been accustomed to read that same paper, and ponder over it in private.

The next day he went to Fuller's Meadow. He had done only right in believing her so implicitly—she was there, punctual to a minute, to answer for herself. The last-left faint defences in Isaac's heart against the fascination which a word or look from her began inscrutably to exercise over him, sank down and vanished before her for ever on that memorable morning.

When a man, previously insensible to the influence of women, forms an attachment in middle life, the instances are rare indeed, let the warning circumstances be what they may, in which he is found capable of freeing himself from the tyranny of the new ruling passion. The charm of being spoken to familiarly, fondly, and gratefully by a woman whose language and manners still retained enough of their early refinement to hint at the high social station that she had lost, would have been a dangerous luxury to a man of Isaac's rank at the age of twenty. But it was far more than that—it was certain ruin to him—now that his heart was opening unworthily to a new influence, at that middle time of life when strong feelings of all kinds, once implanted, strike root most stubbornly in a man's moral nature. A few more stolen interviews after that first morning in Fuller's Meadow completed his infatuation. In less than a month from the time when he first met her, Isaac Scatchard had consented to give Rebecca Murdoch a new interest in existence, and a chance of recovering the character she had lost, by promising to make her his wife.

She had taken possession, not of his passions only, but of his faculties as well. All arrangements for the present and all plans for the future were of her devising. All the mind he had he put into her keeping. She directed him on every point; even instructing him how to break the news of his approaching marriage in the safest manner to his mother.

'If you tell her how you met me and who I am at first,' said the cunning woman, 'she will move heaven and earth to prevent our marriage. Say I am the sister of one of your fellow-servants—ask her to see me before you go into any more particulars—and leave it to me to do the rest. I want to make her love me next best to you, Isaac, before she knows anything of who I really am.'

The motive of the deceit was sufficient to sanctify it to Isaac. The stratagem proposed relieved him of his one great anxiety, and quieted his uneasy conscience on the subject of his mother. Still, there was something wanting to perfect his happiness, something that he could not realise, something mysteriously untraceable, and yet, something that perpetually made itself felt; not when he was absent from Rebecca Murdoch, but, strange to say, when he was actually in her presence! She was kindness itself with him; she never made him feel his inferior capacities, and inferior manners,—she showed the sweetest anxiety to please him in the smallest trifles; but, in spite of all these attractions, he never could feel quite at his ease with her. At their first meeting, there had mingled with his admiration when he looked in her face, a faint involuntary feeling of doubt whether that face was entirely strange to him. No after familiarity had the slightest effect on this inexplicable, wearisome uncertainty.

Concealing the truth as he had been directed, he announced his marriage engagement precipitately and confusedly to his mother, on the day when he contracted it. Poor Mrs Scatchard showed her perfect confidence in her son by flinging her arms round his neck, and giving him joy of having found at last, in the sister of one of his fellow-servants, a woman to comfort and care for him after his mother was gone. She was all eagerness to see the woman of her son's choice; and the next day was fixed for the introduction.

It was a bright sunny morning, and the little cottage parlour was full of light, as Mrs Scatchard, happy and expectant, dressed for the occasion in her Sunday gown, sat waiting for her son and her future daughter-in-law. Punctual to the appointed time, Isaac hurriedly and nervously led his promised wife into the room. His mother rose to receive her—advanced a few steps, smiling—looked Rebecca full in the eyes—and suddenly stopped. Her face, which had been flushed the moment before, turned white in an instant—her eyes lost their expression of softness and kindness, and assumed a blank look of terror—her outstretched hands fell to her sides, and she staggered back a few steps with a low cry to her son.

'Isaac!' she whispered, clutching him fast by the arm, when he asked alarmedly if she was taken ill. 'Isaac! Does that woman's face remind you of nothing?'

Before he could answer; before he could look round to where Rebecca, astonished and angered by her reception, stood, at the lower end of the room; his mother pointed impatiently to her writing-desk, and gave him the key.

'Open it,' she said, in a quick, breathless whisper.

'What does this mean? Why am I treated as if I had no business here? Does your mother want to insult me?' asked Rebecca, angrily.

'Open it, and give me the paper in the left-hand drawer. Quick! quick, for Heaven's sake!' said Mrs Scatchard, shrinking further back in terror. Isaac gave her the paper. She looked it over eagerly for a moment—then followed Rebecca, who was now turning away haughtily to leave the room, and caught her by the shoulder—abruptly raised the long, loose sleeve of her gown, and glanced at her hand and arm. Something like fear began to steal over the angry expression of Rebecca's face as she shook herself free from the old woman's grasp. 'Mad!' she said to herself; 'and Isaac never told me.' With these few words she left the room.

Isaac was hastening after her when his mother turned and stopped his further progress. It wrung his heart to see the misery and terror in her face as she looked at him.

'Light grey eyes,' she said, in low, mournful, awe-struck tones, pointing towards the open door. 'A droop in the left eyelid. Flaxen hair with a gold-yellow streak in it. White arms with a down on them. Little, lady's hand, with a reddish look under the finger-nails. *The woman of the dream!*—Oh, Heaven! Isaac, the woman of the dream!'

That faint cleaving doubt which he had never been able to shake off in Rebecca Murdoch's presence, was fatally set at rest for ever. He *had* seen her face, then, before—seven years before, on his birthday, in the bedroom of the lonely inn. 'The woman of the dream!'

'Be warned, Oh, my son! be warned! Isaac! Isaac! let her go, and do you stop with me!'

Something darkened the parlour window, as those words were said. A sudden chill ran through him; and he glanced sidelong at the shadow. Rebecca Murdoch had come back. She was peering in curiously at them over the low window blind.

'I have promised to marry, mother,' he said, 'and marry I must.'

The tears came into his eyes as he spoke, and dimmed his sight; but he could just discern the fatal face outside moving away again from the window.

His mother's head sank lower.

'Are you faint?' he whispered.

'Broken-hearted, Isaac.'

He stooped down and kissed her. The shadow, as he did so, returned to the window; and the fatal face peered in curiously once more.

Three weeks after that day, Isaac and Rebecca were man and wife. All that was hopelessly dogged and stubborn in the man's moral nature, seemed to have closed round his fatal passion, and to have fixed it unassailably in his heart.

After that first interview in the cottage parlour, no consideration would induce Mrs Scatchard to see her son's wife again, or even to talk of her when Isaac tried hard to plead her cause after their marriage. This course of conduct was not in any degree occasioned by a discovery of the degradation in which Rebecca had lived. There was no question of that between mother and son. There was no question of anything but the fearfully exact resemblance between the living breathing woman and the spectre woman of Isaac's dream. Rebecca, on her side, neither felt nor expressed the slightest sorrow at the estrangement between herself and her mother-in-law. Isaac, for the sake of peace, had never contradicted her first idea that age and long illness had affected Mrs Scatchard's mind. He even allowed his wife to upbraid him for not having confessed this to her at the time of their marriage engagement, rather than risk anything by hinting at the truth. The sacrifice of his integrity before his one all-mastering delusion, seemed but a small thing, and cost his conscience but little, after the sacrifices he had already made.

The time of waking from his delusion—the cruel and the rueful time—was not far off. After some quiet months of married life, as the summer was ending, and the year was getting on towards the month of his birthday, Isaac found his wife altering towards him. She grew sullen and con-temptuous—she formed acquaintances of the most danger-ous kind, in defiance of his objections, his entreaties, and his commands,—and, worst of all, she learnt, ere long, after every fresh difference with her husband, to seek the deadly self-oblivion of drink. Little by little, after the first miserable discovery that his wife was keeping company with drunk-ards, the shocking certainty forced itself on Isaac that she had grown to be a drunkard herself.

He had been in a sadly desponding state for some time before the occurrence of these domestic calamities. His mother's health, as he could but too plainly discern every time he went to see her at the cottage, was failing fast; and he upbraided himself in secret as the cause of the bodily and mental suffering she endured. When, to his remorse on his mother's account, was added the shame and misery occa-sioned by the discovery of his wife's degradation, he sank under the double trial—his face began to alter fast, and he looked what he was, a spirit-broken man. His mother, still struggling bravely against the illness that was hurrying her to the grave, was the first to notice the sad alteration in him, and the first to hear of his last bitterest trouble with his wife. She could only weep bitterly, on the day when he made his humiliating confession; but on the next occasion when he went to see her, she had taken a resolution, in reference to his domestic afflictions, which astonished, and even alarmed him. He found her dressed to go out, and on asking the reason, received this answer:

'I am not long for this world, Isaac,' said she; 'and I shall not feel easy on my death-bed, unless I have done my best to the last, to make my son happy. I mean to put my own fears and my own feelings out of the question, and to go with you to your wife, and try what I can do to reclaim her. Give me your arm, Isaac; and let me do the last thing I can in this world to help my son before it is too late.'

He could not disobey her: and they walked together slowly towards his miserable home. It was only one o'clock in the afternoon when they reached the cottage where he lived. It was their dinner hour, and Rebecca was in the kitchen. He was thus able to take his mother quietly into the parlour, and then prepare his wife for the interview. She had fortunately drank but little at that early hour, and she was less sullen and capricious than usual. He returned to his mother, with his mind tolerably at ease. His wife soon followed him into the parlour, and the meeting between her and Mrs Scatchard passed off better than he had ventured to anticipate: though he observed, with secret apprehension, that his mother, resolutely as she controlled herself in other respects, could not look his wife in the face when she spoke to her. It was a relief to him, therefore, when Rebecca began to lay the cloth.

She laid the cloth—brought in the bread-tray, and cut a slice from the loaf for her husband—then returned to the kitchen. At that moment, Isaac, still anxiously watching his mother, was startled by seeing the same ghastly change pass over her face, which had altered it so awfully on the morning when Rebecca and she first met. Before he could say a word she whispered with a look of horror: —

'Take me back!—home, home, again, Isaac! Come with me, and never come back again.'

He was afraid to ask for an explanation,—he could only sign to her to be silent, and help her quickly to the door. As they passed the bread-tray on the table she stopped and pointed to it.

'Did you see what your wife cut your bread with?' she asked, in a low, still whisper.

'No, mother,—I was not noticing—what was it?'

'Look!'

He did look. A new clasp-knife, with a buck-horn handle lay with the loaf in the bread-tray. He stretched out his hand, shudderingly, to possess himself of it; but, at the same time, there was a noise in the kitchen, and his mother caught at his arm.

'The knife of the dream!—Isaac, I'm faint with fear— take me away! before she comes back!'

He was hardly able to support her—the visible, tangible reality of the knife struck him with a panic, and utterly destroyed any faint doubts that he might have entertained up to this time, in relation to the mysterious dream-warning of nearly eight years before. By a last desperate effort, he summoned self-possession enough to help his mother quietly out of the house,—so quietly, that the 'dream-woman' (he thought of her by that name, now!) did not hear them departing, from the kitchen.

'Don't go back, Isaac,—don't go back!' implored Mrs Scatchard, as he turned to go away, after seeing her safely seated again in her own room.

'I must get the knife,' he answered, under his breath. She tried to stop him again; but he hurried out without another word.

On his return, he found that his wife had discovered their secret departure from the house. She had been drinking, and was in a fury of passion. The dinner in the kitchen was flung under the grate; the cloth was off the parlour-table. Where was the knife? Unwisely, he asked for it. She was only too glad of the opportunity of irritating him, which the request afforded her. 'He wanted the knife, did he? Could he give her a reason why?—No!—Then he should not have it,—not if he went down on his knees to ask for it.' Further recriminations elicited the fact that she had bought it a bargain—and that she considered it her own especial property. Isaac saw the uselessness of attempting to get the knife by fair means, and determined to search for it, later in the day, in secret. The search was unsuccessful. Night came on, and he left the house to walk about the streets. He was afraid now to sleep in the same room with her.

Three weeks passed. Still sullenly enraged with him, she would not give up the knife; and still that fear of sleeping in the same room with her, possessed him. He walked about at night, or dozed in the parlour, or sat watching by his mother's bed-side. Before the expiration of the first week in the new month his mother died. It wanted then but ten days' of her son's birthday. She had longed to live till that anniversary. Isaac was present at her death; and her last words in this world were addressed to him: 'Don't go back, my son, don't go back!'

He was obliged to go back, if it were only to watch his wife. Exasperated to the last degree by his distrust of her, she had revengefully sought to add a sting to his grief, during the last days of his mother's illness, by declaring that she would assert her right to attend the funeral. In spite of all that he could do, or say, she held with wicked pertinacity to her word; and, on the day appointed for the burial, forced herself—inflamed and shameless with drink— into her husband's presence, and declared that she would walk in the funeral procession to his mother's grave.

This last worst outrage, accompanied by all that was most insulting in word and look, maddened him for the moment. He struck her. The instant the blow was dealt, he repented it. She crouched down, silent in a corner of the room, and eyed him steadily; it was a look that cooled his hot blood, and made him tremble. But there was no time now to think of a means of making atonement. Nothing remained, but to risk the worst till the funeral was over. There was but one way of making sure of her. He locked her into her bed-room.

When he came back some hours after, he found her sitting, very much altered in look and bearing, by the bed-side, with a bundle on her lap. She rose, and faced him quietly, and spoke with a strange stillness in her voice, a strange repose in her eyes, a strange composure in her manner.

'No man has ever struck me twice,' she said, 'and my husband shall have no second opportunity. Set the door open and let me go. From this day forth we see each other no more.'

Before he could answer she passed him, and left the room. He saw her walk away up the street.

Would she return? All that night he watched and waited; but no footstep came near the house. The next night, over-powered by fatigue, he lay down in bed, in his clothes, with the door locked, the key on the table, and the candle burn-ing. His slumber was not disturbed. The third night, the fourth, the fifth, the sixth, passed, and nothing happened. He lay down on the seventh, still in his clothes, still with the door locked, the key on the table, and the candle burning; but easier in his mind.

Easier in his mind, and in perfect health of body, when he fell off to sleep. But his rest was disturbed. He woke twice, without any sensation of uneasiness. But the third time it was that never-to-be-forgotten shivering of the night at the lonely inn, that dreadful sinking pain at the heart, which once more aroused him in an instant.

His eyes opened towards the left hand side of the bed, and there stood——The woman of the dream, again?—No! His wife; the living reality, with the dream-spectre's face—in the dream-spectre's attitude; the fair arm up—the knife clasped in the delicate, white hand.

He sprang upon her, almost at the instant of seeing her, and yet not quickly enough to prevent her from hiding the knife. Without a word from him—without a cry from her—he pinioned her in a chair. With one hand he felt up her sleeve—and, there, where the dream-woman had hidden the knife, she had hidden it,—the knife with the buck-horn handle, that looked like new.

In the despair of that fearful moment his brain was steady, his heart was calm. He looked at her fixedly, with the knife in his hand, and said these last words:

'You told me we should see each other no more, and you have come back. It is my turn, now, to go, and to go for ever. *I* say that we shall see each other no more; and *my* word shall not be broken.'

He left her, and set forth into the night. There was a bleak wind abroad, and the smell of recent rain was in the air. The distant church-clocks chimed the quarter as he walked rapidly beyond the last houses in the suburb. He asked the first policeman he met, what hour that was, of which the quarter past had just struck.

The man referred sleepily to his watch, and answered: 'Two o'clock.' Two in the morning. What day of the month was this day that had just begun? He reckoned it up from the date of his mother's funeral. The fatal parallel was complete—it was his birthday!

Had he escaped the mortal peril which his dream foretold? or had he only received a second warning? As that ominous doubt forced itself on his mind, he stopped, reflected, and turned back again towards the city. He was still resolute to hold to his word, and never to let her see him more; but there was a thought now in his mind of having her watched and followed. The knife was in his possession—the world was before him; but, a new distrust of her—a vague, unspeakable, superstitious dread—had overcome him.

'I must know where she goes, now she thinks I have left her,' he said to himself, as he stole back wearily to the precincts of his house.

It was still dark. He had left the candle burning in the bedchamber: but when he looked up at the window of the room now, there was no light in it. He crept cautiously to the house-door. On going away, he remembered to have closed it: on trying it now, he found it open.

He waited outside, never losing sight of the house, till daylight. Then he ventured indoors—listened, and heard nothing—looked into kitchen, scullery, parlour; and found nothing: went up, at last, into the bedroom—it was empty. A pick-lock lay on the floor, betraying how she had gained entrance in the night; and that was the only trace of her.

Whither had she gone? That no mortal tongue could tell him. The darkness had covered her flight; and when the day broke, no man could say where the light found her.

Before leaving the house and the town for ever, he gave instructions to a friend and neighbour to sell his furniture for anything that it would fetch, and apply the proceeds to employing the police to trace her. The directions were honestly followed, and the money was all spent; but the enquiries led to nothing. The pick-lock on the bedroom floor remained the one last useless trace of her.

At this point of the narrative the landlord paused, and looked towards the stable-door.

'So far,' he said, 'I tell you what was told to me. The little that remains to be added lies within my own experience. Between two and three months after the events I have just been relating, Isaac Scatchard came to me, withered and old-looking before his time, just as you saw him today. He had his testimonials to character with him, and he asked for employment here. I gave him a trial, and liked him in spite of his queer habits. He is as sober, honest, and willing a man as there is in England. As for his restlessness at night, and his sleeping away his leisure time in the day, who can wonder at it after hearing his story? Besides, he never objects to being roused up, when he's wanted, so there's not much inconvenience to complain of, after all.'

'I suppose he is afraid of waking out of that dreadful dream in the dark?' said I.

'No,' returned the landlord. 'The dream comes back to him so often, that he has got to bear with it by this time resignedly enough. It's his wife keeps him waking at night, as he has often told me.'

'What! Has she never been heard of yet?'

'Never. Isaac himself has the one perpetual thought about her, that she is alive and looking for him. I believe he wouldn't let himself drop off to sleep towards two in the morning for a king's ransom. Two in the morning, he says, is the time when she will find him, one of these days. Two in the morning is the time all the year round, when he likes to be most certain that he has got that clasp-knife safe about him. He does not mind being alone, as long as he is awake, except on the night before his birthday, when he firmly believes himself to be in peril of his life. The birthday has only come round once since he has been here; and then he sat up, along with the night-porter. "She's looking for me," he always says, when I speak to him on the one theme of his life; "she's looking for me." He may be right. She *may* be looking for him. Who can tell?'

'Who can tell!' said I.

THE DIARY OF ANNE RODWAY

MARCH 3rd, 1840. A long letter today from Robert, which surprised and vexed and fluttered me so, that I have been sadly behind-hand with my work ever since. He writes in worse spirits than last time, and absolutely declares that he is poorer even than when he went to America, and that he has made up his mind to come home to London. How happy I should be at this news, if he only returned to me a prosperous man! As it is, though I love him dearly, I cannot look forward to the meeting him again, disappointed and broken down and poorer than ever, without a feeling almost of dread for both of us. I was twenty-six last birthday and he was thirty-three; and there seems less chance now than ever of our being married. It is all I can do to keep myself by my needle; and his prospects, since he failed in the small stationery business three years ago, are worse, if possible, than mine. Not that I mind so much for myself; women, in all ways of life, and especially in my dress-making way, learn, I think, to be more patient than men. What I dread is Robert's despondency, and the hard struggle he will have in this cruel city to get his bread—let alone making money enough to marry me. So little as poor people want to set up in house-keeping and be happy together, it seems hard that they can't get it when they are honest and hearty, and willing to work. The clergyman said in his sermon, last Sunday evening, that all things were ordered for the best, and we are all put into the stations in life that are properest for us. I suppose he was right, being a very clever gentleman who fills the church to crowding; but I think I should have understood him better if I had not been very hungry at the time, in consequence of my own station in life being nothing but Plain Needlewoman.

March 4th. Mary Mallinson came down to my room to take a cup of tea with me. I read her bits of Robert's letter, to show her that if she has her troubles, I have mine too; but I could not succeed in cheering her. She says she is born to misfortune, and that, as long back as she can remember, she has never had the least morsel of luck to be thankful for. I told her to go and look in my glass, and to say if she had nothing to be thankful for then; for Mary is a very pretty girl, and would look still prettier if she could be more cheerful and dress neater. However, my compliment did no good. She rattled her spoon impatiently in her tea-cup, and said, 'If I was only as good a hand at needlework as you are, Anne, I would change faces with the ugliest girl in London.' 'Not you!' says I, laughing. She looked at me for a moment, and shook her head, and was out of the room before I could get up and stop her. She always runs off in that way when she is going to cry, having a kind of pride about letting other people see her in tears.

March 5th.—A fright about Mary. I had not seen her all day, as she does not work at the same place where I do; and in the evening she never came down to have tea with me, or sent me word to go to her. So just before I went to bed I ran upstairs to say good-night. She did not answer when I knocked; and when I stepped softly into the room I saw her in bed, asleep, with her work not half done, lying about the room in the untidiest way. There was nothing remarkable in that, and I was just going away on tip-toe, when a tiny bottle and wine-glass on the chair by her bed-side caught my eye. I thought she was ill and had been taking physic, and looked at the bottle. It was marked in large letters, 'Laudanum—Poison.' My heart gave a jump as if it was going to fly out of me. I laid hold of her with both hands, and shook her with all my might. She was sleeping heavily, and woke slowly, as it seemed to me—but still she did wake. I tried to pull her out of bed, having heard that people ought to be always walked up and down when they have taken laudanum; but she resisted, and pushed me away violently.

'Anne!' says she in a fright. 'For gracious sake, what's come to you! Are you out of your senses?'

'O, Mary! Mary!' says I, holding up the bottle before her, 'If I hadn't come in when I did——' And I laid hold of her to shake her again.

She looked puzzled at me for a moment—then smiled (the first time I had seen her do so for many a long day)—then put her arms round my neck.

'Don't be frightened about me, Anne,' she says, 'I am not worth it, and there is no need.'

'No need!' says I, out of breath. 'No need, when the bottle has got Poison marked on it!'

'Poison, dear, if you take it all,' says Mary, looking at me very tenderly; 'and a night's rest if you only take a little.'

I watched her for a moment; doubtful whether I ought to believe what she said, or to alarm the house. But there was no sleepiness now in her eyes, and nothing drowsy in her voice; and she sat up in bed quite easily without anything to support her.

'You have given me a dreadful fright, Mary,' says I, sitting down by her in the chair, and beginning, by this time, to feel rather faint after being startled so.

She jumped out of bed to get me a drop of water; and kissed me, and said how sorry she was, and how undeserving of so much interest being taken in her. At the same time, she tried to possess herself of the landanum-bottle which I still kept cuddled up tight in my own hands.

'No,' says I. 'You have got into a low-spirited despairing way. I won't trust you with it.'

'I am afraid I can't do without it,' says Mary, in her usual quiet, hopeless voice. 'What with work that I can't get through as I ought, and troubles that I can't help thinking of, sleep won't come to me unless I take a few drops out of that bottle. Don't keep it away from me, Anne; it's the only thing in the world that makes me forget myself.'

'Forget yourself!' says I. 'You have no right to talk in that way, at your age. There's something horrible in the notion of a girl of eighteen sleeping with a bottle of laudanum by her bedside every night. We all of us have our troubles. Haven't I got mine?'

'You can do twice the work I can, twice as well as me,' says Mary. 'You are never scolded and rated at for awkwardness with your needle; and I always am. You can pay for your room every week; and I am three weeks in debt for mine.'

'A little more practice,' says I, 'and a little more courage, and you will soon do better. You have got all your life before you—'

'I wish I was at the end of it,' says she, breaking in. 'I'm alone in the world, and my life's no good to me.'

'You ought to be ashamed of yourself for saying so,' says I. 'Haven't you got me for a friend? Didn't I take a fancy to you when first you left your stepmother, and came to lodge in this house? And haven't I been sisters with you ever since? Suppose you are alone in the world, am I much better off? I'm an orphan, like you. I've almost as many things in pawn as you; and, if your pockets are empty, mine have only got nine-pence in them, to last me for all the rest of the week.'

'Your father and mother were honest people,' says Mary, obstinately. 'My mother ran away from home, and died in a hospital. My father was always drunk, and always beating me. My stepmother is as good as dead, for all she cares about me. My only brother is thousands of miles away in foreign parts, and never writes to me, and never helps me with a farthing. My sweetheart—'

She stopped, and the red flew into her face. I knew, if she went on that way, she would only get to the saddest part of her sad story, and give both herself and me unnecessary pain.

'My sweetheart is too poor to marry me, Mary,' I said. 'So I'm not so much to be envied, even there. But let's give over disputing which is worst off. Lie down in bed, and let me tuck you up. I'll put a stitch or two into that work of yours while you go to sleep.'

Instead of doing what I told her, she burst out crying (being very like a child in some of her ways), and hugged me so tight round the neck, that she quite hurt me. I let her go on, till she had worn herself out, and was obliged to lie down. Even then, her last few words, before she dropped off to sleep, were such as I was half-sorry, half-frightened, to hear.

'I won't plague you long, Anne,' she said. 'I haven't courage to go out of the world as you seem to fear I shall.

But I began my life wretchedly, and wretchedly I am sentenced to end it.'

It was of no use lecturing her again, for she closed her eyes. I tucked her up as neatly as I could, and put her petticoat over her; for the bed-clothes were scanty, and her hands felt cold. She looked so pretty and delicate as she fell asleep, that it quite made my heart ache to see her, after such talk as we had held together. I just waited long enough to be quite sure that she was in the land of dreams; then emptied the horrible landanum-bottle into the grate, took up her half-done work, and, going out softly, left her for that night.

March 6th. Sent off a long letter to Robert, begging and entreating him not to be so down-hearted, and not to leave America without making another effort. I told him I could bear any trial except the wretchedness of seeing him come back a helpless, broken-down man, trying uselessly to begin life again, when too old for a change. It was not till after I had posted my own letter, and read over parts of Robert's again, that the suspicion suddenly floated across me, for the first time, that he might have sailed for England immediately after writing to me. There were expressions in the letter which seemed to indicate that he had some such headlong project in his mind. And yet, surely if it were so, I ought to have noticed them at the first reading. I can only hope I am wrong in my present interpretation of much of what he has written to me—hope it earnestly for both our sakes.

This has been a doleful day for me. I have been uneasy about Robert, and uneasy about Mary. My mind is haunted by those last words of hers: 'I began my life wretchedly, and wretchedly I am sentenced to end it.' Her usual melancholy way of talking never produced the same impression on me that I feel now. Perhaps the discovery of the laudanum-bottle is the cause of this. I would give many a hard day's work to know what to do for Mary's good. My heart warmed to her when we first met in the same lodging-house, two years ago; and, although I am not one of the over-affectionate sort myself, I feel as if I could go to the world's end to serve that girl. Yet, strange to say, if I was asked why I was so fond of her, I don't think I should know how to answer the question.

March 7th. I am almost ashamed to write it down, even in this journal, which no eyes but mine ever look on; yet I must honestly confess to myself, that here I am, at nearly one in the morning, sitting up in a state of serious uneasiness, because Mary has not yet come home. I walked with her, this morning, to the place where she works, and tried to lead her into talking of the relations she has got who are still alive. My motive in doing this was to see if she dropped anything in the course of conversation which might suggest a way of helping her interests with those who are bound to give her all reasonable assistance. But the little I could get her to say to me led to nothing. Instead of answering my questions about her stepmother and her brother, she persisted at first, in the strangest way, in talking of her father, who was dead and gone, and of one Noah Truscott, who had been the worst of all the bad friends he had, and had taught him to drink and game. When I did get her to speak of her brother, she only knew that he had gone out to a place called Assam, where they grew tea. How he was doing, or whether he was there still, she did not seem to know, never having heard a word from him for years and years past. As for her stepmother, Mary, not unnaturally, flew into a passion the moment I spoke of her. She keeps an eating-house at Hammersmith, and could have given Mary good employment in it; but she seems always to have hated her, and to have made her life so wretched with abuse and ill-usage, that she had no refuge left but to go away from home, and do her best to make a living for herself. Her husband (Mary's father) appears to have behaved badly to her; and, after his death, she took the wicked course of revenging herself on her step-daughter. I felt, after this, that it was impossible Mary could go back, and that it was the hard necessity of her position, as it is of mine, that she should struggle on to make a decent livelihood without assistance from any of her relations. I confessed as much as this to her; but I added that I would try to get her employment with the persons for whom I work, who pay higher wages, and show a little more indulgence to those under them, than the people to whom she is now obliged to look for support. I spoke much more confidently than I felt, about being able to do this; and left her, as I thought, in better spirits than usual. She promised to be back tonight to tea, at nine o'clock, and now it is nearly one in the morning, and she is not home yet. If it was any other girl I should not feel uneasy, for I should make up my mind that there was extra work to be done in a hurry, and that they were keeping her late, and I should go to bed. But Mary is so unfortunate in everything that happens to her, and her own melancholy talk about herself keeps hanging on my mind so, that I have fears on her account which would not distress me about any one else. It seems inexcusably silly to think such a thing, much more to write it down; but I have a kind of nervous dread upon me that some accident—

What does that loud knocking at the street door mean? And those voices and heavy footsteps outside? Some lodger who has lost his key, I suppose. And yet, my heart——What a coward I have become all of a sudden!

More knocking and louder voices. I must run to the door and see what it is. O, Mary! Mary! I hope I am not going to have another fright about you; but I feel sadly like it.

March 8th.

March 9th.

March 10th.

March 11th. O, me! all the troubles I have ever had in my life are as nothing to the trouble I am in now. For three days I have not been able to write a single line in this journal, which I have kept so regularly, ever since I was a girl. For three days I have not once thought of Robert—I, who am always thinking of him at other times. My poor, dear, unhappy Mary, the worst I feared for you on that night when I sat up alone was far below the dreadful calamity that has really happened. How can I write about it, with my eyes full of tears and my hand all of a tremble? I don't even know why I am sitting down at my desk now, unless it is habit that keeps me to my old everyday task, in spite of all the grief and fear which seem to unfit me entirely for performing it.

The people of the house were asleep and lazy on that dreadful night, and I was the first to open the door. Never, never, could I describe in writing, or even say in plain talk, though it is so much easier, what I felt when I saw two policemen come in, carrying between them what seemed to me to be a dead girl, and that girl Mary! I caught hold of her and gave a scream that must have alarmed the whole house; for, frightened people came crowding downstairs in their night-dresses. There was a dreadful confusion and noise of loud talking, but I heard nothing, and saw nothing, till I had got her into my room, and laid on my bed. I stooped down, frantic-like, to kiss her, and saw an awful mark of a blow on her left temple, and felt, at the same time, a feeble flutter of her breath on my cheek. The discovery that she was not dead seemed to give me back my senses again. I told one of the policemen where the nearest doctor was to be found, and sat down by the bedside while he was gone, and bathed her poor head with cold water. She never opened her eyes, or moved, or spoke; but she breathed, and that was enough for me, because it was enough for life.

The policeman left in the room was a big, thick-voiced, pompous man, with a horrible unfeeling pleasure in hearing himself talk before an assembly of frightened, silent people. He told us how he had found her, as if he had been telling a story in a tap-room, and began with saying, 'I don't think the young woman was drunk.' Drunk! My Mary, who might have been a born lady for all the spirits she ever touched— drunk! I could have struck the man for uttering the word, with her lying, poor suffering angel, so white and still and helpless before him. As it was, I gave him a look; but he was too stupid to understand it, and went droning on, saying the same thing over and over again in the same words. And yet the story of how they found her was, like all the sad stories I have ever heard told in real life, so very, very short. They had just seen her lying along on the kerb-stone, a few streets off, and had taken her to the station-house. There she had been searched, and one of my cards, that I give to ladies who promise me employment, had been found in her pocket, and so they had brought her to our house. This was all the man really had to tell. There was nobody near her when she was found, and no evidence to show how the blow on her temple had been inflicted.

What a time it was before the doctor came, and how dreadful to hear him say, after he had looked at her, that he was afraid all the medical men in the world could be of no use here! He could not get her to swallow anything; and the more he tried to bring her back to her senses, the less chance there seemed of his succeeding. He examined the blow on her temple, and said he thought she must have fallen down in a fit of some sort, and struck her head against the pavement, and so have given her brain what he was afraid was a fatal shake. I asked what was to be done if she showed any return to sense in the night. He said, 'Send for me directly;' and stopped for a little while afterwards stroking her head gently with his hand, and whispering to himself, 'Poor girl, so young and so pretty!' I had felt, some minutes before, as if I could have struck the policeman; and I felt now as if I could have thrown my arms round the doctor's neck and kissed him. I did put out my hand, when he took up his hat, and he shook it in the friendliest way. 'Don't hope, my dear,' he said, and went out.

The rest of the lodgers followed him, all silent and shocked, except the inhuman wretch who owns the house, and lives in idleness on the high rents he wrings from poor people like us. 'She's three weeks in my debt,' says he, with a frown and an oath. 'Where the devil is my money to come from now?' Brute! brute!

I had a long cry alone with her that seemed to ease my heart a little. She was not the least changed for the better when I had wiped away the tears, and could see her clearly again. I took up her right hand, which lay nearest to me. It was tight clenched. I tried to unclasp the fingers, and succeeded after a little time. Something dark fell out of the palm of her hand as I straightened it. I picked the thing up, and smoothed it out, and saw that it was an end of a man's cravat.

A very old, rotten, dingy strip of black silk, with thin lilac lines, all blurred and deadened with dirt, running across and across the stuff in a sort of trellis-work pattern. The small end of the cravat was hemmed in the usual way, but the other end was all jagged, as if the morsel then in my hands had been torn off violently from the rest of the stuff. A chill ran all over me as I looked at it; for that poor, stained, crumpled end of a cravat seemed to be saying to me, as though it had been in plain words, 'If she dies, she has come to her death by foul means, and I am the witness of it.'

I had been frightened enough before, lest she should die suddenly and quietly without my knowing it, while we were alone together; but I got into a perfect agony now for fear this last worst affliction should take me by surprise. I don't suppose five minutes passed all that woeful night through, without my getting up and putting my cheek close to her mouth, to feel if the faint breaths still fluttered out of it. They came and went just the same as at first, though the fright I was in often made me fancy they were stilled for ever. Just as the church clocks were striking four, I was startled by seeing the room door open. It was only Dusty Sal (as they call her in the house) the maid-of-all-work. She was wrapped up in the blanket off her bed; her hair was all tumbled over her face; and her eyes were heavy with sleep, as she came up to the bedside where I was sitting.

'I've two hours good before I begin to work,' says she, in her hoarse, drowsy voice, 'and I've come to sit up and take my turn at watching her. You lay down and get some sleep on the rug. Here's my blanket for you—I don't mind the cold—it will keep me awake.'

'You are very kind—very, very kind and thoughtful, Sally,' says I, 'but I am too wretched in my mind to want sleep, or rest, or to do anything but wait where I am, and try and hope for the best.'

'Then I'll wait, too,' says Sally. 'I must do something; if there's nothing to do but waiting, I'll wait.'

And she sat down opposite me at the foot of the bed, and drew the blanket close round her with a shiver.

'After working so hard as you do, I'm sure you must want all the little rest you can get,' says I.

'Excepting only you,' says Sally, putting her heavy arm very clumsily, but very gently at the same time, round Mary's feet, and looking hard at the pale, still face on the pillow. 'Excepting you, she's the only soul in this house as never swore at me, or give me a hard word that I can remember. When you made puddings on Sundays, and give her half, she always give me a bit. The rest of 'em calls me Dusty Sal. Excepting only you, again, she always called me Sally, as if she knowed me in a friendly way. I ain't no good here, but I ain't no harm neither; and I shall take my turn at the sitting up—that's what I shall do!'

She nestled her head down close at Mary's feet as she spoke those words, and said no more. I once or twice thought she had fallen asleep, but whenever I looked at her, her heavy eyes were always wide open. She never changed her position an inch till the church clocks struck six; then she gave one little squeeze to Mary's feet with her arm, and shuffled out of the room without a word. A minute or two after, I heard her down below, lighting the kitchen fire just as usual.

A little later, the doctor stepped over before his breakfast time, to see if there had been any change in the night. He only shook his head when he looked at her, as if there was no hope. Having nobody else to consult that I could put trust in, I showed him the end of the cravat, and told him of the dreadful suspicion that had arisen in my mind, when I found it in her hand.

'You must keep it carefully, and produce it at the inquest,' he said. 'I don't know though, that it is likely to lead to anything. The bit of stuff may have been lying on the pavement near her, and her hand may have unconsciously clutched it when she fell. Was she subject to fainting fits?'

'Not more so, sir, than other young girls who are hard-worked and anxious, and weakly from poor living,' I answered.

'I can't say that she may not have got that blow from a fall,' the doctor went on, looking at her temple again. 'I can't say that it presents any positive appearance of having been inflicted by another person. It will be important, however, to ascertain what state of health she was in last night. Have you any idea where she was yesterday evening?'

I told him where she was employed at work, and said I imagined she must have been kept there later than usual.

'I shall pass the place this morning,' said the doctor, 'in going my rounds among my patients, and I'll just step in and make some inquiries.'

I thanked him, and we parted. Just as he was closing the door, he looked in again.

'Was she your sister?' he asked.

'No, sir, only my dear friend.'

He said nothing more; but I heard him sigh, as he shut the door softly. Perhaps he once had a sister of his own, and lost her? Perhaps she was like Mary in the face?

The doctor was hours gone away. I began to feel unspeakably forlorn and helpless. So much so, as even to wish selfishly that Robert might really have sailed from America, and might get to London in time to assist and console me. No living creature came into the room but Sally. The first time she brought me some tea; the second and third times she only looked in to see if there was any change, and glanced her eye towards the bed. I had never known her so silent before; it seemed almost as if this dreadful accident had struck her dumb. I ought to have spoken to her, perhaps, but there was something in her face that daunted me; and, besides, the fever of anxiety I was in began to dry up my lips as if they would never be able to shape any words again. I was still tormented by that frightful apprehension of the past night, that she would die without my knowing it—die without saying one word to clear up the awful mystery of this blow, and set the suspicions at rest for ever which I still felt whenever my eyes fell on the end of the old cravat.

At last the doctor came back.

'I think you may safely clear your mind of any doubts to which that bit of stuff may have given rise,' he said. 'She was, as you supposed, detained late by her employers, and she fainted in the work-room. They most unwisely and

unkindly let her go home alone, without giving her any
stimulant, as soon as she came to her senses again. Nothing
is more probable, under these circumstances, than that she
should faint a second time on her way here. A fall on the
pavement, without any friendly arm to break it, might have
produced even a worse injury than the injury we see. I
believe that the only ill-usage to which the poor girl was
exposed was the neglect she met with in the work-room.'

'You speak very reasonably, I own, sir,' said I, not yet
quite convinced. 'Still, perhaps she may——'

'My poor girl, I told you not to hope,' said the doctor,
interrupting me. He went to Mary, and lifted up her eyelids,
and looked at her eyes while he spoke, then added: 'If you
still doubt how she came by that blow, do not encourage the
idea that any words of hers will ever enlighten you. She will
never speak again.'

'Not dead! O, sir, don't say she's dead!'

'She is dead to pain and sorrow—dead to speech and recognition. There is more animation in the life of the feeblest insect
that flies, than in the life that is left in her. When you look at
her now, try to think that she is in Heaven. That is the best
comfort I can give you, after telling the hard truth.'

I did not believe him. I could not believe him. So long as
she breathed at all, so long I was resolved to hope. Soon
after the doctor was gone, Sally came in again, and found
me listening (if I may call it so) at Mary's lips. She went to
where my little hand-glass hangs against the wall, took it
down, and gave it to me.

'See if the breath marks it,' she said.

Yes; her breath did mark it, but very faintly. Sally cleaned
the glass with her apron, and gave it back to me. As she did
so, she half stretched out her hand to Mary's face, but drew
it in again suddenly, as if she was afraid of soiling Mary's
delicate skin with her hard, horny fingers. Going out, she
stopped at the foot of the bed, and scraped away a little
patch of mud that was on one of Mary's shoes.

'I always used to clean 'em for her,' said Sally, 'to save her
hands from getting blacked. May I take 'em off now, and
clean 'em again?'

I nodded my head, for my heart was too heavy to speak. Sally took the shoes off with a slow, awkward tenderness, and went out.

An hour or more must have passed, when, putting the glass over her lips again, I saw no mark on it. I held it closer and closer. I dulled it accidentally with my own breath, and cleaned it. I held it over her again. O, Mary, Mary, the doctor was right! I ought to have only thought of you in Heaven!

Dead, without a word, without a sign,—without even a look to tell the true story of the blow that killed her! I could not call to anybody, I could not cry, I could not so much as put the glass down and give her a kiss for the last time. I don't know how long I had sat there with my eyes burning, and my hands deadly cold, when Sally came in with the shoes cleaned, and carried carefully in her apron for fear of a soil touching them. At the sight of that——

I can write no more. My tears drop so fast on the paper that I can see nothing.

March 12th. She died on the afternoon of the eighth. On the morning of the ninth, I wrote, as in duty bound, to her stepmother, at Hammersmith. There was no answer. I wrote again: my letter was returned to me this morning, unopened. For all that woman cares, Mary might be buried with a pauper's funeral. But this shall never be, if I pawn everything about me, down to the very gown that is on my back. The bare thought of Mary being buried by the workhouse gave me the spirit to dry my eyes, and go to the undertaker's, and tell him how I was placed. I said, if he would get me an estimate of all that would have to be paid, from first to last, for the cheapest decent funeral that could be had, I would undertake to raise the money. He gave me the estimate, written in this way, like a common bill:

A walking funeral complete	1	13	8
Vestry	0	4	4
Rector	0	4	4
Clerk	0	1	0
Sexton	0	1	0
Beadle	0	1	0

Bell	0	1	0
Six feet of ground	0	2	0
Total	£2	8	4

If I had the heart to give any thought to it, I should be inclined to wish that the Church could afford to do without so many small charges for burying poor people, to whose friends even shillings are of consequence. But it is useless to complain; the money must be raised at once. The charitable doctor—a poor man himself, or he would not be living in our neighbourhood—has subscribed ten shillings towards the expenses; and the coroner, when the inquest was over, added five more. Perhaps others may assist me. If not, I have fortunately clothes and furniture of my own to pawn. And I must set about parting with them without delay; for the funeral is to be tomorrow, the thirteenth. The funeral— Mary's funeral! It is well that the straits and difficulties I am in, keep my mind on the stretch. If I had leisure to grieve, where should I find the courage to face tomorrow?

Thank God, they did not want me at the inquest. The verdict given—with the doctor, the policeman, and two persons from the place where she worked, for witnesses— was Accidental Death. The end of the cravat was produced, and the coroner said that it was certainly enough to suggest suspicion; but the jury, in the absence of any positive evidence, held to the doctor's notion that she had fainted and fallen down, and so got the blow on her temple. They reproved the people where Mary worked for letting her go home alone, without so much as a drop of brandy to support her, after she had fallen into a swoon from exhaustion before their eyes. The coroner added, on his own account, that he thought the reproof was thoroughly deserved. After that, the cravat-end was given back to me, by my own desire; the police saying that they could make no investigations with such a slight clue to guide them. They may think so, and the coroner, and doctor, and jury may think so; but, in spite of all that has passed, I am now more firmly persuaded than ever that there is some dreadful mystery in connection with that blow on my poor lost Mary's temple which has yet to be revealed, and which may come to be discovered through this very fragment of a cravat that I found in her hand. I cannot give any good reason for why I think so; but I know that if I had been one of the jury at the inquest, nothing should have induced me to consent to such a verdict as Accidental Death.*

After I had pawned my things, and had begged a small advance of wages at the place where I work, to make up what was still wanting to pay for Mary's funeral, I thought I might have had a little quiet time to prepare myself as I best could for tomorrow. But this was not to be. When I got home, the landlord met me in the passage. He was in liquor, and more brutal and pitiless in his way of looking and speaking than ever I saw him before.

'So you're going to be fool enough to pay for her funeral, are you?' were his first words to me.

I was too weary and heart-sick to answer—I only tried to get by him to my own door.

'If you can pay for burying her,' he went on, putting himself in front of me, 'you can pay her lawful debts. She owes me three weeks' rent. Suppose you raise the money for that next, and hand it over to me? I'm not joking, I can promise you. I mean to have my rent; and if somebody don't pay it, I'll have her body seized and sent to the workhouse!'

Between terror and disgust, I thought I should have dropped to the floor at his feet. But I determined not to let him see how he had horrified me, if I could possibly control myself. So I mustered resolution enough to answer that I did not believe the law gave him any such wicked power over the dead.

'I'll teach you what the law is!' he broke in; 'you'll raise money to bury her like a born lady, when she's died in my debt, will you! And you think I'll let my rights be trampled upon like that, do you? See if I do! I give you till tonight to think about it. If I don't have the three weeks she owes before tomorrow, dead or alive, she shall go to the work-house!'

This time I managed to push by him, and get to my own room, and lock the door in his face. As soon as I was alone,

I fell into a breathless, suffocating fit of crying that seemed to be shaking me to pieces. But there was no good and no help in tears; I did my best to calm myself, after a little while, and tried to think who I should run to for help and protection. The doctor was the first friend I thought of; but I knew he was always out seeing his patients of an afternoon. The beadle was the next person who came into my head. He had the look of being a very dignified, unapproachable kind of man when he came about the inquest; but he talked to me a little then, and said I was a good girl, and seemed, I really thought, to pity me. So to him I determined to apply in my great danger and distress.

Most fortunately I found him at home. When I told him of the landlord's infamous threats, and of the misery I was in in consequence of them, he rose up with a stamp of his foot, and sent for his gold-laced cocked-hat that he wears on Sundays, and his long cane with the ivory top to it.

'I'll give it him,' said the beadle. 'Come along with me, my dear. I think I told you you were a good girl at the inquest—if I didn't, I tell you so now. I'll give it to him! Come along with me.'

And he went out, striding on with his cocked-hat and his great cane, and I followed him.

'Landlord!' he cries the moment he gets into the passage, with a thump of his cane on the floor. 'Landlord!' with a look all round him as if he was king of England calling to a beast, 'come out!'

The moment the landlord came out and saw who it was, his eye fixed on the cocked-hat and he turned as pale as ashes.

'How dare you frighten this poor girl?' said the beadle. 'How dare you bully her at this sorrowful time with threatening to do what you know you can't do? How dare you be a cowardly, bullying, braggadocio of an unmanly landlord? Don't talk to me—I won't hear you! I'll pull you up, sir! If you say another word to the young woman, I'll pull you up before the authorities of this metropolitan parish! I've had my eye on you, and the authorities have had their eye on you, and the rector has had his eye on you. We don't like the

look of your small shop round the corner; we don't like
the look of some of the customers who deal at it; we don't
like disorderly characters; and we don't by any manner of
means like you. Go away! Leave the young woman alone!
Hold your tongue, or I'll pull you up! If he says another
word, or interferes with you again, my dear, come and tell
me; and, as sure as he's a bullying, unmanly, braggadocio of
a landlord, I'll pull him up!'

With those words, the beadle gave a loud cough to clear
his throat, and another thump of his cane on the floor—and
so went striding out again before I could open my lips to
thank him. The landlord slunk back into his room without
a word. I was left alone and unmolested at last, to
strengthen myself for the hard trial of my poor love's funeral
tomorrow.

March 13th. It is all over. A week ago, her head rested on
my bosom. It is laid in the churchyard now—the fresh earth
lies heavy over her grave. I and my dearest friend, the sister
of my love, are parted in this world for ever.

I followed her funeral alone through the cruel, bustling
streets. Sally, I thought, might have offered to go with me;
but she never so much as came into my room. I did not like
to think badly of her for this, and I am glad I restrained
myself—for, when we got into the churchyard, among the
two or three people who were standing by the open grave, I
saw Sally, in her ragged grey shawl and her patched black
bonnet. She did not seem to notice me till the last words of
the service had been read, and the clergyman had gone
away. Then she came up and spoke to me.

'I couldn't follow along with you,' she said, looking at her
ragged shawl; 'for I haven't a decent suit of clothes to walk
in. I wish I could get vent in crying for her, like you; but I
can't; all the crying's been drudged and starved out of me,
long ago. Don't you think about lighting your fire when you
get home. I'll do that, and get you a drop of tea to comfort
you.'

She seemed on the point of saying a kind word or two
more, when, seeing the Beadle coming towards me, she drew
back, as if she was afraid of him, and left the churchyard.

'Here's my subscription towards the funeral,' said the Beadle, giving me back his shilling fee. 'Don't say anything about it, for it mightn't be approved of in a business point of view, if it came to some people's ears. Has the landlord said anything more to you? No, I thought not. He's too polite a man to give me the trouble of pulling him up. Don't stop crying here, my dear. Take the advice of a man familiar with funerals, and go home.'

I tried to take his advice; but it seemed like deserting Mary to go away when all the rest forsook her. I waited about till the earth was thrown in, and the man had left the place—then I returned to the grave. Oh, how bare and cruel it was, without so much as a bit of green turf to soften it! Oh, how much harder it seemed to live than to die, when I stood alone, looking at the heavy piled-up lumps of clay, and thinking of what was hidden beneath them!

I was driven home by my own despairing thoughts. The sight of Sally lighting the fire in my room eased my heart a little. When she was gone, I took up Robert's letter again to keep my mind employed on the only subject in the world that has any interest for it now. This fresh reading increased the doubts I had already felt relative to his having remained in America after writing to me. My grief and forlornness have made a strange alteration in my former feelings about his coming back. I seem to have lost all my prudence and self-denial, and to care so little about his poverty, and so much about himself, that the prospect of his return is really the only comforting thought I have now to support me. I know this is weak in me, and that his coming back poor can lead to no good result for either of us. But he is the only living being left me to love, and—I can't explain it—but I want to put my arms round his neck and tell him about Mary.

March 14th. I locked up the end of the cravat in my writing-desk. No change in the dreadful suspicions that the bare sight of it rouses in me. I tremble if I so much as touch it.

March 15th, 16th, 17th. Work, work, work. If I don't knock up,* I shall be able to pay back the advance in another week; and then, with a little more pinching in my daily expenses, I may succeed in saving a shilling or two to get some turf to put over Mary's grave—and perhaps even a few flowers besides, to grow round it.

March 18th. Thinking of Robert all day long. Does this mean that he is really coming back? If it does, reckoning the distance he is at from New York, and the time ships take to get to England, I might see him by the end of April or the beginning of May.

March 19th. I don't remember my mind running once on the end of the cravat yesterday, and I am certain I never looked at it. Yet I had the strangest dream concerning it at night. I thought it was lengthened into a long clue,* like the silken thread that led to Rosamond's Bower.* I thought I took hold of it, and followed it a little way, and then got frightened and tried to go back, but found that I was obliged, in spite of myself, to go on. It led me through a place like the Valley of the Shadow of Death, in an old print I remember in my mother's copy of the Pilgrim's Progress. I seemed to be months and months following it, without any respite, till at last it brought me, on a sudden, face to face with an angel whose eyes were like Mary's. He said to me, 'Go on, still; the truth is at the end, waiting for you to find it.' I burst out crying, for the angel had Mary's voice as well as Mary's eyes, and woke with my heart throbbing and my cheeks all wet. What is the meaning of this? Is it always superstitious, I wonder, to believe that dreams may come true?

April 30th. I have found it! God knows to what results it may lead; but it is as certain as that I am sitting here before my journal, that I have found the cravat from which the end in Mary's hand was torn! I discovered it last night; but the flutter I was in, and the nervousness and uncertainty I felt, prevented me from noting down this most extraordinary and most unexpected event at the time when it happened. Let me try if I can preserve the memory of it in writing now.

I was going home rather late from where I work, when I suddenly remembered that I had forgotten to buy myself any candles the evening before, and that I should be left in the dark if I did not manage to rectify this mistake in some way. The shop close to me, at which I usually deal, would be shut up, I knew, before I could get to it; so I determined to go into the first place I passed where candles were sold. This turned out to be a small shop with two counters, which did business on one side in the general grocery way, and on the other in the rag and bottle and old iron line. There were several customers on the grocery side when I went in, so I waited on the empty rag side till I could be served. Glancing about me here at the worthless-looking things by which I was surrounded, my eye was caught by a bundle of rags lying on the counter, as if they had just been brought in and left there. From mere idle curiosity, I looked close at the rags, and saw among them something like an old cravat. I took it up directly, and held it under a gas-light. The pattern was blurred lilac lines, running across and across the dingy black ground in a trellis-work form. I looked at the ends: one of them was torn off.

How I managed to hide the breathless surprise into which this discovery threw me, I cannot say; but I certainly contrived to steady my voice somehow, and to ask for my candles calmly, when the man and woman serving in the shop, having disposed of their other customers, inquired of me what I wanted. As the man took down the candles, my brain was all in a whirl with trying to think how I could get possession of the old cravat without exciting any suspicion. Chance, and a little quickness on my part in taking advantage of it, put the object within my reach in a moment. The man, having counted out the candles, asked the woman for some paper to wrap them in. She produced a piece much too small and flimsy for the purpose, and declared, when he called for something better, that the day's supply of stout paper was all exhausted. He flew into a rage with her for managing so badly. Just as they were beginning to quarrel violently, I stepped back to the rag-counter, took the old cravat carelessly out of the bundle, and said, in as light a tone as I could possibly assume—

'Come, come! don't let my candles be the cause of hard words between you. Tie this ragged old thing round them with a bit of string, and I shall carry them home quite comfortably.'

The man seemed disposed to insist on the stout paper being produced; but the woman, as if she was glad of an opportunity of spiting him, snatched the candles away, and tied them up in a moment in the torn old cravat. I was afraid he would have struck her before my face, he seemed in such a fury; but, fortunately, another customer came in, and obliged him to put his hands to peaceable and proper uses.

'Quite a bundle of all-sorts on the opposite counter there,' I said to the woman, as I paid her for the candles.

'Yes, and all hoarded up for sale by a poor creature with a lazy brute of a husband, who lets his wife do all the work while he spends all the money,' answered the woman, with a malicious look at the man by her side.

'He can't surely have much money to spend, if his wife has no better work to do than picking up rags,' said I.

'It isn't her fault if she hasn't got no better,' says the woman, rather angrily. 'She's ready to turn her hand to anything. Charing, washing, laying-out, keeping empty houses—nothing comes amiss to her. She's my half-sister; and I think I ought to know.'

'Did you say she went out charing?' I asked, making believe as if I knew of somebody who might employ her.

'Yes, of course I did,' answered the woman; 'and if you can put a job into her hands, you'll be doing a good turn to a poor hard-working creature as wants it. She lives down the Mews here to the right—name of Horlick, and as honest a woman as ever stood in shoe-leather. Now then, ma'am, what for you?'

Another customer came in just then, and occupied her attention. I left the shop, passed the turning that led down to the Mews, looked up at the name of the street, so as to know how to find it again, and then ran home as fast as I could. Perhaps it was the remembrance of my strange dream striking me on a sudden, or perhaps it was the shock of the discovery I had just made, but I began to feel frightened without knowing why, and anxious to be under shelter in my own room.

If Robert should come back! O, what a relief and help it would be now if Robert should come back!

May 1st. On getting indoors last night, the first thing I did, after striking a light, was to take the ragged cravat off the candles and smooth it out on the table. I then took the end that had been in poor Mary's hand out of my writing-desk, and smoothed that out too. It matched the torn side of the cravat exactly. I put them together, and satisfied myself that there was not a doubt of it.

Not once did I close my eyes that night. A kind of fever got possession of me—a vehement yearning to go on from this first discovery and find out more, no matter what the risk might be. The cravat now really became, to my mind, the clue that I thought I saw in my dream—the clue that I was resolved to follow. I determined to go to Mrs Horlick this evening on my return from work.

I found the Mews easily. A crook-backed dwarf of a man was lounging at the corner of it smoking his pipe. Not liking his looks, I did not enquire of him where Mrs Horlick lived, but went down the Mews till I met with a woman, and asked her. She directed me to the right number. I knocked at the door, and Mrs Horlick herself—a lean, ill-tempered, miserable-looking woman—answered it. I told her at once that I had come to ask what her terms were for charing. She stared at me for a moment, then answered my question civilly enough.

'You look surprised at a stranger like me finding you out,' I said. 'I first came to hear of you last night from a relation of yours, in rather an odd way.' And I told her all that had happened in the chandler's shop, bringing in the bundle of rags, and the circumstance of my carrying home the candles in the old torn cravat, as often as possible.

'It's the first time I've heard of anything belonging to him turning out any use,' said Mrs Horlick, bitterly.

'What, the spoilt old neck-handkerchief belonged to your husband, did it?' said I at a venture.

'Yes; I pitched his rotten rag of a neck-'andkercher into the bundle along with the rest; and I wish I could have pitched him in after it,' said Mrs Horlick. 'I'd sell him cheap at any rag-shop. There he stands, smoking his pipe at the end of the Mews, out of work for weeks past, the idlest hump-backed pig in all London!'

She pointed to the man whom I had passed on entering the Mews. My cheeks began to burn and my knees to tremble; for I knew that in tracing the cravat to its owner I was advancing a step towards a fresh discovery. I wished Mrs Horlick good evening, and said I would write and mention the day on which I wanted her.

What I had just been told put thought into my mind that I was afraid to follow out. I have heard people talk of being light-headed, and I felt as I have heard them say they felt, when I retraced my steps up the Mews. My head got giddy, and my eyes seemed able to see nothing but the figure of the little crook-back man still smoking his pipe in his former place. I could see nothing but that; I could think of nothing but the mark of the blow on my poor lost Mary's temple. I know that I must have been light-headed, for as I came close to the crook-backed man, I stopped without meaning it. The minute before, there had been no idea in me of speaking to him. I did not know how to speak, or in what way it would be safest to begin. And yet, the moment I came face to face with him something out of myself seemed to stop me, and to make me speak, without considering before-hand, without thinking of consequences, without knowing, I may almost say, what words I was uttering till the instant when they rose to my lips.

'When your old neck-tie was torn, did you know that one end of it went to the rag-shop and the other fell into my hands?' I said these bold words to him suddenly, and, as it seemed, without my own will taking any part in them.

He started, stared, changed colour. He was too much amazed by my sudden speaking to find an answer for me. When he did open his lips it was to say rather to himself than me:

'You're not the girl.'

'No,' I said, with a strange choking at my heart. 'I'm her friend.'

By this time he had recovered his surprise, and he seemed to be aware that he had let out more than he ought.

'You may be anybody's friend you like,' he said brutally, 'so long as you don't come jabbering nonsense here. I don't know you, I don't understand your jokes.' He turned quickly away from me when he had said the last words. He had never once looked fairly at me since I first spoke to him.

Was it his hand that had struck the blow?

I had only sixpence in my pocket, but I took it out and followed him. If it had been a five-pound note, I should have done the same in the state I was in then.

'Would a pot of beer help you to understand me?' I said, and offered him the sixpence.

'A pot ain't no great things,' he answered, taking the sixpence doubtfully.

'It may lead to something better,' I said.

His eyes began to twinkle, and he came close to me. Oh, how my legs trembled!—how my head swam!

'This is all in a friendly way, is it?' he asked in a whisper.

I nodded my head. At that moment, I could not have spoken for worlds.

'Friendly, of course,' he went on to himself, 'or there would have been a policeman in it. She told you, I suppose, that I wasn't the man?'

I nodded my head again. It was all I could do to keep myself standing upright.

'I suppose it's a case of threatening to have him up, and making him settle it quietly for a pound or two? How much for me if you lay hold of him?'

'Half.' I began to be afraid that he would suspect something if I was still silent. The wretch's eyes twinkled again, and he came yet closer.

'I drove him to the Red Lion, corner of Dodd Street and Rudgely Street. The house was shut up, but he was let in at the Jug-and-Bottle-door, like a man who was known to the landlord. That's as much as I can tell you, and I'm certain I'm right. He was the last fare I took up at night. The next morning master gave me the sack. Said I cribbed* his corn and his fares. I wish I had!'

I gathered from this that the crook-backed man had been a cab-driver.

'Why don't you speak,' he asked suspiciously. 'Has she been telling you a pack of lies about me? What did she say when she came home?'

'What ought she to have said?'

'She ought to have said my fare was drunk, and she came in the way as he was going to get into the cab. That's what she ought to have said to begin with.'

'But, after?'

'Well, after, my fare by way of larking with her, puts out his leg for to trip her up, and she stumbles and catches at me for to save herself, and tears off one of the limp ends of my rotten old tie. "What do you mean by that, you brute," says she, turning round as soon as she was steady on her legs, again, to my fare. Says my fare to her, "I means to teach you to keep a civil tongue in your head. And he ups with his fist, and——"What's come to you, now? What are you looking at me like that, for? How do you think a man of my size was to take her part, against a man big enough to have eaten me up? Look as much as you like, in my place you would have done what I done—drew off when he shook his fist at you, and swore he'd be the death of you if you didn't start your horse in no time.'

I saw he was working himself into a rage; but I could not, if my life had depended on it, have stood near him, or looked at him any longer. I just managed to stammer out that I had been walking a long way, and that, not being used to much exercise, I felt faint and giddy with fatigue. He only changed from angry to sulky, when I made that excuse. I got a little further away from him, and then added, that if he would be at the Mews entrance the next evening, I should have something more to say and something more to give him. He grumbled a few suspicious words in answer, about doubting whether he should trust me to come back. Fortunately, at that moment, a policeman passed on the opposite side of the way, he slunk down the Mews immediately, and I was free to make my escape.

How I got home I can't say, except that I think I ran the greater part of the way. Sally opened the door, and asked if anything was the matter the moment she saw my face. I answered, 'Nothing! nothing!' She stopped me as I was going into my room, and said,

'Smooth your hair a bit, and put your collar straight. There's a gentleman in there waiting for you.'

My heart gave one great bound—I knew who it was in an instant, and rushed into the room like a mad woman.

'Oh, Robert! Robert!'

All my heart went out to him in those two little words.

'Good God, Anne! has anything happened? Are you ill?'

'Mary! my poor, lost, murdered, dear, dear Mary!'

That was all I could say before I fell on his breast.

May 2nd. Misfortunes and disappointments have sad-dened him a little; but towards me he is unaltered. He is as good, as kind, as gently and truly affectionate as ever. I believe no other man in the world could have listened to the story of Mary's death with such tenderness and pity as he. Instead of cutting me short anywhere, he drew me on to tell more than I had intended; and his first generous words, when I had done, were to assure me that he would see himself to the grass being laid and the flowers planted on Mary's grave. I could have almost gone on my knees and worshipped him when he made me that promise.

Surely, this best, and kindest, and noblest of men cannot always be unfortunate! My cheeks burn when I think that he has come back with only a few pounds in his pocket, after all his hard and honest struggles to do well in America. They must be bad people there when such a man as Robert cannot get on among them. He now talks calmly and re-signedly of trying for any one of the lowest employments by which a man can earn his bread honestly in this great city—he, who knows French, who can write so beautifully! Oh, if the people who have places to give away only knew Robert as well as I do, what a salary he would have, what a post he would be chosen to occupy!

I am writing these lines alone, while he has gone to the Mews to treat with the dastardly, heartless wretch with whom I spoke yesterday. He says the creature—I won't call him a man—must be humoured and kept deceived about poor Mary's end, in order that we may discover and bring to justice the monster whose drunken blow was the death of her. I shall know no ease of mind till her murderer is secured, and till I am certain that he will be made to suffer for his crimes. I wanted to go with Robert to the Mews; but he said it was best that he should carry out the rest of the investigation alone; for my strength and resolution had been too hardly taxed already. He said more words in praise of me for what I have been able to do up to this time, which I am almost ashamed to write down with my own pen. Besides, there is no need—praise from his lips is one of the things that I can trust my memory to preserve to the latest day of my life.

May 3rd. Robert very long last night before he came back to tell me what he had done. He easily recognised the hunchback at the corner of the mews by my description of him; but he found it a hard matter, even with the help of money, to overcome the cowardly wretch's distrust of him as a stranger and a man. However, when this had been accomplished, the main difficulty was conquered. The hunchback, excited by the promise of more money, went at once to the Red Lion to enquire about the person whom he had driven there in his cab. Robert followed him, and waited at the corner of the street. The tidings brought by the cabman were of the most unexpected kind. The murderer—I can write of him by no other name—had fallen ill on the very night when he was driven to the Red Lion, had taken to his bed there and then, and was still confined to it at that very moment. His disease was of a kind that is brought on by excessive drinking, and that affects the mind as well as the body. The people at the public-house called it the Horrors. Hearing these things, Robert determined to see if he could not find out something more for himself, by going and enquiring at the public-house, in the character of one of the friends of the sick man in bed upstairs. He made two important discoveries. First, he found out the name and address of the doctor in attendance. Secondly, he entrapped the barman into mentioning the murderous wretch by his name. This last discovery adds an unspeakably fearful interest to the dreadful catastrophe of Mary's death. Noah Truscott, as she told me herself in the last conversation I ever had with her, was the name of the man whose drunken example ruined her father, and Noah Truscott is also the name of the man whose drunken fury killed her. There is something that makes one shudder, something fatal and supernatural in this awful fact. Robert agrees with me that the hand of Providence must have guided my steps to that shop from which all the discoveries since made took their rise. He says he believes we are the instruments of effecting a righteous retribution; and, if he spends his last farthing, he will have the investigation brought to its full end in a court of justice.

May 4th. Robert went today to consult a lawyer whom he knew in former times. The lawyer much interested, though not so seriously impressed as he ought to have been, by the story of Mary's death and of the events that have followed it. He gave Robert a confidential letter to take to the doctor in attendance on the double-dyed villain at the Red Lion. Robert left the letter, and called again and saw the doctor, who said his patient was getting better, and would most likely be up again in ten days or a fortnight. This statement Robert communicated to the lawyer, and the lawyer has undertaken to have the public-house properly watched, and the hunchback (who is the most important witness) sharply looked after for the next fortnight, or longer if necessary. Here, then, the progress of this dreadful business stops for awhile.

May 5th. Robert has got a little temporary employment in copying for his friend the lawyer. I am working harder than ever at my needle to make up for the time that has been lost lately.

May 6th. Today was Sunday, and Robert proposed that we should go and look at Mary's grave. He, who forgets nothing where a kindness is to be done, has found time to perform the promise he made to me on the night when we first met. The grave is already, by his orders, covered with turf, and planted round with shrubs. Some flowers, and a low headstone, are to be added to make the place look worthier of my poor lost darling who is beneath it. Oh, I hope I shall live long after I am married to Robert! I want so much time to show him all my gratitude!

May 20th. A hard trial to my courage today. I have given evidence at the police-office, and have seen the monster who murdered her.

I could only look at him once. I could just see that he was a giant in size, and that he kept his dull, lowering, bestial face turned towards the witness-box, and his bloodshot, vacant eyes staring on me. For an instant I tried to confront that look; for an instant I kept my attention fixed on him—on his blotched face, on the short grizzled hair above it—on his knotty, murderous right hand hanging loose over the bar in front of him, like the paw of a wild beast over the edge of his den. Then the horror of him—the double horror of confronting him, in the first place, and afterwards of seeing that he was an old man—overcame me; and I turned away faint, sick, and shuddering. I never faced him again; and at the end of my evidence, Robert considerately took me out.

When we met once more at the end of the examination, Robert told me that the prisoner never spoke, and never changed his position. He was either fortified by the cruel composure of the savage, or his faculties had not yet thoroughly recovered from the disease that had so lately shaken them. The magistrate seemed to doubt if he was in his right mind; but the evidence of the medical man relieved his uncertainty, and the prisoner was committed for trial on a charge of manslaughter.

Why not on a charge of murder? Robert explained the law to me when I asked that question. I accepted the explanation, but it did not satisfy me. Mary Mallinson was killed by a blow from the hand of Noah Truscott. That is murder in the sight of God. Why not murder in the sight of the law also?

June 18th. Tomorrow is the day appointed for the trial at the Old Bailey. Before sunset this evening I went to look at Mary's grave. The turf has grown so green since I saw it last; and the flowers are springing up so prettily. A bird was perched dressing his feathers, on the low white headstone that bears the inscription of her name and age. I did not go near enough to disturb the little creature. He looked innocent and pretty on the grave, as Mary herself was in her life-time. When he flew away, I went and sat for a little by the headstone, and read the mournful lines on it. Oh, my love, my love! what harm or wrong had you ever done in this world, that you should die at eighteen by a blow from a drunkard's hand?

June 19th. The trial. My experience of what happened at it is limited, like my experience of the examination at the police-office, to the time occupied in giving my own evidence. They made me say much more than I said before the magistrate. Between examination and cross-examination, I had to go into almost all the particulars about poor Mary and her funeral that I have written in this journal; the jury listening to every word I spoke with the most anxious attention. At the end, the judge said a few words to me approving of my conduct, and then there was a clapping of hands among the people in court. I was so agitated and excited that I trembled all over when they let me go out into the air again. I looked at the prisoner both when I entered the witness-box and when I left it. The lowering brutality of his face was unchanged, but his faculties seemed to be more alive and observant than they were at the police-office. A frightful blue change passed over his face, and he drew his breath so heavily that the gasps were distinctly audible, while I mentioned Mary by name, and described the mark of the blow on her temple. When they asked me if I knew anything of the prisoner, and I answered that I only knew what Mary herself had told me about his having been her father's ruin, he gave a kind of groan, and struck both his hands heavily on the dock. And when I passed beneath him on my way out of the court, he leaned over suddenly, whether to speak to me or to strike me I can't say, for he was immediately made to stand upright again by the turnkeys on either side of him. While the evidence proceeded (as Robert described it to me), the signs that he was suffering under superstitious terror became more and more apparent; until, at last, just as the lawyer appointed to defend him was rising to speak, he suddenly cried out, in a voice that startled every one, up to the very judge on the bench, 'Stop!' There was a pause, and all eyes looked at him. The perspiration was pouring over his face like water, and he made strange, uncouth signs with his hands to the judge opposite. 'Stop all this!' he cried again; 'I've been the ruin of the father and the death of the child. Hang me before I do more harm! Hang me, for God's sake, out of the way!' As soon as the shock produced by this extraordinary interruption had subsided, he was removed, and there followed a long discussion about whether he was of sound mind or not. The point was left to the jury to decide by their verdict. They found him guilty of the charge of manslaughter, without the excuse of insanity. He was brought up again, and condemned to transportation for life. All he did on hearing the sentence was to reiterate his desperate words, 'Hang me before I do more harm! Hang me, for God's sake, out of the way!'

June 20th. I made yesterday's entry in sadness of heart, and I have not been better in my spirits today. It is some-thing to have brought the murderer to the punishment that he deserves. But the knowledge that this most righteous act of retribution is accomplished, brings no consolation with it. The law does indeed punish Noah Truscott for his crime; but can it raise up Mary Mallinson from her last resting-place in the churchyard?

While writing of the law, I ought to record that the heartless wretch who allowed Mary to be struck down in his presence without making any attempt to defend her, is not likely to escape with perfect impunity. The policeman who looked after him to insure his attendance at the trial, dis-covered that he had committed past offences, for which the law can make him answer. A summons was executed upon him, and he was taken before the magistrate the moment he left the court after giving his evidence.

I had just written these few lines, and was closing my journal, when there came a knock at the door. I answered it, thinking Robert had called in his way home to say good-night, and found myself face to face with a strange gentle-

man, who immediately asked for Anne Rodway. On hearing
that I was the person inquired for, he requested five minutes'
conversation with me. I showed him into the little empty
room at the back of the house, and waited, rather surprised
and fluttered, to hear what he had to say.

He was a dark man, with a serious manner, and a short
stern way of speaking. I was certain that he was a stranger,
and yet there seemed something in his face not unfamiliar
to me. He began by taking a newspaper from his pocket,
and asking me if I was the person who had given evidence
at the trial of Noah Truscott on a charge of manslaughter. I
answered immediately that I was.

'I have been for nearly two years in London seeking Mary
Mallinson, and always seeking her in vain,' he said. 'The
first and only news I have had of her I found in the newspaper report of the trial yesterday.'

He still spoke calmly, but there was something in the look
of his eyes which showed me that he was suffering in spirit.
A sudden nervousness overcame me, and I was obliged to
sit down.

'You knew Mary Mallinson, sir?' I asked, as quietly as I
could.

'I am her brother.'

I clasped my hands and hid my face in despair. O! the
bitterness of heart with which I heard him say those simple
words!

'You were very kind to her,' said the calm, tearless man.
'In her name and for her sake, I thank you.'

'O! sir,' I said, 'why did you never write to her when you
were in foreign parts?'

'I wrote often,' he answered, 'but each of my letters
contained a remittance of money. Did Mary tell you she had
a step-mother? If she did, you may guess why none of my
letters were allowed to reach her. I now know that this
woman robbed my sister. Has she lied in telling me that she
was never informed of Mary's place of abode?'

I remembered that Mary had never communicated with
her step-mother after the separation, and could therefore
assure him that the woman had spoken the truth.

He paused for a moment, after that, and sighed. Then he took out a pocket-book and said:

'I have already arranged for the payment of any legal expenses that may have been incurred by the trial; but I have still to reimburse you for the funeral charges which you so generously defrayed. Excuse my speaking bluntly on this subject, I am accustomed to look on all matters where money is concerned purely as matters of business.'

I saw that he was taking several bank-notes out of the pocket-book, and stopped him.

'I will gratefully receive back the little money I actually paid, sir, because I am not well off, and it would be an ungracious act of pride in me to refuse it from you,' I said. 'But I see you handling bank-notes, any one of which is far beyond the amount you have to repay me. Pray put them back, sir. What I did for your poor lost sister, I did from my love and fondness for her. You have thanked me for that; and your thanks are all I can receive.'

He had hitherto concealed his feelings, but I saw them now begin to get the better of him. His eyes softened, and he took my hand and squeezed it hard.

'I beg your pardon,' he said. 'I beg your pardon, with all my heart.'

There was silence between us, for I was crying; and I believe, at heart, he was crying too. At last, he dropped my hand, and seemed to change back, by an effort, to his former calmness.

'Is there no one belonging to you to whom I can be of service?' he asked. 'I see among the witnesses on the trial the name of a young man who appears to have assisted you in the enquiries which led to the prisoner's conviction. Is he a relation?'

'No, sir—at least, not now—but I hope——'

'What?'

'I hope that he may, one day, be the nearest and dearest relation to me that a woman can have.' I said those words boldly, because I was afraid of his otherwise taking some wrong view of the connection between Robert and me.

'One day?' he repeated. 'One day may be a long time hence.'

'We are neither of us well off, sir,' I said. 'One day, means the day when we are a little richer than we are now.'

'Is the young man educated? Can he produce testimonials to his character? Oblige me by writing his name and address down on the back of that card.'

When I had obeyed, in a handwriting which I am afraid did me no credit, he took out another card, and gave it to me.

'I shall leave England tomorrow,' he said. 'There is nothing now to keep me in my own country. If you are ever in any difficulty or distress (which, I pray God, you may never be), apply to my London agent, whose address you have there.' He stopped, and looked at me attentively—then took my hand again. 'Where is she buried?' he said suddenly, in a quick whisper, turning his head away.

I told him, and added that we had made the grave as beautiful as we could with grass and flowers.

I saw his lips whiten and tremble.

'God bless and reward you!' he said, and drew me towards him quickly and kissed my forehead. I was quite overcome, and sank down and hid my face on the table. When I looked up again he was gone.

June 25th, 1841. I write these lines on my wedding morning, when little more than a year has passed since Robert returned to England.

His salary was increased yesterday to one hundred and fifty pounds a-year. If I only knew where Mr Mallinson was, I would write and tell him of our present happiness. But for the situation which his kindness procured for Robert, we might still have been waiting vainly for the day that has now come.

I am to work at home for the future, and Sally is to help us in our new abode. If Mary could have lived to see this day! I am not ungrateful for my blessings; but, oh, how I miss that sweet face, on this morning of all others!

I got up today early enough to go alone to the grave, and to gather the nosegay that now lies before me from the

flowers that grow round it. I shall put it in my bosom when
Robert comes to fetch me to the church. Mary would have
been my bridesmaid if she had lived; and I can't forget
Mary, even on my wedding-day.

THE LADY OF GLENWITH GRANGE

PROLOGUE

MY practice in the art of portrait-painting, if it has done nothing else, has at least fitted me to turn my talents (such as they are) to a great variety of uses. I have not only taken the likenesses of men, women, and children, but have also extended the range of my brush, under stress of circumstances, to horses, dogs, houses, and in one case even to a bull—the terror and glory of his parish, and the most truculent sitter I ever had. The beast was appropriately named 'Thunder and Lightning,' and was the property of a gentleman-farmer named Garthwaite, a distant connexion of my wife's family.

How it was that I escaped being gored to death before I had finished my picture, is more than I can explain to this day. 'Thunder and Lightning' resented the very sight of me and my colour-box, as if he viewed the taking of his likeness in the light of a personal insult. It required two men to coax him, while a third held him by a ring in his nostrils, before I could venture on beginning to work. Even then he always lashed his tail, and jerked his huge head, and rolled his fiery eyes with a devouring anxiety to have me on his horns for daring to sit down quietly and look at him. Never, I can honestly say, did I feel more heartily grateful for the blessings of soundness of limb and wholeness of skin, than when I had completed the picture of the bull!

One morning, when I had but little more than half done my unwelcome task, my friend and I were met on our way to the bull's stable by the farm-bailiff, who informed us gravely that 'Thunder and Lightning' was just then in such an especially surly state of temper as to render it quite unsafe for me to think of painting him. I looked inquiringly at Mr Garthwaite, who smiled with an air of comic resignation, and said:—'Very well, then, we have nothing for it but to wait till tomorrow. What do you say to a morning's fishing, Mr Kerby, now that my bull's bad temper has given us a holiday?'

I replied, with perfect truth, that I knew nothing about fishing. But Mr Garthwaite, who was as ardent an angler in his way as Izaak Walton* himself, was not to be appeased even by the best of excuses. 'It is never too late to learn', cried he. 'I will make a fisherman of you in no time, if you will only attend to my directions.' It was impossible for me to make any more apologies, without the risk of appearing discourteous. So I thanked my host for his friendly intentions, and with some secret misgivings, accepted the first fishing rod that he put into my hands.

'We shall soon get there,' said Mr Garthwaite. 'I am taking you to the best mill-stream in the neighbourhood.' It was all one to me whether we got there soon or late, and whether the stream was good or bad. However, I did my best to conceal my unsportsmanlike apathy; and tried to look quite happy and very impatient to begin, as we drew near to the mill, and heard louder and louder the gushing of many waters all around it.

Leading the way immediately to a place beneath the falling stream, where there was a deep, eddying pool, Mr Garthwaite baited and threw in his line before I had fixed the joints of my fishing rod. This first difficulty overcome, I involuntarily plunged into some excellent, but rather embarrassing, sport with my line and hook. I caught every one of my garments, from head to foot; I angled for my own clothes with the dexterity and success of Izaak Walton himself. I caught my hat, my jacket, my waistcoat, my trousers, my fingers, and my thumbs—some devil possessed my hook; some more than eel-like vitality twirled and twisted in every inch of my line. By the time my host arrived to assist me, I had attached myself to my fishing rod, apparently for life. All difficulties yielded, however, to his patience and skill; my hook was baited for me, and thrown in; my rod was put into my hand; my friend went back to his place; and we began at last to angle in earnest.

We certainly caught a few fish (in my case, I mean, of course, that the fish caught themselves); but they were

scanty in number and light in weight. Whether it was the
presence of the miller's foreman—a gloomy personage, who
stood staring disastrously upon us from a little flower-gar-
den on the opposite bank—that cast an adverse influence
over our sport; or whether my want of faith and earnestness
as an angler acted retributively on my companion as well as
myself, I know not; but it is certain that he got almost as
little reward for his skill as I got for my patience. After
nearly two hours of intense expectation on my part, and
intense angling on his, Mr Garthwaite jerked his line out of
the water in a rage, and bade me follow him to another
place, declaring that the stream must have been netted by
poachers in the night, who had taken all the large fish away
with them, and had thrown in the small ones to grow until
their next visit. We moved away, further down the bank,
leaving the imperturbable foreman still in the flower-gar-
den, staring at us speechlessly on our departure, exactly as
he had already stared at us on our approach.

'Stop a minute,' said Mr Garthwaite suddenly, after we
had walked some distance in silence by the side of the
stream, 'I have an idea. Now we *are* out for a day's angling,
we won't be baulked. Instead of trying the water here again,
we will go where I know, by experience, that the fishing is
excellent. And, what is more, you shall be introduced to a
lady whose appearance is sure to interest you, and whose
history, I can tell you beforehand, is a very remarkable one.'

'Indeed,' I said. 'May I ask in what way.'

'She is connected,' answered Mr Garthwaite, 'with an
extraordinary story, which relates to a family once settled in
an old house in this neighbourhood. Her name is Miss
Welwyn; but she is less formally known among the poor
people about here, who love her dearly, and honour her
almost superstitiously, as The Lady of Glenwith Grange.
Wait till you have seen her before you ask me to say anything more. She lives in the strictest retirement: I am almost
the only visitor who is admitted. Don't say you had rather
not go in. Any friend of mine will be welcome at the Grange
(the scene of the story, remember), for my sake—the more
especially because I have never abused my privilege of

introduction. The place is not above two miles from here, and the stream (which we call in our county dialect, Glenwith Beck), runs through the grounds.

As we walked on, Mr Garthwaite's manner altered. He became unusually silent and thoughtful. The mention of Miss Welwyn's name had evidently called up some recollections which were not in harmony with his everyday mood. Feeling that to talk to him on any indifferent subject would be only to interrupt his thoughts to no purpose, I walked by his side in perfect silence, looking out already with some curiosity and impatience for a first view of Glenwith Grange. We stopped, at last, close by an old church, standing on the outskirts of a pretty village. The low wall of the churchyard was bounded on one side by a plantation, and was joined by a park paling, in which I noticed a small wicket-gate. Mr Garthwaite opened it, and led me along a shrubbery-path, which conducted us circuitously to the dwelling-house.

We had evidently entered by a private way, for we approached the building by the back. I looked up at it curiously, and saw standing at one of the windows on the lower floor a little girl watching us as we advanced. She seemed to be about nine or ten years old. I could not help stopping a moment to look up at her, her clear complexion, and her long dark hair were so beautiful. And yet there was something in her expression—a dimness and vacancy in her large eyes, a changeless unmeaning smile on her parted lips—which seemed to jar with all that was naturally attractive in her face; which perplexed, disappointed, and even shocked me, though I hardly knew why. Mr Garthwaite, who had been walking along thoughtfully, with his eyes on the ground, turned back when he found me lingering behind him; looked up where I was looking; started a little, I thought; and then took my arm, whispered rather impatiently, 'Don't say anything about having seen that poor child when you are introduced to Miss Welwyn; I'll tell you why afterwards,' and led me round hastily to the front of the building.

It was a very dreary old house, with a lawn in front thickly sprinkled with flowerbeds, and creepers of all sorts climbing in profusion about the heavy stone porch and the mullions of the lower windows. In spite of these prettiest of all ornaments clustering brightly round the building—in spite of the perfect repair in which it was kept from top to bottom—there was something repellent to me in the aspect of the whole place: a deathly stillness hung over it, which fell oppressively on my spirits. When my companion rang the loud, deep-toned bell, the sound startled me as if we had been committing a crime in disturbing the silence. And when the door was opened by an old female servant (while the hollow echo of the bell was still vibrating in the air), I could hardly imagine it possible that we should be let in. We were admitted, however, without the slightest demur. I remarked that there was the same atmosphere of dreary repose inside the house which I had already observed, or rather felt, outside it. No dogs barked at our approach—no doors banged in the servants' offices—no heads peeped over the banisters—not one of the ordinary domestic consequences of an unexpected visit in the country met either eye or ear. The large shadowy apartment, half library, half break-fast-room, into which we were ushered, was as solitary as the hall of entrance; unless I except such drowsy evidences of life as were here presented to us, in the shape of an Angola cat* and a gray parrot—the first lying asleep in a chair, the second sitting ancient, solemn, and voiceless in a large cage. Mr Garthwaite walked to the window when we entered, without saying a word. Determining to let his taciturn humour have its way, I asked him no questions, but looked around the room to see what information it would give me (and rooms often do give such information) about the character and habits of the owner of the house.

Two tables covered with books were the first objects that attracted me. On approaching them, I was surprised to find that the all-influencing periodical literature of the present day—whose sphere is already almost without limit; whose readers, even in our time, may be numbered by millions—was entirely unrepresented on Miss Welwyn's table. Noth-ing modern, nothing contemporary in the world of books, presented itself. Of all the volumes beneath my hand, not one bore the badge of the circulating library, or wore the flaring modern livery of gilt cloth. Every work that I took up had been written at least fifteen or twenty years since. The prints hanging round the walls (towards which I next looked) were all engraved from devotional subjects by the old masters: the music-stand contained no music of later date than the compositions of Haydn and Mozart. Whatever I examined besides, told me, with the same consistency, the same strange tale. The owner of these possessions lived in the bygone time; lived among old recollections and old associations—a voluntary recluse from all that was connected with the passing day. In Miss Welwyn's house, the stir, the tumult, the 'idle business' of the world, evidently appealed in vain to sympathies which grew no longer with the growing hour.

As these thoughts were passing through my mind, the door opened, and the lady herself appeared.

She looked certainly past the prime of life; longer past it, as I afterwards discovered, than she really was. But I never remember, in any other face, to have seen so much of the better part of the beauty of early womanhood still remaining, as I saw in hers. Sorrow had evidently passed over the fair calm countenance before me, but had left resignation there as its only trace. Her expression was still youthful— youthful in its kindness and its candour especially. It was only when I looked at her hair, that was now growing gray— at her wan thin hands—at the faint lines marked round her mouth—at the sad serenity of her eyes, that I fairly detected the mark of age; and, more than that, the token of some great grief, which had been conquered; but not banished. Even from her voice alone—from the peculiar uncertainty of its low calm tones when she spoke—it was easy to conjecture that she must have passed through sufferings, at some time of her life, which had tried to the quick the noble nature that they could not subdue.

Mr Garthwaite and she met each other almost like brother and sister: it was plain that the friendly intimacy between them had been of very long duration. Our visit was a short one. The conversation never advanced beyond the commonplace topics suited to the occasion: it was, therefore, from what I saw, and not from what I heard, that I was enabled to form my judgement of Miss Welwyn. Deeply as she had interested me—far more deeply than I at all know how to explain in fitting words—I cannot say that I was unwilling to depart when we rose to take leave. Though nothing could be more courteous and more kind than her manner towards me during the whole interview, I could still perceive that it cost her some effort to repress in my presence the shades of sadness and reserve which seemed often ready to steal over her. And I must confess that when I once or twice heard the half-sigh stifled, and saw the momentary relapse into thoughtfulness suddenly restrained, I felt an indefinable awkwardness in my position which made me ill at ease: which set me doubting whether, as a perfect stranger, I had done right in suffering myself to be introduced where no new faces could awaken either interest or curiosity; where no new sympathies could ever be felt, no new friendships ever be formed.

As soon as we had taken leave of Miss Welwyn, and were on our way to the stream in her grounds, I more than satisfied Mr Garthwaite that the impression the lady had produced on me was of no transitory kind, by overwhelming him with questions about her—not omitting one or two incidental inquiries on the subject of the little girl whom I had seen at the back window. He only rejoined that his story would answer all my questions; and that he would begin to tell it as soon as we had arrived at Glenwith Beck, and were comfortably settled to fishing.

Five minutes more of walking brought us to the bank of the stream, and showed us the water running smoothly and slowly, tinged with the softest green lustre from the reflections of trees which almost entirely arched it over. Leaving me to admire the view at my ease, Mr Garthwaite occupied himself with the necessary preparations for angling, baiting my hook as well as his own. Then, desiring me to sit near him on the bank, he at last satisfied my curiosity by beginning his story. I shall relate it in his own manner, and, as nearly as possible, in his own words.

THE LADY OF GLENWITH GRANGE

I have known Miss Welwyn long enough to be able to bear
personal testimony to the truth of many of the particulars
which I am now about to relate. I knew her father, and her
younger sister Rosamond; and I was acquainted with the
Frenchman who became Rosamond's husband. These are
the persons of whom it will be principally necessary for me
to speak; they are the only prominent characters in my story.

Miss Welwyn's father died some years since. I remember
him very well—though he never excited in me, or in any one
else that I ever heard of, the slightest feeling of interest.
When I have said that he inherited a very large fortune,
amassed during his father's time, by speculations of a very
daring, very fortunate, but not always very honourable kind,
and that he bought this old house with the notion of raising
his social position, by making himself a member of our
landed aristocracy in these parts, I have told you as much
about him, I suspect, as you would care to hear. He was a
thoroughly commonplace man, with no great virtues and no
great vices in him. He had a little heart, a feeble mind, an
amiable temper, a tall figure, and a handsome face. More
than this need not, and cannot, be said on the subject of Mr
Welwyn's character.

I must have seen the late Mrs Welwyn very often as a
child; but I cannot say that I remember anything more of
her than that she was tall and handsome, and very generous
and sweet-tempered towards me when I was in her company. She was her husband's superior in birth, as in everything else; was a great reader of books in all languages; and
possessed such admirable talents as a musician, that her
wonderful playing on the organ is remembered and talked
of to this day among the old people in our country houses
about here. All her friends, as I have heard, were disappointed when she married Mr Welwyn, rich as he was; and
were afterwards astonished to find her preserving the appearance, at least, of being perfectly happy with a husband
who, neither in mind nor heart, was worthy of her.

It was generally supposed (and I have no doubt correctly), that she found her great happiness and her great consolation in her little girl Ida—now the lady from whom we have just parted. The child took after her mother from the first—inheriting her mother's quick sensibilities, and, more than all, her mother's quiet firmness, patience, and loving-kindness of disposition. From Ida's earliest years, Mrs Welwyn undertook the whole superintendence of her education. The two were hardly ever apart, within doors or without. Neighbours and friends said that the little girl was being brought up too fancifully, was not enough among other children, was sadly neglected as to all reasonable and practical teaching, and was perilously encouraged in those dreamy and imaginative tendencies of which she had naturally more than her due share. There was, perhaps, some truth in this; and there might have been still more, if Ida had possessed an ordinary character, or had been reserved for an ordinary destiny. But she was a strange child from the first, and a strange future was in store for her.

Little Ida reached her eleventh year without either brother or sister to be her playfellow and companion at home. Immediately after that period, however, her sister Rosamond was born. Though Mr Welwyn's own desire was to have had a son, there were, nevertheless, great rejoicings yonder in the old house on the birth of this second daughter. But they were all turned, only a few months afterwards, to the bitterest grief and despair: the Grange lost its mistress. While Rosamond was still an infant in arms, her mother died.

Mrs Welwyn had been afflicted with some disorder after the birth of her second child, the name of which I am not learned enough in medical science to be able to remember. I only know that she recovered from it, to all appearance, in an unexpectedly short time; that she suffered a fatal relapse, and that she died a lingering and a painful death. Mr Welwyn (who, in after-years, had a habit of vaingloriously describing his marriage as 'a love-match on both sides') was really fond of his wife in his own frivolous feeble way, and suffered as acutely as such a man could suffer, during the latter days of her illness, and at the terrible time when the doctors, one and all, confessed that her life was a thing to be despaired of. He burst into irrepressible passions of tears, and was always obliged to leave the sick-room whenever Mrs Welwyn spoke of her approaching end. The last solemn words of the dying woman, the tenderest messages that she could give, the dearest parting wishes that she could express, the most earnest commands that she could leave behind her, the gentlest reasons for consolation that she could suggest to the survivors among those who loved her, were not poured into her husband's ear, but into her child's. From the first period of her illness, Ida had persisted in remaining in the sick-room, rarely speaking, never showing outwardly any signs of terror or grief, except when she was removed from it; and then bursting into hysterical passions of weeping, which no expostulations, no arguments, no commands—nothing, in short, but bringing her back to the bedside—ever availed to calm. Her mother had been her playfellow, her companion, her dearest and most familiar friend; and there seemed something in the remembrance of this which, instead of overwhelming the child with despair, strengthened her to watch faithfully and bravely by her dying parent to the very last.

When the parting moment was over, and when Mr Welwyn, unable to bear the shock of being present in the house of death at the time of his wife's funeral, left home and went to stay with one of his relations in a distant part of England, Ida, whom it had been his wish to take away with him, petitioned earnestly to be left behind. 'I promised mamma before she died that I would be as good to my little sister Rosamond as she had been to me,' said the child simply; 'and she told me in return that I might wait here and see her laid in her grave.' There happened to be an aunt of Mrs Welwyn, and an old servant of the family, in the house at this time, who understood Ida much better than her father did, and they persuaded him not to take her away. I have heard my mother say that the effect of the child's appearance at the funeral on her, and on all who went to see it, was something that she could never think of without the tears coming into her eyes, and could never forget to the last day of her life.

It must have been very shortly after this period that I saw Ida for the first time.

I remember accompanying my mother on a visit to the old house we have just left, in the summer, when I was at home for the holidays. It was a lovely, sunshiny morning; there was nobody indoors, and we walked out into the garden. As we approached that lawn yonder, on the other side of the shrubbery, I saw, first, a young woman in mourning (apparently a servant) sitting reading; then a little girl, dressed all in black, moving towards us slowly over the bright turf, and holding up before her a baby whom she was trying to teach to walk. She looked, to my ideas, so very young to be engaged in such an occupation as this, and her gloomy black frock appeared to be such an unnaturally grave garment for a mere child of her age, and looked so doubly dismal by contrast with the brilliant sunny lawn on which she stood, that I quite started when I first saw her, and eagerly asked my mother who she was. The answer informed me of the sad family story, which I have just been relating to you. Mrs Welwyn had then been buried, about three months; and Ida, in her childish way, was trying, as she had promised, to supply her mother's place to her infant sister Rosamond.

I only mention this simple incident, because it is necessary, before I proceed to the eventful part of my narrative, that you should know exactly in what relation the sisters stood towards one another from the first. Of all the last parting words that Mrs Welwyn had spoken to her child, none had been oftener repeated, none more solemnly urged, than those which had commended the little Rosamond to Ida's love and care. To other persons, the full, the all-trusting dependence which the dying mother was known to have placed in a child hardly eleven years old, seemed merely a proof of that helpless desire to cling even to the feeblest consolations which the approach of death so often brings with it. But the event showed that the trust so strangely placed had not been ventured vainly when it was committed to young and tender hands. The whole future existence of the child was one noble proof that she had been worthy of her mother's dying confidence when it was first reposed in her. In that simple incident which I have just mentioned, the new life of the two motherless sisters was all foreshadowed.

Time passed. I left school—went to college—travelled in Germany, and stayed there some time to learn the language. At every interval when I came home, and asked about the Welwyns, the answer was, in substance, almost always the same. Mr Welwyn was giving his regular dinners, performing his regular duties as a county magistrate, enjoying his regular recreations as an amateur farmer and an eager sportsman. His two daughters were never separate. Ida was the same strange, quiet, retiring girl, that she had always been; and was still (as the phrase went) 'spoiling' Rosamond in every way in which it was possible for an elder sister to spoil a younger by too much kindness.

I myself went to the Grange occasionally, when I was in this neighbourhood, in holiday and vacation time; and was able to test the correctness of the picture of life there which had been drawn for me. I remember the two sisters, when Rosamond was four or five years old; and when Ida seemed to me, even then, to be more like the child's mother than her sister. She bore with her little caprices as sisters do not bear with one another. She was so patient at lesson-time, so anxious to conceal any weariness that might overcome her in play-hours, so proud when Rosamond's beauty was noticed, so grateful for Rosamond's kisses when the child thought of bestowing them, so quick to notice all that Rosamond did, and to attend to all that Rosamond said, even when visitors were in the room; that she seemed, to my boyish observations, altogether different from other elder sisters, in other family circles into which I was then received.

I remember them, again, when Rosamond was just growing to womanhood, and was in high spirits at the prospect of spending a season in London, and being presented at Court. She was very beautiful at that time—much handsomer than Ida. Her 'accomplishments' were talked of far and near in our country circles. Few, if any, of the people, however, who applauded her playing and singing, who admired her water-colour drawings, who were delighted at her fluency when she spoke French, and amazed at her ready comprehension when she read German, knew how little of all this elegant mental cultivation and nimble manual dexterity she owed to her governesses and masters, and how much to her elder sister. It was Ida who really found out the means of stimulating her when she was idle; Ida who helped her through all her worst difficulties; Ida who gently conquered her defects of memory over her books, her inaccuracies of ear at the piano, her errors of taste when she took the brush or pencil in hand. It was Ida alone who worked these marvels, and whose all-sufficient reward for her hardest exertions was a chance word of kindness from her sister's lips. Rosamond was not unaffectionate, and not ungrateful; but she inherited much of her father's commonness and frivolity of character. She became so accustomed to owe everything to her sister—to resign all her most trifling difficulties to Ida's ever-ready care—to have all her tastes consulted by Ida's ever watchful kindness—that she never appreciated, as it deserved the deep devoted love of which she was the object. When Ida refused two good offers of marriage, Rosamond was as much astonished as the veriest strangers, who wondered why the elder Miss Welwyn seemed bent on remaining single all her life.

When the journey to London, to which I have already alluded, took place, Ida accompanied her father and sister. If she had consulted her own tastes, she would have remained in the country; but Rosamond declared that she should feel quite lost and helpless twenty times a day, in town, without her sister. It was in the nature of Ida to sacrifice herself to any one whom she loved, on the smallest occasions as well as the greatest. Her affection was as intuitively ready to sanctify Rosamond's slightest caprices as to excuse Rosamond's most thoughtless faults. So she went to London cheerfully, to witness with pride all the little triumphs won by her sister's beauty; to hear, and never tire of hearing, all that admiring friends could say in her sister's praise.

At the end of the season, Mr Welwyn and his daughters returned for a short time to the country; then left home again to spend the latter part of the autumn and the beginning of the winter in Paris.

They took with them excellent letters of introduction, and saw a great deal of the best society in Paris, foreign as well as English. At one of the first of the evening parties which they attended, the general topic of conversation was the conduct of a certain French nobleman, the Baron Franval, who had returned to his native country after a long absence, and who was spoken of in terms of high eulogy by the majority of the guests present. The history of who Franval was, and of what he had done, was readily communicated to Mr Welwyn and his daughters, and was briefly this:—

The Baron inherited little from his ancestors besides his high rank and his ancient pedigree. On the death of his parents, he and his two unmarried sisters (their only surviving children) found the small territorial property of the Franvals, in Normandy, barely productive enough to afford a comfortable subsistence for the three. The Baron, then a young man of three-and-twenty, endeavoured to obtain such military or civil employment as might become his rank; but although the Bourbons were at that time restored to the throne of France, his efforts were ineffectual. Either his interest at Court was bad, or secret enemies were at work to oppose his advancement. He failed to obtain even the slightest favour; and, irritated by undeserved neglect, resolved to leave France, and seek occupation for his energies in foreign countries, where his rank would be no bar to his bettering his fortunes, if he pleased, by engaging in commercial pursuits.

An opportunity of the kind that he wanted unexpectedly offered itself. He left his sisters in care of an old male relative of the family at the château in Normandy, and sailed, in the first instance to the West Indies; afterwards extending his wanderings to the continent of South America, and there engaging in mining transactions on a very large scale. After fifteen years of absence (during the latter part of which time false reports of his death had reached

Normandy), he had just returned to France; having realised a handsome independence, with which he proposed to widen the limits of his ancestral property, and to give his sisters (who were still, like himself, unmarried) all the luxuries and advantages that affluence could bestow. The Baron's independent spirit, and generous devotion to the honour of his family and the happiness of his surviving relatives, were themes of general admiration in most of the social circles of Paris. He was expected to arrive in the capital every day; and it was naturally enough predicted that his reception in society there could not fail to be of the most flattering and most brilliant kind.

The Welwyns listened to this story with some little interest; Rosamond, who was very romantic, being especially attracted by it, and openly avowing to her father and sister, when they got back to their hotel, that she felt as ardent a curiosity as anybody to see the adventurous and generous Baron. The desire was soon gratified. Franval came to Paris, as had been anticipated—was introduced to the Welwyns—met them constantly in society—made no favourable impression on Ida, but won the good opinion of Rosamond from the first; and was regarded with such high approval by their father, that when he mentioned his intention of visiting England in the spring of the new year, he was cordially invited to spend the hunting season at Glenwith Grange.

I came back from Germany about the same time that the Welwyns returned from Paris: and at once set myself to improve my neighbourly intimacy with the family. I was very fond of Ida; more fond, perhaps, than my vanity will now allow me to—but that is of no consequence. It is much more to the purpose to tell you, that I heard the whole of the Baron's story enthusiastically related by Mr Welwyn and Rosamond; that he came to the Grange at the appointed time; that I was introduced to him; and that he produced as unfavourable an impression upon me as he had already produced upon Ida.

It was whimsical enough, but I really could not tell why I disliked him, though I could account very easily, according

to my own notions, for his winning the favour and approval
of Rosamond and her father. He was certainly a handsome
man, as far as features went; he had a winning gentleness
and graceful respect in his manner when he spoke to
women; and he sang remarkably well, with one of the sweetest tenor voices I ever heard. These qualities alone were
quite sufficient to attract any girl of Rosamond's disposition: and I certainly never wondered why he was a favourite
of hers.

Then, as to her father, the Baron was not only fitted to
win his sympathy and regard in the field, by proving himself
an ardent sportsman and an excellent rider, but was also, in
virtue of some of his minor personal peculiarities, just the
man to gain the friendship of his host. Mr Welwyn was as
ridiculously prejudiced, as most weak-headed Englishmen
are, on the subject of foreigners in general. In spite of his
visit to Paris, the vulgar notion of a Frenchman continued
to be his notion, both while he was in France and when he
returned from it. Now, the Baron was as unlike the traditional 'Mounseer'* of English songs, plays, and satires, as a
man could well be; and it was on account of his very
dissimilarity that Mr Welwyn first took a violent fancy to
him, and then invited him to his house. Franval spoke
English remarkably well; wore neither beard, moustachios,
or whiskers; kept his hair cut almost unbecomingly short;
dressed in the extreme of plainness and modest good taste;
talked little in general society; uttered his words, when he
did speak, with singular calmness and deliberation; and, to
crown all, had the greater part of his acquired property
invested in English securities. In Mr Welwyn's estimation,
such a man as this was a perfect miracle of a Frenchman,
and he admired and encouraged him accordingly.

I have said that I disliked him, yet could not assign a
reason for my dislike; and I can only repeat it now. He was
remarkably polite to me; we often rode together in hunting,
and sat near each other at the Grange table; but I could
never become familiar with him. He always gave me the idea
of a man who had some mental reservation in saying the
most trifling thing. There was a constant restraint, hardly

perceptible to most people, but plainly visible, nevertheless, to me, which seemed to accompany his lightest words, and to hang about his most familiar manner. This, however, was no just reason for my secretly disliking and distrusting him as I did. Ida said as much to me, I remember, when I confessed to her what my feelings towards him were, and tried (but vainly) to induce her to be equally candid with me in return. She seemed to shrink from the tacit condemnation of Rosamond's opinion which such a confidence on her part would have implied. And yet she watched the growth of that opinion, or, in other words, the growth of her sister's liking for the Baron, with an apprehension and sorrow which she tried fruitlessly to conceal. Even her father began to notice that her spirits were not so good as usual, and to suspect the cause of her melancholy. I remember he jested, with all the dense insensibility of a stupid man, about Ida having invariably been jealous, from a child, if Rosamond looked kindly upon anybody except her elder sister.

The spring began to get far advanced towards summer. Franval paid a visit to London; came back in the middle of the season to Glenwith Grange; wrote to put off his departure for France; and, at last (not at all to the surprise of anybody who was intimate with the Welwyns) proposed to Rosamond, and was accepted. He was candour and generosity itself when the preliminaries of the marriage settlement were under discussion. He quite overpowered Mr Welwyn and the lawyers with references, papers, and statements of the distribution and extent of his property, which were found to be perfectly correct. His sisters were written to, and returned the most cordial answers: saying that the state of their health would not allow them to come to England for the marriage; but adding a warm invitation to Normandy for the bride and her family. Nothing, in short, could be more straightforward and satisfactory than the Baron's behaviour, and the testimonies to his worth and integrity which the news of the approaching marriage produced from his relatives and his friends.

The only joyless face at the Grange now was Ida's. At any time it would have been a hard trial to her to resign that first and foremost place, which she had held since childhood in her sister's heart, as she knew she must resign it when Rosamond married. But, secretly disliking and distrusting Franval as she did, the thought that he was soon to become the husband of her beloved sister filled her with a vague sense of terror which she could not explain to herself, which it was imperatively necessary that she should conceal, and which, on those very accounts, became a daily and hourly torment to her that was almost more than she could bear.

One consolation alone supported her: Rosamond and she were not to be separated. She knew that the Baron secretly disliked her as much as she disliked him; she knew that she must bid farewell to the brighter and happier part of her life on the day when she went to live under the same roof with her sister's husband; but, true to the promise made years and years ago, by her dying mother's bed, true to the affection which was the ruling and beautiful feeling of her whole existence, she never hesitated about indulging Rosamond's wish, when the girl, in her bright light-hearted way, said that she could never get on comfortably in the marriage state unless she had Ida to live with her and help her just the same as ever. The Baron was too polite a man even to look dissatisfied when he heard of the proposed arrangement; and it was therefore settled from the beginning that Ida was always to live with her sister.

The marriage took place in the summer, and the bride and bridegroom went to spend their honeymoon in Cumberland. On their return to Glenwith Grange, a visit to the Baron's sisters, in Normandy, was talked of; but the execution of this project was suddenly and disastrously suspended by the death of Mr Welwyn from an attack of pleurisy.

In consequence of this calamity, the projected journey was of course deferred: and when autumn and the shooting season came, the Baron was unwilling to leave the well-stocked preserves of the Grange. He seemed, indeed, to grow less and less inclined, as time advanced, for the trip to Normandy; and wrote excuse after excuse to his sisters, when letters arrived from them urging him to pay the promised visit. In the winter-time, he said he would not allow his wife to risk a long journey. In the spring, his health was pronounced to be delicate. In the genial summertime, the accomplishment of the proposed visit would be impossible; for at that period the Baroness expected to become a mother. Such were the apologies which Franval seemed almost glad to be able to send to his sisters in France.

The marriage was, in the strictest sense of the term, a happy one. The Baron, though he never altogether lost the strange restraint and reserve of his manner, was, in his quiet, peculiar way, the fondest and kindest of husbands. He went to town occasionally on business, but always seemed glad to return to the Baroness; he never varied in the politeness of his bearing towards his wife's sister; he behaved with the most courteous hospitality towards all the friends of the Welwyns: in short, he thoroughly justified the good opinion which Rosamond and her father had formed of him when they first met at Paris. And yet no experience of his character thoroughly reassured Ida. Months passed on quietly and pleasantly; and still that secret sadness, that indefinable, unreasonable apprehension on Rosamond's account, hung heavily on her sister's heart.

At the beginning of the first summer months, a little domestic inconvenience happened, which showed the Baroness, for the first time, that her husband's temper could be seriously ruffled—and that by the veriest trifle. He was in the habit of taking in two French provincial newspapers—one published at Bordeaux, and the other at Havre. He always opened these journals the moment they came, looked at one particular column of each with the deepest attention for a few minutes, then carelessly threw them aside into his wastepaper basket. His wife and her sister were at first rather surprised at the manner in which he read his two papers; but they thought no more of it when he explained that he only took them in to consult them about French commercial intelligence, which might be, occasionally, of importance to him.

These papers were published weekly. On the occasion to which I have just referred, the Bordeaux paper came on the proper day, as usual; but the Havre paper never made its appearance. This trifling circumstance seemed to make the Baron seriously uneasy. He wrote off directly to the country post office, and to the newspaper agent in London. His wife, astonished to see his tranquillity so completely overthrown by so slight a cause, tried to restore his good humour by jesting with him about the missing newspaper. He replied by the first angry and unfeeling words that she had heard issue from his lips. She was then within about six weeks of her confinement, and very unfit to bear harsh answers from anybody—least of all from her husband.

On the second day no answer came. On the afternoon of the third, the Baron rode off to the post-town to make inquiries. About an hour after he had gone, a strange gentleman came to the Grange, and asked to see the Baroness. On being informed that she was not well enough to receive visitors, he sent up a message that his business was of great importance, and that he would wait downstairs for a second answer.

On receiving this message, Rosamond turned, as usual to her elder sister for advice. Ida went downstairs immediately to see the stranger. What I am now about to tell you of the extraordinary interview which took place between them, and of the shocking events that followed it, I have heard from Miss Welwyn's own lips.

She felt unaccountably nervous when she entered the room. The stranger bowed very politely, and asked, in a foreign accent, if she were the Baroness Franval. She set him right on this point, and told him she attended to all matters of business for the Baroness; adding, that, if his errand at all concerned her sister's husband, the Baron was not then at home.

The stranger answered that he was aware of it when he called, and that the unpleasant business on which he came could not be confided to the Baron—at least in the first instance.

She asked why. He said he was there to explain; and expressed himself as feeling greatly relieved at having to open his business to her, because she would doubtless, be best able to prepare her sister for the bad news that he was, unfortunately, obliged to bring. The sudden faintness which overcame her, as he spoke those words, prevented her from addressing him in return. He poured out some water for her from a bottle which happened to be standing on the table, and asked if he might depend on her fortitude. She tried to say 'Yes;' but the violent throbbing of her heart seemed to choke her. He took a foreign newspaper from his pocket, saying that he was a secret agent of the French police—that the paper was the *Havre Journal* for the past week, and that it had been expressly kept from reaching the Baron, as usual, through his (the agent's) interference. He then opened the newspaper, and begged that she would nerve herself sufficiently (for her sister's sake) to read certain lines, which would give her some hint of the business that brought him there. He pointed to the passage as he spoke. It was among the 'Shipping Entries,' and was thus expressed:—

'Arrived, the *Berenice*, from San Francisco, with a valuable cargo of hides. She brings one passenger, the Baron Franval, of Chateau Franval, in Normandy.'

As Miss Welwyn read the entry, her heart, which had been throbbing violently but the moment before, seemed suddenly to cease from all action, and she began to shiver, though it was a warm June evening. The agent held the tumbler to her lips, and made her drink a little of the water, entreating her very earnestly to take courage and listen to him. He then sat down, and referred again to the entry; every word he uttered seeming to burn itself in for ever (as she expressed it) on her memory and her heart.

He said: 'It has been ascertained beyond the possibility of doubt that there is no mistake about the name in the lines you have just read. And it is as certain as that we are here, that there is only one Baron Franval now alive. The question, therefore, is, whether the passenger by the *Berenice* is the true Baron, or—I beg you most earnestly to bear with me and to compose yourself— or the husband of your sister. The person who arrived last week at Havre was scouted* as an impostor by the ladies at the château, the moment he presented himself there as their brother, returning to them after sixteen years of absence. The authorities were communicated with, and I and my assistants were instantly sent for from Paris.

'We wasted no time in questioning the supposed impostor. He either was, or affected to be, in a perfect frenzy of grief and indignation. We just ascertained, from competent witnesses, that he bore an extraordinary resemblance to the real Baron, and that he was perfectly familiar with places and persons in and about the château; we just ascertained that, and then proceeded to confer with the local authorities, and to examine their private entries of suspected persons in their jurisdiction, ranging back over a past period of twenty years or more. One of the entries thus consulted contained these particulars:—"Hector Auguste Monbrun, son of a respectable proprietor in Normandy. Well educated; gentlemanlike manners. On bad terms with his family. Character: bold, cunning, unscrupulous, self-possessed. Is a clever mimic. May be easily recognised by his striking likeness to the Baron Franval. Imprisoned at twenty for theft and assault." '

Miss Welwyn saw the agent look up at her after he had read this extract from the police-book, to ascertain if she was still able to listen to him. He asked, with some appearance of alarm, as their eyes met, if she would like some more water. She was just able to make a sign in the negative. He took a second extract from his pocket-book, and went on.

He said: 'The next entry under the same name was dated four years later, and ran thus: "H. A. Monbrun, condemned to the galleys for life, for assassination, and other crimes not officially necessary to be here specified. Escaped from custody at Toulon. Is known, since the expiration of his first term of imprisonment, to have allowed his beard to grow, and to have worn his hair long, with the intention of rendering it impossible for those acquainted with him in his native province to recognise him, as heretofore, by his likeness to the Baron Franval." There were more particulars added, not important enough for extract. We immediately examined the supposed impostor: for, if he was Monbrun, we

knew that we should find on his shoulder the two letters of
the convict brand, "T.F." (standing for *Travaux Forcés*).*
After the minutest examination with the mechanical and
chemical tests used on such occasions, not the slightest
trace of the brand was to be found. The moment this
astounding discovery was made, I started to lay an embargo
on the forthcoming numbers of the *Havre Journal* for that
week, which were about to be sent to the English agent in
London. I arrived at Havre on Saturday (the morning of
publication), in time to execute my design. I waited there
long enough to communicate by telegraph with my superiors in Paris, then hastened to this place. What my errand
here is, you may—'

He might have gone on speaking for some moments
longer; but Miss Welwyn heard no more.

Her first sensation of returning consciousness was the
feeling that water was being sprinkled on her face. Then she
saw that all the windows in the room had been set wide
open, to give her air; and that she and the agent were still
alone. At first, she felt bewildered, and hardly knew who he
was; but he soon recalled to her mind the horrible realities
that had brought him there, by apologising for not having
summoned assistance when she fainted. He said it was of
the last importance, in Franval's absence, that no one in the
house should imagine that anything unusual was taking
place in it. Then, after giving her an interval of a minute or
two to collect what little strength she had left, he added that
he would not increase her sufferings by saying anything
more, just then, on the shocking subject of the investigation
which it was his duty to make—that he would leave her to
recover herself, and to consider what was the best course to
be taken with the Baroness in the present terrible emergency—and that he would privately return to the house
between eight and nine o'clock that evening, ready to act as
Miss Welwyn wished, and to afford her and her sister any
aid and protection of which they might stand in need. With
these words he bowed, and noiselessly quitted the room.

For the first few awful minutes after she was left alone,
Miss Welwyn sat helpless and speechless; utterly numbed in

heart, and mind, and body—then a sort of instinct (she was incapable of thinking) seemed to urge her to conceal the fearful news from her sister as long as possible. She ran upstairs to Rosamond's sitting-room, and called through the door (for she dared not trust herself in her sister's presence) that the visitor had come on some troublesome business from their late father's lawyers, and that she was going to shut herself up, and write some long letters in connexion with that business. After she had got into her own room, she was never sensible of how time was passing —never conscious of any feeling within her, except a baseless, helpless hope that the French police might yet be proved to have made some terrible mistake—until she heard a violent shower of rain come on a little after sunset. The noise of the rain, and freshness it brought with it in the air, seemed to awaken her as if from a painful and fearful sleep. The power of reflection returned to her; her heart heaved and bounded with an overwhelming terror, as the thought of Rosamond came back vividly to it; her memory recurred despairingly to the long past day of her mother's death, and to the farewell promise she had made by her mother's bedside. She burst into an hysterical passion of weeping that seemed to be tearing her to pieces. In the midst of it she heard the clatter of a horse's hoofs in the courtyard, and knew that Rosamond's husband had come back.

Dipping her handkerchief in cold water, and passing it over her eyes as she left the room, she instantly hastened to her sister.

Fortunately, the daylight was fading in the old-fashioned chamber that Rosamond occupied. Before they could say two words to each other, Franval was in the room. He seemed violently irritated; said that he had waited for the arrival of the mail—that the missing newspaper had not come by it—that he had got wet through—that he felt a shivering fit coming on—and that he believed he had caught a violent cold. His wife anxiously suggested some simple remedies. He roughly interrupted her, saying there was but one remedy, the remedy of going to bed; and so left them without another word. She just put her handkerchief to her eyes, and said softly to her sister, 'How he is changed!'—then spoke no more. They sat silent for half an hour or longer. After that, Rosamond went affectionately and forgivingly to see how her husband was. She returned, saying that he was in bed, and in a deep, heavy sleep; and predicting hopefully that he would wake up quite well the next morning. In a few minutes more the clock struck nine, and Ida heard the servant's step ascending the stairs. She suspected what his errand was, and went out to meet him. Her presentiment had not deceived her; the police agent had arrived, and was waiting for her downstairs.

He asked her if she had said anything to her sister, or had thought of any plan of action, the moment she entered the room; and, on receiving a reply in the negative, inquired further if 'the Baron' had come home yet. She answered that he had; that he was ill and tired, and vexed, and that he had gone to bed. The agent asked in an eager whisper if she knew that he was asleep, and alone in bed? and, when he received her reply, said that he must go up into the bedroom directly.

She began to feel the faintness coming over her again, and with it sensations of loathing and terror that she could neither express to others nor define to herself. He said that if she hesitated to let him avail himself of this unexpected opportunity, her scruples might lead to fatal results. He reminded her that if 'the Baron' were really the convict Monbrun, the claims of society and of justice demanded that he should be discovered by the first available means; and that if he were not—if some inconceivable mistake had really been committed—then, such a plan for getting immediately at the truth as was now proposed, would ensure the delivery of an innocent man from suspicion, and at the same time spare him the knowledge that he had ever been suspected. This last argument had its effect on Miss Welwyn. The baseless, helpless hope that the French authorities might yet be proved to be in error, which she had already felt in her own room, returned to her now. She suffered the agent to lead her upstairs.

He took the candle from her hand when she pointed to the door; opened it softly; and, leaving it ajar, went into the room.

She looked through the gap, with a feverish, horrorstruck curiosity. Franval was lying on his side in a profound sleep, with his back turned towards the door. The agent softly placed the candle upon a small reading-table between the door and the bedside, softly drew down the bed-clothes a little way from the sleeper's back, then took a pair of scissors from the toilette table, and very gently and slowly began to cut away, first the loose folds, then the intervening strips of linen from the part of Franval's nightgown, that was over his shoulders. When the upper part of his back had been bared in this way, the agent took the candle and held it near the flesh. Miss Welwyn heard him ejaculate some word under his breath, then saw him looking round to where she was standing, and beckoning to her to come in.

Mechanically she obeyed; mechanically she looked down where his finger was pointing. It was the convict Monbrun—there, just visible under the bright light of the candle, were the fatal letters 'T.F.' branded on the villain's shoulder!

Though she could neither move nor speak, the horror of this discovery did not deprive her of her consciousness. She saw the agent softly draw up the bed-clothes again into their proper position, replace the scissors on the toilet-table, and take from it a bottle of smelling-salts. She felt him removing her from the bedroom, and helping her quickly downstairs, giving her the salts to smell by the way. When they were alone again, he said, with the first appearance of agitation that he had yet exhibited, 'Now, madam, for God's sake, collect all your courage, and be guided by me. You and your sister had better leave the house immediately. Have you any relatives in the neighbourhood, with whom you could take refuge?' They had none. 'What is the name of the nearest town where you could get good accommodation for the night?' Harleybrook (he wrote the name down on his tablets). 'How far off is it?' Twelve miles. 'You had better have the carriage out at once, to go there with as little delay as possible: leaving me to pass the night here. I will communicate with you tomorrow at the principal hotel. Can you compose yourself sufficiently to be able to tell the head-servant, if I ring for him, that he is to obey my orders till further notice?'

The servant was summoned, and received his instruc-tions, the agent going out with him to see that the carriage was got ready quietly and quickly. Miss Welwyn went up-stairs to her sister.

How the fearful news was first broken to Rosamond, I cannot relate to you. Miss Welwyn has never confided to me, has never confided to anybody, what happened at the interview between her sister and herself that night. I can tell you nothing of the shock they both suffered, except that the younger and the weaker died under it; that the elder and the stronger has never recovered from it, and never will.

They went away the same night, with one attendant, to Harleybrook, as the agent had advised. Before daybreak Rosamond was seized with the pains of premature labour. She died three days after, unconscious of the horror of her situation; wandering in her mind about past times, and singing old tunes that Ida had taught her, as she lay in her sister's arms.

The child was born alive, and lives still. You saw her at the window as we came in at the back way to the Grange. I surprised you, I dare say, by asking you not to speak of her to Miss Welwyn. Perhaps you noticed something vacant in the little girl's expression. I am sorry to say that her mind is more vacant still. If 'idiot' did not sound like a mocking word, however tenderly and pityingly one may wish to utter it, I should tell you that the poor thing had been an idiot from her birth.

You will, doubtless, want to hear now what happened at Glenwith Grange, after Miss Welwyn and her sister had left it. I have seen the letter which the police agent sent the next morning to Harleybrook; and, speaking from my recollec-tion of that, I shall be able to relate all you can desire to know.

First, as to the history of the scoundrel Monbrun, I need only tell you that he was identical with an escaped convict, who, for a long term of years, had successfully eluded the vigilance of the authorities all over Europe, and in America as well. In conjunction with two accomplices, he had succeeded in possessing himself of large sums of money by the most criminal means. He also acted secretly as the 'banker' of his convict brethren, whose dishonest gains were all confided to his hands for safe keeping. He would have been certainly captured, on venturing back to France, along with his two associates, but for the daring imposture in which he took refuge; and which, if the true Baron Franval had really died abroad, as was reported, would, in all probability never have been found out.

Besides his extraordinary likeness to the Baron, he had every other requisite for carrying on his deception successfully. Though his parents were not wealthy he had received a good education. He was so notorious for his gentlemanlike manners among the villainous associates of his crimes and excesses, that they nicknamed him 'the Prince.' All his early life had been passed in the neighbourhood of the Château Franval. He knew what were the circumstances which had induced the Baron to leave it. He had been in the country to which the Baron had emigrated. He was able to refer familiarly to persons and localities, at home and abroad, with which the Baron was sure to be acquainted. And, lastly, he had an expatriation of fifteen years to plead for him as his all-sufficient excuse, if he made any slight mistakes before the Baron's sisters, in his assumed character of their long-absent brother. It will be, of course, hardly necessary for me to tell you, in relation to this part of the subject, that the true Franval was immediately and honourably reinstated in the family rights of which the impostor had succeeded for a time in depriving him.

According to Monbrun's own account, he had married poor Rosamond purely for love; and the probabilities certainly are, that the pretty innocent English girl had really struck the villain's fancy for the time; and that the easy, quiet life he was leading at the Grange pleased him, by contrast with his perilous and vagabond existence of former days. What might have happened if he had had time enough to grow wearied of his ill-fated wife and his English home, it is now useless to inquire. What really did happen on the morning when he awoke after the flight of Ida and her sister can be briefly told.

As soon as his eyes opened they rested on the police-agent, sitting quietly by the bedside, with a loaded pistol in his hand. Monbrun knew immediately that he was dis-covered; but he never for an instant lost the self-possession for which he was famous. He said he wished to have five minutes allowed him to deliberate quietly in bed, whether he should resist the French authorities on English ground, and so gain time by obliging the one government to apply specially to have him delivered up by the other—or whether he should accept the terms officially offered to him by the agent, if he quietly allowed himself to be captured. He chose the latter course—it was suspected, because he wished to communicate personally with some of his convict associates in France, whose fradulent gains were in his keeping, and because he felt boastfully confident of being able to escape again, whenever he pleased. Be his secret motives, however, what they might, he allowed the agent to conduct him peaceably from the Grange; first writing a farewell letter to poor Rosamond, full of heartless French sentiment, and glib sophistries about Fate and Society. His own fate was not long in overtaking him. He attempted to escape again, as it had been expected he would, and was shot by the sentinel on duty at the time. I remember hearing that the bullet entered his head and killed him on the spot.

My story is done. It is ten years now since Rosamond was buried in the churchyard yonder; and it is ten years also since Miss Welwyn returned to be the lonely inhabitant of Glenwith Grange. She now lives but in the remembrances that it calls up before her of her happier existence of former days. There is hardly an object in the old house which does not tenderly and solemnly remind her of the mother, whose last wishes she lived to obey; of the sister, whose happiness was once her dearest earthly care. Those prints that you noticed on the library walls, Rosamond used to copy in the past time, when her pencil was often guided by Ida's hand.

Those music-books that you were looking over, she and her mother have played from together, through many a long and quiet summer's evening. She has no ties now to bind her to the present but the poor child whose affliction it is her constant effort to lighten, and the little peasant population around her, whose humble cares and wants and sorrows she is always ready to relieve. Far and near her modest charities have penetrated among us; and far and near she is heartily beloved and blessed in many a labourer's household. There is no poor man's hearth, not in this village only, but for miles away from it as well, at which you would not be received with the welcome given to an old friend, if you only told the cottagers that you knew the Lady of Glenwith Grange!

THE DEAD HAND

WHEN this present nineteenth century was younger by a
good many years than it is now, a certain friend of mine,
named Arthur Holliday, happened to arrive in the town of
Doncaster,* exactly in the middle of the race-week, or, in
other words, in the middle of the month of September. He
was one of those reckless, rattle-pated, open-hearted, and
open-mouthed young gentlemen, who possess the gift of
familiarity in its highest perfection, and who scramble carelessly along the journey of life making friends, as the phrase
is, wherever they go. His father was a rich manufacturer,
and had bought landed property enough in one of the
midland counties to make all the born squires in his neighbourhood thoroughly envious of him. Arthur was his only
son, possessor in prospect of the great estate and the great
business after his father's death; well supplied with money,
and not too rigidly looked after, during his father's lifetime.
Report, or scandal, whichever you please, said that the old
gentleman had been rather wild in his youthful days, and
that, unlike most parents, he was not disposed to be violently indignant when he found that his son took after him.
This may be true or not. I myself only knew the elder Mr
Holliday when he was getting on in years; and then he was
as quiet and as respectable a gentleman as ever I met with.

Well, one September, as I told you, young Arthur comes
to Doncaster, having decided all of a sudden, in his hare-
brained way, that he would go to the races. He did not reach
the town till towards the close of the evening, and he went
at once to see about his dinner and bed at the principal
hotel. Dinner they were ready enough to give him; but as for
a bed, they laughed when he mentioned it. In the race-week
at Doncaster, it is no uncommon thing for visitors who have
not bespoken apartments, to pass the night in their carriages
at the inn doors. As for the lower sort of strangers, I myself
have often seen them, at that full time, sleeping out on the
doorsteps for want of a covered place to creep under. Rich

as he was, Arthur's chance of getting a night's lodging (seeing that he had not written beforehand to secure one) was more than doubtful. He tried the second hotel, and the third hotel, and two of the inferior inns after that; and was met everywhere by the same form of answer. No accommodation for the night of any sort was left. All the bright golden sovereigns in his pocket would not buy him a bed at Doncaster in the race-week.

To a young fellow of Arthur's temperament, the novelty of being turned away into the street, like a penniless vagabond, at every house where he asked for a lodging, presented itself in the light of a new and highly amusing piece of experience. He went on, with his carpet-bag in his hand, applying for a bed at every place of entertainment for travellers that he could find in Doncaster, until he wandered into the outskirts of the town. By this time, the last glimmer of twilight had faded out, the moon was rising dimly in a mist, the wind was getting cold, the clouds were gathering heavily, and there was every prospect that it was soon going to rain.

The look of the night had rather a lowering effect on young Holliday's good spirits. He began to contemplate the houseless situation in which he was placed, from the serious rather than the humorous point of view; and he looked about him, for another public-house to enquire at, with something very like downright anxiety in his mind on the subject of a lodging for the night. The suburban part of the town towards which he had now strayed was hardly lighted at all, and he could see nothing of the houses as he passed them, except that they got progressively smaller and dirtier, the farther he went. Down the winding road before him shone the dull gleam of an oil lamp, the one faint, lonely light that struggled ineffectually with the foggy darkness all round him. He resolved to go on as far as this lamp, and then, if it showed him nothing in the shape of an Inn, to return to the central part of the town and to try if he could not at least secure a chair to sit down on, through the night, at one of the principal Hotels.

As he got near the lamp, he heard voices; and, walking close under it, found that it lighted the entrance to a narrow court, on the wall of which was painted a long hand in faded flesh-colour, pointing, with a lean fore-finger, to this inscription:—

THE TWO ROBINS.

Arthur turned into the court without hesitation, to see what The Two Robins could do for him. Four or five men were standing together round the door of the house which was at the bottom of the court, facing the entrance from the street. The men were all listening to one other man, better dressed than the rest, who was telling his audience something, in a low voice, in which they were apparently very much interested.

On entering the passage, Arthur was passed by a stranger with a knapsack in his hand, who was evidently leaving the house.

'No,' said the traveller with the knapsack, turning round and addressing himself cheerfully to a fat, sly-looking, bald-headed man, with a dirty white apron on, who had followed him down the passage. 'No, Mr Landlord, I am not easily scared by trifles; but, I don't mind confessing that I can't quite stand *that*.'

It occurred to young Holliday, the moment he heard these words, that the stranger had been asked an exorbitant price for a bed at The Two Robins; and that he was unable or unwilling to pay it. The moment his back was turned, Arthur, comfortably conscious of his own well-filled pockets, addressed himself in a great hurry, for fear any other benighted traveller should slip in and forestall him, to the sly-looking landlord with the dirty apron and the bald head.

'If you have got a bed to let,' he said, 'and if that gentleman who has just gone out won't pay you your price for it, I will.'

The sly landlord looked hard at Arthur.

'Will you, sir?' he asked, in a meditative, doubtful way.

'Name your price,' said young Holliday, thinking that the landlord's hesitation sprang from some boorish distrust of him. 'Name your price, and I'll give you the money at once, if you like?'

'Are you game for five shillings?' enquired the landlord, rubbing his stubbly double chin, and looking up thoughtfully at the ceiling above him.

Arthur nearly laughed in the man's face; but thinking it prudent to control himself, offered the five shillings as seriously as he could. The sly landlord held out his hand, then suddenly drew it back again.

'You're acting all fair and above-board by me,' he said: 'and, before I take your money, I'll do the same by you. Look here, this is how it stands. You can have a bed all to yourself for five shillings; but you can't have more than a half-share of the room it stands in. Do you see what I mean, young gentleman?'

'Of course I do,' returned Arthur, a little irritably. 'You mean that it is a double-bedded room, and that one of the beds is occupied?'

The landlord nodded his head, and rubbed his double chin harder than ever. Arthur hesitated, and mechanically moved back a step or two towards the door. The idea of sleeping in the same room with a total stranger, did not present an attractive prospect to him. He felt more than half-inclined to drop his five shillings into his pocket, and to go out into the street once more.

'Is it yes, or no?' asked the landlord. 'Settle it as quick as you can, because there's lots of people wanting a bed at Doncaster tonight, besides you.'

Arthur looked towards the court, and heard the rain falling heavily in the street outside. He thought he would ask a question or two before he rashly decided on leaving the shelter of The Two Robins.

'What sort of a man is it who has got the other bed?' he inquired. 'Is he a gentleman? I mean, is he a quiet, well-behaved person?'

'The quietest man I ever came across,' said the landlord, rubbing his fat hands stealthily one over the other. 'As sober as a judge, and as regular as clock-work in his habits. It hasn't struck nine, not ten minutes ago, and he's in his bed already. I don't know whether that comes up to your notion of a quiet man: it goes a long way ahead of mine, I can tell you.'

'Is he asleep, do you think?' asked Arthur.

'I know he's asleep,' returned the landlord. 'And what's more, he's gone off so fast, that I'll warrant you don't wake him. This way, sir,' said the landlord, speaking over young Holliday's shoulder, as if he was addressing some new guest who was approaching the house.

'Here you are,' said Arthur, determined to be beforehand with the stranger, whoever he might be. 'I'll take the bed.' And he handed the five shillings to the landlord, who nodded, dropped the money carelessly into his waistcoat-pocket, and lighted a candle.

'Come up and see the room,' said the host of The Two Robins, leading the way to the staircase quite briskly, considering how fat he was.

They mounted to the second-floor of the house. The landlord half opened a door, fronting the landing, then stopped, and turned round to Arthur.

'It's a fair bargain, mind, on my side as well as on yours,' he said. 'You give me five shillings, I give you in return a clean, comfortable bed; and I warrant, beforehand, that you won't be interfered with, or annoyed in any way, by the man who sleeps in the same room with you.' Saying those words, he looked hard, for a moment, in young Holliday's face, and then led the way into the room.

It was larger and cleaner than Arthur had expected it would be. The two beds stood parallel with each other—a space of about six feet intervening between them. They were both of the same medium size, and both had the same plain white curtains, made to draw, if necessary, all round them. The occupied bed was the bed nearest the window. The curtains were all drawn round this, except the half curtain at the bottom, on the side of the bed farthest from the window. Arthur saw the feet of the sleeping man raising the scanty clothes into a sharp little eminence, as if he was lying flat on his back. He took the candle, and advanced softly to draw the curtain—stopped half way, and listened for a moment—then turned to the landlord.

'He is a very quiet sleeper,' said Arthur.

'Yes,' said the landlord, 'very quiet.'

Young Holliday advanced with the candle, and looked in at the man cautiously.

'How pale he is!' said Arthur.

'Yes,' returned the landlord, 'pale enough, isn't he?'

Arthur looked closer at the man. The bed-clothes were drawn up to his chin, and they lay perfectly still over the region of his chest. Surprised and vaguely startled, as he noticed this, Arthur stooped down closer over the stranger; looked at his ashy, parted lips; listened breathlessly for an instant; looked again at the strangely still face, and the motionless lips and chest; and turned round suddenly on the landlord, with his own cheeks as pale for the moment as the hollow cheeks of the man on the bed.

'Come here,' he whispered, under his breath. 'Come here, for God's sake! The man's not asleep—he is dead!'

'You have found that out sooner than I thought you would,' said the landlord composedly. 'Yes, he's dead, sure enough. He died at five o'clock today.'

'How did he die? Who is he?' asked Arthur, staggered, for the moment, by the audacious coolness of the answer.

'As to who is he,' rejoined the landlord, 'I know no more about him than you do. There are his books and letters and things, all sealed up in that brown paper parcel, for the Coroner's inquest to open tomorrow or next day. He's been here a week, paying his way fairly enough, and stopping indoors, for the most part, as if he was ailing. My girl brought him up his tea at five today; and as he was pouring of it out, he fell down in a faint, or a fit, or a compound of both, for anything I know. We could not bring him to—and I said he was dead. And the doctor couldn't bring him to—and the doctor said he was dead. And there he is. And the Coroner's inquest's coming as soon as it can. And that's as much as I know about it.'

Arthur held the candle close to the man's lips. The flame still burnt straight up, as steadily as ever. There was a moment of silence; and the rain pattered drearily through it against the panes of the window.

'If you haven't got nothing more to say to me,' continued the landlord, 'I suppose I may go. You don't expect your five shillings back, do you? There's the bed I promised you, clean and comfortable. There's the man I warranted not to disturb you, quiet in this world for ever. If you're frightened to stop alone with him, that's not my look out. I've kept my part of the bargain, and I mean to keep the money. I'm not Yorkshire, myself, young gentleman; but I've lived long enough in these parts to have my wits sharpened; and I shouldn't wonder if you found out the way to brighten up yours, next time you come among us.' With these words, the landlord turned towards the door, and laughed to himself softly, in high satisfaction at his own sharpness.

Startled and shocked as he was, Arthur had by this time sufficiently recovered himself to feel indignant at the trick that had been played on him, and at the insolent manner in which the landlord exulted in it.

'Don't laugh,' he said sharply, 'till you are quite sure you have got the laugh against me. You shan't have the five shillings for nothing, my man. I'll keep the bed.'

'Will you?' said the landlord. 'Then I wish you a good night's rest.' With that brief farewell, he went out, and shut the door after him.

A good night's rest! The words had hardly been spoken, the door had hardly been closed, before Arthur half-repented the hasty words that had just escaped him. Though not naturally over-sensitive, and not wanting in courage of the moral as well as the physical sort, the presence of the dead man had an instantaneously chilling effect on his mind when he found himself alone in the room—alone, and bound by his own rash words to stay there till the next morning. An older man would have thought nothing of those words, and would have acted, without reference to them, as his calmer sense suggested. But Arthur was too young to treat the ridicule, even of his inferiors, with contempt—too young not to fear the momentary humiliation of falsifying his own foolish boast, more than he feared the trial of watching out the long night in the same chamber with the dead.

'It is but a few hours,' he thought to himself, 'and I can get away the first thing in the morning.'

He was looking towards the occupied bed as that idea passed through his mind, and the sharp angular eminence made in the clothes by the dead man's upturned feet again caught his eye. He advanced and drew the curtains, purposely abstaining, as he did so, from looking at the face of the corpse, lest he might unnerve himself at the outset by fastening some ghastly impression of it on his mind. He drew the curtain very gently, and sighed involuntarily as he closed it. 'Poor fellow,' he said, almost as sadly as if he had known the man. 'Ah, poor fellow!'

He went next to the window. The night was black, and he could see nothing from it. The rain still pattered heavily against the glass. He inferred, from hearing it, that the window was at the back of the house; remembering that the front was sheltered from the weather by the court and the buildings over it.

While he was still standing at the window—for even the dreary rain was a relief, because of the sound it made; a relief, also, because it moved, and had some faint suggestion, in consequence, of life and companionship in it—while he was standing at the window, and looking vacantly into the black darkness outside, he heard a distant church-clock strike ten. Only ten! How was he to pass the time till the house was astir the next morning?

Under any other circumstances, he would have gone down to the public-house parlour, would have called for his grog, and would have laughed and talked with the company assembled as familiarly as if he had known them all his life. But the very thought of whiling away the time in this manner was now distasteful to him. The new situation in which he was placed seemed to have altered him to himself already. Thus far, his life had been the common, trifling, prosaic, surface-life of a prosperous young man, with no troubles to conquer, and no trials to face. He had lost no relation whom he loved, no friend whom he treasured. Till this night, what share he had of the immortal inheritance that is divided amongst us all, had lain dormant within him. Till this night, Death and he had not once met, even in thought.

He took a few turns up and down the room—then stopped. The noise made by his boots on the poorly carpeted floor, jarred on his ear. He hesitated a little, and ended by taking the boots off, and walking backwards and forwards noiselessly. All desire to sleep or to rest had left him. The bare thought of lying down on the unoccupied bed instantly drew the picture on his mind of a dreadful mimicry of the position of the dead man. Who was he? What was the story of his past life? Poor he must have been, or he would not have stopped at such a place as The Two Robins Inn—and weakened, probably, by long illness, or he could hardly have died in the manner which the landlord had described. Poor, ill, lonely,—dead in a strange place; dead, with nobody but a stranger to pity him. A sad story: truly, on the mere face of it, a very sad story.

While these thoughts were passing through his mind, he had stopped insensibly at the window, close to which stood the foot of the bed with the closed curtains. At first he looked at it absently; then he became conscious that his eyes were fixed on it; and then, a perverse desire took possession of him to do the very thing which he had resolved not to do, up to this time—to look at the dead man.

He stretched out his hand towards the curtains; but checked himself in the very act of undrawing them, turned his back sharply on the bed, and walked towards the chimney-piece, to see what things were placed on it, and to try if he could keep the dead man out of his mind in that way.

There was a pewter inkstand on the chimney-piece, with some mildewed remains of ink in the bottle. There were two coarse china ornaments of the commonest kind; and there was a square of embossed card, dirty and fly-blown, with a collection of wretched riddles printed on it, in all sorts of zig-zag directions, and in variously coloured inks. He took the card, and went away, to read it, to the table on which the candle was placed; sitting down, with his back resolutely turned to the curtained bed.

He read the first riddle, the second, the third, all in one corner of the card—then turned it round impatiently to look at another. Before he could begin reading the riddles printed here, the sound of the church-clock stopped him. Eleven. He had got through an hour of the time, in the room with the dead man.

Once more he looked at the card. It was not easy to make out the letters printed on it, in consequence of the dimness of the light which the landlord had left him—a common tallow candle, furnished with a pair of heavy old-fashioned steel snuffers. Up to this time, his mind had been too much occupied to think of the light. He had left the wick of the candle unsnuffed, till it had risen higher than the flame, and had burnt into an odd pent-house shape at the top, from which morsels of the charred cotton fell off, from time to time, in little flakes. He took up the snuffers now, and trimmed the wick. The light brightened directly, and the room became less dismal.

Again he turned to the riddles; reading them doggedly and resolutely, now in one corner of the card, now in another. All his efforts, however, could not fix his attention on them. He pursued his occupation mechanically, deriving no sort of impression from what he was reading. It was as if a shadow from the curtained bed had got between his mind and the gaily printed letters—a shadow that nothing could dispel. At last, he gave up the struggle, and threw the card from him impatiently, and took to walking softly up and down the room again.

The dead man, the dead man, the *hidden* dead man on the bed! There was the one persistent idea still haunting him. Hidden! Was it only the body being there, or was it the body being there, concealed, that was preying on his mind? He stopped at the window, with that doubt in him; once more listening to the pattering rain, once more looking out into the black darkness.

Still the dead man! The darkness forced his mind back upon itself, and set his memory at work, reviving, with a painfully-vivid distinctness the momentary impression it had received from his first sight of the corpse. Before long the face seemed to be hovering out in the middle of the darkness, confronting him through the window, with the paleness whiter, with the dreadful dull line of light between the imperfectly-closed eyelids broader than he had seen it—with the parted lips slowly dropping farther and farther away from each other—with the features growing larger and moving closer, till they seemed to fill the window and to silence the rain, and to shut out the night.

The sound of a voice, shouting below stairs, woke him suddenly from the dream of his own distempered fancy. He recognised it as the voice of the landlord. 'Shut up at twelve, Ben,' he heard it say. 'I'm off to bed.'

He wiped away the damp that had gathered on his forehead, reasoned with himself for a little while, and resolved to shake his mind free of the ghastly counterfeit which still clung to it, by forcing himself to confront, if it was only for a moment, the solemn reality. Without allowing himself an instant to hesitate, he parted the curtains at the foot of the bed, and looked through.

There was the sad, peaceful, white face, with the awful mystery of stillness on it, laid back upon the pillow. No stir, no change there! He only looked at it for a moment before he closed the curtains again—but that moment steadied him, calmed him, restored him—mind and body—to himself.

He returned to his old occupation of walking up and down the room; persevering in it, this time, till the clock struck again. Twelve.

As the sound of the clock-bell died away, it was succeeded by the confused noise, downstairs, of the drinkers in the tap-room leaving the house. The next sound, after an interval of silence, was caused by the barring of the door, and the closing of the shutters, at the back of the Inn. Then the silence followed again, and was disturbed no more.

He was alone now—absolutely, utterly, alone with the dead man, till the next morning.

The wick of the candle wanted trimming again. He took up the snuffers—but paused suddenly on the very point of using them, and looked attentively at the candle—then back, over his shoulder, at the curtained bed—then again at the candle. It had been lighted, for the first time, to show him the way upstairs, and three parts of it, at least, were already consumed. In another hour it would be burnt out. In another hour—unless he called at once to the man who had shut up the Inn, for a fresh candle—he would be left in the dark.

Strongly as his mind had been affected since he had entered the room, his unreasonable dread of encountering ridicule, and of exposing his courage to suspicion, had not altogether lost its influence over him, even yet. He lingered irresolutely by the table, waiting till he could prevail on himself to open the door, and call, from the landing, to the man who had shut up the Inn. In his present hesitating frame of mind, it was a kind of relief to gain a few moments only by engaging in the trifling occupation of snuffing the candle. His hand trembled a little, and the snuffers were heavy and awkward to use. When he closed them on the wick, he closed them a hair's breadth too low. In an instant the candle was out, and the room was plunged in pitch darkness.

The one impression which the absence of light immediately produced on his mind, was distrust of the curtained bed—distrust which shaped itself into no distinct idea, but which was powerful enough, in its very vagueness, to bind him down to his chair, to make his heart beat fast, and to set him listening intently. No sound stirred in the room but the familiar sound of the rain against the window, louder and sharper now than he had heard it yet.

Still the vague distrust, the inexpressible dread possessed him, and kept him in his chair. He had put his carpet-bag on the table, when he first entered the room; and he now took the key from his pocket, reached out his hand softly, opened the bag, and groped in it for his travelling writing-case, in which he knew that there was a small store of matches. When he had got one of the matches, he waited before he struck it on the coarse wooden table, and listened intently again, without knowing why. Still there was no sound in the room but the steady, ceaseless, rattling sound of the rain.

He lighted the candle again, without another moment of delay; and, on the instant of its burning up, the first object in the room that his eyes sought for was the curtained bed.

Just before the light had been put out, he had looked in that direction, and had seen no change, no disarrangement of any sort, in the folds of the closely-drawn curtains.

When he looked at the bed, now, he saw, hanging over the side of it, a long white hand.

It lay perfectly motionless, midway on the side of the bed, where the curtain at the head and the curtain at the foot met. Nothing more was visible. The clinging curtains hid everything but the long white hand.

He stood looking at it unable to stir, unable to call out; feeling nothing, knowing nothing; every faculty he possessed gathered up and lost in the one seeing faculty. How long that first panic held him he never could tell afterwards. It might have been only for a moment; it might have been for many minutes together. How he got to the bed—whether he ran to it headlong, or whether he approached it slowly—how he wrought himself up to unclose the curtains and look in, he never has remembered, and never will remember to his dying day. It is enough that he did go to the bed, and that he did look inside the curtains.

The man had moved. One of his arms was outside the clothes; his face was turned a little on the pillow; his eyelids were wide open. Changed as to position, and as to one of the features, the face was otherwise, fearfully and wonderfully unaltered. The dead paleness and the dead quiet were on it still.

One glance showed Arthur this—one glance, before he flew breathlessly to the door, and alarmed the house.

The man whom the landlord called 'Ben,' was the first to appear on the stairs. In three words, Arthur told him what had happened, and sent him for the nearest doctor.

I, who tell you this story, was then staying with a medical friend of mine, in practice at Doncaster, taking care of his patients for him, during his absence in London; and I, for the time being, was the nearest doctor. They had sent for me from the Inn, when the stranger was taken ill in the afternoon; but I was not at home, and medical assistance was sought for elsewhere. When the man from The Two Robins rang the night-bell, I was just thinking of going to bed. Naturally enough, I did not believe a word of his story about 'a dead man who had come to life again.' However, I put on my hat, armed myself with one or two bottles of restorative medicine, and ran to the Inn, expecting to find nothing more remarkable, when I got there, than a patient in a fit.

My surprise at finding that the man had spoken the literal truth was almost, if not quite, equalled by my astonishment at finding myself face to face with Arthur Holliday as soon as I entered the bedroom. It was no time then for giving or seeking explanations. We just shook hands amazedly; and then I ordered everybody but Arthur out of the room, and hurried to the man on the bed.

The kitchen fire had not been long out. There was plenty of hot water in the boiler, and plenty of flannel to be had. With these, with my medicines, and with such help as Arthur could render under my direction, I dragged the man, literally, out of the jaws of death. In less than an hour from the time when I had been called in, he was alive and talking in the bed on which he had been laid out to wait for the Coroner's inquest.

You will naturally ask me, what had been the matter with him; and I might treat you, in reply, to a long theory, plentifully sprinkled with, what the children call, hard words. I prefer telling you that, in this case, cause and effect could not be satisfactorily joined together by any theory whatever. There are mysteries in life, and the conditions of it, which human science has not fathomed yet; and I candidly confess to you, that, in bringing that man back to existence, I was, morally speaking, groping haphazard in the dark. I know (from the testimony of the doctor who attended him in the afternoon) that the vital machinery, so far as its action is appreciable by our senses, had, in this case, unquestionably stopped; and I am equally certain (seeing that I recovered him) that the vital principle was not extinct. When I add, that he had suffered from a long and complicated illness, and that his whole nervous system was utterly deranged, I have told you all I really know of the physical condition of my dead-alive patient at the Two Robins Inn.

When he 'came to,' as the phrase goes, he was a startling object to look at, with his colourless face, his sunken cheeks, his wild black eyes, and his long black hair. The first question he asked me about himself, when he could speak, made me suspect that I had been called in to a man in my own profession. I mentioned to him my surmise; and he told me that I was right.

He said he had come last from Paris, where he had been attached to a hospital. That he had lately returned to England, on his way to Edinburgh, to continue his studies; that he had been taken ill on the journey; and that he had stopped to rest and recover himself at Doncaster. He did not add a word about his name, or who he was: and, of course, I did not question him on the subject. All I inquired, when he ceased speaking, was what branch of the profession he intended to follow.

'Any branch,' he said bitterly, 'which will put bread into the mouth of a poor man.'

At this, Arthur, who had been hitherto watching him in silent curiosity, burst out impetuously in his usual good-humoured way:—

'My dear fellow!' (everybody was 'my dear fellow' with Arthur) 'now you have come to life again, don't begin by being down-hearted about your prospects. I'll answer for it, I can help you to some capital thing in the medical line—or, if I can't, I know my father can.'

The medical student looked at him steadily.

'Thank you,' he said coldly. Then added, 'May I ask who your father is?'

'He's well enough known all about this part of the country,' replied Arthur. 'He is a great manufacturer, and his name is Holliday.'

My hand was on the man's wrist during this brief conversation. The instant the name of Holliday was pronounced I felt the pulse under my fingers flutter, stop, go on suddenly with a bound, and beat afterwards, for a minute or two, at the fever rate.

'How did you come here?' asked the stranger, quickly, excitably, passionately almost.

Arthur related briefly what had happened from the time of his first taking the bed at the inn.

'I am indebted to Mr Holliday's son then for the help that has saved my life,' said the medical student, speaking to himself, with a singular sarcasm in his voice. 'Come here!'

He held out, as he spoke, his long, white, bony right hand.

'With all my heart,' said Arthur, taking the hand cordially. 'I may confess it now,' he continued, laughing, 'Upon my honour, you almost frightened me out of my wits.'

The stranger did not seem to listen. His wild black eyes were fixed with a look of eager interest on Arthur's face, and his long bony fingers kept tight hold of Arthur's hand. Young Holliday, on his side, returned the gaze, amazed and puzzled by the medical student's odd language and manners. The two faces were close together; I looked at them; and, to my amazement, I was suddenly impressed by the sense of a likeness between them—not in features, or complexion, but solely in expression. It must have been a strong likeness, or I should certainly not have found it out, for I am naturally slow at detecting resemblances between faces.

'You have saved my life,' said the strange man, still looking hard in Arthur's face, still holding tightly by his hand. 'If you had been my own brother, you could not have done more for me than that.'

He laid a singularly strong emphasis on those three words 'my own brother,' and a change passed over his face as he pronounced them,—a change that no language of mine is competent to describe.

'I hope I have not done being of service to you yet,' said Arthur. 'I'll speak to my father, as soon as I get home.'

'You seem to be fond and proud of your father,' said the medical student. 'I suppose, in return, he is fond and proud of you?'

'Of course, he is!' answered Arthur, laughing. 'Is there anything wonderful in that? Isn't *your* father fond—'

The stranger suddenly dropped young Holliday's hand, and turned his face away.

'I beg your pardon,' said Arthur. 'I hope I have not unintentionally pained you. I hope you have not lost your father?'

'I can't well lose what I have never had,' retorted the medical student, with a harsh mocking laugh.

'What you have never had!'

The strange man suddenly caught Arthur's hand again, suddenly looked once more hard in his face.

'Yes,' he said, with a repetition of the bitter laugh. 'You have brought a poor devil back into the world, who has no business there. Do I astonish you? Well! I have a fancy of my own for telling you what men in my situation generally keep a secret. I have no name and no father. The merciful law of Society tells me I am Nobody's Son! Ask your father if he will be my father too, and help me on in life with the family name.'

Arthur looked at me, more puzzled than ever. I signed to him to say nothing, and then laid my fingers again on the man's wrist. No! In spite of the extraordinary speech that he had just made, he was not, as I had been disposed to suspect, beginning to get light-headed. His pulse, by this time, had fallen back to a quiet, slow beat, and his skin was moist and cool. Not a symptom of fever or agitation about him.

Finding that neither of us answered him, he turned to me, and began talking of the extraordinary nature of his case, and asking my advice about the future course of medical treatment to which he ought to subject himself. I said the matter required careful thinking over, and suggested that I should submit certain prescriptions to him the next morning. He told me to write them at once, as he would, most likely, be leaving Doncaster, in the morning, before I was up. It was quite useless to represent to him the folly and danger of such a proceeding as this. He heard me politely and patiently, but held to his resolution, without offering any reasons or any explanations, and repeated to me, that if I wished to give him a chance of seeing my prescription, I must write it at once. Hearing this, Arthur volunteered the loan of a travelling writing-case, which, he said, he had with him; and, bringing it to the bed, shook the notepaper out of the pocket of the case forthwith in his usual careless way. With the paper, there fell out on the counterpane of the bed a small packet of sticking-plaster, and a little water-colour drawing of a landscape.

The medical student took up the drawing and looked at it. His eye fell on some initials neatly written, in cypher, in one corner. He started, and trembled; his pale face grew whiter than ever; his wild black eyes turned on Arthur, and looked through and through him.

'A pretty drawing,' he said, in a remarkably quiet tone of voice.

'Ah! and done by such a pretty girl,' said Arthur. 'Oh, such a pretty girl! I wish it was not a landscape—I wish it was a portrait of her!'

'You admire her very much?'

Arthur, half in jest, half in earnest, kissed his hand for answer.

'Love at first sight!' he said, putting the drawing away again. 'But the course of it doesn't run smooth. It's the old story. She's monopolised as usual. Trammelled by a rash engagement to some poor man who is never likely to get money enough to marry her. It was lucky I heard of it in time, or I should certainly have risked a declaration when she gave me that drawing. Here, doctor! Here is pen, ink, and paper all ready for you.'

'When she gave you that drawing? Gave it. Gave it.' He repeated the words slowly to himself, and suddenly closed his eyes. A momentary distortion passed across his face, and I saw one of his hands clutch up the bedclothes and squeeze them hard. I thought he was going to be ill again, and begged that there might be no more talking. He opened his eyes when I spoke, fixed them once more searchingly on Arthur, and said, slowly and distinctly, 'You like her, and she likes you. The poor man may die out of your way. Who can tell that she may not give you herself as well as her drawing, after all?'

Before young Holliday could answer, he turned to me, and said in a whisper, 'Now for the prescription.' From that time, though he spoke to Arthur again, he never looked at him more.

When I had written the prescription, he examined it, approved of it, and then astonished us both by abruptly wishing us good night. I offered to sit up with him, and he shook his head. Arthur offered to sit up with him, and he said, shortly, with his face turned away, 'No.' I insisted on having somebody left to watch him. He gave way when he found I was determined, and said he would accept the services of the waiter at the inn.

'Thank you, both,' he said, as we rose to go. 'I have one last favour to ask—not of you, doctor, for I leave you to exercise your professional discretion—but of Mr Holliday.' His eyes, while he spoke, still rested steadily on me, and never once turned towards Arthur. 'I beg that Mr Holliday will not mention to any one—least of all to his father—the events that have occurred, and the words that have passed, in this room. I entreat him to bury me in his memory, as, but for him, I might have been buried in my grave. I cannot give my reasons for making this strange request. I can only implore him to grant it.'

His voice faltered for the first time, and he hid his face on the pillow. Arthur, completely bewildered, gave the required pledge. I took young Holliday away with me, immediately afterwards, to the house of my friend; determining to go back to the inn, and to see the medical student again before he had left in the morning.

I returned to the inn at eight o'clock, purposely abstaining from waking Arthur, who was sleeping off the past night's excitement on one of my friend's sofas. A suspicion had occurred to me, as soon as I was alone in my bedroom, which made me resolve that Holliday and the stranger whose life he had saved should not meet again, if I could prevent it. I have already alluded to certain reports, or scandals, which I knew of, relating to the early life of Arthur's father. While I was thinking, in my bed, of what had passed at the Inn—of the change in the student's pulse when he heard the name of Holliday; of the resemblance of expression that I had discovered between his face and Arthur's; of the emphasis he had laid on those three words, 'my own brother;' and of his incomprehensible acknowledgment of his own illegitimacy—while I was thinking of these things, the reports I have mentioned suddenly flew into my mind, and linked themselves fast to the chain of my previous reflections. Something within me whispered, 'It is best that those two young men should not meet again.' I felt it before I slept; I felt it when I woke; and I went, as I told you, alone to the Inn the next morning.

I had missed my only opportunity of seeing my nameless patient again. He had been gone nearly an hour when I inquired for him.

I have now told you everything that I know for certain, in relation to the man whom I brought back to life in the double-bedded room of the Inn at Doncaster. What I have next to add is matter for inference and surmise, and is not, strictly speaking, matter of fact.

I have to tell you, first, that the medical student turned out to be strangely and unaccountably right in assuming it as more than probable that Arthur Holliday would marry the young lady who had given him the water-colour drawing of the landscape. That marriage took place a little more than a year after the events occurred which I have just been relating. The young couple came to live in the neighbourhood in which I was then established in practice. I was present at the wedding, and was rather surprised to find that Arthur was singularly reserved with me, both before and after his marriage, on the subject of the young lady's prior engagement. He only referred to it once, when we were alone, merely telling me, on that occasion, that his wife had done all that honour and duty required of her in the matter, and that the engagement had been broken off with the full approval of her parents. I never heard more from him than this. For three years he and his wife lived together happily. At the expiration of that time, the symptoms of a serious illness first declared themselves in Mrs Arthur Holliday. It turned out to be a long, lingering, hopeless malady. I attended her throughout. We had been great friends when she was well, and we became more attached to each other than ever when she was ill. I had many long and interesting conversations with her in the intervals when she suffered least. The result of one of those conversations I may briefly

relate, leaving you to draw any inferences from it that you
please.

The interview to which I refer, occurred shortly before
her death. I called one evening, as usual, and found her
alone, with a look in her eyes which told me that she had
been crying. She only informed me at first, that she had been
depressed in spirits; but, by little and little, she became
more communicative, and confessed to me that she had
been looking over some old letters, which had been addressed to her, before she had seen Arthur, by a man to
whom she had been engaged to be married. I asked her how
the engagement came to be broken off. She replied that it
had not been broken off, but that it had died out in a very
mysterious way. The person to whom she was engaged—her
first love, she called him—was very poor, and there was no
immediate prospect of their being married. He followed my
profession, and went abroad to study. They had corresponded regularly, until the time when, as she believed, he
had returned to England. From that period she heard no
more of him. He was of a fretful, sensitive temperament;
and she feared that she might have inadvertently done or
said something that offended him. However that might be,
he had never written to her again; and, after waiting a year,
she had married Arthur. I asked when the first estrangement
had begun, and found that the time at which she ceased to
hear anything of her first lover exactly corresponded with
the time at which I had been called in to my mysterious
patient at The Two Robins Inn.

A fortnight after that conversation, she died. In course of
time, Arthur married again. Of late years, he has lived principally in London, and I have seen little or nothing of him.

I have many years to pass over before I can approach to
anything like a conclusion of this fragmentary narrative.
And even when that later period is reached, the little that I
have to say will not occupy your attention for more than a
few minutes. Between six and seven years ago, the gentleman to whom I introduced you in this room, came to me,
with good professional recommendations, to fill the position of my assistant. We met, not like strangers, but like

friends —the only difference between us being, that I was very much surprised to see him, and that he did not appear to be at all surprised to see me. If he was my son, or my brother, I believe he could not be fonder of me than he is; but he has never volunteered any confidences since he has been here, on the subject of his past life. I saw something that was familiar to me in his face when we first met; and yet it was also something that suggested the idea of change. I had a notion once that my patient at the Inn might be a natural son of Mr Holliday's; I had another idea that he might also have been the man who was engaged to Arthur's first wife; and I have a third idea, still clinging to me, that Mr Lorn is the only man in England who could really enlighten me, if he chose, on both those doubtful points. His hair is not black, now, and his eyes are dimmer than the piercing eyes that I remember, but, for all that, he is very like the nameless medical student of my young days—very like him. And, sometimes, when I come home late at night, and find him asleep, and wake him, he looks, in coming to, wonderfully like the stranger at Doncaster, as he raised himself in the bed on that memorable night!

THE BITER BIT

FROM CHIEF INSPECTOR THEAKSTONE, OF THE
DETECTIVE POLICE, TO SERGEANT BULMER,
OF THE SAME FORCE.

London, 4th July, 18—.

SERGEANT BULMER,

This is to inform you that you are wanted to assist in
looking up a case of importance, which will require all the
attention of an experienced member of the force. The matter of the robbery on which you are now engaged you will
please to shift over to the young man who brings you this
letter. You will tell him all the circumstances of the case,
just as they stand; you will put him up to the progress you
have made (if any) towards detecting the person or persons
by whom the money has been stolen; and you will leave him
to make the best he can of the matter now in your hands. He
is to have the whole responsibility of the case, and the whole
credit of his success, if he brings it to a proper issue.

So much for the orders that I am desired to communicate
to you. A word in your ear, next, about this new man who
is to take your place. His name is Matthew Sharpin; and
between ourselves, Sergeant, I don't think much of him. He
has not served his time among the rank and file of the force.
You and I mounted up, step by step, to the places we now
fill; but this stranger, it seems, is to have the chance given
him of dashing into our office at one jump,—supposing he
turns out strong enough to take it. You will naturally ask me
how he comes by this privilege. I can only tell you, that he
has some uncommonly strong interest to back him in certain high quarters, which you and I had better not mention
except under our breath. He has been a lawyer's clerk; and
he looks, to my mind, rather a mean, underhand sample of
that sort of man. According to his own account,—by the
bye, I forgot to say that he is wonderfully conceited in his
opinion of himself, as well as mean and underhand to look

at,—according to his own account, he leaves his old trade and joins ours of his own free will and preference. You will no more believe that than I do. My notion is, that he has managed to ferret out some private information, in connection with the affairs of one of his master's clients, which makes him rather an awkward customer to keep in the office for the future, and which, at the same time, gives him hold enough over his employer to make it dangerous to drive him into a corner by turning him away. I think the giving him this unheard-of chance among us is, in plain words, pretty much like giving him hush-money to keep him quiet. However that may be, Mr Matthew Sharpin is to have the case now in your hands; and if he succeeds with it, he pokes his ugly nose into our office, as sure as fate. You have heard tell of some sad stuff they have been writing lately in the newspapers, about improving the efficiency of the Detective Police by mixing up a sharp lawyer's clerk or two along with them. Well, the experiment is now going to be tried; and Mr Matthew Sharpin is the first lucky man who has been pitched on for the purpose. We shall see how this precious move succeeds. I put you up to it, Sergeant, so that you may not stand in your own light by giving the new man any cause to complain of you at head-quarters, and remain yours,

FRANCIS THEAKSTONE.

FROM MR MATTHEW SHARPIN TO CHIEF
INSPECTOR THEAKSTONE

London, 5th July, 18—.

DEAR SIR,

Having now been favoured with the necessary instructions from Sergeant Bulmer, I beg to remind you of certain directions which I have received, relating to the report of my future proceedings, which I am to prepare for examination at head-quarters.

The document in question is to be addressed to you. It is to be not only a daily report, but an hourly report as well, when circumstances may require it. All statements which I send to you, in this way, you are, as I understand, expected to examine carefully before you seal them up and send them in to the higher authorities. The object of my writing and of your examining what I have written is, I am informed, to give me, as an untried hand, the benefit of your advice, in case I want it (which I venture to think I shall not) at any stage of my proceedings. As the extraordinary circumstances of the case on which I am now engaged make it impossible for me to absent myself from the place where the robbery was committed, until I have made some progress towards discovering the thief, I am necessarily precluded from consulting you personally. Hence the necessity of my writing down the various details, which might, perhaps, be better communicated by word of mouth. This, if I am not mistaken, is the position in which we are now placed. I state my own impressions on the subject, in writing, in order that we may clearly understand each other at the outset,—and have the honour to remain your obedient servant,

MATTHEW SHARPIN.

FROM CHIEF INSPECTOR THEAKSTONE TO MR MATTHEW SHARPIN.

London, 5th July, 18—.

SIR,

You have begun by wasting time, ink, and paper. We both of us perfectly well knew the position we stood in towards each other, when I sent you with my letter to Sergeant Bulmer. There was not the least need to repeat it in writing. Be so good as to employ your pen, in future, on the business actually in hand. You have now three separate matters on which to write me. First, you have to draw up a statement of your instructions received from Sergeant Bulmer, in order to show us that nothing has escaped your memory, and that you are thoroughly acquainted with all the circumstances of the case which has been entrusted to you. Secondly, you are to inform me what it is you propose to do. Thirdly, you are to report every inch of your progress, (if you make any) from day to day, and, if need be, from hour to hour as well. This is your duty. As to what *my* duty may be, when I want you to remind me of it, I will write and tell you so. In the mean time I remain yours,

FRANCIS THEAKSTONE.

FROM MR MATTHEW SHARPIN TO CHIEF INSPECTOR THEAKSTONE.

London, 6th July, 18—.

SIR,

You are rather an elderly person, and, as such, naturally inclined to be a little jealous of men like me, who are in the prime of their lives and their faculties. Under these circumstances, it is my duty to be considerate towards you, and not to bear too hardly on your small failings. I decline, therefore, altogether, to take offence at the tone of your letter; I give you the full benefit of the natural generosity of my nature; I sponge the very existence of your surly communication out of my memory; in short, Chief Inspector Theakstone, I forgive you, and proceed to business.

My first duty is to draw up a full statement of the instructions I have received from Sergeant Bulmer. Here they are at your service, according to my version of them.

At Number Thirteen, Rutherford Street, Soho, there is a stationer's shop. It is kept by one Mr Yatman. He is a married man, but has no family. Besides Mr and Mrs Yatman, the other inmates of the house are a lodger, a young single man named Jay, who occupies the front room on the second floor,—a shopman, who sleeps in one of the attics,—and a servant-of-all-work, whose bed is in the back-kitchen. Once a week a charwoman comes to help this servant. These are all the persons who, on ordinary occasions, have means of access to the interior of the house, placed, as a matter of course, at their disposal.

Mr Yatman has been in business for many years,—carrying on his affairs prosperously enough to realise a handsome independence for a person in his position. Unfor-

tunately for himself, he endeavoured to increase the amount
of his property by speculating. He ventured boldly in his
investments, luck went against him, and rather less than two
years ago he found himself a poor man again. All that was
saved out of the wreck of his property was the sum of two
hundred pounds.

Although Mr Yatman did his best to meet his altered
circumstances, by giving up many of the luxuries and com-
forts to which he and his wife had been accustomed, he
found it impossible to retrench so far as to allow of putting
by any money from the income produced by his shop. The
business has been declining of late years,—the cheap adver-
tising stationers having done it injury with the public. Consequently, up to the last week, the only surplus property
possessed by Mr Yatman consisted of the two hundred
pounds which had been recovered from the wreck of his
fortune. This sum was placed as a deposit in a joint-stock
bank of the highest possible character.

Eight days ago, Mr Yatman and his lodger, Mr Jay, held
a conversation together on the subject of the commercial
difficulties, which are hampering trade in all directions at
the present time. Mr Jay (who lives by supplying the newspapers with short paragraphs relating to accidents, offences,
and brief records of remarkable occurrences in general,—
who is, in short, what they call a penny-a-liner) told his
landlord that he had been in the city that day, and heard
unfavourable rumours on the subject of the joint-stock
banks. The rumours to which he alluded had already reached
the ears of Mr Yatman from other quarters; and the con-
firmation of them by his lodger had such an effect on his
mind,—predisposed, as it was, to alarm, by the experience
of his former losses,—that he resolved to go at once to the
bank and withdraw his deposit. It was then getting on
towards the end of the afternoon; and he arrived just in time
to receive his money before the bank closed.

He received the deposit in bank-notes of the following
amounts:—one fifty-pound note, three twenty-pound notes,
six ten-pound notes, and six five-pound notes. His object in
drawing the money in this form was to have it ready to lay

out immediately in trifling loans, on good security, among the small tradespeople of his district,—some of whom are sorely pressed for the very means of existence at the present time. Investments of this kind seemed to Mr Yatman to be the most safe and the most profitable on which he could now venture.

He brought the money back in an envelope placed in his breast pocket; and asked his shopman, on getting home, to look for a small flat tin cash-box, which had not been used for years, and which, as Mr Yatman remembered it, was exactly of the right size to hold the bank-notes. For some time the cash-box was searched for in vain. Mr Yatman called to his wife to know if she had any idea where it was. The question was overheard by the servant-of-all-work, who was taking up the tea-tray at the time, and by Mr Jay, who was coming downstairs on his way out to the theatre. Ultimately the cash-box was found by the shopman. Mr Yatman placed the bank-notes in it, secured them by a padlock, and put the box in his coat pocket. It stuck out of the coat pocket a very little, but enough to be seen. Mr Yatman remained at home, upstairs, all that evening. No visitors called. At eleven o'clock he went to bed, and put the cash-box under his pillow.

When he and his wife woke the next morning, the box was gone. Payment of the notes was immediately stopped at the Bank of England; but no news of the money has been heard of since that time.

So far, the circumstances of the case are perfectly clear. They point unmistakably to the conclusion that the robbery must have been committed by some person living in the house. Suspicion falls, therefore, upon the servant-of-all-work, upon the shopman, and upon Mr Jay. The two first knew that the cash-box was being inquired for by their master, but did not know what it was he wanted to put into it. They would assume, of course, that it was money. They both had opportunities (the servant, when she took away the tea,—and the shopman, when he came, after shutting up, to give the keys of the till to his master) of seeing the cash-box in Mr Yatman's pocket, and of inferring naturally, from its position there, that he intended to take it into his bedroom with him at night.

Mr Jay, on the other hand, had been told, during the afternoon's conversation on the subject of joint-stock banks, that his landlord had a deposit of two hundred pounds in one of them. He also knew that Mr Yatman left him with the intention of drawing that money out; and he heard the inquiry for the cash-box, afterwards, when he was coming downstairs. He must, therefore, have inferred that the money was in the house, and that the cash-box was the receptacle intended to contain it. That he could have had any idea, however, of the place in which Mr Yatman intended to keep it for the night is impossible, seeing that he went out before the box was found, and did not return till his landlord was in bed. Consequently, if he committed the robbery, he must have gone into the bedroom purely on speculation.

Speaking of the bedroom reminds me of the necessity of noticing the situation of it in the house, and the means that exist of gaining easy access to it at any hour of the night. The room in question is the back room on the first floor. In consequence of Mrs Yatman's constitutional nervousness on the subject of fire, which makes her apprehend being burnt alive in her room, in case of accident, by the hampering of the lock, if the key is turned in it, her husband has never been accustomed to lock the bedroom door. Both he and his wife are, by their own admission, heavy sleepers. Consequently, the risk to be run by any evil-disposed persons wishing to plunder the bedroom was of the most trifling kind. They could enter the room by merely turning the handle of the door; and if they moved with ordinary caution, there was no fear of their waking the sleepers inside. This fact is of importance. It strengthens our conviction that the money must have been taken by one of the inmates of the house, because it tends to show that the robbery, in this case, might have been committed by persons not possessed of the superior vigilance and cunning of the experienced thief.

Such are the circumstances, as they were related to Sergeant Bulmer, when he was first called in to discover the guilty parties, and, if possible, to recover the lost bank-notes. The strictest inquiry which he could institute failed of producing the smallest fragment of evidence against any of the persons on whom suspicion naturally fell. Their language and behaviour, on being informed of the robbery, was perfectly consistent with the language and behaviour of innocent people. Sergeant Bulmer felt, from the first, that this was a case for private inquiry and secret observation. He began by recommending Mr and Mrs Yatman to affect a feeling of perfect confidence in the innocence of the persons living under their roof; and he then opened the campaign by employing himself in following the goings and comings, and in discovering the friends, the habits, and the secrets of the maid-of-all-work.

Three days and nights of exertion on his own part, and on that of others who were competent to assist his investigations, were enough to satisfy him that there was no sound cause for suspicion against the girl.

He next practised the same precautions in relation to the shopman. There was more difficulty and uncertainty in privately clearing up this person's character without his knowledge, but the obstacles were at last smoothed away with tolerable success; and though there is not the same amount of certainty, in this case, which there was in the case of the girl, there is still fair reason for believing that the shopman has had nothing to do with the robbery of the cash-box.

As a necessary consequence of these proceedings, the range of suspicion now becomes limited to the lodger, Mr Jay. When I presented your letter of introduction to Sergeant Bulmer, he had already made some inquiries on the subject of this young man. The result, so far, has not been at all favourable. Mr Jay's habits are irregular; he frequents public houses, and seems to be familiarly acquainted with a great many dissolute characters; he is in debt to most of the tradespeople whom he employs; he has not paid his rent to Mr Yatman for the last month; yesterday evening he came home excited by liquor, and last week he was seen talking to a prize-fighter. In short, though Mr Jay does call himself a journalist, in virtue of his penny-a-line contributions to the newspapers, he is a young man of low tastes, vulgar manners, and bad habits. Nothing has yet been discovered, in relation to him, which redounds to his credit in the smallest degree.

I have now reported, down to the very last details, all the particulars communicated to me by Sergeant Bulmer. I believe you will not find an omission anywhere; and I think you will admit, though you are prejudiced against me, that a clearer statement of facts was never laid before you than the statement I have now made. My next duty is to tell you what I propose to do, now that the case is confided to my hands.

In the first place, it is clearly my business to take up the case at the point where Sergeant Bulmer has left it. On his authority, I am justified in assuming that I have no need to trouble myself about the maid-of-all-work and the shopman. Their characters are now to be considered as cleared up. What remains to be privately investigated is the question of the guilt or innocence of Mr Jay. Before we give up the notes for lost, we must make sure, if we can, that he knows nothing about them.

This is the plan that I have adopted, with the full approval of Mr and Mrs Yatman, for discovering whether Mr Jay is or is not the person who has stolen the cash-box:—

I propose, today, to present myself at the house in the character of a young man who is looking for lodgings. The back room on the second floor will be shown to me as the room to let; and I shall establish myself there tonight, as a person from the country, who has come to London to look for a situation in a respectable shop or office. By this means I shall be living next to the room occupied by Mr Jay. The partition between us is mere lath and plaster. I shall make a small hole in it, near the cornice, through which I can see what Mr Jay does in his room, and hear every word that is said when any friend happens to call on him. Whenever he is at home, I shall be at my post of observation. Whenever he goes out, I shall be after him. By employing these means of watching him, I believe I may look forward to the discovery of his secret—if he knows anything about the lost bank-notes—as to a dead certainty.

What you may think of my plan of observation I cannot undertake to say. It appears to me to unite the invaluable merits of boldness and simplicity. Fortified by this conviction, I close the present communication with feelings of the most sanguine description in regard to the future, and remain your obedient servant,

MATTHEW SHARPIN.

FROM THE SAME TO THE SAME.

7th July.

SIR,

As you have not honoured me with any answer to my last communication, I assume, that, in spite of your prejudices against me, it has produced the favourable impression on your mind which I ventured to anticipate. Gratified and encouraged beyond measure by the token of approval which your eloquent silence conveys to me, I proceed to report the progress that has been made in the course of the last twenty-four hours.

I am now comfortably established next door to Mr Jay; and I am delighted to say that I have two holes in the partition, instead of one. My natural sense of humour has led me into the pardonable extravagance of giving them both appropriate names. One I call my Peep-Hole, and the other my Pipe-Hole. The name of the first explains itself; the name of the second refers to a small tin pipe, or tube, inserted in the hole, and twisted so that the mouth of it comes close to my car, when I am standing at my post of observation. Thus, while I am looking at Mr Jay through my Peep-Hole, I can hear every word that may be spoken in his room through my Pipe-Hole.

Perfect candour—a virtue which I have possessed from my childhood—compels me to acknowledge, before I go any farther, that the ingenious notion of adding a Pipe-Hole to my proposed Peep-Hole originated with Mrs Yatman. This lady—a most intelligent and accomplished person, simple, and yet distinguished, in her manners—has entered into all my little plans with an enthusiasm and intelligence which I cannot too highly praise. Mr Yatman is so cast down by his loss, that he is quite incapable of affording me any assistance. Mrs Yatman, who is evidently most tenderly attached to him, feels her husband's sad condition of mind even more acutely than she feels the loss of the money; and is mainly stimulated to exertion by her desire to assist in raising him from the miserable state of prostration into which he has now fallen. 'The money, Mr Sharpin,' she said to me yesterday evening, with tears in her eyes, 'the money may be regained by rigid economy and strict attention to business. It is my husband's wretched state of mind that makes me so anxious for the discovery of the thief. I may be wrong, but I felt hopeful of success as soon as you entered the house; and I believe, that, if the wretch who has robbed us is to be found, you are the man to discover him.' I accepted this gratifying compliment in the spirit in which it was offered,—firmly believing that I shall be found, sooner or later, to have thoroughly deserved it.

Let me now return to business,—that is to say, to my Peep-Hole and my Pipe-Hole.

I have enjoyed some hours of calm observation of Mr Jay. Though rarely at home, as I understand from Mrs Yatman, on ordinary occasions, he has been indoors the whole of this day. That is suspicious, to begin with. I have to report, further, that he rose at a late hour this morning, (always a bad sign in a young man,) and that he lost a great deal of time, after he was up, in yawning and complaining to himself of headache. Like other debauched characters, he ate little or nothing for breakfast. His next proceeding was to smoke a pipe,—a dirty clay pipe, which a gentleman would have been ashamed to put between his lips. When he had done smoking, he took out pen, ink, and paper, and sat down to write, with a groan,—whether of remorse for having taken the bank-notes, or of disgust at the task before him, I am unable to say. After writing a few lines, (too far away from my Peep-Hole to give me a chance of reading over his shoulder,) he bent back in his chair, and amused himself by humming the tunes of popular songs. I recognised 'My Mary Anne,' 'Bobbin' Around,' and 'Old Dog Tray,' among other melodies. Whether these do or do not represent secret signals by which he communicates with his accomplices remains to be seen. After he had amused himself for some time by humming, he got up and began to walk about the room, occasionally stopping to add a sentence to the paper on his desk. Before long, he went to a locked cupboard and opened it. I strained my eyes eagerly, in expectation of making a discovery. I saw him take something carefully out of the cupboard,—he turned round,—it was only a pint-bottle of brandy! Having drunk some of the liquor, this extremely indolent reprobate lay down on his bed again, and in five minutes was fast asleep.

After hearing him snoring for at least two hours, I was recalled to my Peep-Hole by a knock at his door. He jumped up and opened it with suspicious activity. A very small boy, with a very dirty face, walked in, said, 'Please, Sir, I've come for copy,' sat down on a chair with his legs a long way from the ground, and instantly fell asleep! Mr Jay swore an oath, tied a wet towel round his head, and, sitting down to his paper, began to cover it with writing as fast as his fingers could move the pen. Occasionally getting up to dip the towel in water and tie it on again, he continued at this employment for nearly three hours,—then folded up the leaves of writing, woke the boy, and gave them to him, with this remarkable expression: 'Now, then, young sleepy-head, quick, march! If you see the Governor, tell him to have the money ready for me when I call for it.' The boy grinned, and disappeared. I was sorely tempted to follow 'sleepy-head,' but, on reflection, considered it safest still to keep my eye on the proceedings of Mr Jay.

In half an hour's time, he put on his hat and walked out. Of course, I put on my hat and walked out also. As I went downstairs, I passed Mrs Yatman going up. The lady has been kind enough to undertake, by previous arrangement between us, to search Mr Jay's room, while he is out of the way, and while I am necessarily engaged in the pleasing

duty of following him wherever he goes. On the occasion to
which I now refer, he walked straight to the nearest tavern,
and ordered a couple of mutton-chops for his dinner. I
placed myself in the next box to him, and ordered a couple
of mutton-chops for my dinner. Before I had been in the
room a minute, a young man of highly suspicious manners
and appearance, sitting at a table opposite, took his glass of
porter in his hand and joined Mr Jay. I pretended to be
reading the newspaper, and listened, as in duty bound, with
all my might.

'How are you, my boy?' says the young man. 'Jack has
been here, inquiring after you.'

'Did he leave any message?' asks Mr Jay.

'Yes,' says the other. 'He told me, if I met with you, to say
that he wished very particularly to see you tonight; and that
he would give you a look-in, at Rutherford Street, at seven
o'clock.'

'All right,' says Mr Jay. 'I'll get back in time to see him.'

Upon this, the suspicious-looking young man finished his
porter, and, saying that he was rather in a hurry, took leave
of his friend, (perhaps I should not be wrong, if I said his
accomplice?) and left the room.

At twenty-five minutes and a half past six,—in these
serious cases it is important to be particular about time,—
Mr Jay finished his chops and paid his bill. At twenty-six
minutes and three-quarters, I finished my chops and paid
mine. In ten minutes more I was inside the house in Rutherford Street, and was received by Mrs Yatman in the passage. That charming woman's face exhibited an expression
of melancholy and disappointment which it quite grieved
me to see.

'I am afraid, Ma'am,' says I, 'that you have not hit on any
little criminating discovery in the lodger's room?'

She shook her head and sighed. It was a soft, languid,
fluttering sigh,—and, upon my life, it quite upset me. For
the moment, I forgot business, and burned with envy of Mr
Yatman.

'Don't despair, Ma'am.' I said, with an insinuating mild-
ness which seemed to touch her. 'I have heard a mysterious

conversation,—I know of a guilty appointment,—and I expect great things from my Peep-Hole and my Pipe-Hole tonight. Pray, don't be alarmed, but I think we are on the brink of a discovery.'

Here my enthusiastic devotion to business got the better of my tender feelings. I looked,—winked,—nodded,—left her.

When I got back to my observatory, I found Mr Jay digesting his mutton-chops in an arm-chair, with his pipe in his mouth. On his table were two tumblers, a jug of water, and the pint-bottle of brandy. It was then close upon seven o'clock. As the hour struck, the person described as 'Jack' walked in.

He looked agitated,—I am happy to say he looked violently agitated. The cheerful glow of anticipated success diffused itself (to use a strong expression) all over me, from head to foot. With breathless interest I looked through my Peep-Hole, and saw the visitor—the 'Jack' of this delightful case—sit down, facing me, at the opposite side of the table to Mr Jay. Making allowance for the difference in expression which their countenances just now happened to exhibit, these two abandoned villains were so much alike in other respects as to lead at once to the conclusion that they were brothers. Jack was the cleaner man and the better-dressed of the two. I admit that, at the outset. It is, perhaps, one of my failings to push justice and impartiality to their utmost limits. I am no Pharisee; and where Vice has its redeeming point, I say, let Vice have its due,—yes, yes, by all manner of means, let Vice have its due.

'What's the matter now, Jack?' says Mr Jay.

'Can't you see it in my face?' says Jack. 'My dear fellow, delays are dangerous. Let us have done with suspense, and risk it, the day after tomorrow.'

'So soon as that?' cries Mr Jay, looking very much astonished. 'Well, I'm ready, if you are. But, I say, Jack, is Somebody Else ready, too? Are you quite sure of that?'

He smiled, as he spoke,—a frightful smile,—and laid a very strong emphasis on those two words, 'Somebody Else.' There is evidently a third ruffian, a nameless desperado, concerned in the business.

'Meet us tomorrow,' says Jack, 'and judge for yourself. Be in the Regent's Park at eleven in the morning, and look out for us at the turning that leads to the Avenue Road.'

'I'll be there,' says Mr Jay. 'Have a drop of brandy and water. What are you getting up for? You're not going already?'

'Yes, I am,' says Jack. 'The fact is, I'm so excited and agitated, that I can't sit still anywhere for five minutes together. Ridiculous as it may appear to you, I'm in a perpetual state of nervous flutter. I can't, for the life of me, help fearing that we shall be found out. I fancy that every man who looks twice at me in the street is a spy'——

At those words, I thought my legs would have given way under me. Nothing but strength of mind kept me at my Peep-Hole,—nothing else, I give you my word of honour.

'Stuff and nonsense!' cries Mr Jay, with all the effrontery of a veteran in crime. 'We have kept the secret up to this time, and we will manage cleverly to the end. Have a drop of brandy and water, and you will feel as certain about it as I do.'

Jack steadily refused the brandy and water, and steadily persisted in taking his leave. 'I must try if I can't walk it off,' he said. 'Remember tomorrow morning,—eleven o'clock,—Avenue-Road side of the Regent's Park.'

With those words he went out. His hardened relative laughed desperately, and resumed the dirty clay pipe.

I sat down on the side of my bed, actually quivering with excitement. It is clear to me that no attempt has yet been made to change the stolen bank-notes; and I may add, that Sergeant Bulmer was of that opinion also, when he left the case in my hands. What is the natural conclusion to draw from the conversation which I have just set down? Evidently, that the confederates meet tomorrow to take their respective shares in the stolen money, and to decide on the safest means of getting the notes changed the day after. Mr Jay is, beyond a doubt, the leading criminal in this business, and he will probably run the chief risk,—that of changing the fifty-pound note. I shall, therefore, still make it my business to follow him,—attending at the Regent's Park tomorrow, and doing my best to hear what is said there. If another appointment is made for the day after, I shall, of course, go to it. In the mean time, I shall want the immediate assistance of two competent persons (supposing the rascals separate after their meeting) to follow the two minor criminals. It is only fair to add, that, if the rogues all retire together, I shall probably keep my subordinates in reserve. Being naturally ambitious, I desire, if possible, to have the whole credit of discovering this robbery to myself.

8th July.

I have to acknowledge, with thanks, the speedy arrival of my two subordinates,—men of very average abilities, I am afraid; but, fortunately, I shall always be on the spot to direct them.

My first business this morning was, necessarily, to prevent possible mistakes, by accounting to Mr and Mrs Yatman for the presence of the two strangers on the scene. Mr Yatman (between ourselves, a poor, feeble man) only shook his head and groaned. Mrs Yatman (that superior woman) favoured me with a charming look of intelligence. 'Oh, Mr Sharpin!' she said, 'I am so sorry to see those two men! Your sending for their assistance looks as if you were beginning to be doubtful of success.' I privately winked at her, (she is very good in allowing me to do so without taking offence,) and told her, in my facetious way, that she laboured under a slight mistake. 'It is because I am sure of sucess, Ma'am, that I send for them. I am determined to recover the money, not for my own sake only, but for Mr Yatman's sake,— and for yours.' I laid a considerable amount of stress on those last three words. She said, 'Oh, Mr Sharpin!' again,—and blushed of a heavenly red,—and looked down at her work. I could go to the world's end with that woman, if Mr Yatman would only die.

I sent off the two subordinates to wait, until I wanted them, at the Avenue-Road gate of the Regent's Park. Half an hour afterwards I was following the same direction myself, at the heels of Mr Jay.

The two confederates were punctual to the appointed time. I blush to record it, but it is, nevertheless, necessary to state, that the third rogue—the nameless desperado of my report, or, if you prefer it, the mysterious 'Somebody Else' of the conversation between the two brothers—is—— a woman! and, what is worse, a young woman! and, what is more lamentable still, a nice-looking woman! I have long resisted a growing conviction, that, wherever there is mischief in this world, an individual of the fair sex is inevitably certain to be mixed up in it. After the experience of this morning, I can struggle against that sad conclusion no longer. I give up the sex,—excepting Mrs Yatman, I give up the sex.

The man named 'Jack' offered the woman his arm. Mr Jay placed himself on the other side of her. The three then walked away slowly among the trees. I followed them at a respectful distance. My two subordinates, at a respectful distance also, followed me.

It was, I deeply regret to say, impossible to get near enough to them to overhear their conversation, without running too great a risk of being discovered. I could only infer from their gestures and actions that they were all three talking together with extraordinary earnestness on some subject which deeply interested them. After having been engaged in this way a full quarter of an hour, they suddenly turned round to retrace their steps. My presence of mind did not forsake me in this emergency. I signed to the two subordinates to walk on carelessly and pass them, while I myself slipped dexterously behind a tree. As they came by me, I heard 'Jack' address these words to Mr Jay:—

'Let us say half-past ten tomorrow morning. And mind you come in a cab. We had better not risk taking one in this neighbourhood.'

Mr Jay made some brief reply, which I could not overhear. They walked back to the place at which they had met, shaking hands there with an audacious cordiality which it quite sickened me to see. Then they separated. I followed Mr Jay. My subordinates paid the same delicate attention to the other two.

Instead of taking me back to Rutherford Street, Mr Jay led me to the Strand. He stopped at a dingy, disreputable-looking house, which, according to the inscription over the door, was a newspaper office, but which, in my judgment, had all the external appearance of a place devoted to the reception of stolen goods. After remaining inside for a few minutes, he came out, whistling, with his finger and thumb in his waistcoat pocket. Some men would now have arrested him on the spot. I remembered the necessity of catching the two confederates, and the importance of not interfering with the appointment that had been made for the next morning. Such coolness as this, under trying circumstances, is rarely to be found, I should imagine, in a young beginner, whose reputation as a detective policeman is still to make.

From the house of suspicious appearance Mr Jay betook himself to a cigar-divan,* and read the magazines over a cheroot. I sat at a table near him, and read the magazines, likewise, over a cheroot. From the divan he strolled to the tavern, and had his chops. I strolled to the tavern, and had my chops. When he had done, he went back to his lodging. When I had done, I went back to mine. He was overcome with drowsiness early in the evening, and went to bed. As soon as I heard him snoring, I was overcome with drowsiness, and went to bed also.

Early in the morning, my two subordinates came to make their report. They had seen the man named 'Jack' leave the woman at the gate of an apparently respectable villa-residence, not far from the Regent's Park. Left to himself, he took a turning to the right, which led to a sort of suburban street, principally inhabited by shopkeepers. He stopped at the private door of one of the houses, and let himself in with his own key,—looking about him as he opened the door, and staring suspiciously at my men as they lounged along on the opposite side of the way. These were all the particulars which the subordinates had to communicate. I kept them in my room to attend on me, if needful, and mounted to my Peep-Hole to have a look at Mr Jay.

He was occupied in dressing himself, and was taking extraordinary pains to destroy all traces of the natural slovenliness of his appearance. This was precisely what I expected. A vagabond like Mr Jay knows the importance of giving himself a respectable look when he is going to run the risk of changing a stolen bank-note. At five minutes past ten o'clock he had given the last brush to his shabby hat and the last scouring with bread-crumb to his dirty gloves. At ten minutes past ten he was in the street, on his way to the nearest cab-stand, and I and my subordinates were close on his heels.

He took a cab, and we took a cab. I had not overheard them appoint a place of meeting, when following them in the Park on the previous day; but I soon found that we were proceeding in the old direction of the Avenue-Road gate. The cab in which Mr Jay was riding turned into the Park slowly. We stopped outside, to avoid exciting suspicion. I got out to follow the cab on foot. Just as I did so, I saw it stop, and detected the two confederates approaching it from among the trees. They got in, and the cab was turned about directly. I ran back to my own cab, and told the driver to let them pass him, and then to follow as before.

The man obeyed my directions, but so clumsily as to excite their suspicions. We had been driving after them about three minutes, (returning along the road by which we had advanced,) when I looked out of the window to see how far they might be ahead of us. As I did this, I saw two hats popped out of the windows of their cab, and two faces looking back at me. I sank into my place in a cold sweat;— the expression is coarse, but no other form of words can describe my condition at that trying moment.

'We are found out!' I said, faintly, to my two subordinates. They stared at me in astonishment. My feelings changed instantly from the depth of despair to the height of indignation. 'It is the cabman's fault. Get out, one of you,' I said, with dignity,—'get out, and punch his head.'

Instead of following my directions, (I should wish this act of disobedience to be reported at head-quarters,) they both looked out of the window. Before I could pull them back, they both sat down again. Before I could express my just indignation, they both grinned, and said to me, 'Please to look out, Sir!'

I did look out. Their cab had stopped. Where? At a church door!

What effect this discovery might have had upon the ordinary run of men, I don't know. Being of a religious turn myself, it filled me with horror. I have often read of the unprincipled cunning of criminal persons; but I never before heard of three thieves attempting to double on their pursuers by entering a church! The sacrilegious audacity of that proceeding is, I should think, unparalleled in the annals of crime.

I checked my grinning subordinates by a frown. It was easy to see what was passing in their superficial minds. If I had not been able to look below the surface, I might, on observing two nicely dressed men and one nicely dressed woman enter a church before eleven in the morning, on a weekday, have come to the same hasty conclusion at which my inferiors had evidently arrived. As it was, appearances had no power to impose on *me*. I got out, and, followed by one of my men, entered the church. The other man I sent round to watch the vestry door. You may catch a weasel asleep,—but not your humble servant, Matthew Sharpin!

We stole up the gallery-stairs, diverged to the organ-loft, and peeped through the curtains in front. There they were, all three, sitting in a pew below,—yes, incredible as it may appear, sitting in a pew below!

Before I could determine what to do, a clergyman made his appearance in full canonicals, from the vestry door, followed by a clerk. My brain whirled, and my eyesight grew dim. Dark remembrances of robberies committed in vestries floated through my mind. I trembled for the excellent man in full canonicals;—I even trembled for the clerk.

The clergyman placed himself inside the altar rails. The three desperadoes approached him. He opened his book, and began to read. What?—you will ask.

I answer, without the slightest hesitation, the first lines of the Marriage Service.

My subordinate had the audacity to look at me, and then to stuff his pocket-handkerchief into his mouth. I scorned to

pay any attention to him. After my own eyes had satisfied
me that there was a parchment licence in the clergyman's
hand, and that it was consequently useless to come forward
and forbid the marriage,—after I had seen this, and after I
had discovered that the man 'Jack' was the bridegroom, and
that the man Jay acted the part of father and gave away the
bride, I left the church, followed by my man, and joined the
other subordinate outside the vestry door. Some people in
my position would now have felt rather crestfallen, and
would have begun to think that they had made a very foolish
mistake. Not the faintest misgiving of any kind troubled me.
I did not feel in the slightest degree depreciated in my own
estimation. And even now, after a lapse of three hours, my
mind remains, I am happy to say, in the same calm and
hopeful condition.

As soon as I and my subordinates were assembled
together, outside the church, I intimated my intention of
still following the other cab, in spite of what had occurred.
My reason for deciding on this course will appear presently.
The two subordinates appeared to be astonished at my
resolution. One of them had the impertinence to say to me,
'If you please, Sir, who is it we are after? A man who has
stolen money, or a man who has stolen a wife?' The other
low person encouraged him by laughing. Both have deserved
an official reprimand; and both, I sincerely trust, will be
sure to get it.

When the marriage ceremony was over, the three got into
their cab; and, once more, our vehicle (neatly hidden round
the corner of the church, so that they could not suspect it to
be near them) started to follow theirs. We traced them to
the terminus of the South-Western Railway. The newly
married couple took tickets for Richmond,—paying their
fare with a half sovereign, and so depriving me of the
pleasure of arresting them, which I should certainly have
done, if they had offered a bank-note. They parted from Mr
Jay, saying, 'Remember the address,—14, Babylon Terrace.
You dine with us tomorrow week.' Mr Jay accepted the
invitation, and added, jocosely, that he was going home at
once to get off his clean clothes, and to be comfortable and

dirty again for the rest of the day. I have to report that I saw him home safely, and that he is comfortable and dirty again (to use his own disgraceful language) at the present moment.

Here the affair rests, having by this time reached what I may call its first stage. I know very well what persons of hasty judgments will be inclined to say of my proceedings thus far. They will assert that I have been deceiving myself, all through, in the most absurd way; they will declare that the suspicious conversations which I have reported referred solely to the difficulties and dangers of successfully carrying out a runaway match; and they will appeal to the scene in the church, as offering undeniable proof of the correctness of their assertions. So let it be. I dispute nothing, up to this point. But I ask a question, out of the depths of my own sagacity as a man of the world, which the bitterest of my enemies will not, I think, find it particularly easy to answer. Granted the fact of the marriage, what proof does it afford me of the innocence of the three persons concerned in that clandestine transaction? It gives me none. On the contrary, it strengthens my suspicions against Mr Jay and his confederates, because it suggests a distinct motive for their stealing the money. A gentleman who is going to spend his honeymoon at Richmond wants money; and a gentleman who is in debt to all his tradespeople wants money. Is this an unjustifiable imputation of bad motives? In the name of outraged Morality, I deny it. These men have combined together, and have stolen a woman. Why should they not combine together and steal a cash-box? I take my stand on the logic of rigid Virtue; and I defy all the sophistry of Vice to move me an inch out of my position.

Speaking of virtue, I may add that I have put this view of the case to Mr and Mrs Yatman. That accomplished and charming woman found it difficult, at first, to follow the close chain of my reasoning. I am free to confess that she shook her head, and shed tears, and joined her husband in premature lamentation over the loss of the two hundred pounds. But a little careful explanation on my part, and a little attentive listening on hers, ultimately changed her opinion. She now agrees with me, that there is nothing in this unexpected circumstance of the clandestine marriage which absolutely tends to divert suspicion from Mr Jay, or Mr 'Jack,' or the runaway lady,—'audacious hussey' was the term my fair friend used in speaking of her, but let that pass. It is more to the purpose to record, that Mrs Yatman has not lost confidence in me, and that Mr Yatman promises to follow her example and do his best to look hopefully for future results.

I have now, in the new turn that circumstances have taken, to await advice from your office. I pause for fresh orders with all the composure of a man who has got two strings to his bow. When I traced the three confederates from the church door to the railway terminus, I had two motives for doing so. First, I followed them as a matter of official business, believing them still to have been guilty of the robbery. Secondly, I followed them as a matter of private speculation, with a view of discovering the place of refuge to which the runaway couple intended to retreat, and of making my information a marketable commodity to offer to the young lady's family and friends. Thus, whatever happens, I may congratulate myself beforehand on not having wasted my time. If the office approves of my conduct, I have my plan ready for further proceedings. If the office blames me, I shall take myself off, with my marketable information, to the genteel villa-residence in the neighbourhood of the Regent's Park. Any way, the affair puts money into my pocket, and does credit to my penetration, as an uncommonly sharp man.

I have only one word more to add, and it is this:—If any individual ventures to assert that Mr Jay and his confederates are innocent of all share in the stealing of the cash-box, I, in return, defy that individual—though he may even be Chief Inspector Theakstone himself—to tell me who has committed the robbery at Rutherford Street, Soho.

Strong in that conviction,
I have the honour to be
Your very obedient servant,
MATTHEW SHARPIN.

FROM CHIEF INSPECTOR THEAKSTONE TO
SERGEANT RULMER.

Birmingham, July 9th.

SERGEANT BULMER,

That empty-headed puppy, Mr Matthew Sharpin, has
made a mess of the case at Rutherford Street, exactly as I
expected he would. Business keeps me in this town; so I
write to you to set the matter straight. I enclose, with this,
the pages of feeble scribble-scrabble which the creature,
Sharpin, calls a report. Look them over; and when you have
made your way through all the gabble, I think you will agree
with me that the conceited booby has looked for the thief in
every direction but the right one. The case is perfectly
simple, now. Settle it at once; forward your report to me at
this place; and tell Mr Sharpin that he is suspended till
further notice.

Yours,
FRANCIS THEAKSTONE.

FROM SERGEANT BULMER TO CHIEF INSPECTOR
THEAKSTONE.

London, July 10th.

INSPECTOR THEAKSTONE,

Your letter and enclosure came safe to hand. Wise men,
they say, may always learn something, even from a fool. By
the time I had got through Sharpin's maundering report of
his own folly, I saw my way clear enough to the end of the
Rutherford-Street case, just as you thought I should. In half
an hour's time I was at the house. The first person I saw
there was Mr Sharpin himself.

'Have you come to help me?' says he.

'Not exactly,' says I. 'I've come to tell you that you are
suspended till further notice.'

'Very good,' says he, not taken down, by so much as a
single peg, in his own estimation. 'I thought you would be
jealous of me. It's very natural; and I don't blame you. Walk

in, pray, and make yourself at home. I'm off to do a little detective business on my own account, in the neighbourhood of the Regent's Park. Ta-ta, Sergeant, ta-ta!'

With those words he took himself out of my way,—which was exactly what I wanted him to do. As soon as the maid-servant had shut the door, I told her to inform her master that I wanted to say a word to him in private. She showed me into the parlour behind the shop; and there was Mr Yatman, all alone, reading the newspaper.

'About this matter of the robbery, Sir,' says I.

He cut me short, peevishly enough,—being naturally a poor, weak, womanish sort of man. 'Yes, yes, I know,' says he. 'You have come to tell me that your wonderfully clever man, who has bored holes in my second-floor partition, has made a mistake, and is off the scent of the scoundrel who has stolen my money.'

'Yes, Sir,' says I. 'That *is* one of the things I came to tell you. But I have got something else to say, besides that.'

'Can you tell me who the thief is?' says he, more pettish than ever.

'Yes, Sir,' says I, 'I think I can.'

He put down the newspaper, and began to look rather anxious and frightened.

'Not my shopman?' says he. 'I hope, for the man's own sake, it's not my shopman.'

'Guess again, Sir,' says I.

'That idle slut, the maid?' says he.

'She is idle, Sir,' says I, 'and she is also a slut; my first inquiries about her proved as much as that. But she's not the thief.'

'Then, in the name of Heaven, who is?' says he.

'Will you please to prepare yourself for a very disagreeable surprise, Sir?' says I. 'And in case you lose your temper, will you excuse my remarking, that I am the stronger man of the two, and that, if you allow yourself to lay hands on me, I may unintentionally hurt you, in pure self-defence?'

He turned as pale as ashes, and pushed his chair two or three feet away from me.

'You have asked me to tell you, Sir, who has taken your money,' I went on. 'If you insist on my giving you an answer'——

'I do insist,' he said, faintly. 'Who has taken it?'

'Your wife has taken it,' I said, very quietly, and very positively at the same time.

He jumped out of the chair as if I had put a knife into him, and struck his fist on the table, so heavily that the wood cracked again.

'Steady, Sir,' says I. 'Flying into a passion won't help you to the truth.'

'It's a lie!' says he, with another smack of his fist on the table,—'a base, vile, infamous lie! How dare you'——

He stopped, and fell back into the chair again, looked about him in a bewildered way, and ended by bursting out crying.

'When your better sense comes back to you, Sir,' says I, 'I am sure you will be gentleman enough to make me an apology for the language you have just used. In the mean time, please to listen, if you can, to a word of explanation. Mr Sharpin has sent in a report to our Inspector, of the most irregular and ridiculous kind; setting down, not only all his own foolish doings and sayings, but the doings and sayings of Mrs Yatman as well. In most cases, such a document would have been fit only for the waste-paper basket; but, in this particular case, it so happens that Mr Sharpin's budget of nonsense leads to a certain conclusion which the simpleton of a writer has been quite innocent of suspecting from the beginning to the end. Of that conclusion I am so sure, that I will forfeit my place, if it does not turn out that Mrs Yatman has been practising upon the folly and conceit of this young man, and that she has tried to shield herself from discovery by purposely encouraging him to suspect the wrong persons. I tell you that confidently; and I will even go farther. I will undertake to give a decided opinion as to why Mrs Yatman took the money, and what she has done with it, or with a part of it. Nobody can look at that lady, Sir, without being struck by the great taste and beauty of her dress'——

As I said those last words, the poor man seemed to find his powers of speech again. He cut me short directly, as haughtily as if he had been a duke instead of a stationer. 'Try some other means of justifying your vile calumny against my wife,' says he. 'Her milliner's bill, for the past year, is on my file of receipted accounts, at this moment.'

'Excuse me, Sir,' says I, 'but that proves nothing. Milliners, I must tell you, have a certain rascally custom which comes within the daily experience of our office. A married lady who wishes it can keep two accounts at her dressmaker's;—one is the account which her husband sees and pays; the other is the private account, which contains all the extravagant items, and which the wife pays secretly, by instalments, whenever she can. According to our usual experience, these instalments are mostly squeezed out of the housekeeping money. In your case, I suspect no instalments have been paid; proceedings have been threatened; Mrs Yatman, knowing your altered circumstances, has felt herself driven into a corner; and she has paid her private account out of your cash-box.'

'I won't believe it!' says he. 'Every word you speak is an abominable insult to me and to my wife.'

'Are you man enough, Sir,' says I, taking him up short, in order to save time and words, 'to get that receipted bill you spoke of just now, off the file, and to come with me at once to the milliner's shop where Mrs Yatman deals?'

He turned red in the face at that, got the bill directly, and put on his hat. I took out of my pocket-book the list containing the numbers of the lost notes, and we left the house together immediately.

Arrived at the milliner's, (one of the expensive West-End houses, as I expected,) I asked for a private interview, on important business, with the mistress of the concern. It was not the first time that she and I had met over the same delicate investigation. The moment she set eyes on me, she sent for her husband. I mentioned who Mr Yatman was, and what we wanted.

'This is strictly private?' says the husband. I nodded my head.

'And confidential?' says the wife. I nodded again.

'Do you see any objection, dear, to obliging the Sergeant with a sight of the books?' says the husband.

'None in the world, love, if you approve of it,' says the wife.

All this while poor Mr Yatman sat looking the picture of astonishment and distress, quite out of place at our polite conference. The books were brought,—and one minute's look at the pages in which Mrs Yatman's name figured was enough, and more than enough, to prove the truth of every word that I had spoken.

There, in one book, was the husband's account, which Mr Yatman had settled. And there, in the other, was the private account, crossed off also; the date of settlement being the very day after the loss of the cash-box. This said private account amounted to the sum of a hundred and seventy-five pounds, odd shillings; and it extended over a period of three years. Not a single instalment had been paid on it. Under the last line was an entry to this effect: 'Written to for the third time, June 23d.' I pointed to it, and asked the milliner if that meant 'last June.' Yes, it did mean last June; and she now deeply regretted to say that it had been accompanied by a threat of legal proceedings.

'I thought you gave good customers more than three years' credit?' says I.

The milliner looks at Mr Yatman, and whispers to me,— 'Not when a lady's husband gets into difficulties.'

She pointed to the account as she spoke. The entries after the time when Mr Yatman's circumstances became involved were just as extravagant, for a person in his wife's situation, as the entries for the year before that period. If the lady had economised in other things, she had certainly not economised in the matter of dress.

There was nothing left now but to examine the cash-book, for form's sake. The money had been paid in notes, the amounts and numbers of which exactly tallied with the figures set down in my list.

After that, I thought it best to get Mr Yatman out of the house immediately. He was in such a pitiable condition, that I called a cab and accompanied him home in it. At first, he cried and raved like a child; but I soon quieted him,— and I must add, to his credit, that he made me a most handsome apology for his language, as the cab drew up at his house-door. In return, I tried to give him some advice about how to set matters right, for the future, with his wife. He paid very little attention to me, and went upstairs muttering to himself about a separation. Whether Mrs Yatman will come cleverly out of the scrape or not seems doubtful. I should say, myself, that she will go into screeching hysterics, and so frighten the poor man into forgiving her. But this is no business of ours. So far as we are concerned, the case is now at an end; and the present report may come to a conclusion along with it.

I remain, accordingly, yours to command,

THOMAS BULMER.

P. S.—I have to add, that, on leaving Rutherford Street, I met Mr Matthew Sharpin coming back to pack up his things.

'Only think!' says he, rubbing his hands in great spirits, 'I've been to the genteel villa-residence; and the moment I mentioned my business, they kicked me out directly. There were two witnesses of the assault; and it's worth a hundred pounds to me, if it's worth a farthing.'

'I wish you joy of your luck,' says I.

'Thank you,' says he. 'When may I pay you the same compliment on finding the thief?'

'Whenever you like,' says I, 'for the thief is found.'

'Just what I expected,' says he. 'I've done all the work; and now you cut in, and claim all the credit.—Mr Jay, of course?'

'No,' says I.

'Who is it, then?' says he.

'Ask Mrs Yatman,' says I. 'She'll tell you.'

'All right! I'd much rather hear it from her than from you,' says he,—and goes into the house in a mighty hurry.

What do you think of that, Inspector Theakstone? Would you like to stand in Mr Sharpin's shoes? I shouldn't, I can promise you!

FROM CHIEF INSPECTOR THEAKSTONE TO MR
MATTHEW SHARPIN.

July 12th.

SIR,

Sergeant Bulmer has already told you to consider yourself
suspended until further notice. I have now authority to add,
that your services as a member of the Detective Police are
positively declined. You will please to take this letter as
notifying officially your dismissal from the force.

I may inform you, privately, that your rejection is not
intended to cast any reflections on your character. It merely
implies that you are not quite sharp enough for our purpose.
If we are to have a new recruit among us, we should infinite-
ly prefer Mrs Yatman.

Your obedient servant,

FRANCIS THEAKSTONE.

NOTE ON THE PRECEDING CORRESPONDENCE.—The editor is,
unfortunately, not in a position to add any explanations of importance to the last of the published letters of Chief Inspector Theakstone. It has been discovered that Mr Matthew Sharpin left the
house in Rutherford Street a quarter of an hour after his interview
outside of it with Sergeant Bulmer,—his manner expressing the
liveliest emotions of terror and astonishment, and his left cheek
displaying a bright patch of red, which looked as if it might have
been the result of what is popularly termed a smart box on the ear.
He was also heard, by the shopman at Rutherford Street, to use a
very shocking expression in reference to Mrs Yatman; and was
seen to clinch his fist vindictively, as he ran round the corner of the
street. Nothing more has been heard of him; and it is conjectured
that he has left London with the intention of offering his valuable
services to the provincial police.

On the interesting domestic subject of Mr and Mrs Yatman still
less is known. It has however, been positively ascertained that the
medical attendant of the family was sent for in a great hurry on
the day when Mr Yatman returned from the milliner's shop. The
neighbouring chemist received, soon afterwards, a prescription of
a soothing nature to make up for Mrs Yatman. The day after, Mr
Yatman purchased some smelling-salts at the shop, and afterwards
appeared at the circulating library to ask for a novel that would

amuse an invalid lady. It has been inferred from these circumstances that he has not thought it desirable to carry out his threat of separating himself from his wife,—at least in the present (presumed) condition of that lady's sensitive nervous system.

JOHN JAGO'S GHOST

I

'HEART all right,' said the doctor. 'Lungs all right. No organic disease that I can discover. Philip Lefrank, don't alarm yourself. You are not going to die yet. The disease you are suffering from is—overwork. The remedy in your case is—rest.'

So the doctor spoke, in my chambers in the Temple (London); having been sent for to see me about half an hour after I had alarmed my clerk by fainting at my desk. I have no wish to intrude myself needlessly on the reader's attention; but it may be necessary to add, in the way of explanation, that I am a 'junior' barrister in good practice. I come from the Channel Island of Jersey. The French spelling of my name (Lefranc) was Anglicised generations since, in the days when the letter 'k' was still used in England at the end of words which now terminate in 'c'. We hold our heads high, nevertheless, as a Jersey family. It is to this day a trial to my father to hear his son described as a member of the English bar.

'Rest!' I repeated, when my medical adviser had done. 'My good friend, are you aware that it is term time? The courts are sitting. Look at the briefs waiting for me on that table! Rest means ruin in my case.'

'And work,' added the doctor, quietly, 'means death.'

I started. He was not trying to frighten me: he was plainly in earnest.

'It is merely a question of time,' he went on. 'You have a fine constitution; you are a young man; but you cannot deliberately overwork your brain, and derange your nervous system much longer. Go away at once. If you are a good sailor, take a sea-voyage. The ocean-air is the best of all air to build you up again. No: I don't want to write a prescription. I decline to physic you. I have no more to say.'

With those words my medical friend left the room. I was obstinate: I went into court the same day.

The senior counsel in the case on which I was engaged applied to me for some information which it was my duty to give him. To my horror and amazement, I was perfectly unable to collect my ideas: facts and dates all mingled together confusedly in my mind. I was led out of court thoroughly terrified about myself. The next day my briefs went back to the attorneys; and I followed my doctor's advice by taking my passage for America in the first steamer that sailed for New York.

I had chosen the voyage to America in preference to any other trip by sea, with a special object in view. A relative of my mother's had emigrated to the United States many years since, and had thriven there as a farmer. He had given me a general invitation to visit him if I ever crossed the Atlantic. The long period of inaction, under the name of *rest*, to which the doctor's decision had condemned me, could hardly be more pleasantly occupied, as I thought, than by paying a visit to my relation, and seeing what I could of America in that way. After a brief sojourn at New York, I started by railway for the residence of my host—Mr Isaac Meadowcroft, of Morwick Farm.

There are some of the grandest natural prospects on the face of creation in America. There is also to be found in certain States of the Union, by way of wholesome contrast, scenery as flat, as monotonous, and as uninteresting to the traveller, as any that the earth can show. The part of the country in which Mr Meadowcroft's farm was situated fell within this latter category. I looked round me when I stepped out of the railway carriage on the platform at Morwick Station; and I said to myself, 'If to be cured means, in my case, to be dull, I have accurately picked out the very place for the purpose.'

I look back at those words by the light of later events; and I pronounce them, as you will soon pronounce them, to be the words of an essentially rash man, whose hasty judgment never stopped to consider what surprises time and chance together might have in store for him.

Mr Meadowcroft's eldest son, Ambrose, was waiting at the station to drive me to the farm.

There was no forewarning, in the appearance of Ambrose Meadowcroft, of the strange and terrible events that were to follow my arrival at Morwick. A healthy, handsome young fellow, one of thousands of other healthy, handsome young fellows, said, 'How d'ye do, Mr Lefrank? Glad to see you, sir. Jump into the buggy: the man will look after your portmanteau.' With equally conventional politeness I answered, 'Thank you. How are you all at home?' So we started on the way to the farm.

Our conversation on the drive began with the subjects of agriculture and breeding. I displayed my total ignorance of crops and cattle before we had travelled ten yards on our journey. Ambrose Meadowcroft cast about for another topic, and failed to find it. Upon this I cast about on my side, and asked, at a venture, if I had chosen a convenient time for my visit. The young farmer's stolid brown face instantly brightened. I had evidently hit, haphazard, on an interesting subject.

'You couldn't have chosen a better time,' he said. 'Our house has never been so cheerful as it is now.'

'Have you any visitors staying with you?'

'It's not exactly a visitor. It's a new member of the family who has come to live with us.'

'A new member of the family? May I ask who it is?'

Ambrose Meadowcroft considered before he replied; touched his horse with the whip; looked at me with a certain sheepish hesitation; and suddenly burst out with the truth, in the plainest possible words:

'It's just the nicest girl, sir, you ever saw in your life.'

'Ay ay! A friend of your sister's, I suppose?'

'A friend! Bless your heart! it's our little American cousin—Naomi Colebrook.'

I vaguely remembered that a younger sister of Mr Meadowcroft's had married an American merchant in the remote past, and had died many years since, leaving an only child. I was now further informed that the father also was dead. In his last moments he had committed his helpless daughter to the compassionate care of his wife's relations at Morwick.

'He was always a speculating man,' Ambrose went on. 'Tried one thing after another, and failed in all. Died, sir, leaving barely enough to bury him. My father was a little doubtful, before she came here, how his American niece would turn out. We are English, you know; and, though we do live in the United States, we stick fast to our English ways and habits. We don't much like American women in general, I can tell you; but when Naomi made her appearance, she conquered us all. Such a girl! Took her place as one of the family directly. Learnt to make herself useful in the dairy in a week's time. I tell you this—she hasn't been with us quite two months yet; and we wonder already how we ever got on without her!'

Once started on the subject of Naomi Colebrook, Ambrose held to that one topic, and talked on it without intermission. It required no great gift of penetration to discover the impression which the American cousin had produced in this case. The young fellow's enthusiasm communicated itself, in a certain tepid degree, to me. I really felt a mild flutter of anticipation at the prospect of seeing Naomi, when we drew up, towards the close of evening, at the gates of Morwick Farm.

II

Immediately on my arrival, I was presented to Mr Meadow-croft, the father.

The old man had become a confirmed invalid, confined by chronic rheumatism to his chair. He received me kindly, and a little wearily as well. His only unmarried daughter (he had long since been left a widower) was in the room, in attendance on her father. She was a melancholy, middle-aged woman, without visible attractions of any sort—one of those persons who appear to accept the obligation of living, under protest, as a burden which they would never have consented to bear if they had only been consulted first. We three had a dreary little interview in a parlour of bare walls;

and then I was permitted to go upstairs, and unpack my portmanteau in my own room.

'Supper will be at nine o'clock, sir,' said Miss Meadowcroft.

She pronounced those words as if 'supper' was a form of domestic offence, habitually committed by the men, and endured by the women. I followed the groom up to my room, not over well pleased with my first experience of the farm.

No Naomi, and no romance, thus far!

My room was clean—oppressively clean. I quite longed to see a little dust somewhere. My library was limited to the Bible and the Prayer Book. My view from the window showed me a dead flat in a partial state of cultivation, fading sadly from view in the waning light. Above the head of my spruce white bed hung a scroll, bearing a damnatory quotation from scripture in emblazoned letters of red and black. The dismal presence of Miss Meadowcroft had passed over my bedroom, and had blighted it. My spirits sank as I looked round me. Supper-time was still an event in the future. I lit the candles, and took from my portmanteau what I firmly believe to have been the first French novel ever produced at Morwick Farm. It was one of the masterly and charming stories of Dumas the elder.* In five minutes I was in a new world, and my melancholy room was full of the liveliest French company. The sound of an imperative and uncompromising bell recalled me in due time to the regions of reality. I looked at my watch. Nine o'clock.

Ambrose met me at the bottom of the stairs, and showed me the way to the supper-room.

Mr Meadowcroft's invalid-chair had been wheeled to the head of the table. On his right-hand side sat his sad and silent daughter. She signed to me, with a ghostly solemnity, to take the vacant place on the left of her father. Silas Meadowcroft came in at the same moment, and was presented to me by his brother. There was a strong family likeness between them, Ambrose being the taller and handsomer man of the two. But there was no marked character in either face. I set them down as men with undeveloped qualities, waiting (the good and evil qualities alike) for time and circumstances to bring them to their full growth.

The door opened again while I was still studying the two brothers, without, I honestly confess, being very favourably impressed by either of them. A new member of the family circle, who instantly attracted my attention, entered the room.

He was short, spare, and wiry; singularly pale for a person whose life was passed in the country. The face was in other respects, beside this, a striking face to see. As to the lower part, it was covered with a thick black beard and moustache, at a time when shaving was the rule, and beards the rare exception in America. As to the upper part of the face, it was irradiated by a pair of wild, glittering brown eyes, the expression of which suggested to me that there was something not quite right with the man's mental balance. A perfectly sane person in all his sayings and doings, so far as I could see, there was still something in those wild brown eyes which suggested to me, that, under exceptionally trying circumstances, he might surprise his oldest friends by acting in some exceptionally violent or foolish way. 'A little cracked'—that, in the popular phrase, was my impression of the stranger who now made his appearance in the supper-room.

Mr Meadowcroft the elder, having not spoken one word thus far, himself introduced the newcomer to me, with a side-glance at his sons, which had something like defiance in it—a glance which, as I was sorry to notice, was returned with a similar appearance of defiance by the two young men.

'Philip Lefrank, this is my overlooker, Mr Jago,' said the old man, formally presenting us. 'John Jago, this is my young relative by marriage, Mr Lefrank. He is not well! he has come over the ocean for rest, and change of scene. Mr Jago is an American, Philip. I hope you have no prejudice against Americans. Make acquaintance with Mr Jago. Sit together.' He cast another dark look at his sons; and the sons again returned it. They pointedly drew back from John Jago as he approached the empty chair next to me, and moved round to the opposite side of the table. It was plain that the man with the beard stood high in the father's favour, and that he was cordially disliked for that or for some other reason by the sons.

The door opened once more. A young lady quietly joined the party at the supper-table.

Was the young lady Naomi Colebrook? I looked at Ambrose, and saw the answer in his face. Naomi at last!

A pretty girl, and so far as I could judge by appearances, a good girl too. Describing her generally, I may say that she had a small head, well carried, and well set on her shoulders; bright grey eyes, that looked at you honestly, and meant what they looked; a trim, slight little figure—too slight for our English notions of beauty; a strong American accent; and (a rare thing in America) a pleasantly-toned voice, which made the accent agreeable to English ears. Our first impressions of people are, in nine cases out of ten, the right impressions. I liked Naomi Colebrook at first sight; liked her pleasant smile; liked her hearty shake of the hand when we were presented to each other. 'If I get on well with nobody else in this house,' I thought to myself, 'I shall certainly get on well with *you*.'

For once in a way, I proved a true prophet. In the atmosphere of smouldering enmities at Morwick Farm, the pretty American girl and I remained firm and true friends from first to last.

Ambrose made room for Naomi to sit between his brother and himself. She changed colour for a moment, and looked at him, with a pretty reluctant tenderness, as she took her chair. I strongly suspected the young farmer of squeezing her hand privately, under cover of the tablecloth.

The supper was not a merry one. The only cheerful conversation was the conversation across the table between Naomi and me.

For some incomprehensible reason, John Jago seemed to be ill at ease in the presence of his young countrywoman. He looked up at Naomi doubtingly from his plate, and looked down again slowly with a frown. When I addressed him, he answered constrainedly. Even when he spoke to Mr Meadow-

croft, he was still on his guard— on his guard against the
two young men, as I fancied by the direction which his eyes
took on these occasions. When we began our meal, I had
noticed for the first time that Silas Meadowcroft's left hand
was strapped up with surgical plaster; and I now further
observed that John Jago's wandering brown eyes, furtively
looking at everybody round the table in turn, looked with a
curious cynical scrutiny at the young man's injured hand.

By way of making my first evening at the farm all the more
embarrassing to me as a stranger, I discovered before long
that the father and sons were talking indirectly *at* each
other, through Mr Jago and through me. When old Mr
Meadowcroft spoke disparagingly to his overlooker of some
past mistake made in the cultivation of the arable land of the
farm, old Mr Meadowcroft's eyes pointed the application of
his hostile criticism straight in the direction of his two sons.
When the two sons seized a stray remark of mine about
animals in general, and applied it satirically to the misman-
agement of sheep and oxen in particular, they looked at
John Jago, while they talked to me. On occasions of this
sort—and they happened frequently—Naomi struck in resolutely at the right moment, and turned the talk to some
harmless topic. Every time she took a prominent part in this
way in keeping the peace, melancholy Miss Meadowcroft
looked slowly round at her in stern and silent disparagement
of her interference. A more dreary and more disunited
family party I never sat at the table with. Envy, hatred,
malice, and uncharitableness are never so essentially detest-
able to my mind as when they are animated by a sense of
propriety, and work under the surface. But for my interest
in Naomi, and my other interest in the little love-looks
which I now and then surprised passing between her and
Ambrose, I should never have sat through that supper. I
should certainly have taken refuge in my French novel and
my own room.

At last the unendurably long meal, served with ostenta-
tious profusion, was at an end. Miss Meadowcroft rose with
her ghostly solemnity, and granted me my dismissal in these
words:

'We are early people at the farm, Mr Lefrank. I wish you good-night.'

She laid her bony hands on the back of Mr Meadowcroft's invalid-chair, cut him short in his farewell salutation to me, and wheeled him out to his bed as if she were wheeling him out to his grave.

'Do you go to your room immediately, sir? If not, may I offer you a cigar?—provided the young gentlemen will permit it.'

So, picking his words with painful deliberation, and pointing his reference to 'the young gentlemen' with one sardonic side-look at them, Mr John Jago performed the duties of hospitality on his side. I excused myself from accepting the cigar. With studied politeness, the man of the glittering brown eyes wished me a good night's rest, and left the room.

Ambrose and Silas both approached me hospitably, with their open cigar cases in their hands.

'You were quite right to say "No,"' Ambrose began. 'Never smoke with John Jago. His cigars will poison you.'

'And never believe a word John Jago says to you,' added Silas. 'He is the greatest liar in America, let the other be whom he may.'

Naomi shook her forefinger reproachfully at them, as if the two sturdy young farmers had been two children.

'What will Mr Lefrank think,' she said, 'if you talk in that way of a person whom your father respects and trusts? Go and smoke. I am ashamed of both of you.'

Silas slunk away without a word of protest. Ambrose stood his ground, evidently bent on making his peace with Naomi before he left her.

Seeing that I was in the way, I walked aside towards a glass door at the lower end of the room. The door opened on the trim little farm-garden, bathed at that moment in lovely moonlight. I stepped out to enjoy the scene, and found my way to a seat under an elm tree. The grand repose of Nature had never looked so unutterably solemn and beautiful as it now appeared, after what I had seen and heard inside the house. I understood, or thought I understood, the sad despair of humanity which led men into monasteries in the old time. The misanthropical side of my nature (where is the sick man who is not conscious of that side of him?) was fast getting the upper hand of me—when I felt a light touch laid on my shoulder, and found myself reconciled to my species once more by Naomi Colebrook.

III

'I want to speak to you,' Naomi began. 'You don't think ill of me for following you out here? We are not accustomed to stand much on ceremony in America.'

'You are quite right in America. Pray sit down.'

She seated herself by my side, looking at me frankly and fearlessly by the light of the moon.

'You are related to the family here,' she resumed, 'and I am related too. I guess I may say to *you* what I couldn't say to a stranger. I am right glad you have come here, Mr Lefrank; and for a reason, sir, which you don't suspect.'

'Thank you for the compliment you pay me Miss Colebrook, whatever the reason may be.'

She took no notice of my reply: she steadily pursued her own train of thought.

'I guess you may do some good, sir, in this wretched house,' the girl went on, with her eyes still fixed earnestly on my face. 'There is no love, no trust, no peace at Morwick Farm. They want somebody here—except Ambrose: don't think ill of Ambrose; he is only thoughtless—I say, the rest of them want somebody here to make them ashamed of their hard hearts, and their horrid, false, envious ways. You are a gentleman; you know more than they know: they can't help themselves, they must look up to *you*. Try, Mr Lefrank, when you have the opportunity—pray try, sir, to make peace among them. You heard what went on at supper-time; and you were disgusted with it. Oh, yes, you were! I saw you frown to yourself; and I know what *that* means in you Englishmen.'

There was no choice but to speak one's mind plainly to Naomi. I acknowledged the impression which had been produced on me at supper-time just as plainly as I have acknowledged it in these pages. Naomi nodded her head in undisguised approval of my candour.

'That will do; that's speaking out,' she said. 'But—oh, my! you put it a deal too mildly, sir, when you say the men don't seem to be on friendly terms together here. They hate each other. That's the word, Mr Lefrank—hate; bitter, bitter, bitter, hate!' She clenched her little fists; she shook them vehemently, by way of adding emphasis to her last words; and then she suddenly remembered Ambrose. 'Except Ambrose,' she added, opening her hand again, and laying it very earnestly on my arm. 'Don't go and misjudge Ambrose, sir. There is no harm in poor Ambrose.'

The girl's innocent frankness was really irresistible.

'Should I be altogether wrong,' I asked, 'if I guessed that you were a little partial to Ambrose?'

An Englishwoman would have felt, or would at least have assumed, some little hesitation at replying to my question. Naomi did not hesitate for an instant.

'You are quite right, sir,' she said, with the most perfect composure. 'If things go well, I mean to marry Ambrose.'

'If things go well,' I repeated. 'What does that mean? Money?'

She shook her head.

'It means a fear that I have in my own mind,' she answered—'a fear, Mr Lefrank, of matters taking a bad turn among the men here—the wicked, hard-hearted, unfeeling men. I don't mean Ambrose, sir: I mean his brother Silas, and John Jago. Did you notice Silas's hand? John Jago did that, sir, with a knife.'

'By accident?' I asked.

'On purpose,' she answered. 'In return for a blow.'

This plain revelation of the state of things at Morwick Farm rather staggered me. Blows and knives under the rich and respectable roof-tree of old Mr Meadowcroft!—blows and knives not among the labourers, but among the masters! My first impression was like *your* first impression, no doubt. I could hardly believe it.

'Are you sure of what you say?' I enquired.

'I have it from Ambrose. Ambrose would never deceive me. Ambrose knows all about it.'

My curiosity was powerfully excited. To what sort of household had I rashly voyaged across the ocean in search of rest and quiet?

'May I know all about it too?' I said.

'Well, I will try and tell you what Ambrose told me. But you must promise me one thing first, sir. Promise you won't go away and leave us when you know the whole truth. Shake hands on it, Mr Lefrank; come, shake hands on it.'

There was no resisting her fearless frankness. I shook hands on it. Naomi entered on her narrative the moment I had given her my pledge, without wasting a word by way of preface.

'When you are shown over the farm here,' she began, 'you will really see that it is really two farms in one. On this side of it, as we look from under this tree, they raise crops: on the other side—on much the larger half of the land, mind— they raise cattle. When Mr Meadowcroft got too old and too sick to look after his farm himself, the boys (I mean Ambrose and Silas) divided the work between them. Ambrose looked after the crops, and Silas after the cattle. Things didn't go well, somehow, under their management. I can't tell you why. I am only sure Ambrose was not in fault. The old man got more and more dissatisfied, especially about his beasts. His pride is in his beasts. Without saying a word to the boys, he looked about privately (*I* think he was wrong in that, sir; don't you?)—he looked about privately for help; and, in an evil hour, he heard of John Jago. Do you like John Jago, Mr Lefrank?'

'So far, no. I don't like him.'

'Just my sentiments, sir. But I don't know: it's likely we may be wrong. There's nothing against John Jago, except that he is so odd in his ways. They do say he wears all that nasty hair on his face (I hate hair on a man's face) on account of a vow he made when he lost his wife. Don't you think, Mr Lefrank, a man must be a little mad who shows his grief at losing his wife by vowing that he will never shave himself again? Well, that's what they do say John Jago vowed. Perhaps it's a lie. People are such liars here! Anyway, it's truth (the boys themselves confess *that*), when John came to the farm he came with a first-rate character. The old man here isn't easy to please; and he pleased the old father. Yes, that's so. Mr Meadowcroft don't like my countrymen in general. He's like his sons—English, bitter English, to the marrow of his bones. Somehow, in spite of that, John Jago got round him; maybe because John does certainly know his business. Oh, yes! Cattle and crops, John knows his business. Since he's been overlooker, things have prospered as they didn't prosper in the time of the boys. Ambrose owned as much to me himself. Still, sir, it's hard to be set aside for a stranger isn't it? John gives the orders now. The boys do the work; but they have no voice in it when John and the old man put their heads together over the business of the farm. I have been long in telling you of it, sir; but now you know how the envy and the hatred grew among the men, before my time. Since I have been here, things seem to get worse and worse. There's hardly a day goes by that hard words don't pass between the boys and John, or the boys and their father. The old man has an aggravating way, Mr Lefrank—a nasty way, as we do call it—of taking John Jago's part. Do speak to him about it when you get the chance. The main blame of the quarrel between Silas and John the other day lies at his door, I think. I don't want to excuse Silas, either. It was brutal of him—though he *is* Ambrose's brother—to strike John, who is the smaller and weaker man of the two. But it was worse than brutal in John, to out with his knife, and try to stab Silas. Oh, he did it! If Silas had not caught the knife in his hand (his hand's awfully cut, I can tell you: I dressed it myself), it might have ended, for anything I know, in murder——'

She stopped as the word passed her lips, looked back over her shoulder, and started violently.

I looked where my companion was looking. The dark figure of a man was standing, watching us, in the shadow of the elm tree. I rose directly to approach him. Naomi recovered her self-possession, and checked me before I could interfere.

'Who are you?' she asked, turning sharply towards the stranger. 'What do you want there?'

The man stepped out from the shadow into the moonlight, and stood revealed to us as John Jago.

'I hope I am not intruding?' he said, looking hard at me.

'What do you want?' Naomi repeated.

'I don't wish to disturb you, or to disturb this gentleman,' he proceeded. 'When you are quite at leisure, Miss Naomi, you would be doing me a favour if you would permit me to say a few words to you in private.'

He spoke with the most scrupulous politeness; trying, and trying vainly, to conceal some strong agitation which was in possession of him. His wild brown eyes—wilder than ever in the moonlight—rested entreatingly, with a strange underlying expression of despair, on Naomi's face. His hands, clasped tightly in front of him, trembled incessantly. Little as I liked the man, he did really impress me as a pitiable object at that moment.

'Do you mean that you want to speak to me tonight?' Naomi asked, in undisguised surprise.

'Yes, miss, if you please, at your leisure and at Mr Lefrank's.'

Naomi hesitated.

'Won't it keep till tomorrow?' she said.

'I shall be away on farm business tomorrow, miss, for the whole day. Please to give me a few minutes this evening.' He advanced a step towards her: his voice faltered, and dropped timidly to a whisper. 'I really have something to say to you, Miss Naomi. It would be a kindness on your part—a very, very great kindness—if you will let me say it before I rest tonight.'

I rose again to resign my place to him. Once more Naomi checked me.

'No,' she said. 'Don't stir.' She addressed John Jago very reluctantly: 'If you are so much in earnest about it, Mr John, I suppose it must be. I can't guess what *you* can possibly have to say to me which cannot be said before a third person. However, it wouldn't be civil, I suppose, to say "No" in my place. You know it's my business to wind up the hall-clock at ten every night. If you choose to come and help me, the chances are that we shall have the hall to ourselves. Will that do?'

'Not in the hall, miss, if you will excuse me.'

'Not in the hall!'

'And not in the house either, if I may make so bold.'

'What do you mean?' She turned impatiently, and appealed to me. 'Do *you* understand him?'

John Jago signed to me imploringly to let him answer for himself.

'Bear with me, Miss Naomi,' he said. 'I think I can make you understand me. There are eyes on the watch, and ears on the watch, in the house; and there are some footsteps—I won't say whose—so soft, that no person can hear them.'

The last allusion evidently made itself understood. Naomi stopped him before he could say more.

'Well, where is it to be?' she asked, resignedly. 'Will the garden do, Mr John?'

'Thank you kindly, miss: the garden will do.' He pointed to a gravel-walk beyond us, bathed in the full flood of the moonlight. 'There,' he said, 'where we can see all round us, and be sure that nobody is listening. At ten o'clock.' He paused and addressed himself to me. 'I beg to apologise, sir, for intruding myself on your conversation. Please to excuse me.'

His eyes rested with a last anxious pleading look on Naomi's face. He bowed to us, and melted away into the shadow of the tree. The distant sound of a door, closed softly, came to us through the stillness of the night. John Jago had re-entered the house.

Now that he was out of hearing, Naomi spoke to me very earnestly:

'Don't suppose, sir, I have any secrets with *him*,' she said. 'I know no more than you do what he wants with me. I have half a mind not to keep the appointment. It's close on ten now. What would you do in my place?'

'Having made the appointment,' I answered, 'it seems to be due to yourself to keep it. If you feel the slightest alarm, I will wait in another part of the garden, so that I can hear if you call me.'

She received my proposal with a saucy toss of the head, and a smile of pity for my ignorance.

'You are a stranger, Mr Lefrank, or you would never talk to me in that way. In America, we don't do the men the honour of letting them alarm us. In America, the women take care of themselves. He has got my promise to meet him, as you say; and I must keep my promise. Only think,' she added, speaking more to herself than to me, 'of John Jago finding out Miss Meadowcroft's nasty, sly, underhand ways in the house! Most men would never had noticed her!'

I was completely taken by surprise. Sad and severe Miss Meadowcroft a listener and a spy! What next at Morwick Farm?

'Was that hint at the watchful eyes and ears, and the soft footsteps, really an allusion to Mr Meadowcroft's daughter?' I asked.

'Of course it was. Ah! she has imposed on you as she imposes on everybody else. The false wretch! She is secretly at the bottom of half the bad feeling among the men. I am certain of it—she keeps Mr Meadowcroft's mind bitter towards the boys. Old as she is, Mr Lefrank, and ugly as she is, she wouldn't object (if she could only make him ask her) to be John Jago's second wife. No, sir; and she wouldn't break her heart if the boys were not left a stick or a stone on the farm when the father dies. I have watched her, and I know it. Ah! I could tell you such things. But there's no time now—there's ten o'clock striking! we must say good-night. I am right glad I have spoken to you, sir. I say again, at parting, what I have said already: use your influence, pray use your influence, to soften them, and to make them ashamed of themselves, in this wicked house. We will have more talk about what you can do tomorrow, when you are shown over the farm. Say good-bye now; I must keep my appointment. Look! here is John Jago stealing out again in the shadow of the tree! Good-night, friend Lefrank; and pleasant dreams.'

With one hand she took mine, and pressed it cordially: with the other she pushed me away without ceremony in the direction of the house. A charming girl!—an irresistible girl!

I was nearly as bad as the boys. I declare, *I* almost hated
John Jago, too, as we crossed each other in the shadow of
the tree.

Arrived at the glass door, I stopped, and looked back at
the gravel-walk.

They had met. I saw the two shadowy figures slowly
pacing backwards and forwards in the moonlight, the woman
a little in advance of the man. What was he saying to her?
Why was he so anxious that not a word of it should be
heard? Our presentiments are sometimes, in certain rare
cases, the faithful prophecy of the future. A vague distrust
of that moonlight-meeting stealthily took a hold on my
mind. 'Will mischief come of it?' I asked myself, as I closed
the door and entered the house.

Mischief *did* come of it. You shall hear how.

IV

Persons of sensitive nervous temperament, sleeping for the
first time in a strange house, and in a bed that is new to
them, must make up their minds to pass a wakeful night.
My first night at Morwick Farm was no exception to this
rule. The little sleep I had was broken and disturbed by
dreams. Towards six o'clock in the morning my bed became
unendurable to me. The sun was shining in brightly at the
window. I determined to try the reviving influence of a stroll
in the fresh morning air.

Just as I got out of bed, I heard footsteps and voices under
my window.

The footsteps stopped, and the voices became recognis-
able. I had passed the night with my window open: I was
able, without exciting notice from below, to look out.

The persons beneath me were Silas Meadowcroft,
John Jago, and three strangers, whose dress and appearance indicated plainly enough that they were labourers on
the farm. Silas was swinging a stout beechen stick in his
hand, and was speaking to Jago, coarsely and insolently
enough, of his moonlight-meeting with Naomi on the previous night.

'Next time you go courting a young lady in secret,' said Silas, 'make sure that the moon goes down first, or wait for a cloudy sky. You were seen in the garden, Master Jago; and you may as well tell us the truth for once in a way. Did you find her open to persuasion, sir? Did she say "Yes?" '

John Jago kept his temper.

'If you must have your joke, Mr Silas,' he said, quietly and firmly, 'be pleased to joke on some other subject. You are quite wrong, sir, in what you suppose to have passed between the young lady and me.'

Silas turned about, and addressed himself ironically to the three labourers.

'You hear him, boys? He can't tell the truth, try him as you may. He wasn't making love to Naomi in the garden last night—oh, dear, no! He has had one wife already; and he knows better than to take the yoke on his shoulders for the second time!'

Greatly to my surprise, John Jago met this clumsy jesting with a formal and serious reply.

'You are quite right, sir,' he said. 'I have no intention of marrying for the second time. What I was saying to Miss Naomi doesn't matter to you. It was not at all what you choose to suppose; it was something of quite another kind, with which you have no concern. Be pleased to understand once for all, Mr Silas, that not so much as the thought of making love to the young lady has ever entered my head. I respect her; I admire her good qualities: but if she was the only woman left in the world, and if I was a much younger man than I am, I should never think of asking her to be my wife.' He burst out suddenly into a harsh uneasy laugh. 'No, no! not my style, Mr Silas—not my style!'

Something in those words, or in his manner of speaking them, appeared to exasperate Silas. He dropped his clumsy irony, and addressed himself directly to John Jago in a tone of savage contempt.

'Not your style?' he repeated. 'Upon my soul, that's a cool way of putting it, for a man in your place! What do you mean by calling her "not your style"? You impudent beggar! Naomi Colebrook is meat for your master!'

John Jago's temper began to give way at last. He approached defiantly a step or two nearer to Silas Meadowcroft.

'Who is my master?' he asked.

'Ambrose will show you, if you go to him,' answered the other. 'Naomi is *his* sweetheart, not mine. Keep out of his way, if you want to keep a whole skin on your bones.'

John Jago cast one of his sardonic sidelooks at the farmer's wounded left hand. 'Don't forget your own skin, Mr Silas, when you threaten mine! I have set my mark on you once, sir. Let me by on my business, or I may mark you for a second time.'

Silas lifted his beechen stick. The labourers, roused to some rude sense of the serious turn which the quarrel was taking, got between the two men, and parted them. I had been hurriedly dressing myself while the altercation was proceeding; and now I ran downstairs to try what my influence could do towards keeping the peace at Morwick Farm.

The war of angry words was still going on when I joined the men outside.

'Be off with you on your business, you cowardly hound!' I heard Silas say. 'Be off with you to the town! and take care you don't meet Ambrose on the way!'

'Take *you* care you don't feel my knife again before I go!' cried the other man.

Silas made a desperate effort to break away from the labourers who were holding him.

'Last time you only felt my fist!' he shouted. 'Next time you shall feel *this*!'

He lifted the stick as he spoke. I stepped up, and snatched it out of his hand.

'Mr Silas,' I said, 'I am an invalid, and I am going out for a walk. Your stick will be useful to me. I beg leave to borrow it.'

The labourers burst out laughing. Silas fixed his eyes on me with a stare of angry surprise. John Jago, immediately recovering his self-possession, took off his hat, and made me a deferential bow.

'I had no idea, Mr Lefrank, that we were disturbing you,' he said. 'I am very much ashamed of myself, sir. I beg to apologise.'

'I accept your apology, Mr Jago,' I answered, 'on the understanding that you, as the older man, will set the example of forbearance, if your temper is tried on any future occasion as it has been tried today. And I have further to request,' I added, addressing myself to Silas, 'that you will do me a favour, as your father's guest. The next time your good spirits lead you into making jokes at Mr Jago's expense, don't carry them quite so far. I am sure you meant no harm, Mr Silas. Will you gratify me by saying so yourself? I want to see you and Mr Jago shake hands.'

John Jago instantly held out his hand, with an assumption of good feeling which was a little overacted, to my thinking. Silas Meadowcroft made no advance of the same friendly sort on his side.

'Let him go about his business,' said Silas. 'I won't waste any more words on him, Mr Lefrank, to please *you*. But (saving your presence) I'm damned if I take his hand!'

Further persuasion was plainly useless, addressed to such a man as this. Silas gave me no further opportunity of remonstrating with him, even if I had been inclined to do so. He turned about in sulky silence, and, retracing his steps along the path, disappeared round the corner of the house. The labourers withdrew next, in different directions, to begin the day's work. John Jago and I were alone.

I left it to the man of the wild brown eyes to speak first.

'In half an hour's time, sir,' he said, 'I shall be going on business to Narrabee, our market-town here. Can I take any letters to the post for you? or is there anything else that I can do in the town?'

I thanked him, and declined both proposals. He made me another deferential bow, and withdrew into the house. I mechanically followed the path, in the direction which Silas had taken before me.

Turning the corner of the house, and walking on for a little way, I found myself at the entrance to the stables, and face to face with Silas Meadowcroft once more. He had his elbows on the gate of the yard, swinging it slowly backwards and forwards, and turning and twisting a straw between his teeth. When he saw me approaching him, he advanced a step from the gate, and made an effort to excuse himself, with a very ill grace.

'No offence, mister. Ask me what you will besides, and I'll do it for you. But don't ask me to shake hands with John Jago; I hate him too badly for that. If I touched him with one hand, sir, I tell you this, I should throttle him with the other!'

'That's your feeling towards the man, Mr Silas, is it?'

'That's my feeling, Mr Lefrank; and I'm not ashamed of it, either.'

'Is there any such place as a church in your neighbour-hood, Mr Silas?'

'Of course there is.'

'And do you ever go to it?'

'Of course I do.'

'At long intervals, Mr Silas?'

'Every Sunday, sir, without fail.'

Some third person behind me burst out laughing; some third person had been listening to our talk. I turned round, and discovered Ambrose Meadowcroft.

'I understand the drift of your catechism, though my brother doesn't,' he said. 'Don't be hard on Silas, sir. He isn't the only Christian who leaves his Christianity in the pew when he goes out of church. You will never make us friends with John Jago, try as you may. Why, what have you got there, Mr Lefrank? May I die if it isn't my stick! I have been looking for it everywhere!'

The thick beechen stick had been feeling uncomfortably heavy in my invalid hand for some time past. There was no sort of need for my keeping it any longer. John Jago was going away to Narrabee, and Silas Meadowcroft's savage temper was subdued to a sulky repose. I handed the stick back to Ambrose. He laughed as he took it from me.

'You can't think how strange it feels, Mr Lefrank, to be without one's stick,' he said. 'A man gets used to his stick, sir; doesn't he? Are you ready for your breakfast?'

'Not just yet. I thought of taking a little walk first.'

'All right, sir. I wish I could go with you; but I have got my work to do this morning, and Silas has his work too. If you go back by the way you came, you will find yourself in the garden. If you want to go further, the wicket-gate at the end will lead you into the lane.'

Through sheer thoughtlessness, I did a very foolish thing. I turned back as I was told, and left the brothers together at the gate of the stable-yard.

V

Arrived at the garden, a thought struck me. The cheerful speech and easy manner of Ambrose plainly indicated that he was ignorant thus far of the quarrel which had taken place under my window. Silas might confess to having taken his brother's stick, and might mention whose head he had threatened with it. It was not only useless, but undesirable, that Ambrose should know of the quarrel. I retraced my steps to the stable-yard. Nobody was at the gate. I called alternately to Silas and to Ambrose. Nobody answered. The brothers had gone away to their work.

Returning to the garden, I heard a pleasant voice wishing me 'Good morning'. I looked round. Naomi Colebrook was standing at one of the lower windows of the farm. She had her working-apron on, and she was industriously brightening the knives for the breakfast table, on an old-fashioned board. A sleek black cat balanced himself on her shoulder watching the flashing motion of the knife as she passed it rapidly to and fro on the leather-covered surface of the board.

'Come here,' she said: 'I want to speak to you.'

I noticed as I approached, that her pretty face was cloudy and anxious. She pushed the cat irritably off her shoulder: she welcomed me with only the faint reflection of her bright customary smile.

'I have seen John Jago,' she said. 'He has been hinting at something which he says happened under your bedroom window this morning. When I begged him to explain himself he only answered, "Ask Mr Lefrank: I must be off to Narrabee." What does it mean? Tell me right away, sir! I'm out of temper, and I can't wait!'

Except that I made the best instead of the worst of it, I told her what had happened under my window as plainly as I have told it here. She put down the knife that she was cleaning, and folded her hands before her, thinking.

'I wish I had never given John Jago that meeting,' she said. 'When a man asks anything of a woman, the woman, I find, mostly repents it if she says "Yes".'

She made that quaint reflection with a very troubled brow. The moonlight-meeting had left some unwelcome remembrances in her mind. I saw that as plainly as I saw Naomi herself.

What had John Jago said to her? I put the question with all needful delicacy, making my apologies beforehand.

'I should like to tell *you*,' she began, with a strong emphasis on the last word.

There she stopped. She turned pale; then suddenly flushed again to the deepest red. She took up the knife once more, and went on cleaning it as industriously as ever.

'I mustn't tell you,' she resumed, with her head down over the knife. 'I have promised not to tell anybody. That's the truth. Forget all about it, sir, as soon as you can. Hush! here's the spy who saw us last night on the walk, and who told Silas!'

Dreary Miss Meadowcroft opened the kitchen door. She carried an ostentatiously large Prayer Book; and she looked at Naomi as only a jealous woman of middle age *can* look at a younger and prettier woman than herself.

'Prayers, Miss Colebrook,' she said, in her sourest manner. She paused, and noticed me standing under the window. 'Prayers, Mr Lefrank,' she added, with a look of devout pity, directed exclusively to my address.

'We will follow you directly, Miss Meadowcroft,' said Naomi.

'I have no desire to intrude on your secrets, Miss Colebrook.'

With that acrid answer, our priestess took herself and her Prayer Book out of the kitchen. I joined Naomi, entering the room by the garden door. She met me eagerly.

'I am not quite easy about something,' she said. 'Did you tell me that you left Ambrose and Silas together?'

'Yes.'

'Suppose Silas tells Ambrose of what happened this morning?'

The same idea, as I have already mentioned, had occurred to my mind. I did my best to reassure Naomi.

'Mr Jago is out of the way,' I replied. 'You and I can easily put things right in his absence.'

She took my arm.

'Come into prayers,' she said. 'Ambrose will be there, and I shall find an opportunity of speaking to him.'

Neither Ambrose nor Silas was in the breakfast-room when we entered it. After waiting vainly for ten minutes, Mr Meadowcroft told his daughter to read the prayers. Miss Meadowcroft read, thereupon, in the tone of an injured woman taking the throne of mercy by storm, and insisting on her rights. Breakfast followed; and still the brothers were absent. Miss Meadowcroft looked at her father, and said, 'From bad to worse, sir. What did I tell you?' Naomi instantly applied the antidote: 'The boys are no doubt detained over their work, uncle.' She turned to me. 'You want to see the farm, Mr Lefrank. Come and help me to find the boys.'

For more than an hour we visited one part of the farm after another, without discovering the missing men. We found them at last near the outskirts of a small wood, sitting, talking together, on the trunk of a felled tree.

Silas rose as we approached, and walked away without a word of greeting or apology, into the wood. As he got on his feet I noticed that his brother whispered something in his ear; and I heard him answer, 'All right!'

'Ambrose, does that mean you have something to keep a secret from us?' asked Naomi, approaching her lover with a smile. 'Is Silas ordered to hold his tongue?'

Ambrose kicked sulkily at the loose stones lying about him. I noticed, with a certain surprise, that his favourite stick was not in his hand, and was not lying near him.

'Business,' he said, in answer to Naomi, not very gra-
ciously— 'business between Silas and me. That's what it
means, if you must know.'

Naomi went on, woman-like, with her questions, heedless
of the reception which they might meet with from an irritated man.

'Why were you both away at prayers and breakfast time?'
she asked next.

'We had too much to do,' Ambrose gruffly replied, 'and
we were too far from the house.'

'Very odd,' said Naomi. 'This has never happened before,
since I have been at the farm.'

'Well, live and learn. It has happened now.'

The tone in which he spoke would have warned any man
to let him alone. But warnings which speak by implication
only are thrown away on women. The woman, having still
something in her mind to say, said it.

'Have you seen anything of John Jago this morning?'

The smouldering ill-temper of Ambrose burst suddenly—
why, it was impossible to guess—into a flame.

'How many more questions am I to answer?' he
broke out, violently. 'Are you the parson, putting me
through my catechism? I have seen nothing of John Jago,
and I have got my work to go on with. Will that do for
you?'

He turned with an oath, and followed his brother into the
wood. Naomi's bright eyes looked up at me, flashing with
indignation.

'What does he mean, Mr Lefrank, by speaking to me in
that way? Rude brute! How dare he do it?' She paused: her
voice, look, and manner suddenly changed. 'This has never
happened before, sir. Has anything gone wrong? I declare,
I shouldn't know Ambrose again, he is so changed. Say,
how does it strike you?'

I made the best of a bad case.

'Something has upset his temper,' I said. 'The merest
trifle, Miss Colebrook, upsets a man's temper sometimes. I
speak as a man, and I know it. Give him time, and he will
make his excuses, and all will be well again.'

My presentation of the case entirely failed to reassure my pretty companion. We went back to the house. Dinner-time came, and the brothers appeared. Their father spoke to them of their absence from morning prayers—with needless severity, as I thought. They resented the reproof with needless indignation on their side, and left the room. A sour smile of satisfaction showed itself on Miss Meadowcroft's thin lips. She looked at her father; then raised her eyes sadly to the ceiling, and said, 'We can only pray for them, sir.'

Naomi disappeared after dinner. When I saw her again, she had some news for me.

'I have been with Ambrose,' she said, 'and he has begged my pardon. We have made it up, Mr Lefrank. Still—still——'

'Still—*what*, Miss Naomi?'

'He is not like himself, sir. He denies it; but I can't help thinking he is hiding something from me.'

The day wore on: the evening came. I returned to my French novel. But not even Dumas himself could keep my attention to the story. What else I was thinking of I cannot say. Why I was out of spirits I am unable to explain. I wished myself back in England: I took a blind unreasonable hatred to Morwick Farm.

Nine o'clock struck; and we all assembled again at supper, with the exception of John Jago. He was expected back to supper; and we waited for him a quarter of an hour, by Mr Meadowcroft's own directions. John Jago never appeared.

The night wore on, and still the absent man failed to return. Miss Meadowcroft volunteered to sit up for him. Naomi eyed her, a little maliciously I must own, as the two women parted for the night. I withdrew to my room; and again I was unable to sleep. When sunrise came, I went out, as before, to breathe the morning air.

On the staircase I met Miss Meadowcroft ascending to her own room. Not a curl of her stiff grey hair was disarranged: nothing about the impenetrable woman betrayed that she had been watching through the night.

'Has Mr Jago not returned?' I asked.

Miss Meadowcroft slowly shook her head, and frowned at me.

'We are in the hands of Providence, Mr Lefrank. Mr Jago must have been detained for the night at Narrabee.'

The daily routine of the meals resumed its unalterable course. Breakfast-time came and dinner-time came, and no John Jago darkened the doors of Morwick Farm. Mr Meadowcroft and his daughter consulted together, and determined to send in search of the missing man. One of the more intelligent of the labourers was despatched to Narrabee to make inquiries.

The man returned late in the evening, bringing startling news to the farm. He had visited all the inns and all the places of business resort in Narrabee; he had made endless inquiries in every direction, with this result—no one had set eyes on John Jago. Everybody declared that John Jago had not entered the town.

We all looked at each other, excepting the two brothers, who were seated together in a dark corner of the room. The conclusion appeared to be inevitable. John Jago was a lost man.

VI

Mr Meadowcroft was the first to speak.

'Somebody must find John,' he said.

'Without losing a moment,' added his daughter.

Ambrose suddenly stepped out of the dark corner of the room.

'*I* will inquire,' he said.

Silas followed him.

'I will go with you,' he added.

Mr Meadowcroft interposed his authority.

'One of you will be enough; for the present, at least. You go, Ambrose. Your brother may be wanted later. If any accident has happened (which God forbid), we may have to inquire in more than one direction. Silas, you will stay at the farm.'

The brothers withdrew together—Ambrose to prepare for his journey, Silas to saddle one of the horses for him. Naomi slipped out after them: left in company with Mr Meadow-croft and his daughter (both devoured by anxiety about the missing man, and both trying to conceal it under an assumption of devout resignation to circumstances), I need hardly add that I too, retired, as soon as it was politely possible for me to leave the room. Ascending the stairs on my way to my own quarters, I discovered Naomi half-hidden in a recess formed by an old-fashioned window-seat on the first landing. My bright little friend was in sore trouble. Her apron was over her face, and she was crying bitterly. Ambrose had not taken his leave as tenderly as usual. She was more firmly persuaded than ever that 'Ambrose was hiding something from her'. We all waited anxiously for the next day. The next day made the mystery deeper than ever.

The horse which had taken Ambrose to Narrabee was ridden back to the farm by a groom from the hotel. He delivered a written message from Ambrose which startled us. Further inquiries had positively proved that the missing man had never been near Narrabee. The only attainable tidings of his whereabouts were tidings derived from vague report. It was said that a man like John Jago had been seen the previous day in a railway car, travelling on the line to New York. Acting on this imperfect information, Ambrose had decided on verifying the truth of the report by extending his enquiries to New York.

This extraordinary proceeding forced the suspicion on me that something had really gone wrong. I kept my doubts to myself; but I was prepared, from that moment, to see the disappearance of John Jago followed by very grave results.

The same day the results declared themselves.

Time enough had now elapsed for report to spread through the district the news of what had happened at the farm. Already aware of the bad feeling existing between the men, the neighbours had been now informed (no doubt by the labourers present) of the deplorable scene that had taken place under my bedroom window. Public opinion declares itself in America without the slightest reserve, or the slightest care for consequences. Public opinion declared on this occasion that the lost man was the victim of foul play, and held one or both of the brothers Meadowcroft responsible for his disappearance. Later in the day, the reasonableness of this serious view of the case was confirmed in the popular mind by a startling discovery. It was announced that a Methodist preacher lately settled at Morwick, and greatly respected throughout the district, had dreamed of John Jago in the character of a murdered man, whose bones were hidden at Morwick Farm. Before night the cry was general for a verification of the preacher's dream. Not only in the immediate district, but in the town of Narrabee itself, the public voice insisted on the necessity of a search for the mortal remains of John Jago at Morwick Farm.

In the terrible turn which matters had now taken, Mr Meadowcroft the elder displayed a spirit and an energy for which I was not prepared.

'My sons have their faults,' he said—'serious faults, and nobody knows it better than I do. My sons have behaved badly and ungratefully towards John Jago; I don't deny that either. But Ambrose and Silas are not murderers. Make your search. I ask for it; no, I insist on it, after what has been said, in justice to my family and my name!'

The neighbours took him at his word. The Morwick section of the American nation organised itself on the spot. The sovereign people met in committee, made speeches, elected competent persons to represent the public interests, and began the search the next day. The whole proceeding, ridiculously informal from a legal point of view, was carried on by these extraordinary people with as stern and strict a sense of duty as if it had been sanctioned by the highest tribunal in the land.

Naomi met the calamity that had fallen on the household as resolutely as her uncle himself. The girl's courage rose with the call which was made on it. Her one anxiety was for Ambrose.

'He ought to be here,' she said to me. 'The wretches in this neighbourhood are wicked enough to say that his absence is a confession of his guilt.'

She was right. In the present temper of the popular mind the absence of Ambrose was a suspicious circumstance in itself.

'We might telegraph to New York,' I suggested, 'if you only knew where a message would be likely to find him.'

'I know the hotel which the Meadowcrofts use at New York,' she replied. 'I was sent there after my father's death, to wait till Miss Meadowcroft could take me to Morwick.'

We decided on telegraphing to the hotel. I was writing the message, and Naomi was looking over my shoulder, when we were startled by a strange voice speaking close behind us.

'Oh! that's his address, is it?' said the voice. 'We wanted his address rather badly.'

The speaker was a stranger to me. Naomi recognised him as one of the neighbours.

'What do you want his address for?' she asked, sharply.

'I guess we've found the mortal remains of John Jago, miss,' the man replied. 'We have got Silas already, and we want Ambrose, too, on suspicion of murder.'

'It's a lie!' cried Naomi, furiously—'a wicked lie!'

The man turned to me.

'Take her into the next room, mister,' he said, 'and let her see for herself.'

We went together into the next room.

In one corner, sitting by her father, and holding his hand, we saw stern and stony Miss Meadowcroft, weeping silently. Opposite to them, crouched on the window-seat—his eyes wandering, his hands hanging helpless—we next discovered Silas Meadowcroft, plainly self-betrayed as a panic-stricken man. A few of the persons who had been engaged in the search were seated near, watching him. The mass of the strangers present stood congregated round a table in the middle of the room. They drew aside as I approached with Naomi, and allowed us to have a clear view of certain objects placed on the table.

The centre object of the collection was a little heap of charred bones. Round this were ranged a knife, two metal buttons, and a stick partially burnt. The knife was recognised by the labourers as the weapon John Jago habitually carried about with him—the weapon with which he had wounded Silas Meadowcroft's hand. The buttons Naomi herself declared to have a peculiar pattern on them, which had formerly attracted her attention to John Jago's coat. As for the stick, burnt as it was, I had no difficulty in identifying the quaintly-carved knob at the top. It was the heavy beechen stick which I had restored to Ambrose on his claiming it as his own. In reply to my inquiries, I was informed that the bones, the knife, the buttons and the stick, had all been found together in a lime-kiln then in use on the farm.

'Is it serious?' Naomi whispered to me, as we drew back from the table.

It would have been sheer cruelty to deceive her now.

'Yes,' I whispered back; 'it *is* serious.'

The search committee conducted its proceedings with the strictest regularity. The proper applications were made forthwith to a justice of the peace, and the justice issued his warrant. That night Silas was committed to prison; and an officer was despatched to arrest Ambrose in New York.

For my part, I did the little I could to make myself useful. With the silent sanction of Mr Meadowcroft and his daughter, I went to Narrabee, and secured the best legal assistance for the defence which the town could place at my disposal. This done, there was no choice but to wait for news of Ambrose, and for the examination before the magistrate which was to follow. I shall pass over the misery in the house during the interval of expectation: no useful purpose could be served by describing it now. Let me only say that Naomi's conduct strengthened me in the conviction that she possessed a noble nature. I was unconscious of the state of my own feelings at the time; but I am now disposed to think that this was the epoch at which I began to envy Ambrose the wife whom he had won.

The telegraph brought us our first news of Ambrose. He had been arrested at the hotel, and he was on his way to Morwick. The next day he arrived, and followed his brother to prison. The two were confined in separate cells, and were forbidden all communication with each other.

Two days later, the preliminary examination took place. Ambrose and Silas Meadowcroft were charged before the magistrate with the wilful murder of John Jago. I was cited to appear as one of the witnesses; and, at Naomi's own request, I took the poor girl into court, and sat by her during the proceedings. My host also was present in his invalid-chair, with his daughter by his side.

Such was the result of my voyage across the ocean in search of rest and quiet; and thus did time and chance fulfil my first hasty forebodings of the dull life I was to lead at Morwick Farm!

VII

On our way to the chairs allotted to us in the magistrate's court, we passed the platform on which the prisoners were standing together.

Silas took no notice of us. Ambrose made a friendly sign of recognition, and then rested his hand on the 'bar' in front of him. As she passed beneath him, Naomi was just tall enough to reach his hand on tiptoe. She took it. 'I know you are innocent,' she whispered, and gave him one look of loving encouragement as she followed me to her place. Ambrose never lost his self-control. I may have been wrong; but I thought this a bad sign.

The case, as stated for the prosecution, told strongly against the suspected men.

Ambrose and Silas Meadowcroft were charged with the murder of John Jago (by means of the stick or by use of some other weapon), and with the deliberate destruction of the body by throwing it into the quicklime. In proof of this latter assertion, the knife which the deceased habitually carried about him, and the metal buttons which were known to belong to his coat, were produced. It was argued that these indestructible substances, and some fragments of the larger bones, had alone escaped the action of the burning lime. Having produced medical witnesses to support this theory by declaring the bones to be human, and having thus circumstantially asserted the discovery of the remains in the kiln, the prosecution next proceeded to prove that the missing man had been murdered by the two brothers, and had been by them thrown into the quicklime as a means of concealing their guilt.

Witness after witness deposed to the inveterate enmity against the deceased displayed by Ambrose and Silas. The threatening language they habitually used towards him; their violent quarrels with him, which had become a public scandal throughout the neighbourhood, and which had ended (on one occasion at least) in a blow; the disgraceful scene which had taken place under my window; and the restoration to Ambrose, on the morning of the fatal quarrel, of the very stick which had been found among the remains of the dead man—these facts and events, and a host of minor circumstances besides, sworn to by witnesses whose credit was unimpeachable, pointed with terrible directness to the conclusion at which the prosecution had arrived.

I looked at the brothers as the weight of the evidence pressed more and more heavily against them. To outward view, at least, Ambrose still maintained his self-possession. It was far otherwise with Silas. Abject terror showed itself in his ghastly face; in his great knotty hands, clinging convulsively to the bar at which he stood; in his staring eyes, fixed in vacant horror on each witness who appeared. Public feeling judged him on the spot. There he stood, self-betrayed already, in the popular opinion, as a guilty man!

The one point gained in cross-examination by the defence related to the charred bones.

Pressed on this point, a majority of the medical witnesses admitted that their examination had been a hurried one, and that it was just possible that the bones might yet prove to be the remains of an animal, and not of a man. The presiding magistrate decided upon this, that a second examination should be made, and that the number of the medical experts should be increased.

Here the preliminary proceedings ended. The prisoners were remanded for three days.

The prostration of Silas at the close of the inquiry was so complete, that it was found necessary to have two men to support him on his leaving the court. Ambrose leaned over the bar to speak to Naomi before he followed the gaoler out.

'Wait,' he whispered confidently, 'till they hear what I have to say!' Naomi kissed her hand to him affectionately, and turned to me with the bright tears in her eyes.

'Why don't they hear what he has to say at once?' she asked. 'Anybody can see that Ambrose is innocent. It's a crying shame, sir, to send him back to prison. Don't you think so yourself?'

If I had confessed what I really thought, I should have said that Ambrose had proved nothing to my mind, except that he possessed rare powers of self-control. It was impossible to acknowledge this to my little friend. I diverted her mind from the question of her lover's innocence, by proposing that we should get the necessary order and visit him in his prison on the next day. Naomi dried her tears, and gave me a little grateful squeeze of the hand.

'Oh, my! what a good fellow you are!' cried the outspoken American girl. 'When your time comes to be married, sir, I guess the woman won't repent saying "Yes" to *you*!'

Mr Meadowcroft preserved unbroken silence as we walked back to the farm on either side of his invalid-chair. His last reserves of resolution seemed to have given way under the overwhelming strain laid on them by the proceedings in court. His daughter, in stern indulgence to Naomi, mercifully permitted her opinion to glimmer on us only, through the medium of quotation from scripture-texts. If the texts meant anything, they meant that she had foreseen all that had happened, and that the one sad aspect of the case, to her mind, was the death of John Jago, unprepared to meet his end.

I obtained the order of admission to the prison the next morning.

We found Ambrose still confident of the favourable result, for his brother and for himself, of the inquiry before the magistrate. He seemed to be almost as eager to tell, as Naomi was to hear, the true story of what had happened at the lime-kiln. The authorities of the prison—present, of course, at the interview—warned him to remember that what he said might be taken down in writing and produced against him in court.

'Take it down, gentlemen, and welcome,' Ambrose replied. 'I have nothing to fear; I am only telling the truth.'

With that he turned to Naomi, and began his narrative, as nearly as I can remember, in these words:

'I may as well make a clean breast of it at starting, my girl. After Mr Lefrank left us that morning, I asked Silas how he came by my stick. In telling me how, Silas also told me of the words that had passed between him and John Jago under Mr Lefrank's window. I was angry and jealous; and I own it freely, Naomi, I thought the worst that could be thought about you and John.'

Here Naomi stopped him without ceremony.

'Was that what made you speak to me as you spoke when we found you at the wood?' she asked.

'Yes.'

'And was that what made you leave me, when you went away to Narrabee, without giving me a kiss at parting?'

'It was.'

'Beg my pardon for it before you say a word more.'

'I beg your pardon.'

'Say you are ashamed of yourself.'

'I am ashamed of myself,' Ambrose answered, penitently.

'Now you may go on,' said Naomi. 'Now I'm satisfied.'

Ambrose went on.

'We were on our way to the clearing at the other side of the wood while Silas was talking to me; and, as ill luck would have it, we took the path that led by the lime-kiln. Turning the corner, we met John Jago on his way to Narrabee. I was too angry, I tell you, to let him pass quietly. I gave him a bit of my mind. His blood was up too, I suppose; and he spoke out, on his side, as freely as I did. I own I threatened him with the stick; but I'll swear to it I meant him no harm. You know—after dressing Silas's hand— that John Jago is ready with his knife. He comes from out West, where they are always ready with one weapon or another handy in their pockets. It's likely enough *he* didn't mean to harm me, either; but how could I be sure of that? When he stepped up to me, and showed his weapon, I dropped the stick, and closed with him. With one hand I wrenched the knife away from him; and with the other I caught him by the collar of his rotten old coat, and gave him a shaking that made his bones rattle in his skin. A big piece of the cloth came away in my hand. I shied it into the quicklime close by us, and I pitched the knife after the cloth; and, if Silas hadn't stopped me, I think it's likely I might have shied John Jago himself into the lime next. As it was, Silas kept hold of me. Silas shouted out to him, 'Be off with you! and don't come back again, if you don't want to be burnt in the kiln!' He stood looking at us for a minute, fetching his breath, and holding his torn coat round him. Then he spoke with a deadly-quiet voice and a deadly-quiet look: "Many a true word, Mr Silas," he says, "is spoken in jest. *I shall not come back again.*" He turned about, and left us. We stood staring at each other like a couple of fools. "You don't think he means it?" I says. "Bosh!" says Silas. "He's too sweet on Naomi not to come back." What's the matter now, Naomi?'

I had noticed it too. She started and turned pale, when Ambrose repeated to her what Silas had said to him.

'Nothing is the matter,' Naomi answered. 'Your brother has no right to take liberties with my name. Go on. Did Silas say any more while he was about it?'

'Yes: he looked into the kiln; and he says "What made you throw away the knife, Ambrose?"—"How does a man know why he does anything," I says, "when he does it in a passion?"—"It's a ripping-good knife," says Silas: "in your place, I should have kept it." I picked up the stick off the ground. "Who says I've lost it yet?" I answered him; and with that I got up on the side of the kiln, and began sounding for the knife, to bring it, you know, by means of the stick, within easy reach of a shovel, or some such thing. "Give us your hand," I says to Silas. "Let me stretch out a bit, and I'll have it in no time." Instead of finding the knife, I came nigh to falling myself into the burning lime. The vapour overpowered me, I suppose. All I know is, I turned giddy, and dropped the stick in the kiln. I should have followed the stick, to a dead certainty, but for Silas pulling me back by the hand. "Let it be," says Silas. "If I hadn't had hold of you, John Jago's knife might have been the death of you, after all!" He led me away by the arm, and we went on together on the road to the wood. We stopped where you found us, and sat down on the felled tree. We had a little more talk about John Jago. It ended in our agreeing to wait and see what happened, and to keep our own counsel in the meantime. You and Mr Lefrank came upon us, Naomi, while we were still talking; and you guessed right when you guessed that we had a secret from you. You know the secret now.'

There he stopped. I put the question to him—the first that I had asked yet.

'Had you or your brother any fear at that time of the charge which has since been brought against you?' I said.

'No such thought entered our heads, sir,' Ambrose answered. 'How could *we* foresee that the neighbours would search the kiln, and say what they have said of us? All we feared was, that the old man might hear of the quarrel, and be bitterer against us than ever. I was the more anxious of the two to keep things secret, because I had Naomi to consider as well as the old man. Put yourself in my place, and you will own, sir, that the prospect at home was not a pleasant one for *me*, if John Jago really kept away from the farm, and if it came out that it was all my doing.'

(This was certainly an explanation of his conduct; but it was not quite satisfactory to my mind.)

'As *you* believe, then,' I went on, 'John Jago has carried out his threat of not returning to the farm? According to you, he is now alive and in hiding somewhere?'

'Certainly!' said Ambrose.

'Certainly!' repeated Naomi.

'Do you believe the report that he was seen travelling on the railway to New York?'

'I believe it firmly, sir; and, what is more, I believe I was on his track. I was only too anxious to find him; and I say I could have found him, if they would have let me stay in New York.'

I looked at Naomi.

'I believe it too,' she said. 'John Jago is keeping away.'

'Do you suppose he is afraid of Ambrose and Silas?'

She hesitated.

'He *may* be afraid of them,' she replied, with a strong emphasis on the word 'may'.

'But you don't think it likely?'

She hesitated again. I pressed her again.

'Do you think there is any other motive for his absence?'

Her eyes dropped to the floor. She answered obstinately, almost doggedly—

'I can't say.'

I addressed myself to Ambrose.

'Have you anything more to tell us?' I asked.

'No,' he said. 'I have told you all I know about it.'

I rose to speak to the lawyer whose services I had retained. He had helped us to get the order of admission, and he had accompanied us to the prison. Seated apart, he had kept silence throughout, attentively watching the effect of Ambrose Meadowcroft's narrative on the officers of the prison and on me.

'Is this the defence?' I inquired, in a whisper.

'This is the defence, Mr Lefrank. What do you think between ourselves?'

'Between ourselves, I think the magistrate will commit them for trial.'

'On the charge of murder?'

'Yes; on the charge of murder.'

VIII

My replies to the lawyer accurately expressed the conviction in my mind. The narrative related by Ambrose had all the appearance, in my eyes, of a fabricated story, got up, and clumsily got up, to pervert the plain meaning of the circumstantial evidence produced by the prosecution. I reached this conclusion reluctantly and regretfully, for Naomi's sake. I said all I could say to shake the absolute confidence which she felt in the discharge of the prisoners at the next examination.

The day of the adjourned inquiry arrived.

Naomi and I again attended the court together. Mr Meadowcroft was unable, on this occasion, to leave the house. His daughter was present, walking to the court by herself, and occupying a seat by herself.

On his second appearance at the 'bar', Silas was more composed, and more like his brother: no new witnesses were called by the prosecution. We began the battle over the medical evidence relating to the charred bones; and, to some extent, we won the victory. In other words we forced the doctors to acknowledge that they differed widely in their opinions. They confessed that they were not certain. Two went still further, and declared that the bones were the bones of an animal, not of a man. We made the most of this; and then we entered upon the defence, founded on Ambrose Meadowcroft's story.

Necessarily, no witnesses could be called on our side. Whether this circumstance discouraged him, or whether he privately shared my opinion of his client's statement, I cannot say—it is only certain that the lawyer spoke mechanically, doing his best, no doubt, but doing it without genuine conviction or earnestness on his own part. Naomi cast an anxious glance at me as he sat down. The girl's hand, when I took it, turned cold in mine. She saw plain signs of the failure of the defence in the look and manner of the counsel for the prosecution; but she waited resolutely until the presiding magistrate announced his decision. I had only too clearly foreseen what he would feel it to be his duty to do. Naomi's head dropped on my shoulder as he said the terrible words which committed Ambrose and Silas Meadowcroft to take their trial on the charge of murder.

I led her out of the court into the air. As I passed the 'bar', I saw Ambrose, deadly pale, looking after us as we left him; the magistrate's decision had evidently daunted him. His brother Silas had dropped in abject terror on the gaoler's chair; the miserable wretch shook and shuddered dumbly like a cowed dog.

Miss Meadowcroft returned with us to the farm, preserving unbroken silence on the way back. I could detect nothing in her bearing which suggested any compassionate

feeling for the prisoners in her stern and secret nature. On
Naomi's withdrawal to her own room, we were left together
for a few minutes; and then, to my astonishment, the outwardly merciless woman showed me that she, too, was one
of Eve's daughters, and could feel and suffer, in her own
hard way, like the rest of us. She suddenly stepped close up
to me, and laid her hand on my arm.

'You are a lawyer, ain't you?' she asked.

'Yes.'

'Have you had any experience in your profession?'

'Ten years' experience.'

'Do *you* think——' She stopped abruptly, her hard face
softened; her eyes dropped to the ground. 'Never mind,'
she said, confusedly. 'I'm upset by all this misery, though I
may not look like it. Don't notice me.'

She turned away. I waited, in the firm persuasion that the
unspoken question in her mind would sooner or later force
its way to utterance by her lips. I was right. She came back
to me unwillingly, like a woman acting under some influence
which the utmost exertion of her will was powerless to resist.

'Do *you* believe John Jago is still a living man?'

She put the question vehemently, desperately, as if the
words rushed out of her mouth in spite of her.

'I do *not* believe it,' I answered.

'Remember what John Jago has suffered at the hands of
my brothers,' she persisted. 'Is it not in your experience that
he should take a sudden resolution to leave the farm?'

I replied, as plainly as before—

'It is *not* in my experience.'

She stood looking at me for a moment with a face of blank
despair; then bowed her grey head in silence, and left me.
As she crossed the room to the door, I saw her look upward;
and I heard her say to herself softly, between her teeth,
'Vengeance is mine, I will repay, saith the Lord.'

It was the requiem of John Jago, pronounced by the
woman who loved him.

When I next saw her, her mask was on once more. Miss
Meadowcroft was herself again. Miss Meadowcroft could
sit by, impenetrably calm, while the lawyers discussed the

terrible position of her brothers, with the scaffold in view as one of the possibilities of the 'case'.

Left by myself, I began to feel uneasy about Naomi. I went upstairs, and, knocking softly at her door, made my inquiries from outside. The clear young voice answered me sadly, 'I am trying to bear it: I won't distress you when we meet again.' I descended the stairs, feeling my first suspicion of the true nature of my interest in the American girl. Why had her answer brought the tears into my eyes? I went out walking, alone, to think undisturbedly. Why did the tones of her voice dwell on my ear all the way? Why did my hand still feel the last cold faint pressure of her fingers when I led her out of court?

I took a sudden resolution to go back to England.

When I returned to the farm, it was evening. The lamp was not yet lit in the hall. Pausing to accustom my eyes to the obscurity indoors, I heard the voice of the lawyer whom we had employed for the defence, speaking to someone very earnestly.

'I'm not to blame,' said the voice. 'She snatched the paper out of my hand before I was aware of her.'

'Do you want it back?' asked the voice of Miss Meadow-croft.

'No: it's only a copy. If keeping it will help to quiet her, let her keep it by all means. Good evening.'

Saying those last words, the lawyer approached me on his way out of the house. I stopped him without ceremony: I felt an ungovernable curiosity to know more.

'Who snatched the paper out of your hand?' I asked, bluntly.

The lawyer started. I had taken him by surprise. The instinct of professional reticence made him pause before he answered me.

In the brief interval of silence, Miss Meadowcroft replied to my question from the other end of the hall.

'Naomi Colebrook snatched the paper out of his hand.'

'What paper?'

A door opened softly behind me. Naomi herself appeared on the threshold; Naomi herself answered my question.

'I will tell you,' she whispered. 'Come in here.'

One candle only was burning in the room. I looked at her by the dim light. My resolution to return to England instantly became the last one of the lost ideas of my life.

'Good God!' I exclaimed, 'what has happened now?'

She gave me the paper which she had taken from the lawyer's hand.

The 'copy' to which he had referred was a copy of the written confession of Silas Meadowcroft on his return to prison. He accused his brother Ambrose of the murder of John Jago. He declared on his oath that he had seen his brother Ambrose commit the crime.

In the popular phrase, I could 'hardly believe my own eyes'. I read the last sentences of the confession for the second time:

> . . . I heard their voices at the lime-kiln. They were having words about Cousin Naomi. I ran to the place to part them. I was not in time. I saw Ambrose strike the deceased a terrible blow on the head with his (Ambrose's) heavy stick. The deceased dropped without a cry. I put my hand on his heart. He was dead. I was horribly frightened. Ambrose threatened to kill *me* next if I said a word to any living soul. He took up the body and cast it into the quicklime, and threw the stick in after it. We went on together to the wood. We sat down on a felled tree outside the wood. Ambrose made up the story that we were to tell if what he had done was found out. He made me repeat it after him like a lesson. We were still at it when Cousin Naomi and Mr Lefrank came up to us. They know the rest. This, on my oath, is a true confession. I make it of my own free will, repenting me sincerely that I did not make it before.

(Signed) 'SILAS MEADOWCROFT'

I laid down the paper, and looked at Naomi once more. She spoke to me with a strange composure. Immovable determination was in her eye, immovable determination was in her voice.

'Silas has lied away his brother's life to save himself,' she said. 'I see cowardly falsehood and cowardly cruelty in every line on that paper. Ambrose is innocent, and the time has come to prove it.'

'You forget,' I said, 'that we have just failed to prove it.'
She took no notice of my objection.

'John Jago is alive, in hiding from us,' she went on. 'Help me, friend Lefrank, to advertise for him in the newspapers.'

I drew back from her in speechless distress. I own I believed that the new misery which had fallen on her had affected her brain.

'You don't believe it?' she said. 'Shut the door.'

I obeyed her. She seated herself, and pointed to a chair near her.

'Sit down,' she proceeded. 'I am going to do a wrong thing, but there is no help for it. I am going to break a sacred promise. You remember that moonlight night when I met him on the garden-walk?'

'John Jago?'

'Yes. Now listen. I am going to tell you what passed between John Jago and me.'

IX

I waited in silence for the disclosure that was now to come. Naomi began by asking me a question.

'You remembered when we went to see Ambrose in prison?' she said.

'Perfectly.'

'Ambrose told us of something which his villain of a brother said of John Jago and me. Do you remember what it was?'

I remembered perfectly. Silas had said, 'John Jago is too sweet on Naomi not to come back.'

'That's so,' Naomi remarked, when I had repeated the words. 'I couldn't help starting when I heard what Silas had said; and I thought you noticed me.'

'I did notice you.'

'Did you wonder what it meant?'

'Yes.'

'I'll tell you. It meant this: what Silas Meadowcroft said to his brother of John Jago, was what I myself was thinking of John Jago at that very moment. It startled me to find my own thought in a man's mind, spoken for me by a man. I am the person, sir, who has driven John Jago away from Morwick Farm; and I am the person who can and will bring him back again.'

There was something in her manner, more than in her words, which let the light in suddenly on my mind.

'You have told me the secret,' I said. 'John Jago is in love with you.'

'Mad about me!' she rejoined, dropping her voice to a whisper. 'Stark, staring mad!—that's the only word for him. After we had taken a few turns on the gravel-walk, he suddenly broke out like a man beside himself. He fell down on his knees; he kissed my gown, he kissed my feet; he sobbed and cried for love of me. I'm not badly off for courage, sir, considering I'm a woman. No man, that I can call to mind, every really scared me before. But, I own, John Jago frightened me: oh, my! he did frighten me! My heart was in my mouth, and my knees shook under me. I begged and prayed of him to get up and go away. No; there he knelt, and held by the skirt of my gown. The words poured out from him like—well, like nothing I can think of but water from a pump. His happiness and his life, and his hopes in earth and heaven, and Lord only knows what besides, all depended, he said, on a word from me. I plucked up spirit enough at that to remind him that I was promised to Ambrose. "I think you ought to be ashamed of youself," I said, "to own that you are wicked enough to love me when you know I am promised to another man!" When I spoke to him, he took a new turn: he began abusing Ambrose. *That* straightened me up. I snatched my gown out of his hand, and I gave him my whole mind. "I hate you!" I said. "Even if I wasn't promised to Ambrose, I wouldn't marry you; no! not if there wasn't another man left in the world to ask me. I hate you, Mr Jago! I hate you!" He saw I was in earnest at last. He got up from my feet, and he settled down quiet again, all on a sudden. "You have said enough" (that was how he answered me). "You have broken my life. I have no hopes and no prospects now. I had a pride in the farm, miss, and a pride in my work; I bore with your brutish cousins' hatred of me; I was faithful to Mr Meadowcroft's interests; all for your sake, Naomi Colebrook—all for your sake! I have done with it now; I have done with my life at the farm. You will never be troubled with me again. I am going away, as the dumb creatures go when they are sick, to hide myself in a corner, and die. Do me one last favour. Don't make me the laughing-stock of the whole neighbourhood. I can't bear that: it maddens me, only to think of it. Give me your promise never to tell any living soul what I have said to you tonight—your sacred promise to the man whose life you have broken!" I did as he bade me: I gave him my sacred promise with the tears in my eyes. Yes; that is so. After telling him I hated him (and I did hate him), I cried over his misery; I did. Mercy, what fools women are! What is the horrid perversity, sir, which makes us always ready to pity the men? He held out his hand to me; and he said, "Good-bye for ever!" and I pitied him. I said, "I'll shake hands with you if you will give me your promise in exchange for mine. I beg of you not to leave the farm. What will my uncle do if you go away? Stay here and be friends with me; and forget and forgive, Mr John." He gave me his promise (he can refuse me nothing); and he gave it again when I saw him again the next morning. Yes, I'll do him justice, though I do hate him! I believe he honestly meant to keep his word as long as my eye was on him. It was only when he was left to himself that the Devil tempted him to break his promise, and leave the farm. I was brought up to believe in the Devil, Mr Lefrank; and I find it explains many things. It explains John Jago. Only let me find out where he has gone, and I'll engage he shall come back and clear Ambrose of the suspicion which his vile brother has cast on him. Here is the pen all ready for you. Advertise for him, friend Lefrank; and do it right away, for my sake!'

I let her run on, without attempting to dispute her conclusions, until she could say no more. When she put the pen into my hand, I began the composition of the advertisement, as obediently as if I, too, believed that John Jago was a living man.

In the case of anyone else, I should have openly acknowledged that my own convictions remained unshaken. If no quarrel had taken place at the lime-kiln, I should have been quite ready, as I viewed the case, to believe that John Jago's disappearance was referable to the terrible disappointment which Naomi had inflicted on him. The same morbid dread of ridicule which had led him to assert that he cared nothing for Naomi, when he and Silas had quarrelled under my bedroom window, might also have impelled him to withdraw himself secretly and suddenly from the scene of his discomfiture. But to ask me to believe, after what had happened at the lime-kiln, that he was still living, was to ask me to take Ambrose Meadowcroft's statement for granted as a true statement of facts.

I had refused to do this from the first; and I still persisted in taking that course. If I had been called upon to decide the balance of probability between the narrative related by Ambrose in his defence and the narrative related by Silas in his confession, I must have owned, no matter how unwillingly, that the confession was, to my mind, the least incredible story of the two.

Could I say this to Naomi? I would have written fifty advertisements inquiring for John Jago rather than say it; and you would have done the same, if you had been so fond of her as I was.

I drew out the advertisement, for insertion in 'The Morwick Mercury', in these terms:

MURDER.—Printers of newspapers throughout the United States are desired to publish that Ambrose Meadowcroft and Silas Meadowcroft, of Morwick Farm, Morwick Country, are committed for trial on the charge of murdering John Jago, now missing from the farm and from the neighbourhood. Any person who can give information of the existence of said Jago may save the lives of two wrongly accused men by making immediate communication. Jago is about five feet four inches high. He is spare and wiry; his complexion is extremely pale; his eyes are dark, and very bright and restless. The lower part of his face is concealed by a thick black beard and moustache. The whole appearance of the man is wild and flighty.

I added the date and address. That evening a servant was sent on horseback to Narrabee to procure the insertion of the advertisement in the next issue of the newspaper.

When we parted that night, Naomi looked almost like her brighter and happier self. Now that the advertisement was on its way to the printing-office, she was more than sanguine: she was certain of the result.

'You don't know how you have comforted me,' she said, in her frank, warm-hearted way, when we parted for the night. 'All the newspapers will copy it, and we shall hear of John Jago before the week is out.' She turned to go, and came back again to me. 'I will never forgive Silas for writing that confession!' she whispered in my ear. 'If he ever lives under the same roof with Ambrose again, I—well, I believe I wouldn't marry Ambrose if he did! There!'

She left me. Through the wakeful hours of the night my mind dwelt on her last words. That she should contemplate, under any circumstances, even the bare possibility of not marrying Ambrose, was, I am ashamed to say, a direct encouragement to certain hopes which I had already begun to form in secret. The next day's mail brought me a letter on business. My clerk wrote to inquire if there was any chance of my returning to England in time to appear in court at the opening of next law term. I answered, without hesitation, 'It is still impossible for me to fix the date of my return.' Naomi was in the room while I was writing. How would she have answered, I wonder, if I had told her the truth, and said, 'You are responsible for this letter'?

X

The question of time was now a serious question at Morwick Farm. In six weeks, the court for the trial of criminal cases was to be opened at Narrabee.

During this interval, no new event of any importance occurred.

Many idle letters reached us relating to the advertisement for John Jago; but no positive information was received. Not the slightest trace of the lost man turned up; not the shadow of a doubt was cast on the assertion of the prosecution, that his body had been destroyed in the kiln. Silas Meadowcroft held firmly to the horrible confession that he had made. His brother Ambrose, with equal resolution, asserted his innocence, and reiterated the statement which he had already advanced. At regular periods I accompanied Naomi to visit him in the prison. As the day appointed for the opening of the court approached, he seemed to falter a little in his resolution; his manner became restless; and he grew irritably suspicious about the merest trifles. This change did not necessarily imply the consciousness of guilt: it might merely have indicated natural nervous agitation as the time for the trial drew near. Naomi noticed the alteration in her lover. It greatly increased her anxiety, though it never shook her confidence in Ambrose. Except at meal-times, I was left, during the period of which I am now writing, almost constantly alone with the charming American girl. Miss Meadowcroft searched the newspapers for tidings of the living John Jago in the privacy of her own room. Mr Meadowcroft would see nobody but his daughter and his doctor, and occasionally one or two old friends. I have since had reason to believe that Naomi, in these days of our intimate association, discovered the true nature of the feeling with which she had inspired me. But she kept her secret. Her manner towards me steadily remained the manner of a sister: she never overstepped by a hair's breadth the safe limits of the character she had assumed.

The sittings of the court began. After hearing the evidence, and examining the confession of Silas Meadowcroft, the grand jury found a true bill against both the prisoners. The day appointed for the trial was the first day in the new week.

I had carefully prepared Naomi's mind for the decision of the grand jury. She bore the new blow bravely.

'If you are not tired of it,' she said, 'come with me to the prison tomorrow. Ambrose will need a little comfort by that time.' She paused, and looked at the day's letters lying on the table. 'Still not a word about John Jago,' she said. 'And all the papers have copied the advertisement. I felt so sure we should hear of him long before this!'

'Do you still feel sure that he is living?' I ventured to ask.

'I am as certain of it as ever,' she replied firmly. 'He is somewhere in hiding: perhaps he is in disguise. Suppose we know no more of him than we know now, when the trial begins? Suppose the jury——' She stopped, shuddering. Death—shameful death on the scaffold—might be the terrible result of the consultation of the jury. 'We have waited for news to come to us long enough,' Naomi resumed. 'We must find the tracks of John Jago for ourselves. There is a week yet before the trial begins. Who will help me to make inquiries? Will you be the man, friend Lefrank?'

It is needless to add (though I knew nothing would come of it) that I consented to be the man.

We arranged to apply that day for the order of admission to the prison, and, having seen Ambrose, to devote ourselves immediately to the contemplated search. How that search was to be conducted was more than I could tell, and more than Naomi could tell. We were to begin by applying to the police to help us to find John Jago, and we were then to be guided by circumstances. Was there ever a more hopeless programme than this?

'Circumstances' declared themselves against us at starting. I applied, as usual, for the order of admission to the prison, and the order was for the first time refused; no reason being assigned by the persons in authority for taking this course. Inquire as I might, the only answer given was, 'Not today'.

At Naomi's suggestion, we went to the prison to seek the explanation which was refused to us at the office. The gaoler on duty at the outer gate was one of Naomi's many admirers. He solved the mystery cautiously in a whisper. The sheriff and the governor of the prison were then speaking privately with Ambrose Meadowcroft in his cell: they had expressly directed that no persons should be admitted to see the prisoner that day but themselves.

What did it mean? We returned, wondering, to the farm. There Naomi, speaking by chance to one of the female servants, made certain discoveries.

Early that morning the sheriff had been brought to Morwick by an old friend of the Meadowcrofts. A long interview had been held between Mr Meadowcroft and his daughter and the official personage introduced by the friend. Leaving the farm, the sheriff had gone straight to the prison, and had proceeded with the governor to visit Ambrose in his cell. Was some potent influence being brought privately to bear on Ambrose? Appearances certainly suggested that inquiry. Supposing the influence to have been really exerted, the next question followed: What was the object in view? We could only wait and see.

Our patience was not severely tried. The event of the next day enlightened us in a very unexpected manner. Before noon, the neighbours brought startling news from the prison to the farm.

Ambrose Meadowcroft had confessed himself to be the murderer of John Jago! He had signed the confession in the presence of the sheriff and the governor on that very day!

I saw the document. It is needless to reproduce it here. In substance, Ambrose confessed what Silas had confessed; claiming, however, to have only struck Jago under intolerable provocation, so as to reduce the nature of his offence against the law from murder to manslaughter. Was the confession really the true statement of what had taken place? or had the sheriff and the governor, acting in the interests of the family name, persuaded Ambrose to try this desperate means of escaping the ignominy of death on the scaffold? The sheriff and the governor preserved impenetrable silence until the pressure put on them judicially at the trial obliged them to speak.

Who was to tell Naomi of this last and saddest of all the calamities which had fallen on her? Knowing how I loved her in secret, I felt an invincible reluctance to be the person who revealed Ambrose Meadowcroft's degradation to his betrothed wife. Had any other member of the family told her what had happened? The lawyer was able to answer me: Miss Meadowcroft had told her.

I was shocked when I heard it. Miss Meadowcroft was the last person in the house to spare the poor girl: Miss Meadowcroft would make the hard tidings doubly terrible to bear in the telling. I tried to find Naomi, without success. She had been always accessible at other times. Was she hiding herself from me now? The idea occurred to me as I was descending the stairs after vainly knocking at the door of her room. I was determined to see her. I waited a few minutes, and then ascended the stairs again suddenly. On the landing I met her, just leaving her room.

She tried to run back. I caught her by the arm, and detained her. With her free hand she held her handkerchief over her face so as to hide it from me.

'You once told me I had comforted you,' I said to her, gently. 'Won't you let me comfort you now?'

She still struggled to get away, and still kept her head turned from me.

'Don't you see that I am ashamed to look you in the face?' she said, in low broken tones. 'Let me go.'

I still persisted in trying to soothe her. I drew her to the window-seat. I said I would wait until she was able to speak to me.

She dropped on the seat, and wrung her hands on her lap. Her downcast eyes still obstinately avoided meeting mine.

'Oh!' she said to herself, 'what madness possessed me? Is it possible that I ever disgraced myself by loving Ambrose Meadowcroft?' She shuddered as the idea found its way to expression on her lips. The tears rolled slowly over her cheeks. 'Don't despise me, Mr Lefrank!' she said, faintly.

I tried, honestly tried, to put the confession before her in its least unfavourable light.

'His resolution has given way,' I said. 'He has done this, despairing of proving his innocence, in terror of the scaffold.'

She rose, with an angry stamp of her foot. She turned her face on me with the deep-red flush of shame in it, and the big tears glistening in her eyes.

'No more of him!' she said, sternly. 'If he is not a murderer, what else is he? A liar and a coward! In which of his characters does he disgrace me most? I have done with him for ever! I will never speak to him again!' She pushed me furiously away from her; advanced a few steps towards her own door; stopped, and came back to me. The generous nature of the girl spoke in her next words. 'I am not ungrateful to *you*, friend Lefrank. A woman in my place is only a woman; and, when she is shamed as I am, she feels it very bitterly. Give me your hand! God bless you!'

She put my hand to her lips before I was aware of her, and kissed it, and ran back to her room.

I sat down on the place which she had occupied. She had looked at me for one moment when she kissed my hand. I forgot Ambrose and his confession; I forgot the coming trial; I forgot my professional duties and my English friends. There I sat, in a fool's Elysium of my own making, with absolutely nothing in my mind but the picture of Naomi's face at the moment when she had last looked at me!

I have already mentioned that I was in love with her. I merely add this to satisfy you that I tell the truth.

XI

Miss Meadowcroft and I were the only representatives of the family at the farm who attended the trial. We went separately to Narrabee. Excepting the ordinary greetings at morning and night, Miss Meadowcroft had not said one word to me since the time when I told her that I did *not* believe John Jago to be a living man.

I have purposely abstained from encumbering my narrative with legal details. I now propose to state the nature of the defence in the briefest outline only.

We insisted on making both the prisoners plead 'Not guilty'. This done, we took an objection to the legality of the proceedings at starting. We appealed to the old English law, that there should be no conviction for murder until the body of the murdered person was found, or proof of its destruction obtained beyond a doubt. We denied that sufficient proof had been obtained in the case now before the court.

The judges consulted, and decided that the trial should go on. We took our next objection when the Confessions were produced in evidence. We declared that they had been extorted by terror, or by undue influence; and we pointed out certain minor particulars in which the two confessions failed to corroborate each other. For the rest, our defence on this occasion was, as to essentials, what our defence had been at the inquiry before the magistrate. Once more the judges consulted, and once more they overruled our objection. The Confessions were admitted in evidence.

On their side, the prosecution produced one new witness in support of their case. It is needless to waste time in recapitulating his evidence. He contradicted himself gravely on cross-examination. We showed plainly, and after investigation proved, that he was not to be believed on his oath.

The Chief Justice summed up.

He charged, in relation to the Confessions, that no weight should be attached to confession incited by hope or fear; and he left it to the jury to determine whether the Confessions in this case had been so influenced. In the course of the trial, it had been shown for the defence that the sheriff and the governor of the prison had told Ambrose, with his father's knowledge and sanction, that the case was clearly against him; that the only chance of sparing his family the disgrace of his death by public execution lay in making a confession; and that they would do their best, if he did confess, to have his sentence commuted to transportation for life. As for Silas, he was proved to have been beside himself with terror when he made his abominable charge against his brother. We had vainly trusted to the evidence on these two points to induce the court to reject the Confessions; and we were destined to be once more disappointed in anticipating that the same evidence would influence the verdict of the jury on the side of mercy. After an absence of an hour, they returned into court with a verdict of 'Guilty' against both the prisoners.

Being asked in due form if they had anything to say in mitigation of their sentence, Ambrose and Silas solemnly declared their innocence, and publicly acknowledged that their respective confessions had been wrung from them with the hope of escaping the hangman's hands. This statement was not noticed by the bench. The prisoners were both sentenced to death.

On my return to the farm, I did not see Naomi. Miss Meadowcroft informed her of the result of the trial. Half an hour later, one of the women servants handed to me an envelope bearing my name on it in Naomi's handwriting.

The envelope enclosed a letter, and with it a slip of paper on which Naomi had hurriedly written these words: 'For God's sake, read the letter I send to you, and do something about it immediately!'

I looked at the letter. It assumed to be written by a gentleman in New York. Only the day before, he had, by the merest accident, seen the advertisement for John Jago, cut out of a newspaper and pasted into a book of 'curiosities' kept by a friend. Upon this he wrote to Morwick Farm to say that he had seen a man exactly answering to the description of John Jago, but bearing another name, working as a clerk in a merchant's office in Jersey City. Having time to spare before the mail went out, he had returned to the office to take another look at the man before he posted his letter. To his surprise, he was informed that the clerk had not appeared at his desk that day. His employer had sent to his lodgings, and had been informed that he had suddenly packed up his bag after reading the newspaper at breakfast; had paid his rent honestly, and had gone away, nobody knew where!

It was late in the evening when I read these lines. I had time for reflection before it would be necessary for me to act.

Assuming the letter to be genuine, and adopting Naomi's explanation of the motive which had led John Jago to absent himself secretly from the farm, I reached the conclusion that the search for him might be usefully limited to Narrabee and to the surrounding neighbourhood.

The newspaper at his breakfast had no doubt given him his first information of the 'finding' of the grand jury, and of the trial to follow. It was in my experience of human nature that he should venture back to Narrabee under these circumstances, and under the influence of his infatuation for Naomi. More than this, it was again in my experience, I am sorry to say, that he should attempt to make the critical position of Ambrose a means of extorting Naomi's consent to listen favourably to his suit. Cruel indifference to the injury and the suffering which his sudden absence might inflict on others, was plainly implied in his secret withdrawal from the farm. The same cruel indifference, pushed to a further extreme, might well lead him to press his proposals privately on Naomi, and to fix her acceptance of them as the price to be paid for saving her cousin's life.

To these conclusions I arrived after much thinking. I had determined, on Naomi's account, to clear the matter up; but it is only candid to add, that my doubts of John Jago's existence remained unshaken by the letter. I believed it to be nothing more or less than a heartless and stupid 'hoax'.

The striking of the hall clock roused me from my meditations. I counted the strokes—midnight!

I rose to go up to my room. Everybody else in the farm had retired to bed, as usual, more than an hour since. The stillness in the house was breathless. I walked softly, by instinct, as I crossed the room to look out at the night. A lovely moonlight met my view: it was like the moonlight on the fatal evening when Naomi had met John Jago on the garden walk.

My bedroom candle was on the side-table: I had just lit it. I was just leaving the room, when the door suddenly opened, and Naomi herself stood before me!

Recovering the first shock of her sudden appearance, I saw instantly, in her eager eyes, in her deadly pale cheeks, that something serious had happened. A large cloak was thrown over her; a white handkerchief was tied over her head. Her hair was in disorder: she had evidently just risen in fear and in haste from her bed.

'What is it?' I asked, advancing to meet her.

She clung trembling with agitation to my arm.

'John Jago!' she whispered.

You will think my obstinacy invincible. I could hardly believe it, even then!

'Do you mean John Jago's ghost?' I asked.

'I have seen John Jago himself,' she answered.

'Where?'

'In the back yard, under my bedroom window!'

The emergency was far too serious to allow of any consideration for the small proprieties of everyday life.

'Let *me* see him!' I said.

'I am here to fetch you,' she replied, in her frank and fearless way. 'Come upstairs with me.'

Her room was on the first floor of the house, and was the only bedroom which looked out on the back yard. On our way up the stairs she told me what had happened.

'I was in bed,' she said, 'but not asleep, when I heard a pebble strike against the window-pane. I waited, wondering what it meant. Another pebble was thrown against the glass. So far I was surprised, but not frightened. I got up, and ran to the window to look out. There was John Jago, looking up at me in the moonlight!'

'Did he see you?'

'Yes. He said, "Come down and speak to me! I have something serious to say to you!" '

'Did you answer him?'

'As soon as I could fetch my breath, I said, "Wait a little," and ran downstairs to you. What shall I do?'

'Let *me* see him, and I will tell you.'

We entered her room. Keeping cautiously behind the window-curtain, I looked out.

There he was! His beard and moustache were shaved off: his hair was cut close. But there was no disguising his wild brown eyes, or the peculiar movement of his spare wiry figure, as he walked slowly to and fro in the moonlight, waiting for Naomi. For the moment, my own agitation almost overpowered me: I had so firmly disbelieved that John Jago was a living man!

'What shall I do?' Naomi repeated.

'Is the door of the dairy open?' I asked.

'No; but the door of the tool-house, round the corner, is not locked.'

'Very good. Show yourself at the window, and say to him, "I am coming directly".'

The brave girl obeyed me without a moment's hesitation.

There had been no doubt about his eyes and his gait; there was no doubt now about his voice as he answered softly from below—

'All right!'

'Keep him talking to you where he is now,' I said to Naomi, 'until I have time to get round by the other way to the tool-house. Then pretend to be fearful of discovery at the dairy; and bring him round the corner, so that I can hear him behind the door.'

We left the house together, and separated silently. Naomi followed my instructions with a woman's quick intelligence where stratagems are concerned. I had hardly been a minute in the tool-house before I heard him speaking to Naomi on the other side of the door.

The first words which I caught distinctly related to his motive for secretly leaving the farm. Mortified pride— doubly mortified by Naomi's contemptuous refusal, and by the personal indignity offered to him by Ambrose—was at the bottom of his conduct in absenting himself from Mor-wick. He owned that he had seen the advertisement, and that it had actually encouraged him to keep in hiding!

'After being laughed at and insulted and denied, I was glad,' said the miserable wretch, 'to see that some of you had serious reason to wish me back again. It rests with you, Miss Naomi, to keep me here, and to persuade me to save Ambrose by showing myself, and owning to my name.'

'What do you mean?' I heard Naomi ask, sternly.

He lowered his voice; but I could still hear him.

'Promise you will marry me,' he said, 'and I will go before the magistrate tomorrow, and show him that I am a living man.'

'Suppose I refuse?'

'In that case you will lose me again, and none of you will find me till Ambrose is hanged.'

'Are you villain enough, John Jago, to mean what you say?' asked the girl, raising her voice.

'If you attempt to give the alarm,' he answered, 'as true as God's above us, you will feel my hand on your throat! It's my turn, now, miss; and I am not to be trifled with. Will you have me for your husband—yes or no?'

'No!' she answered, loudly and firmly.

I threw open the door, and seized him as he lifted his hand on her. He had not suffered from the nervous derangement which had weakened me, and he was the stronger man of the two. Naomi saved my life. She struck up his pistol as he pulled it out of his pocket with his free hand and presented it at my head. The bullet was fired into the air. I tripped up his heels at the same moment. The report of the pistol had alarmed the house. We two together kept him on the ground until help arrived.

XII

John Jago was brought before the magistrate, and John Jago was identified the next day.

The lives of Ambrose and Silas were, of course, no longer in peril, so far as human justice was concerned. But there were legal delays to be encountered, and legal formalities to be observed, before the brothers could be released from prison in the characters of innocent men.

During the interval which thus elapsed, certain events happened which may be briefly mentioned here before I close my narrative.

Mr Meadowcroft the elder, broken by the suffering which he had gone through, died suddenly of a rheumatic affection of the heart. A codicil attached to his will abundantly justified what Naomi had told me of Miss Meadowcroft's influence over her father, and of the end she had in view in exercising it. A life-income only was left to Mr Meadowcroft's sons. The freehold of the farm was bequeathed to his daughter, with the testator's recommendation added, that she should marry his 'best and dearest friend, Mr John Jago'.

Armed with the power of the will, the heiress of Morwick sent an insolent message to Naomi requesting her no longer to consider herself one of the inmates at the farm. Miss Meadowcroft, it should be here added, positively refused to believe that John Jago had ever asked Naomi to be his wife, or had ever threatened her, as I had heard him threaten her, if she refused. She accused me, as she accused Naomi, of trying meanly to injure John Jago in her estimation, out of hatred towards 'that much injured man'; and she sent to me, as she had sent to Naomi, a formal notice to leave the house.

We two banished ones met the same day in the hall, with our travelling bags in our hands.

'We are turned out together, friend Lefrank,' said Naomi, with her quaintly comical smile. 'You will go back to England, I guess; and I must make my own living in my own country. Women can get employment in the States if they have a friend to speak for them. Where shall I find somebody who can give me a place?'

I saw my way to saying the right word at the right moment.

'I have got a place to offer you,' I replied, 'if you see no objection to accepting it.'

She suspected nothing, so far.

'That's lucky, sir,' was all she said. 'Is it in a telegraph-office or in a dry-goods store?'

I astonished my little American friend by taking her then and there in my arms, and giving her my first kiss.

'The office is by my fireside,' I said. 'The salary is anything in reason you like to ask me for. And the place, Naomi, if you have no objection to it, is the place of my wife.'

I have no more to say, except that years have passed since I spoke those words, and that I am as fond of Naomi as ever.

Some months after our marriage, Mrs Lefrank wrote to a friend at Narrabee for news of what was going on at the farm. The answer informed us that Ambrose and Silas had emigrated to New Zealand, and that Miss Meadowcroft was alone at Morwick Farm. John Jago had refused to marry her. John Jago had disappeared again, nobody knew where.

THE CLERGYMAN'S CONFESSION

I

MY brother, the elergyman, looked over my shoulder before I was aware of him, and discovered that the volume which completely absorbed my attention was a collection of famous Trials, published in a new edition and in a popular form.

He laid his finger on the Trial which I happened to be reading at the moment. I looked up at him; his face startled me. He had turned pale. His eyes were fixed on the open page of the book with an expression which puzzled and alarmed me.

'My dear fellow,' I said, 'what in the world is the matter with you?'

He answered in an odd absent manner, still keeping his finger on the open page.

'I had almost forgotten,' he said. 'And this reminds me.'

'Reminds you of what?' I asked. 'You don't mean to say you know anything about the Trial?'

'I know this,' he said. 'The prisoner was guilty.'

'Guilty?' I repeated. 'Why, the man was acquitted by the jury, with the full approval of the judge! What can you possibly mean?'

'There are circumstances connected with that Trial,' my brother answered, 'which were never communicated to the judge or the jury—which were never so much as hinted or whispered in court. *I* know them—of my own knowledge, by my own personal experience. They are very sad, very strange, very terrible. I have mentioned them to no mortal creature. I have done my best to forget them. You—quite innocently—have brought them back to my mind. They oppress, they distress me. I wish I had found you reading any book in your library, except *that* book!'

My curiosity was now strongly excited. I spoke out plainly.

'Surely,' I suggested, 'you might tell your brother what you are unwilling to mention to persons less nearly related to you. We have followed different professions, and have lived in different countries, since we were boys at school. But you know you can trust me.'

He considered a little with himself.

'Yes,' he said. 'I know I can trust you.' He waited a moment; and then he surprised me by a strange question.

'Do you believe,' he asked, 'that the spirits of the dead can return to earth, and show themselves to the living?'

I answered cautiously—adopting as my own the words of a great English writer, touching the subject of ghosts.

'You ask me a question,' I said, 'which, after five thousand years, is yet undecided. On that account alone, it is a question not to be trifled with.'

My reply seemed to satisfy him.

'Promise me,' he resumed, 'that you will keep what I tell you a secret as long as I live. After my death I care little what happens. Let the story of my strange experience be added to the published experience of those other men who have seen what I have seen, and who believe what I believe. The world will not be the worse, and may be the better, for knowing one day what I am now about to trust to your ear alone.'

My brother never again alluded to the narrative which he had confided to me, until the later time when I was sitting by his deathbed. He asked if I still remembered the story of Jéromette. 'Tell it to others,' he said, 'as I have told it to you.'

I repeat it, after his death—as nearly as I can in his own words.

II

On a fine summer evening, many years since, I left my chambers in the Temple,* to meet a fellow-student, who had proposed to me a night's amusement in the public gardens at Cremorne.*

You were then on your way to India; and I had taken my degree at Oxford. I had sadly disappointed my father by choosing the Law as my profession, in preference to the Church. At that time, to own the truth, I had no serious intention of following any special vocation. I simply wanted an excuse for enjoying the pleasures of a London life. The study of the Law supplied me with that excuse. And I chose the Law as my profession accordingly.

On reaching the place at which we had arranged to meet, I found that my friend had not kept his appointment. After waiting vainly for ten minutes, my patience gave way, and I went into the Gardens by myself.

I took two or three turns round the platform devoted to the dancers, without discovering my fellow-student, and without seeing any other person with whom I happened to be acquainted at that time.

For some reason which I cannot now remember, I was not in my usual good spirits that evening. The noisy music jarred on my nerves, the sight of the gaping crowd round the platform irritated me, the blandishments of the painted ladies of the profession of pleasure saddened and disgusted me. I opened my cigar-case, and turned aside into one of the quiet by-walks of the Gardens.

A man who is habitually careful in choosing his cigar has this advantage over a man who is habitually careless. He can always count on smoking the best cigar in his case, down to the last. I was still absorbed in choosing *my* cigar, when I heard these words behind me—spoken in a foreign accent and in a woman's voice:

'Leave me directly, sir! I wish to have nothing to say to you.'

I turned round and discovered a little lady very simply and tastefully dressed, who looked both angry and alarmed as she rapidly passed me on her way to the more frequented part of the Gardens. A man (evidently the worse for the wine he had drunk in the course of the evening) was following her, and was pressing his tipsy attentions on her with the coarsest insolence of speech and manner. She was young and pretty, and she cast one entreating look at me as she went by, which it was not in manhood—perhaps I ought to say, in young-manhood—to resist.

I instantly stepped forward to protect her, careless whether I involved myself in a discreditable quarrel with a black-guard or not. As a matter of course, the fellow resented my interference, and my temper gave way. Fortunately for me, just as I lifted my hand to knock him down, a police-man appeared who had noticed that he was drunk, and who settled the dispute officially by turning him out of the Gardens.

I led her away from the crowd that had collected. She was evidently frightened—I felt her hand trembling on my arm—but she had one great merit: she made no fuss about it.

'If I can sit down for a few minutes,' she said in her pretty foreign accent, 'I shall soon be myself again, and I shall not trespass any farther on your kindness. I thank you very much, sir, for taking care of me.'

We sat down on a bench in a retired part of the Gardens, near a little fountain. A row of lighted lamps ran round the outer rim of the basin. I could see her plainly.

I have said that she was 'a little lady.' I could not have described her more correctly in three words.

Her figure was slight and small: she was a well-made miniature of a woman from head to foot. Her hair and her eyes were both dark. The hair curled naturally; the expres-sion of the eyes was quiet, and rather sad; the complexion, as I then saw it, very pale; the little mouth perfectly charming. I was especially attracted, I remember, by the carriage of her head; it was strikingly graceful and spirited; it distinguished her, little as she was and quiet as she was, among the thousands of other women in the Gardens, as a creature apart. Even the one marked defect in her—a slight 'cast' in the left eye—seemed to add, in some strange way, to the quaint attractiveness of her face. I have already spoken of the tasteful simplicity of her dress. I ought now to add that it was not made of any costly material, and that she wore no jewels or ornaments of any sort. My little lady was not rich: even a man's eye could see that.

She was perfectly unembarrassed and unaffected. We fell as easily into talk as if we had been friends instead of strangers.

I asked how it was that she had no companion to take care of her. 'You are too young and too pretty,' I said in my blunt English way, 'to trust yourself alone in such a place as this.'

She took no notice of the compliment. She calmly put it away from her as if it had not reached her ears.

'I have no friend to take care of me,' she said simply. 'I was sad and sorry this evening, all by myself, and I thought I would go to the Gardens and hear the music, just to amuse me. It is not much to pay at the gate; only a shilling.'

'No friend to take care of you?' I repeated. 'Surely there must be one happy man who might have been here with you tonight?'

'What man do you mean?' she asked.

'The man,' I answered thoughtlessly, 'whom we call, in England, a Sweetheart.'

I would have given worlds to have recalled those foolish words the moment they passed my lips. I felt that I had taken a vulgar liberty with her. Her face saddened; her eyes dropped to the ground. I begged her pardon.

'There is no need to beg my pardon,' she said. 'If you wish to know, sir—yes, I had once a sweetheart, as you call it in England. He has gone away and left me. No more of him, if you please. I am rested now. I will thank you again, and go home.'

She rose to leave me.

I was determined not to part with her in that way. I begged to be allowed to see her safely back to her own door. She hesitated. I took a man's unfair advantage of her, by appealing to her fears. I said, 'Suppose the blackguard who annoyed you should be waiting outside the gates?' That decided her. She took my arm. We went away together by the bank of the Thames, in the balmy summer night.

A walk of half an hour brought us to the house in which she lodged—a shabby little house in a by-street, inhabited evidently by very poor people.

She held out her hand at the door, and wished me goodnight. I was too much interested in her to consent to leave my little foreign lady without the hope of seeing her again.

I asked permission to call on her the next day. We were standing under the light of the street-lamp. She studied my face with a grave and steady attention before she made any reply.

'Yes,' she said at last. 'I think I do know a gentleman when I see him. You may come, sir, if you please, and call upon me tomorrow.'

So we parted. So I entered—doubting nothing, foreboding nothing—on a scene in my life, which I now look back on with unfeigned repentance and regret.

III

I am speaking at this later time in the position of a clergyman, and in the character of a man of mature age. Remember that; and you will understand why I pass as rapidly as possible over the events of the next year of my life—why I say as little as I can of the errors and the delusions of my youth.

I called on her the next day. I repeated my visits during the days and weeks that followed, until the shabby little house in the by-street had become a second and (I say it with shame and self-reproach) a dearer home to me.

All of herself and her story which she thought fit to confide to me under these circumstances may be repeated to you in few words.

The name by which letters were addressed to her was 'Mademoiselle Jéromette.' Among the ignorant people of the house and the small tradesmen of the neighbourhood— who found her name not easy of pronunciation by the average English tongue—she was known by the friendly nickname of 'The French Miss.' When I knew her, she was resigned to her lonely life among strangers. Some years had elapsed since she had lost her parents, and had left France. Possessing a small, very small, income of her own, she added to it by colouring miniatures for the photographers. She had relatives still living in France; but she had long since ceased to correspond with them. 'Ask me nothing more about my family,' she used to say. 'I am as good as dead in my own country and among my own people.'

This was all—literally all—that she told me of herself. I have never discovered more of her sad story from that day to this.

She never mentioned her family name—never even told me what part of France she came from, or how long she had lived in England. That she was, by birth and breeding, a lady, I could entertain no doubt; her manners, her accomplishments, her ways of thinking and speaking, all proved it. Looking below the surface, her character showed itself in aspects not common among young women in these days. In her quiet way, she was an incurable fatalist, and a firm believer in the ghostly reality of apparitions from the dead. Then again, in the matter of money, she had strange views of her own. Whenever my purse was in my hand, she held me resolutely at a distance from first to last. She refused to move into better apartments; the shabby little house was clean inside, and the poor people who lived in it were kind to her —and that was enough. The most expensive present that she ever permitted me to offer her was a little enamelled ring, the plainest and cheapest thing of the kind in the jeweller's shop. In all her relations with me she was sincerity itself. On all occasions, and under all circumstances, she spoke her mind (as the phrase is) with the same uncompromising plainness.

'I like you,' she said to me; 'I respect you; I shall always be faithful to you while you are faithful to me. But my love has gone from me. There is another man who has taken it away with him, I know not where.'

Who was the other man?

She refused to tell me. She kept his rank and his name strict secrets from me. I never discovered how he had met with her, or why he had left her, or whether the guilt was his of making her an exile from her country and her friends. She despised herself for still loving him; but the passion was too strong for her—she owned it and lamented it with the frankness which was so pre-eminently a part of her character. More than this, she plainly told me, in the early days of our acquaintance, that she believed he would return to her. It might be tomorrow, or it might be years hence. Even if he failed to repent of his own cruel conduct, the man would still miss her, as something lost out of his life; and, sooner or later, he would come back.

'And will you receive him if he does come back?' I asked.

'I shall receive him,' she replied, 'against my own better judgment—in spite of my own firm persuasion that the day of his return to me will bring with it the darkest days of my life.'

I tried to remonstrate with her.

'You have a will of your own,' I said. 'Exert it, if he attempts to return to you.'

'I have no will of my own,' she answered quietly, 'where *he* is concerned. It is my misfortune to love him.' Her eyes rested for a moment on mine, with the utter self-abandonment of despair. 'We have said enough about this,' she added abruptly. 'Let us say no more.'

From that time we never spoke again of the unknown man. During the year that followed our first meeting, she heard nothing of him directly or indirectly. He might be living, or he might be dead. There came no word of him, or from him. I was fond enough of her to be satisfied with this—he never disturbed us.

IV

The year passed—and the end came. Not the end as you may have anticipated it, or as I might have foreboded it.

You remember the time when your letters from home informed you of the fatal termination of our mother's illness? It is the time of which I am now speaking. A few hours only before she breathed her last, she called me to her bedside, and desired that we might be left together alone. Reminding me that her death was near, she spoke of my prospects in life; she noticed my want of interest in the studies which were then supposed to be engaging my attention, and she ended by entreating me to reconsider my refusal to enter the Church.

'Your father's heart is set upon it,' she said. 'Do what I ask of you, my dear, and you will help to comfort him when I am gone.'

Her strength failed her: she could say no more. Could I refuse the last request she would ever make to me? I knelt at the bedside, and took her wasted hand in mine, and solemnly promised her the respect which a son owes to his mother's last wishes.

Having bound myself by this sacred engagement, I had no choice but to accept the sacrifice which it imperatively exacted from me. The time had come when I must tear myself free from all unworthy associations. No matter what the effort cost me, I must separate myself at once and for ever from the unhappy woman who was not, who never could be, my wife.

At the close of a dull foggy day I set forth with a heavy heart to say the words which were to part us for ever.

Her lodging was not far from the banks of the Thames. As I drew near the place the darkness was gathering, and the broad surface of the river was hidden from me in a chill white mist. I stood for a while, with my eyes fixed on the vaporous shroud that brooded over the flowing water—I stood, and asked myself in despair the one dreary question: 'What am I to say to her?'

The mist chilled me to the bones. I turned from the riverbank, and made my way to her lodgings hard by. 'It must be done!' I said to myself, as I took out my key and opened the house door.

She was not at her work, as usual, when I entered her little sitting-room. She was standing by the fire, with her head down, and with an open letter in her hand.

The instant she turned to meet me, I saw in her face that something was wrong. Her ordinary manner was the manner of an unusually placid and self-restrained person. Her temperament had little of the liveliness which we associate in England with the French nature. She was not ready with her laugh; and, in all my previous experience, I had never yet known her to cry. Now, for the first time, I saw the quiet face disturbed; I saw tears in the pretty brown eyes. She ran to meet me, and laid her head on my breast, and burst into a passionate fit of weeping that shook her from head to foot.

Could she by any human possibility have heard of the coming change in my life? Was she aware, before I had opened my lips, of the hard necessity which had brought me to the house?

It was simply impossible; the thing could not be.

I waited until her first burst of emotion had worn itself out. Then I asked—with an uneasy conscience, with a sinking heart—what had happened to distress her.

She drew herself away from me, sighing heavily, and gave me the open letter which I had seen in her hand.

'Read that,' she said. 'And remember I told you what might happen when we first met.'

I read the letter.

It was signed in initials only; but the writer plainly revealed himself as the man who had deserted her. He had repented; he had returned to her. In proof of his penitence he was willing to do her the justice which he had hitherto refused—he was willing to marry her; on the condition that she would engage to keep the marriage a secret, so long as his parents lived. Submitting this proposal, he waited to know whether she would consent, on her side, to forgive and forget.

I gave her back the letter in silence. This unknown rival had done me the service of paving the way for our separation. In offering her the atonement of marriage, he had made it, on my part, a matter of duty to *her*, as well as to myself, to say the parting words. I felt this instantly. And yet, I hated him for helping me!

She took my hand, and led me to the sofa. We sat down, side by side. Her face was composed to a sad tranquillity. She was quiet; she was herself again.

'I have refused to see him,' she said, 'until I had first spoken to you. You have read his letter. What do you say?'

I could make but one answer. It was my duty to tell her what my own position was in the plainest terms. I did my duty—leaving her free to decide on the future for herself. Those sad words said, it was useless to prolong the wretchedness of our separation. I rose, and took her hand for the last time.

I see her again now, at that final moment, as plainly as if it had happened yesterday. She had been suffering from an affection of the throat; and she had a white silk handkerchief tied loosely round her neck. She wore a simple dress of purple merino, with a black-silk apron over it. Her face was deadly pale; her fingers felt icily cold as they closed round my hand.

'Promise me one thing,' I said, 'before I go. While I live, I am your friend—if I am nothing more. If you are ever in trouble, promise that you will let me know it.'

She started, and drew back from me as if I had struck her with a sudden terror.

'Strange!' she said, speaking to herself. 'He feels as I feel. *He* is afraid of what may happen to me, in my life to come.'

I attempted to reassure her. I tried to tell her what was indeed the truth—that I had only been thinking of the ordinary chances and changes of life, when I spoke.

She paid no heed to me; she came back and put her hands on my shoulders, and thoughtfully and sadly looked up in my face.

'My mind is not your mind in this matter,' she said. 'I once owned to you that I had my forebodings, when we first spoke of this man's return. I may tell you now, more than I told you then. I believe I shall die young, and die miserably. If I am right, have you interest enough still left in me to wish to hear of it?'

She paused, shuddering—and added these startling words:

'You *shall* hear of it.'

The tone of steady conviction in which she spoke alarmed and distressed me. My face showed her how deeply and how painfully I was affected.

'There, there!' she said, returning to her natural manner; 'don't take what I say too seriously. A poor girl who has led a lonely life like mine thinks strangely and talks strangely—sometimes. Yes; I give you my promise. If I am ever in trouble, I will let you know it. God bless you—you have been very kind to me—good-bye!'

A tear dropped on my face as she kissed me. The door closed between us. The dark street received me.

It was raining heavily. I looked up at her window, through the drifting shower. The curtains were parted: she was standing in the gap, dimly lit by the lamp on the table behind her, waiting for our last look at each other. Slowly lifting her hand, she waved her farewell at the window, with the unsought native grace which had charmed me on the night when we first met. The curtains fell again—she disappeared—nothing was before me, nothing was round me, but the darkness and the night.

V

In two years from that time, I had redeemed the promise given to my mother on her deathbed. I had entered the Church.

My father's interest made my first step in my new profession an easy one. After serving my preliminary apprenticeship as a curate, I was appointed, before I was thirty years of age, to a living in the West of England.

My new benefice offered me every advantage that I could possibly desire—with the one exception of a sufficient income. Although my wants were few, and although I was still an unmarried man, I found it desirable, on many accounts, to add to my resources. Following the example of other young clergymen in my position, I determined to receive pupils who might stand in need of preparation for a career at the Universities. My relatives exerted themselves; and my good fortune still befriended me. I obtained two pupils to start with. A third would complete the number which I was at present prepared to receive. In course of time, this third pupil made his appearance, under circumstances sufficiently remarkable to merit being mentioned in detail.

It was the summer vacation; and my two pupils had gone home. Thanks to a neighbouring clergyman, who kindly undertook to perform my duties for me, I too obtained a fortnight's holiday, which I spent at my father's house in London.

During my sojourn in the metropolis, I was offered an opportunity of preaching in a church, made famous by the eloquence of one of the popular pulpit-orators of our time. In accepting the proposal, I felt naturally anxious to do my best, before the unusually large and unusually intelligent congregation which would be assembled to hear me.

At the period of which I am now speaking, all England had been startled by the discovery of a terrible crime, perpetrated under circumstances of extreme provocation. I chose this crime as the main subject of my sermon. Admitting that the best among us were frail mortal creatures, subject to evil promptings and provocations like the worst among us, my object was to show how a Christian man may find his certain refuge from temptation in the safeguards of his religion. I dwelt minutely on the hardship of the Christian's first struggle to resist the evil influence—on the help which his Christianity inexhaustibly held out to him in the worst relapses of the weaker and viler part of his nature—on the steady and certain gain which was the ultimate reward of his faith and his firmness—and on the blessed sense of peace and happiness which accompanied the final triumph. Preaching to this effect, with the fervent conviction which I really felt, I may say for myself, at least, that I did no discredit to the choice which had placed me in the pulpit. I held the attention of my congregation, from the first word to the last.

While I was resting in the vestry on the conclusion of the service, a note was brought to me written in pencil. A member of my congregation—a gentleman—wished to see me, on a matter of considerable importance to himself. He would call on me at any place, and at any hour, which I might choose to appoint. If I wished to be satisfied of his respectability, he would beg leave to refer me to his father, with whose name I might possibly be acquainted.

The name given in the reference was undoubtedly familiar to me, as the name of a man of some celebrity and influence in the world of London. I sent back my card, appointing an hour for the visit of my correspondent on the afternoon of the next day.

VI

The stranger made his appearance punctually. I guessed him to be some two or three years younger than myself. He was undeniably handsome; his manners were the manners of a gentleman—and yet, without knowing why, I felt a strong dislike to him the moment he entered the room.

After the first preliminary words of politeness had been exchanged between us, my visitor informed me as follows of the object which he had in view.

'I believe you live in the country, sir?' he began.

'I live in the West of England,' I answered.

'Do you make a long stay in London?'

'No. I go back to my rectory tomorrow.'

'May I ask if you take pupils?'

'Yes.'

'Have you any vacancy?'

'I have one vacancy.'

'Would you object to let me go back with you tomorrow, as your pupil?'

The abruptness of the proposal took me by surprise. I hesitated.

In the first place (as I have already said), I disliked him. In the second place, he was too old to be a fit companion for my other two pupils—both lads in their teens. In the third place, he had asked me to receive him at least three weeks before the vacation came to an end. I had my own pursuits and amusements in prospect during that interval, and saw no reason why I should inconvenience myself by setting them aside.

He noticed my hesitation, and did not conceal from me that I had disappointed him.

'I have it very much at heart,' he said, 'to repair without delay the time that I have lost. My age is against me, I know. The truth is—I have wasted my opportunities since I left school, and I am anxious, honestly anxious, to mend my ways, before it is too late. I wish to prepare myself for one of the Universities—I wish to show, if I can, that I am not quite unworthy to inherit my father's famous name. You are

the man to help me, if I can only persuade you to do it. I was
struck by your sermon yesterday; and, if I may venture to
make the confession in your presence, I took a strong liking
to you. Will you see my father, before you decide to say No?
He will be able to explain whatever may seem strange in my
present application; and he will be happy to see you this
afternoon, if you can spare the time. As to the question of
terms, I am quite sure it can be settled to your entire
satisfaction.'

He was evidently in earnest—gravely, vehemently in earnest. I unwillingly consented to see his father.

Our interview was a long one. All my questions were
answered fully and frankly.

The young man had led an idle and desultory life. He was
weary of it, and ashamed of it. His disposition was a peculiar one. He stood sorely in need of a guide, a teacher, and
a friend, in whom he was disposed to confide. If I disappointed the hopes which he had centred in me, he would be
discouraged, and he would relapse into the aimless and
indolent existence of which he was now ashamed. Any
terms for which I might stipulate were at my disposal if I
would consent to receive him, for three months to begin
with, on trial.

Still hesitating, I consulted my father and my friends.

They were all of opinion (and justly of opinion so far) that
the new connection would be an excellent one for me. They
all reproached me for taking a purely capricious dislike to a
well-born and well-bred young man, and for permitting it to
influence me, at the outset of my career, against my own
interests. Pressed by these considerations, I allowed myself
to be persuaded to give the new pupil a fair trial. He accompanied me, the next day, on my way back to the rectory.

VII

Let me be careful to do justice to a man whom I personally
disliked. My senior pupil began well: he produced a decidedly favourable impression on the persons attached to
my little household.

The women, especially, admired his beautiful light hair, his crisply-curling beard, his delicate complexion, his clear blue eyes, and his finely-shaped hands and feet. Even the inveterate reserve in his manner, and the downcast, almost sullen, look which had prejudiced *me* against him, aroused a common feeling of romantic enthusiasm in my servants' hall. It was decided, on the high authority of the house-keeper herself, that 'the new gentleman' was in love—and, more interesting still, that he was the victim of an unhappy attachment which had driven him away from his friends and his home.

For myself, I tried hard, and tried vainly, to get over my first dislike to the senior pupil.

I could find no fault with him. All his habits were quiet and regular; and he devoted himself conscientiously to his reading. But, little by little, I became satisfied that his heart was not in his studies. More than this, I had my reasons for suspecting that he was concealing something from me, and that he felt painfully the reserve on his own part which he could not, or dared not, break through. There were moments when I almost doubted whether he had not chosen my remote country rectory, as a safe place of refuge from some person or persons of whom he stood in dread.

For example, his ordinary course of proceeding, in the matter of his correspondence, was, to say the least of it, strange.

He received no letters at my house. They waited for him at the village post-office. He invariably called for them himself, and invariably forbore to trust any of my servants with his own letters for the post. Again, when we were out walking together, I more than once caught him look-ing furtively over his shoulder, as if he suspected some person of following him, for some evil purpose. Being con-stitutionally a hater of mysteries, I determined, at an early stage of our intercourse, on making an effort to clear mat-ters up. There might be just a chance of my winning the senior pupil's confidence, if I spoke to him while the last days of the summer vacation still left us alone together in the house.

'Excuse me for noticing it,' I said to him one morning, while we were engaged over our books—'I cannot help observing that you appear to have some trouble on your mind. Is it indiscreet, on my part, to ask if I can be of any use to you?'

He changed colour—looked up at me quickly—looked down again at his book—struggled hard with some secret fear or secret reluctance that was in him—and suddenly burst out with this extraordinary question:

'I suppose you were in earnest when you preached that sermon in London?'

'I am astonished that you should doubt it,' I replied.

He paused again; struggled with himself again; and startled me by a second outbreak, even stranger than the first.

'I am one of the people you preached at in your sermon,' he said. 'That's the true reason why I asked you to take me for your pupil. Don't turn me out! When you talked to your congregation of tortured and tempted people, you talked of Me.'

I was so astonished by the confession, that I lost my presence of mind. For the moment, I was unable to answer him.

'Don't turn me out!' he repeated. 'Help me against myself. I am telling you the truth. As God is my witness, I am telling you the truth!'

'Tell me the *whole* truth,' I said; 'and rely on my consoling and helping you—rely on my being your friend.'

In the fervour of the moment, I took his hand. It lay cold and still in mine: it mutely warned me that I had a sullen and a secret nature to deal with.

'There must be no concealment between us,' I resumed. 'You have entered my house, by your own confession, under false pretences. It is your duty to me, and your duty to yourself, to speak out.'

The man's inveterate reserve—cast off for the moment only—renewed its hold on him. He considered, carefully considered, his next words before he permitted them to pass his lips.

'A person is in the way of my prospects in life,' he began slowly, with his eyes cast down on his book. 'A person provokes me horribly. I feel dreadful temptations (like the man you spoke of in your sermon) when I am in the person's company. Teach me to resist temptation! I am afraid of myself, if I see the person again. You are the only man who can help me. Do it while you can.'

He stopped, and passed his handkerchief over his forehead.

'Will that do?' he asked—still with his eyes on his book.

'It will *not* do,' I answered. 'You are so far from really opening your heart to me, that you won't even let me know whether it is a man or a woman who stands in the way of your prospects in life. You use the word "person," over and over again—rather than say "he" or "she" when you speak of the provocation which is trying you. How can I help a man who has so little confidence in me as that?'

My reply evidently found him at the end of his resources. He tried, tried desperately, to say more than he had said yet. No! The words seemed to stick in his throat. Not one of them would pass his lips.

'Give me time,' he pleaded piteously. 'I can't bring myself to it, all at once. I mean well. Upon my soul, I mean well. But I am slow at this sort of thing. Wait till tomorrow.'

Tomorrow came—and again he put it off.

'One more day!' he said. 'You don't know how hard it is to speak plainly. I am half afraid; I am half ashamed. Give me one more day.'

I had hitherto only disliked him. Try as I might (and did) to make merciful allowance for his reserve, I began to despise him now.

VIII

The day of the deferred confession came, and brought an event with it, for which both he and I were alike unprepared. Would he really have confided in me but for that event? He must either have done it, or have abandoned the purpose which had led him into my house.

We met as usual at the breakfast-table. My housekeeper brought in my letters of the morning. To my surprise, instead of leaving the room again as usual, she walked round to the other side of the table, and laid a letter before my senior pupil—the first letter, since his residence with me, which had been delivered to him under my roof.

He started, and took up the letter. He looked at the address. A spasm of suppressed fury passed across his face; his breath came quickly; his hand trembled as it held the letter. So far, I said nothing. I waited to see whether he would open the envelope in my presence or not.

He was afraid to open it, in my presence. He got on his feet; he said, in tones so low that I could barely hear him: 'Please excuse me for a minute'—and left the room.

I waited for half an hour—for a quarter of an hour, after that—and then I sent to ask if he had forgotten his breakfast.

In a minute more, I heard his footstep in the hall. He opened the breakfast-room door, and stood on the threshold, with a small travelling-bag in his hand.

'I beg your pardon,' he said, still standing at the door. 'I must ask for leave of absence for a day or two. Business in London.'

'Can I be of any use?' I asked. 'I am afraid your letter has brought you bad news?'

'Yes,' he said shortly. 'Bad news. I have no time for breakfast.'

'Wait a few minutes,' I urged. 'Wait long enough to treat me like your friend—to tell me what your trouble is before you go.'

He made no reply. He stepped into the hall, and closed the door—then opened it again a little way, without showing himself.

'Business in London,' he repeated—as if he thought it highly important to inform me of the nature of his errand. The door closed for the second time. He was gone.

I went into my study, and carefully considered what had happened.

The result of my reflections is easily described. I determined on discontinuing my relations with my senior pupil.

In writing to his father (which I did, with all due courtesy and respect, by that day's post), I mentioned as my reason for arriving at this decision:—First, that I had found it impossible to win the confidence of his son. Secondly, that his son had that morning suddenly and mysteriously left my house for London, and that I must decline accepting any further responsibility towards him, as the necessary consequence.

I had put my letter in the post-bag, and was beginning to feel a little easier after having written it, when my house-keeper appeared in the study, with a very grave face, and with something hidden apparently in her closed hand.

'Would you please look, sir, at what we have found in the gentleman's bedroom, since he went away this morning?'

I knew the housekeeper to possess a woman's full share of that amiable weakness of the sex which goes by the name of 'Curiosity'. I had also, in various indirect ways, become aware that my senior pupil's strange departure had largely increased the disposition among the women of my house-hold to regard him as the victim of an unhappy attachment. The time was ripe, as it seemed to me, for checking any further gossip about him, and any renewed attempts at prying into his affairs in his absence.

'Your only business in my pupil's bedroom,' I said to the housekeeper, 'is to see that it is kept clean, and that it is properly aired. There must be no interference, if you please, with his letters, or his papers, or with anything else that he has left behind him. Put back directly whatever you may have found in his room.'

The housekeeper had her full share of a woman's temper as well as of a woman's curiosity. She listened to me with a rising colour, and a just perceptible toss of the head.

'Must I put it back, sir, on the floor, between the bed and the wall?' she inquired, with an ironical assumption of the humblest deference to my wishes. '*That's* where the girl found it when she was sweeping the room. Anybody can see for themselves,' pursued the housekeeper indignantly, 'that the poor gentleman has gone away broken-hearted. And there, in my opinion, is the hussy who is the cause of it!'

With those words, she made me a low curtsey, and laid a small photographic portrait on the desk at which I was sitting.

I looked at the photograph.

In an instant, my heart was beating wildly—my head turned giddy—the housekeeper, the furniture, the walls of the room, all swayed and whirled round me.

The portrait that had been found in my senior pupil's bedroom was the portrait of Jéromette!

IX

I had sent the housekeeper out of my study. I was alone, with the photograph of the Frenchwoman on my desk.

There could surely be little doubt about the discovery that had burst upon me. The man who had stolen his way into my house, driven by the terror of a temptation that he dared not reveal, and the man who had been my unknown rival in the bygone time, were one and the same!

Recovering self-possession enough to realise this plain truth, the inferences that followed forced their way into my mind as a matter of course. The unnamed person who was the obstacle to my pupil's prospects in life, the unnamed person in whose company he was assailed by temptations which made him tremble for himself, stood revealed to me now as being, in all human probability, no other than Jéromette. Had she bound him in the fetters of the marriage which he had himself proposed? Had she discovered his place of refuge in my house? And was the letter that had been delivered to him of her writing? Assuming these questions to be answered in the affirmative, what, in that case, was his 'business in London'? I remembered how he had spoken to me of his temptations, I recalled the expression that had crossed his face when he recognised the handwriting on the letter—and the conclusion that followed literally shook me to the soul. Ordering my horse to be saddled, I rode instantly to the railway-station.

The train by which he had travelled to London had reached the terminus nearly an hour since. The one useful course that I could take, by way of quieting the dreadful misgivings crowding one after another on my mind, was to telegraph to Jéromette at the address at which I had last seen her. I sent the subjoined message—prepaying the reply:

'If you are in any trouble, telegraph to me. I will be with you by the first train. Answer, in any case.'

There was nothing in the way of the immediate despatch of my message. And yet the hours passed, and no answer was received. By the advice of the clerk, I sent a second telegram to the London office, requesting an explanation. The reply came back in these terms:

'Improvements in street. Houses pulled down. No trace of person named in telegram.'

I mounted my horse, and rode back slowly to the rectory.

'The day of his return to me will bring with it the darkest days of my life.' . . . 'I shall die young, and die miserably. Have you interest enough still left in me to wish to hear of it?' . . . 'You *shall* hear of it.' Those words were in my memory while I rode home in the cloudless moonlight night. They were so vividly present to me that I could hear again her pretty foreign accent, her quiet clear tones, as she spoke them. For the rest, the emotions of that memorable day had worn me out. The answer from the telegraph-office had struck me with a strange and stony despair. My mind was a blank. I had no thoughts. I had no tears.

I was about half-way on my road home, and I had just heard the clock of a village church strike ten, when I became conscious, little by little, of a chilly sensation slowly creeping through and through me to the bones. The warm balmy air of a summer night was abroad. It was the month of July. In the month of July, was it possible that any living creature (in good health) could feel cold? It was *not* possible—and yet, the chilly sensation still crept through and through me to the bones.

I looked up. I looked all round me.

My horse was walking along an open high-road. Neither trees nor waters were near me. On either side, the flat fields stretched away bright and broad in the moonlight.

I stopped my horse, and looked round me again.

Yes: I saw it. With my own eyes I saw it. A pillar of white mist—between five and six feet high, as well as I could judge—was moving beside me at the edge of the road, on my left hand. When I stopped, the white mist stopped. When I went on, the white mist went on. I pushed my horse to a trot—the pillar of mist was with me. I urged him to a gallop—the pillar of mist was with me. I stopped him again—the pillar of mist stood still.

The white colour of it was the white colour of the fog which I had seen over the river—on the night when I had gone to bid her farewell. And the chill which had then crept through me to the bones was the chill that was creeping through me now.

I went on again slowly. The white mist went on again slowly— with the clear bright night all round it.

I was awed rather than frightened. There was one moment, and one only, when the fear came to me that my reason might be shaken. I caught myself keeping time to the slow tramp of the horse's feet with the slow utterance of these words, repeated over and over again: 'Jéromette is dead. Jéromette is dead.' But my will was still my own: I was able to control myself, to impose silence on my own muttering lips. And I rode on quietly. And the pillar of mist went quietly with me.

My groom was waiting for my return at the rectory gate. I pointed to the mist, passing through the gate with me.

'Do you see anything there?' I said.

The man looked at me in astonishment.

I entered the rectory. The housekeeper met me in the hall. I pointed to the mist, entering with me.

'Do you see anything at my side?' I asked.

The housekeeper looked at me as the groom had looked at me.

'I am afraid you are not well, sir,' she said. 'Your colour is all gone—you are shivering. Let me get you a glass of wine.'

I went into my study, on the ground-floor, and took the chair at my desk. The photograph still lay where I had left it. The pillar of mist floated round the table, and stopped opposite to me, behind the photograph.

The housekeeper brought in the wine. I put the glass to my lips, and set it down again. The chill of the mist was in the wine. There was no taste, no reviving spirit in it. The presence of the housekeeper oppressed me. My dog had followed her into the room. The presence of the animal oppressed me. I said to the woman, 'Leave me by myself, and take the dog with you.'

They went out, and left me alone in the room.

I sat looking at the pillar of mist, hovering opposite to me.

It lengthened slowly, until it reached to the ceiling. As it lengthened, it grew bright and luminous. A time passed, and a shadowy appearance showed itself in the centre of the light. Little by little, the shadowy appearance took the outline of a human form. Soft brown eyes, tender and melancholy, looked at me through the unearthly light in the mist. The head and the rest of the face broke next slowly on my view. Then the figure gradually revealed itself, moment by moment, downward and downward to the feet. She stood before me as I had last seen her, in her purple-merino dress, with the black-silk apron, with the white handkerchief tied loosely round her neck. She stood before me, in the gentle beauty that I remembered so well; and looked at me as she had looked when she gave me her last kiss—when her tears had dropped on my cheek.

I fell on my knees at the table. I stretched out my hands to her imploringly. I said, 'Speak to me—O, once again speak to me, Jéromette.'

Her eyes rested on me with a divine compassion in them. She lifted her hand, and pointed to the photograph on my desk, with a gesture which bade me turn the card. I turned it. The name of the man who had left my house that morning was inscribed on it, in her own handwriting.

I looked up at her again, when I had read it. She lifted her hand once more, and pointed to the handkerchief round her neck. As I looked at it, the fair white silk changed horribly in colour—the fair white silk became darkened and drenched in blood.

A moment more—and the vision of her began to grow dim. By slow degrees, the figure, then the face, faded back into the shadowy appearance that I had first seen. The luminous inner light died out in the white mist. The mist itself dropped slowly downwards—floated a moment in airy circles on the floor—vanished. Nothing was before me but the familiar wall of the room, and the photograph lying face downwards on my desk.

X

The next day, the newspapers reported the discovery of a murder in London. A Frenchwoman was the victim. She had been killed by a wound in the throat. The crime had been discovered between ten and eleven o'clock on the previous night.

I leave you to draw your conclusion from what I have related. My own faith in the reality of the apparition is immovable. I say, and believe, that Jéromette kept her word with me. She died young, and died miserably. And I heard of it from herself.

Take up the Trial again, and look at the circumstances that were revealed during the investigation in court. His motive for murdering her is there.

You will see that she did indeed marry him privately; that they lived together contentedly, until the fatal day when she discovered that his fancy had been caught by another woman; that violent quarrels took place between them, from that time to the time when my sermon showed him his own deadly hatred towards her, reflected in the case of another man; that she discovered his place of retreat in my house, and threatened him by letter with the public assertion of her conjugal rights; lastly, that a man, variously described by different witnesses, was seen leaving the door of her lodgings on the night of the murder. The Law—advancing no farther than this—may have discovered circumstances of suspicion, but no certainty. The Law, in default of direct evidence to convict the prisoner, may have rightly decided in letting him go free.

But *I* persist in believing that the man was guilty. *I* declare that he, and he alone, was the murderer of Jéromette. And now, you know why.

THE CAPTAIN'S LAST LOVE

I

'THE Captain is still in the prime of life,' the widow remarked. 'He has given up his ship; he possesses a sufficient income, and he has nobody to live with him. I should like to know why he doesn't marry.'

'The Captain was excessively rude to Me,' the widow's younger sister added, on her side. 'When we took leave of him in London, I asked if there was any chance of his joining us at Brighton this season. He turned his back on me as if I had mortally offended him; and he made me this extraordinary answer: "Miss! I hate the sight of the sea." The man has been a sailor all his life. What does he mean by saying that he hates the sight of the sea?'

These questions were addressed to a third person present—and the person was a man. He was entirely at the mercy of the widow and the widow's sister. The other ladies of the family—who might have taken him under their protection—had gone to an evening concert. He was known to be the Captain's friend, and to be well acquainted with events in the Captain's later life. As it happened, he had reasons for hesitating to revive associations connected with those events. But what polite alternative was left to him? He must either inflict disappointment, and, worse still, aggravate curiosity—or he must resign himself to circumstances, and tell the ladies why the Captain would never marry, and why (sailor as he was) he hated the sight of the sea. They were both young women and handsome women—and the person to whom they had appealed (being a man) followed the example of submission to the sex, first set in the garden of Eden. He enlightened the ladies, in the terms that follow:

II

The British merchantman, *Fortuna*, sailed from the port of
Liverpool (at a date which it is not necessary to specify) with
the morning tide. She was bound for certain islands in the
Pacific Ocean, in search of a cargo of sandal-wood—a commodity which, in those days, found a ready and profitable
market in the Chinese Empire.

A large discretion was reposed in the Captain by the
owners, who knew him to be not only trustworthy, but a
man of rare ability, carefully cultivated during the leisure
hours of a seafaring life. Devoted heart and soul to his
professional duties, he was a hard reader and an excellent
linguist as well. Having had considerable experience among
the inhabitants of the Pacific Islands, he had attentively
studied their characters, and had mastered their language in
more than one of its many dialects. Thanks to the valuable
information thus obtained, the Captain was never at a loss
to conciliate the islanders. He had more than once succeeded in finding a cargo, under circumstances in which
other captains had failed.

Possessing these merits, he had also his fair share of
human defects. For instance, he was a little too conscious of
his own good looks—of his bright chestnut hair and whiskers, of his beautiful blue eyes, of his fair white skin, which
many a woman had looked at with the admiration that is
akin to envy. His shapely hands were protected by gloves; a
broad-brimmed hat sheltered his complexion in fine
weather from the sun. He was nice in the choice of his
perfumes; he never drank spirits, and the smell of tobacco
was abhorrent to him. New men among his officers and his
crew, seeing him in his cabin, perfectly dressed, washed,
and brushed until he was an object speckless to look upon—
a merchant-captain soft of voice, careful in his choice of
words, devoted to study in his leisure hours—were apt to
conclude that they had trusted themselves at sea under a
commander who was an anomalous mixture of a schoolmas-
ter and a dandy. But if the slightest infraction of discipline
took place, or if the storm rose and the vessel proved to be

in peril, it was soon discovered that the gloved hands held a
rod of iron; that the soft voice could make itself heard
through wind and sea from one end of the deck to the other;
and that it issued orders which the greatest fool on board
discovered to be orders that had saved the ship. Throughout
his professional life, the general impression that this variously gifted man produced on the little world about him was
always the same. Some few liked him; everybody respected
him; nobody understood him. The Captain accepted these
results. He persisted in reading his books and protecting his
complexion, with this result: his owners shook hands with
him, and put up with his gloves.

The *Fortuna* touched at Rio for water, and for supplies of
food which might prove useful in case of scurvy. In due time
the ship rounded Cape Horn, favoured by the finest weather
ever known in those latitudes by the oldest hand on board.
The mate—one Mr Duncalf—a boozing, wheezing, self-
confident old sea-dog, with a flaming face and a vast voca-
bulary of oaths, swore that he didn't like it. 'The foul
weather's coming, my lads,' said Mr Duncalf. 'Mark my
words, there'll be wind enough to take the curl out of the
Captain's whiskers before we are many days older!'

For one uneventful week, the ship cruised in search of the
islands to which the owners had directed her. At the end of
that time the wind took the predicted liberties with the
Captain's whiskers; and Mr Duncalf stood revealed to an
admiring crew in the character of a true prophet.

For three days and three nights the *Fortuna* ran before the
storm, at the mercy of wind and sea. On the fourth morning
the gale blew itself out, the sun appeared again towards
noon, and the Captain was able to take an observation. The
result informed him that he was in a part of the Pacific
Ocean with which he was entirely unacquainted. Thereupon, the officers were called to a council in the cabin.

Mr Duncalf, as became his rank, was consulted first. His
opinion possessed the merit of brevity. 'My lads, this ship's
bewitched. Take my word for it, we shall wish ourselves
back in our own latitudes before we are many days older.'
Which, being interpreted, meant that Mr Duncalf was lost,

like his superior officer, in a part of the ocean of which he knew nothing.

The remaining members of the council, having no suggestions to offer, left the Captain to take his own way. He decided (the weather being fine again) to stand on under an easy press of sail for four-and-twenty hours more, and to see if anything came of it.

Soon after night-fall, something did come of it. The look-out forward hailed the quarter-deck with the dreadful cry, 'Breakers ahead!' In less than a minute more, everybody heard the crash of the broken water. The *Fortuna* was put about, and came round slowly in the light wind. Thanks to the timely alarm and the fine weather, the safety of the vessel was easily provided for. They kept her under short sail; and they waited for the morning.

The dawn showed them in the distance a glorious green island, not marked in the ship's charts—an island girt about by a coral-reef, and having in its midst a high-peaked mountain which looked, through the telescope, like a mountain of volcanic origin. Mr Duncalf, taking his morning draught of rum and water, shook his groggy old head, and said (and swore): 'My lads, I don't like the look of that island.' The Captain was of a different opinion. He had one of the ship's boats put into the water; he armed himself and four of his crew who accompanied him; and away he went in the morning sunlight to visit the island.

Skirting round the coral-reef, they found a natural breach, which proved to be broad enough and deep enough not only for the passage of the boat, but of the ship herself if needful. Crossing the broad inner belt of smooth water, they approached the golden sands of the island, strewed with magnificent shells, and crowded by the dusky island-ers—men, women, and children, all waiting in breathless astonishment to see the strangers land.

The Captain kept the boat off, and examined the islanders carefully. The innocent simple people danced, and sang, and ran into the water, imploring their wonderful white visitors by gestures to come on shore. Not a creature among them carried arms of any sort; a hospitable curiosity anim-

ated the entire population. The men cried out, in their
smooth musical language, 'Come and eat!' and the plump
black-eyed women, all laughing together, added their own
invitation, 'Come and be kissed!' Was it in mortals to resist
such temptations as these? The Captain led the way on
shore, and the women surrounded him in an instant, and
screamed for joy at the glorious spectacle of his whiskers,
his complexion, and his gloves. So, the mariners from the
far north were welcomed to the newly-discovered island.

III

The morning wore on. Mr Duncalf, in charge of the ship,
cursing the island over his rum and water, as a 'beastly
green strip of a place, not laid down in any Christian chart,'
was kept waiting four mortal hours before the Captain
returned to his command, and reported himself to his officers as follows:

He had found his knowledge of the Polynesian dialects
sufficient to make himself in some degree understood by the
natives of the new island. Under the guidance of the chief
he had made a first journey of exploration, and had seen for
himself that the place was a marvel of natural beauty and
fertility. The one barren spot in it was the peak of the
volcanic mountain, composed of crumbling rock; originally
no doubt lava and ashes, which had cooled and consolid-
ated with the lapse of time. So far as he could see, the crater
at the top was now an extinct crater. But, if he had understood rightly, the chief had spoken of earthquakes and
eruptions at certain bygone periods, some of which lay
within his own earliest recollections of the place.

Adverting next to considerations of practical utility, the
Captain announced that he had seen sandal-wood enough
on the island to load a dozen ships, and that the natives
were willing to part with it for a few toys and trinkets
generally distributed amongst them. To the mate's disgust,
the *Fortuna* was taken inside the reef that day, and was
anchored before sunset in a natural harbour. Twelve hours
of recreation, beginning with the next morning, were

granted to the men, under the wise restrictions in such cases established by the Captain. That interval over, the work of cutting the precious wood and loading the ship was to be unremittingly pursued.

Mr Duncalf had the first watch after the *Fortuna* had been made snug. He took the boatswain aside (an ancient sea-dog like himself), and he said in a gruff whisper: 'My lad, this here ain't the island laid down in our sailing orders. See if mischief don't come of disobeying orders before we are many days older.'

Nothing in the shape of mischief happened that night. But at sunrise the next morning a suspicious circumstance occurred; and Mr Duncalf whispered to the boatswain: 'What did I tell you?' The Captain and the chief of the islanders held a private conference in the cabin; and the Captain, after first forbidding any communication with the shore until his return, suddenly left the ship, alone with the chief, in the chief's own canoe.

What did this strange disappearance mean? The Captain himself, when he took his seat in the canoe, would have been puzzled to answer that question. He asked, in the nearest approach that his knowledge could make to the language used in the island, whether he would be a long time or a short time absent from his ship.

The chief answered mysteriously (as the Captain understood him) in these words: 'Long time or short time, your life depends on it, and the lives of your men.'

Paddling his light little boat in silence over the smooth water inside the reef, the chief took his visitor ashore at a part of the island which was quite new to the Captain. The two crossed a ravine, and ascended an eminence beyond. There the chief stopped, and silently pointed out to sea.

The Captain looked in the direction indicated to him, and discovered a second and a smaller island, lying away to the south-west. Taking out his telescope from the case by which it was slung at his back, he narrowly examined the place. Two of the native canoes were lying off the shore of the new island; and the men in them appeared to be all kneeling or crouching in curiously chosen attitudes. Shifting the range of his glass, he next beheld a white-robed figure, tall and solitary—the one inhabitant of the island whom he could discover. The man was standing on the highest point of a rocky cape. A fire was burning at his feet. Now he lifted his arms solemnly to the sky; now he dropped some invisible fuel into the fire, which made a blue smoke; and now he cast other invisible objects into the canoes floating beneath him, which the islanders reverently received with bodies that crouched in abject submission. Lowering his telescope, the Captain looked round at the chief for an explanation. The chief gave the explanation readily. His language was interpreted by the English stranger in these terms:

'Wonderful white man! the island you see yonder is a Holy Island. As such it is *Taboo*—an island sanctified and set apart. The honourable person whom you notice on the rock is an all-powerful favourite of the gods. He is by vocation a Sorcerer, and by rank a Priest. You now see him casting charms and blessings into the canoes of our fishermen, who kneel to him for fine weather and great plenty of fish. If any profane person, native or stranger, presumes to set foot on that island, my otherwise peaceful subjects will (in the performance of a religious duty) put that person to death. Mention this to your men. They will be fed by my male people, and fondled by my female people, so long as they keep clear of the Holy Isle. As they value their lives, let them respect this prohibition. Is it understood between us? Wonderful white man! my canoe is waiting for you. Let us go back.'

Understanding enough of the chief's language (illustrated by his gestures) to receive in the right spirit the communication thus addressed to him, the Captain repeated the warning to the ship's company in the plainest possible English. The officers and men then took their holiday on shore, with the exception of Mr Duncalf, who positively refused to leave the ship. For twelve delightful hours they were fed by the male people, and fondled by the female people, and then they were mercilessly torn from the flesh-pots and the arms of their new friends, and set to work on the sandal-wood in good earnest. Mr Duncalf superintended the loading, and

waited for the mischief that was to come of disobeying the
owners' orders with a confidence worthy of a better cause.

IV

Strangely enough, chance once more declared itself in favour of the mate's point of view. The mischief did actually
come; and the chosen instrument of it was a handsome
young islander, who was one of the sons of the chief.

The Captain had taken a fancy to the sweet-tempered
intelligent lad. Pursuing his studies in the dialect of the
island, at leisure hours, he had made the chief's son his
tutor, and had instructed the youth in English by way of
return. More than a month had passed in this intercourse,
and the ship's lading was being rapidly completed—when,
in an evil hour, the talk between the two turned on the
subject of the Holy Island.

'Does nobody live on the island but the Priest?' the Captain asked.

The chief's son looked round him suspiciously. 'Promise
me you won't tell anybody!' he began very earnestly.

The Captain gave his promise.

'There is one other person on the island,' the lad whispered; 'a person to feast your eyes upon, if you could only
see her! She is the Priest's daughter. Removed to the island
in her infancy, she has never left it since. In that sacred
solitude she has only looked on two human beings—her
father and her mother. I once saw her from my canoe,
taking care not to attract her notice, or to approach too near
the holy soil. Oh, so young, dear master, and, oh, so beautiful!' The chief's son completed the description by kissing
his own hands as an expression of rapture.

The Captain's fine blue eyes sparkled. He asked no more
questions; but, later on that day, he took his telescope with
him, and paid a secret visit to the eminence which overlooked the Holy Island. The next day, and the next, he
privately returned to the same place. On the fourth day,
fatal Destiny favoured him. He discovered the nymph of the
island.

Standing alone upon the cape on which he had already seen her father, she was feeding some tame birds which looked like turtle-doves. The glass showed the Captain her white robe, fluttering in the sea-breeze; her long black hair falling to her feet; her slim and supple young figure; her simple grace of attitude, as she turned this way and that, attending to the wants of her birds. Before her was the blue ocean; behind her rose the lustrous green of the island forest. He looked and looked until his eyes and arms ached. When she disappeared among the trees, followed by her favourite birds, the Captain shut up his telescope with a sigh, and said to himself: 'I have seen an angel!'

From that hour he became an altered man; he was languid, silent, interested in nothing. General opinion, on board his ship, decided that he was going to be taken ill.

A week more elapsed, and the officers and crew began to talk of the voyage to their market in China. The Captain refused to fix a day for sailing. He even took offence at being asked to decide. Instead of sleeping in his cabin, he went ashore for the night.

Not many hours afterwards (just before daybreak), Mr Duncalf, snoring in his cabin on deck, was aroused by a hand laid on his shoulder. The swinging lamp, still alight, showed him the dusky face of the chief's son, convulsed with terror. By wild signs, by disconnected words in the little English which he had learnt, the lad tried to make the mate understand him. Dense Mr Duncalf, understanding nothing, hailed the second officer, on the opposite side of the deck. The second officer was young and intelligent; he rightly interpreted the terrible news that had come to the ship.

The Captain had broken his own rules. Watching his opportunity, under cover of the night, he had taken a canoe, and had secretly crossed the channel to the Holy Island. No one had been near him at the time, but the chief's son. The lad had vainly tried to induce him to abandon his desperate enterprise, and had vainly waited on the shore in the hope of hearing the sound of the paddle announcing his return. Beyond all reasonable doubt, the infatuated man had set foot on the shores of the tabooed island.

The one chance for his life was to conceal what he had done, until the ship could be got out of the harbour, and then (if no harm had come to him in the interval) to rescue him after nightfall. It was decided to spread the report that he had really been taken ill, and that he was confined to his cabin. The chief's son, whose heart the Captain's kindness had won, could be trusted to do this, and to keep the secret faithfully for his good friend's sake.

Towards noon, the next day, they attempted to take the ship to sea, and failed for want of wind. Hour by hour, the heat grew more oppressive. As the day declined, there were ominous appearances in the western heaven. The natives, who had given some trouble during the day by their anxiety to see the Captain, and by their curiosity to know the cause of the sudden preparations for the ship's departure, all went ashore together, looking suspiciously at the sky, and re-appeared no more. Just at midnight, the ship (still in her snug berth inside the reef) suddenly trembled from her keel to her uppermost masts. Mr Duncalf, surrounded by the startled crew, shook his knotty fist at the island as if he could see it in the dark. 'My lads, what did I tell you? That was a shock of earthquake.'

With the morning the threatening aspect of the weather unexpectedly disappeared. A faint hot breeze from the land, just enough to give the ship steerage-way, offered Mr Duncalf a chance of getting to sea. Slowly the *Fortuna*, with the mate himself at the wheel, half sailed, half drifted into the open ocean. At a distance of barely two miles from the island the breeze was felt no more, and the vessel lay becalmed for the rest of the day.

At night the men waited their orders, expecting to be sent after their Captain in one of the boats. The intense darkness, the airless heat, and a second shock of earthquake (faintly felt in the ship at her present distance from the land) warned the mate to be cautious. 'I smell mischief in the air,' said Mr Duncalf. 'The Captain must wait till I am surer of the weather.'

Still no change came with the new day. The dead calm continued, and the airless heat. As the day declined, another ominous appearance became visible. A thin line of smoke was discovered through the telescope, ascending from the topmost peak of the mountain on the main island. Was the volcano threatening an eruption? The mate, for one, entertained no doubt of it. 'By the Lord, the place is going to burst up!' said Mr Duncalf. 'Come what may of it, we must find the Captain tonight!'

V

What was the lost Captain doing? and what chance had the crew of finding him that night?

He had committed himself to his desperate adventure, without forming any plan for the preservation of his own safety; without giving even a momentary consideration to the consequences which might follow the risk that he had run. The charming figure that he had seen haunted him night and day. The image of the innocent creature, secluded from humanity in her island-solitude, was the one image that filled his mind. A man, passing a woman in the street, acts on the impulse to turn and follow her, and in that one thoughtless moment shapes the destiny of his future life. The Captain had acted on a similar impulse, when he took the first canoe he found on the beach, and shaped his reckless course for the tabooed island.

Reaching the shore while it was still dark, he did one sensible thing—he hid the canoe so that it might not betray him when the daylight came. That done, he waited for the morning on the outskirts of the forest.

The trembling light of dawn revealed the mysterious solitude around him. Following the outer limits of the trees, first in one direction, then in another, and finding no trace of any living creature, he decided on penetrating to the interior of the island. He entered the forest.

An hour of walking brought him to rising ground. Continuing the ascent, he got clear of the trees, and stood on the grassy top of a broad cliff which overlooked the sea. An open hut was on the cliff. He cautiously looked in, and

discovered that it was empty. The few household utensils
left about, and the simple bed of leaves in a corner, were
covered with fine sandy dust. Night-birds flew blundering
out of inner cavities in the roof, and took refuge in the
shadows of the forest below. It was plain that the hut had
not been inhabited for some time past.

Standing at the open doorway and considering what he
should do next, the Captain saw a bird flying towards him
out of the forest. It was a turtle-dove, so tame that it
fluttered close up to him. At the same moment the sound of
sweet laughter became audible among the trees. His heart
beat fast; he advanced a few steps and stopped. In a moment more the nymph of the island appeared, in her white
robe, ascending the cliff in pursuit of her truant bird. She
saw the strange man, and suddenly stood still; struck motionless by the amazing discovery that had burst upon her.
The Captain approached, smiling and holding out his hand.
She never moved; she stood before him in helpless wonder-
ment—her lovely black eyes fixed spell-bound on his face:
her dusky bosom palpitating above the fallen folds of her
robe; her rich red lips parted in mute astonishment. Feast-
ing his eyes on her beauty in silence, the Captain after a
while ventured to speak to her in the language of the main
island. The sound of his voice, addressing her in the words
that she understood, roused the lovely creature to action.
She started, stepped close up to him, and dropped on her
knees at his feet.

'My father worships invisible deities,' she said softly. 'Are
you a visible deity? Has my mother sent you?' She pointed
as she spoke to the deserted hut behind them. 'You appear,'
she went on, 'in the place where my mother died. Is it for
her sake that you show yourself to her child? Beautiful deity,
come to the Temple—come to my father!'

The Captain gently raised her from the ground. If her
father saw him, he was a doomed man.

Infatuated as he was, he had sense enough left to an-
nounce himself plainly in his own character, as a mortal
creature arriving from a distant land. The girl instantly drew
back from him with a look of terror.

'He is not like my father,' she said to herself; 'he is not like me. Is he the lying demon of the prophecy? Is he the predestined destroyer of our island?'

The Captain's experience of the sex showed him the only sure way out of the awkward position in which he was now placed. He appealed to his personal appearance.

'Do I look like a demon?' he asked.

Her eyes met his eyes; a faint smile trembled on her lips. He ventured on asking what she meant by the predestined destruction of the island. She held up her hand solemnly, and repeated the prophecy.

The Holy Island was threatened with destruction by an evil being, who would one day appear on its shores. To avert the fatality the place had been sanctified and set apart, under the protection of the gods and their priest. Here was the reason for the taboo, and for the extraordinary rigour with which it was enforced. Listening to her with the deepest interest, the Captain took her hand and pressed it gently.

'Do I feel like a demon?' he whispered.

Her slim brown fingers closed frankly on his hand. 'You feel soft and friendly,' she said with the fearless candour of a child. 'Squeeze me again. I like it!'

The next moment she snatched her hand away from him; the sense of his danger had suddenly forced itself on her mind. 'If my father sees you,' she said, 'he will light the signal fire at the Temple, and the people from the other island will come here and put you to death. Where is your canoe? No! It is daylight. My father may see you on the water.' She considered a little, and, approaching him, laid her hands on his shoulders. 'Stay here till nightfall,' she resumed. 'My father never comes this way. The sight of the place where my mother died is horrible to him. You are safe here. Promise to stay where you are till night-time.'

The Captain gave his promise.

Freed from anxiety so far, the girl's mobile temperament recovered its native cheerfulness, its sweet gaiety and spirit. She admired the beautiful stranger as she might have admired a new bird that had flown to her to be fondled with the rest. She patted his fair white skin, and wished she had a skin like it. She lifted the great glossy folds of her long black hair, and compared it with the Captain's bright curly locks, and longed to change colours with him from the bottom of her heart. His dress was a wonder to her; his watch was a new revelation. She rested her head on his shoulder to listen delightedly to the ticking, as he held the watch to her ear. Her fragrant breath played on his face, her warm supple figure rested against him softly. The Captain's arm stole round her waist, and the Captain's lips gently touched her cheek. She lifted her head with a look of pleased surprise. 'Thank you,' said the child of nature simply. 'Kiss me again; I like it. May I kiss you?' The tame turtle-dove perched on her shoulder as she gave the Captain her first kiss, and diverted her thoughts to the pets that she had left, in pursuit of the truant dove. 'Come,' she said, 'and see my birds. I keep them on this side of the forest. There is no danger, so long as you don't show yourself on the other side. My name is Aimata. Aimata will take care of you. Oh, what a beautiful white neck you have!' She put her arm admiringly round his neck. The Captain's arm held her tenderly to him. Slowly the two descended the cliff, and were lost in the leafy solitudes of the forest. And the tame dove fluttered before them, a winged messenger of love, cooing to his mate.

VI

The night had come, and the Captain had not left the island.

Aimata's resolution to send him away in the darkness was a forgotten resolution already. She had let him persuade her that he was in no danger, so long as he remained in the hut on the cliff; and she had promised, at parting, to return to him while the Priest was still sleeping, at the dawn of day.

He was alone in the hut. The thought of the innocent creature whom he loved was sorrowfully as well as tenderly present to his mind. He almost regretted his rash visit to the island. 'I will take her with me to England,' he said to himself. 'What does a sailor care for the opinion of the world? Aimata shall be my wife.'

The intense heat oppressed him. He stepped out on the cliff, towards midnight, in search of a breath of air.

At that moment, the first shock of earthquake (felt in the ship while she was inside the reef) shook the ground he stood on. He instantly thought of the volcano on the main island. Had he been mistaken in supposing the crater to be extinct? Was the shock that he had just felt a warning from the volcano, communicated through a submarine connection between the two islands? He waited and watched through the hours of darkness, with a vague sense of apprehension, which was not to be reasoned away. With the first light of daybreak he descended into the forest, and saw the lovely being whose safety was already precious to him as his own, hurrying to meet him through the trees.

She waved her hand distractedly, as she approached him. 'Go!' she cried; 'go away in your canoe before our island is destroyed!'

He did his best to quiet her alarm. Was it the shock of earthquake that had frightened her? No: it was more than the shock of earthquake—it was something terrible which had followed the shock. There was a lake near the Temple, the waters of which were supposed to be heated by subterranean fires. The lake had risen with the earthquake, had bubbled furiously, and had then melted away into the earth and been lost. Her father, viewing the portent with horror, had gone to the cape to watch the volcano on the main island, and to implore by prayers and sacrifices the protection of the gods. Hearing this, the Captain entreated Aimata to let him see the emptied lake, in the absence of the Priest. She hesitated; but his influence was all-powerful. He prevailed on her to turn back with him through the forest.

Reaching the farthest limit of the trees, they came out upon open rocky ground which sloped gently downward towards the centre of the island. Having crossed this space, they arrived at a natural amphitheatre of rock. On one side of it, the Temple appeared, partly excavated, partly formed by a natural cavern. In one of the lateral branches of the cavern was the dwelling of the Priest and his daughter. The mouth of it looked out on the rocky basin of the lake. Stooping over the edge, the Captain discovered, far down in the empty depths, a light cloud of steam. Not a drop of water was visible, look where he might.

Aimata pointed to the abyss, and hid her face on his bosom. 'My father says,' she whispered, 'that it is your doing.'

The Captain started. 'Does your father know that I am on the island?'

She looked up at him with a quick glance of reproach. 'Do you think I would tell him, and put your life in peril?' she asked. 'My father felt the destroyer of the island in the earthquake; my father saw the coming destruction in the disappearance of the lake.' Her eyes rested on him with a loving languor. 'Are you indeed the demon of the prophecy?' she said, winding his hair round her finger. 'I am not afraid of you, if you are. I am a creature bewitched; I love the demon.' She kissed him passionately. 'I don't care if I die,' she whispered between the kisses, 'if I only die with you!'

The Captain made no attempt to reason with her. He took the wiser way—he appealed to her feelings.

'You will come and live with me happily in my own country,' he said. 'My ship is waiting for us. I will take you home with me, and you shall be my wife.'

She clapped her hands for joy. Then she thought of her father, and drew back from him in tears.

The Captain understood her. 'Let us leave this dreary place,' he suggested. 'We will talk about it in the cool glades of the forest, where you first said you loved me.'

She gave him her hand. 'Where I first said I loved you!' she repeated, smiling tenderly as she looked at him. They left the lake together.

VII

The darkness had fallen again; and the ship was still becalmed at sea.

Mr Duncalf came on deck after his supper. The thin line of smoke, seen rising from the peak of the mountain that evening, was now succeeded by ominous flashes of fire from the same quarter, intermittently visible. The faint hot breeze from the land was felt once more. 'There's just an air of wind,' Mr Duncalf remarked. 'I'll try for the Captain while I have the chance.'

One of the boats was lowered into the water—under command of the second mate, who had already taken the bearings of the tabooed island by daylight. Four of the men were to go with him, and they were all to be well-armed. Mr Duncalf addressed his final instructions to the officer in the boat.

'You will keep a look-out, sir, with a lantern in the bows. If the natives annoy you, you know what to do. Always shoot natives. When you get anigh the island, you will fire a gun and sing out for the Captain.'

'Quite needless,' interposed a voice from the sea. 'The Captain is here!'

Without taking the slightest notice of the astonishment that he had caused, the commander of the *Fortuna* paddled his canoe to the side of the ship. Instead of ascending to the deck, he stepped into the boat, waiting alongside. 'Lend me your pistols,' he said quietly to the second officer, 'and oblige me by taking your men back to their duties on board.' He looked up at Mr Duncalf and gave some further directions. 'If there is any change in the weather, keep the ship standing off and on, at a safe distance from the land, and throw up a rocket from time to time to show your position. Expect me on board again by sunrise.'

'What!' cried the mate. 'Do you mean to say you are going back to the island—in that boat—all by yourself?'

'I am going back to the island,' answered the Captain, as quietly as ever; 'in this boat—all by myself.' He pushed off from the ship, and hoisted the sail as he spoke.

'You're deserting your duty!' the old sea-dog shouted, with one of his loudest oaths.

'Attend to my directions,' the Captain shouted back, as he drifted away into the darkness.

Mr Duncalf—violently agitated for the first time in his life—took leave of his superior officer, with a singular mixture of solemnity and politeness, in these words:

'The Lord have mercy on your soul! I wish you good-evening.'

VIII

Alone in the boat, the Captain looked with a misgiving mind at the flashing of the volcano on the main island.

If events had favoured him, he would have removed Aimata to the shelter of the ship on the day when he saw the emptied basin of the lake. But the smoke of the Priest's sacrifice had been discovered by the chief; and he had despatched two canoes with instructions to make inquiries. One of the canoes had returned; the other was kept in waiting off the cape, to place a means of communicating with the main island at the disposal of the Priest. The second shock of earthquake had naturally increased the alarm of the chief. He had sent messages to the Priest, entreating him to leave the island, and other messages to Aimata suggesting that she should exert her influence over her father, if he hesitated. The Priest refused to leave the Temple. He trusted in his gods and his sacrifices—he believed they might avert the fatality that threatened his sanctuary.

Yielding to the holy man, the Chief sent reinforcements of canoes to take their turn at keeping watch off the headland. Assisted by torches, the islanders were on the alert (in superstitious terror of the demon of the prophecy) by night as well as by day. The Captain had no alternative but to keep in hiding, and to watch his opportunity of approaching the place in which he had concealed his canoe. It was only after Aimata had left him as usual, to return to her father at the close of evening, that the chances declared themselves in his favour. The fire-flashes from the mountain, visible when the night came, had struck terror into the hearts of the men on the watch. They thought of their wives, their children, and their possessions on the main island, and they one and all deserted their Priest. The Captain seized the opportunity of communicating with the ship, and of exchanging a frail canoe which he was ill able to manage, for a swift-sailing boat capable of keeping the sea in the event of stormy weather.

As he now neared the land, certain small sparks of red, moving on the distant water, informed him that the canoes of the sentinels had been ordered back to their duty.

Carefully avoiding the lights, he reached his own side of the island without accident, and guided by the boat's lantern, anchored under the cliff. He climbed the rocks, advanced to the door of the hut, and was met, to his delight and astonishment, by Aimata on the threshold.

'I dreamed that some dreadful misfortune had parted us for ever,' she said; 'and I came here to see if my dream was true. You have taught me what it is to be miserable; I never felt my heart ache till I looked into the hut and found that you had gone. Now I have seen you, I am satisfied. No! you must not go back with me. My father may be out looking for me. It is you that are in danger, not I. I know the forest as well by dark as by daylight.'

The Captain detained her when she tried to leave him.

'Now you *are* here,' he said, 'why should I not place you at once in safety? I have been to the ship; I have brought back one of the boats. The darkness will befriend us—let us embark while we can.'

She shrank away as he took her hand. 'You forget my father!' she said.

'Your father is in no danger, my love. The canoes are waiting for him at the cape. I saw the lights as I passed.'

With that reply he drew her out of the hut and led her towards the sea. Not a breath of the breeze was now to be felt. The dead calm had returned—and the boat was too large to be easily managed by one man alone at the oars.

'The breeze may come again,' he said. 'Wait here, my angel, for the chance.'

As he spoke, the deep silence of the forest below them was broken by a sound. A harsh wailing voice was heard, calling:

'Aimata! Aimata!'

'My father!' she whispered; 'he has missed me. If he comes here you are lost.'

She kissed him with passionate fervour; she held him to her for a moment with all her strength.

'Expect me at daybreak,' she said, and disappeared down the landward slope of the cliff.

He listened, anxious for her safety. The voices of the father and daughter just reached him from among the trees. The priest spoke in no angry tones; she had apparently found an acceptable excuse for her absence. Little by little, the failing sound of their voices told him that they were on their way back together to the Temple. The silence fell again. Not a ripple broke on the beach. Not a leaf rustled in the forest. Nothing moved but the reflected flashes of the volcano on the mainland over the black sky. It was an airless and an awful calm.

He went into the hut, and lay down on his bed of leaves —not to sleep, but to rest. All his energies might be required to meet the coming events of the morning. After the voyage to and from the ship, and the long watching that had preceded it, strong as he was he stood in need of repose.

For some little time he kept awake, thinking. Insensibly the oppression of the intense heat, aided in its influence by his own fatigue, treacherously closed his eyes. In spite of himself, the weary man fell into a deep sleep.

He was awakened by a roar like the explosion of a park* of artillery. The volcano on the main island had burst into a state of eruption. Smoky flame-light overspread the sky, and flashed through the open doorway of the hut. He sprang from his bed—and found himself up to his knees in water.

Had the sea overflowed the land?

He waded out of the hut, and the water rose to his middle. He looked round him by the lurid light of the eruption. The one visible object within the range of view was the sea, stained by reflections from the blood-red sky, swirling and rippling strangely in the dead calm. In a moment more, he became conscious that the earth on which he stood was sinking under his feet. The water rose to his neck; the last vestige of the roof of the hut disappeared.

He looked round again, and the truth burst on him. The island was sinking—slowly, slowly sinking into volcanic depths, below even the depth of the sea! The highest object was the hut, and that had dropped inch by inch under water before his own eyes. Thrown up to the surface by occult volcanic influences, the island had sunk back, under the same influences, to the obscurity from which it had emerged!

A black shadowy object, turning in a wide circle, came slowly near him as the all-destroying ocean washed its bitter waters into his mouth. The buoyant boat, rising as the sea rose, had dragged its anchor, and was floating round in the vortex made by the slowly-sinking island. With a last desperate hope that Aimata might have been saved as *he* had been saved, he swam to the boat, seized the heavy oars with the strength of a giant, and made for the place (so far as he could guess at it now) where the lake and the Temple had once been.

He looked round and round him; he strained his eyes in the vain attempt to penetrate below the surface of the seething dimpling sea. Had the panic-stricken watchers in the canoes saved themselves, without an effort to preserve the father and daughter? Or had they both been suffocated before they could make an attempt to escape? He called to her in his misery, as if she could hear him out of the fathomless depths, 'Aimata! Aimata!' The roar of the distant eruption answered him. The mounting fires lit the solitary sea far and near over the sinking island. The boat turned slowly and more slowly in the lessening vortex. Never again would those gentle eyes look at him with unutterable love! Never again would those fresh lips touch his lips with their fervent kiss! Alone, amid the savage forces of Nature in conflict, the miserable mortal lifted his hands in frantic supplication—and the burning sky glared down on him in its pitiless grandeur, and struck him to his knees in the boat. His reason sank with his sinking limbs. In the merciful frenzy that succeeded the shock, he saw her afar off, in her white robe, an angel poised on the waters, beckoning him to follow her to the brighter and the better world. He loosened the sail, he seized the oars; and the faster he pursued it, the faster the mocking vision fled from him over the empty and endless sea.

IX

The boat was discovered, on the next morning, from the ship.

All that the devotion of the officers of the *Fortuna* could do for their unhappy commander was done on the homeward voyage. Restored to his own country, and to skilled medical help, the Captain's mind by slow degrees recovered its balance. He has taken his place in society again—he lives and moves and manages his affairs like the rest of us. But his heart is dead to all new emotions; nothing remains in it but the sacred remembrance of his lost love. He neither courts nor avoids the society of women. Their sympathy finds him grateful, but their attractions seem to be lost on him; they pass from his mind as they pass from his eyes—they stir nothing in him but the memory of Aimata.

'Now you know, ladies, why the Captain will never marry, and why (sailor as he is) he hates the sight of the sea.'

WHO KILLED ZEBEDEE?

A FIRST WORD FOR MYSELF

BEFORE the Doctor left me one evening, I asked him how much longer I was likely to live. He answered: 'It's not easy to say; you may die before I can get back to you in the morning, or you may live to the end of the month.'

I was alive enough on the next morning to think of the needs of my soul, and (being a member of the Roman Catholic Church) to send for the priest.

The history of my sins, related in confession, included blameworthy neglect of a duty which I owed to the laws of my country. In the priest's opinion—and I agreed with him—I was bound to make public acknowledgement of my fault, as an act of penance becoming to a Catholic Englishman. We concluded, thereupon, to try a division of labour. I related the circumstances, while his reverence took the pen, and put the matter into shape.

Here follows what came of it:—

I

When I was a young man of five-and-twenty, I became a member of the London police force. After nearly two years' ordinary experience of the responsible and ill-paid duties of that vocation, I found myself employed on my first serious and terrible case of official inquiry—relating to nothing less than the crime of Murder.

The circumstances were these:—

I was then attached to a station in the northern district of London—which I beg permission not to mention more particularly. On a certain Monday in the week, I took my turn of night duty. Up to four in the morning, nothing occured at the station-house out of the ordinary way. It was then spring time, and, between the gas and the fire, the room became rather hot. I went to the door to get a breath of fresh air—much to the surprise of our Inspector on duty, who was constitutionally a chilly man. There was a fine rain falling; and a nasty damp in the air sent me back to the fireside. I don't suppose I had sat down for more than a minute when the swinging-door was violently pushed open. A frantic woman ran in with a scream, and said: 'Is this the station-house?'

Our Inspector (otherwise an excellent officer) had, by some perversity of nature, a hot temper in his chilly constitution. 'Why, bless the woman, can't you *see* it is?' he says. 'What's the matter now?'

'Murder's the matter!' she burst out. 'For God's sake come back with me. It's at Mrs Crosscapel's lodging-house, number 14, Lehigh Street. A young woman has murdered her husband in the night! With a knife, sir. She says she thinks she did it in her sleep.'

I confess I was startled by this; and the third man on duty (a sergeant) seemed to feel it too. She was a nice-looking young woman, even in her terrified condition, just out of bed, with her clothes huddled on anyhow. I was partial in those days to a tall figure—and she was, as they say, my style. I put a chair for her; and the sergeant poked the fire. As for the Inspector, nothing ever upset *him*. He questioned her as coolly as if it had been a case of petty larceny.

'Have you seen the murdered man?' he asked.

'No, sir.'

'Or the wife?'

'No, sir. I didn't dare go into the room; I only heard about it!'

'Oh? And who are You? One of the lodgers?'

'No, sir. I'm the cook.'

'Isn't there a master in the house?'

'Yes, sir. He's frightened out of his wits. And the housemaid's gone for the Doctor. It all falls on the poor servants, of course. Oh, why did I ever set foot in that horrible house?'

The poor soul burst out crying, and shivered from head to foot. The Inspector made a note of her statement, and then asked her to read it, and sign it with her name. The object of this proceeding was to get her to come near enough to give him the opportunity of smelling her breath. 'When people make extraordinary statements,' he afterwards said to me, 'it sometimes saves trouble to satisfy yourself that they are not drunk. I've known them to be mad—but not often. You will generally find *that* in their eyes.'

She roused herself, and signed her name—'Priscilla Thurlby.' The Inspector's own test proved her to be sober; and her eyes—of a nice light blue colour, mild and pleasant, no doubt, when they were not staring with fear, and red with crying—satisfied him (as I supposed) that she was not mad. He turned the case over to me, in the first instance. I saw that he didn't believe in it, even yet.

'Go back with her to the house,' he says. 'This may be a stupid hoax, or a quarrel exaggerated. See to it yourself, and hear what the Doctor says. If it *is* serious, send word back here directly, and let nobody enter the place or leave it till we come. Stop! You know the form if any statement is volunteered?'

'Yes, sir. I am to caution the persons that whatever they say will be taken down, and may be used against them.'

'Quite right. You'll be an Inspector yourself one of these days. Now, Miss!' With that he dismissed her, under my care.

Lehigh Street was not very far off—about twenty minutes' walk from the station. I confess I thought the Inspector had been rather hard on Priscilla. She was herself naturally angry with him. 'What does he mean,' she says, 'by talking of a hoax? I wish he was as frightened as I am. This is the first time I have been out at service, sir—and I did think I had found a respectable place.'

I said very little to her—feeling, if the truth must be told, rather anxious about the duty committed to me. On reaching the house the door was opened from within, before I could knock. A gentleman stepped out, who proved to be the Doctor. He stopped the moment he saw me.

'You must be careful, policeman,' he says. 'I found the man lying on his back, in bed, dead—with the knife that had killed him left sticking in the wound.'

Hearing this, I felt the necessity of sending at once to the station. Where could I find a trustworthy messenger? I took the liberty of asking the Doctor if he would repeat to the police what he had already said to me. The station was not much out of his way home. He kindly granted my request.

The landlady (Mrs Crosscapel) joined us while we were talking. She was still a young woman; not easily frightened, as far as I could see, even by a murder in the house. Her husband was in the passage behind her. He looked old enough to be her father; and he so trembled with terror that some people might have taken him for the guilty person. I removed the key from the street door, after locking it; and I said to the landlady: 'Nobody must leave the house, or enter the house, till the Inspector comes. I must examine the premises to see if anyone has broken in.'

'There is the key of the area gate,' she said, in answer to me. 'It's always kept locked. Come downstairs, and see for yourself.' Priscilla went with us. Her mistress set her to work to light the kitchen fire. 'Some of us,' says Mrs Crosscapel, 'may be the better for a cup of tea.' I remarked that she took things easy, under the circumstances. She answered that the landlady of a London lodging-house could not afford to lose her wits, no matter what might happen.

I found the gate locked, and the shutters of the kitchen window fastened. The back kitchen and back door were secured in the same way. No person was concealed anywhere. Returning upstairs, I examined the front parlour window. There again, the barred shutters answered for the security of that room. A cracked voice spoke through the door of the back parlour. 'The policeman can come in,' it said, 'if he will promise not to look at me.' I turned to the landlady for information. 'It's my parlour lodger, Miss Mybus,' she said, 'a most respectable lady.' Going into the room, I saw something rolled up perpendicularly in the bed curtains. Miss Mybus had made herself modestly invisible in that way. Having now satisfied my mind about the security of the lower part of the house, and having the keys safe in my pocket, I was ready to go upstairs.

On our way to the upper regions I asked if there had been any visitors on the previous day. There had been only two visitors, friends of the lodgers—and Mrs Crosscapel herself had let them both out. My next inquiry related to the lodgers themselves. On the ground floor there was Miss Mybus. On the first floor (occupying both rooms) Mr Barfield, an old bachelor, employed in a merchant's office. On the second floor, in the front room, Mr John Zebedee, the murdered man, and his wife. In the back room, Mr Deluc; described as a cigar agent, and supposed to be a Creole gentleman from Martinique. In the front garret, Mr and Mrs Crosscapel. In the back garret, the cook and the housemaid. These were the inhabitants, regularly accounted for. I asked about the servants. 'Both excellent characters,' says the landlady, 'or they would not be in my service.'

We reached the second floor, and found the housemaid on the watch outside the door of the front room. Not as nice a woman, personally, as the cook, and sadly frightened of course. Her mistress had posted her, to give the alarm in the case of an outbreak on the part of Mrs Zebedee, kept locked up in the room. My arrival relieved the housemaid of further responsibility. She ran downstairs to her fellow-servant in the kitchen.

I asked Mrs Crosscapel how and when the alarm of the murder had been given.

'Soon after three this morning,' says she, 'I was woke by the screams of Mrs Zebedee. I found her out here on the landing, and Mr Deluc, in great alarm, trying to quiet her. Sleeping in the next room, he had only to open his door, when her screams woke him. "My dear John's murdered! I am the miserable wretch—I did it in my sleep!" She repeated those frantic words over and over again, until she dropped in a swoon. Mr Deluc and I carried her back into the bedroom. We both thought the poor creature had been driven distracted by some dreadful dream. But when we got to the bedside—don't ask me what we saw; the Doctor has told you about it already. I was once a nurse in a hospital, and accustomed, as such, to horrid sights. It turned me cold and giddy, notwithstanding. As for Mr Deluc, I thought *he* would have had a fainting fit next.'

Hearing this, I inquired if Mrs Zebedee had said or done any strange things since she had been Mrs Crosscapel's lodger.

'You think she's mad?' says the landlady. 'And anybody would be of your mind, when a woman accuses herself of murdering her husband in her sleep. All I can say is that, up to this morning, a more quiet, sensible, well-behaved little person than Mrs Zebedee I never met with. Only just married, mind, and as fond of her unfortunate husband as a woman could be. I should have called them a pattern couple, in their own line of life.'

There was no more to be said on the landing. We unlocked the door and went into the room.

II

He lay in bed on his back as the Doctor had described him. On the left side of his nightgown, just over his heart, the blood on the linen told its terrible tale. As well as one could judge, looking unwillingly at a dead face, he must have been a handsome young man in his life-time. It was a sight to sadden anybody—but I think the most painful sensation was when my eyes fell next on his miserable wife.

She was down on the floor, crouched up in a corner—a dark little woman, smartly dressed in gay colours. Her black hair and her big brown eyes made the horrid paleness of her face look even more deadly white than perhaps it really was. She stared straight at us without appearing to see us. We spoke to her, and she never answered a word. She might have been dead—like her husband—except that she perpetually picked at her fingers, and shuddered every now and then as if she was cold. I went to her and tried to lift her up. She shrank back with a cry that well-nigh frightened me—not because it was loud, but because it was more like the cry of some animal than of a human being. However quietly she might have behaved in the landlady's previous experience of her, she was beside herself now. I might have been moved by a natural pity for her, or I might have been completely upset in my mind—I only know this, I could not persuade myself that she was guilty. I even said to Mrs Crosscapel, 'I don't believe she did it.'

While I spoke, there was a knock at the door. I went downstairs at once, and admitted (to my great relief) the Inspector, accompanied by one of our men.

He waited downstairs to hear my report, and he approved of what I had done. 'It looks as if the murder had been committed by somebody in the house.' Saying this, he left the man below, and went up with me to the second floor.

Before he had been a minute in the room, he discovered an object which had escaped my observation.

It was the knife that had done the deed.

The Doctor had found it left in the body—had withdrawn it to probe the wound—and had laid it on the bedside table. It was one of those useful knives which contain a saw, a corkscrew, and other like implements. The big blade fastened back, when open, with a spring. Except where the blood was on it, it was as bright as when it had been purchased. A small metal plate was fastened to the horn handle, containing an inscription, only partly engraved, which ran thus: '*To John Zebedee, from——*' There it stopped, strangely enough.

Who or what had interrupted the engraver's work? It was impossible even to guess. Nevertheless, the Inspector was encouraged.

'This ought to help us,' he said—and then he gave an attentive ear (looking all the while at the poor creature in the corner) to what Mrs Crosscapel had to tell him.

The landlady having done, he said he must now see the lodger who slept in the next bedchamber.

Mr Deluc made his appearance, standing at the door of the room, and turning away his head with horror from the sight inside.

He was wrapped in a splendid blue dressing-gown, with a golden girdle and trimmings. His scanty brownish hair curled (whether artificially or not, I am unable to say) in little ringlets. His complexion was yellow; his greenish-brown eyes were of the sort called 'goggle'— they looked as if they might drop out of his face, if you held a spoon under them. His moustache and goat's beard were beautifully oiled; and, to complete his equipment, he had a long black cigar in his mouth.

'It isn't insensibility to this terrible tragedy,' he explained. 'My nerves have been shattered, Mr Policeman, and I can only repair the mischief in this way. Be pleased to excuse and feel for me.'

The Inspector questioned this witness sharply and closely. He was not a man to be misled by appearances; but I could see that he was far from liking, or even trusting, Mr Deluc. Nothing came of the examination, except what Mrs Crosscapel had in substance already mentioned to me. Mr Deluc returned to his room.

'How long has he been lodging with you?' the Inspector asked, as soon as his back was turned.

'Nearly a year,' the landlady answered.

'Did he give you a reference?'

'As good a reference as I could wish for.' Thereupon, she mentioned the names of a well-known firm of cigar merchants in the City. The Inspector noted the information in his pocket-book.

I would rather not relate in detail what happened next: it is too distressing to be dwelt on. Let me only say that the poor demented woman was taken away in a cab to the station-house. The Inspector possessed himself of the knife, and of a book found on the floor, called 'The World of Sleep.' The portmanteau containing the luggage was locked —and then the door of the room was secured, the keys in both cases being left in my charge. My instructions were to remain in the house, and allow nobody to leave it, until I heard again shortly from the Inspector.

III

The coroner's inquest was adjourned; and the examination before the magistrate ended in a remand—Mrs Zebedee being in no condition to understand the proceedings in either case. The surgeon reported her to be completely prostrated by a terrible nervous shock. When he was asked if he considered her to have been a sane woman before the murder took place, he refused to answer positively at that time.

A week passed. The murdered man was buried; his old father attending the funeral. I occasionally saw Mrs Crosscapel, and the two servants, for the purpose of getting such further information as was thought desirable. Both the cook and the housemaid had given their month's notice to quit; declining, in the interest of their characters, to remain in a house which had been the scene of a murder. Mr Deluc's nerves led also to his removal; his rest was now disturbed by frightful dreams. He paid the necessary forfeit-money, and left without notice. The first-floor lodger, Mr Barfield, kept his rooms, but obtained leave of absence from his employers, and took refuge with some friends in the country. Miss Mybus alone remained in the parlours. 'When I am comfortable,' the old lady said, 'nothing moves me, at my age. A murder up two pairs of stairs is nearly the same thing as a murder in the next house. Distance, you see, makes all the difference.'

It mattered little to the police what the lodgers did. We had men in plain clothes watching the house night and day. Everybody who went away was privately followed; and the police in the district to which they retired were warned to keep an eye on them, after that. As long as we failed to put Mrs Zebedee's extraordinary statement to any sort of test— to say nothing of having proved unsuccessful, thus far, in tracing the knife to its purchaser—we were bound to let no person living under Mrs Crosscapel's roof, on the night of the murder, slip through our fingers.

IV

In a fortnight more, Mrs Zebedee had sufficiently recovered to make the necessary statement—after the preliminary caution addressed to persons in such cases. The surgeon had no hesitation, now, in reporting her to be a sane woman.

Her station in life had been domestic service. She had lived for four years in her last place as lady's-maid, with a family residing in Dorsetshire. The one objection to her had been the occasional infirmity of sleep-walking, which made it necessary that one of the other female servants should sleep in the same room, with the door locked and the key under her pillow. In all other respects the lady's-maid was described by her mistress as 'a perfect treasure.'

In the last six months of her service, a young man named John Zebedee entered the house (with a written character*) as footman. He soon fell in love with the nice little lady's-maid, and she heartily returned the feeling. They might have waited for years before they were in a pecuniary position to marry, but for the death of Zebedee's uncle, who left him a little fortune of two thousand pounds. They were now, for persons in their station, rich enough to please themselves; and they were married from the house in which they had served together, the little daughters of the family showing their affection for Mrs Zebedee by acting as her bridesmaids.

The young husband was a careful man. He decided to employ his small capital to the best advantage, by sheep-farming in Australia. His wife made no objection; she was ready to go wherever John went.

Accordingly they spent their short honeymoon in London, so as to see for themselves the vessel in which their passage was to be taken. They went to Mrs Crosscapel's lodging-house because Zebedee's uncle had always stayed there when he was in London. Ten days were to pass before the day of embarkation arrived. This gave the young couple a welcome holiday, and a prospect of amusing themselves to their hearts' content among the sights and shows of the great city.

On their first evening in London they went to the theatre. They were both accustomed to the fresh air of the country, and they felt half stifled by the heat and the gas. However, they were so pleased with an amusement which was new to them that they went to another theatre on the next evening. On this second occasion, John Zebedee found the heat unendurable. They left the theatre, and got back to their lodgings towards ten o'clock.

Let the rest be told in the words used by Mrs Zebedee herself. She said:

'We sat talking for a little while in our room, and John's headache got worse and worse. I persuaded him to go to bed, and I put out the candle (the fire giving sufficient light to undress by), so that he might the sooner fall asleep. But he was too restless to sleep. He asked me to read him something. Books always made him drowsy at the best of times.

'I had not myself begun to undress. So I lit the candle again, and I opened the only book I had. John had noticed it at the railway bookstall by the name of "The World of Sleep." He used to joke with me about my being a sleep-walker; and he said, "Here's something that's sure to interest you"—and he made me a present of the book.

'Before I had read to him for more than half an hour he was fast asleep. Not feeling that way inclined, I went on reading to myself.

'The book did indeed interest me. There was one terrible story which took a hold on my mind—the story of a man who stabbed his own wife in a sleep-walking dream. I thought of putting down my book after that, and then changed my mind again and went on. The next chapters were not so interesting; they were full of learned accounts of why we fall asleep, and what our brains do in that state, and such like. It ended in my falling asleep, too, in my arm-chair by the fireside.

'I don't know what o'clock it was when I went to sleep. I don't know how long I slept, or whether I dreamed or not. The candle and the fire had both burned out, and it was pitch dark when I woke. I can't even say why I woke— unless it was the coldness of the room.

'There was a spare candle on the chimney-piece. I found the match-box, and got a light. Then, for the first time, I turned round towards the bed; and I saw——'

She had seen the dead body of her husband, murdered while she was unconsciously at his side—and she fainted, poor creature, at the bare remembrance of it.

The proceedings were adjourned. She received every possible care and attention; the chaplain looking after her welfare as well as the surgeon.

I have said nothing of the evidence of the landlady and the servants. It was taken as a mere formality. What little they knew proved nothing against Mrs Zebedee. The police made no discoveries that supported her first frantic accusation of herself. Her master and mistress, where she had been last in service, spoke of her in the highest terms. We were at a complete deadlock.

It had been thought best not to surprise Mr Deluc, as yet, by citing him as a witness. The action of the law was, however, hurried in this case by a private communication received from the chaplain.

After twice seeing, and speaking with, Mrs Zebedee, the reverend gentleman was persuaded that she had no more to do than himself with the murder of her husband. He did not consider that he was justified in repeating a confidential communication—he would only recommend that Mr Deluc should be summoned to appear at the next examination. This advice was followed.

The police had no evidence against Mrs Zebedee when the inquiry was resumed. To assist the ends of justice she was now put into the witness-box. The discovery of her murdered husband, when she woke in the small hours of the morning, was passed over as rapidly as possible. Only three questions of importance were put to her.

First, the knife was produced. Had she ever seen it in her husband's possession? Never. Did she know anything about it? Nothing whatever.

Secondly: Did she, or did her husband, lock the bedroom door when they returned from the theatre? No. Did she afterwards lock the door herself? No.

Thirdly: Had she any sort of reason to give for supposing that she had murdered her husband in a sleep-walking dream? No reason, except that she was beside herself at the time, and the book put the thought into her head.

After this the other witnesses were sent out of court. The motive for the chaplain's communication now appeared.

Mrs Zebedee was asked if anything unpleasant had occurred between Mr Deluc and herself.

Yes. He had caught her alone on the stairs at the lodging-
house; had presumed to make love to her; and had carried
the insult still further by attempting to kiss her. She had
slapped his face, and had declared that her husband should
know of it, if his misconduct was repeated. He was in a
furious rage at having his face slapped; and he said to her:
'Madam, you may live to regret this.'

After consultation, and at the request of our Inspector, it
was decided to keep Mr Deluc in ignorance of Mrs Zebedee's statement for the present. When the witnesses were
recalled, he gave the same evidence which he had already
given to the Inspector—and he was then asked if he knew
anything of the knife. He looked at it without any guilty
signs in his face, and swore that he had never seen it until
that moment. The resumed inquiry ended, and still nothing
had been discovered.

But we kept an eye on Mr Deluc. Our next effort was to
try if we could associate him with the purchase of the knife.

Here again (there really did seem to be a sort of fatality in
this case) we reached no useful result. It was easy enough to
find out the wholesale cutlers, who had manufactured the
knife at Sheffield, by the mark on the blade. But they made
tens of thousands of such knives, and disposed of them to
retail dealers all over Great Britain—to say nothing of
foreign parts. As to finding out the person who had engraved the imperfect inscription (without knowing where,
or by whom, the knife had been purchased) we might as well
have looked for the proverbial needle in the bundle of hay.
Our last resource was to have the knife photographed, with
the inscribed side uppermost, and to send copies to every
police-station in the kingdom.

At the same time we reckoned up Mr Deluc—I mean
that we made investigations into his past life—on the
chance that he and the murdered man might have known
each other, and might have had a quarrel, or a rivalry about
a woman, on some former occasion. No such discovery
rewarded us.

We found Deluc to have led a dissipated life, and to have mixed with very bad company. But he had kept out of reach of the law. A man may be a profligate vagabond; may insult a lady; may say threatening things to her, in the first stinging sensation of having his face slapped—but it doesn't follow from these blots on his character that he has murdered her husband in the dead of the night.

Once more, then, when we were called upon to report ourselves, we had no evidence to produce. The photographs failed to discover the owner of the knife, and to explain its interrupted inscription. Poor Mrs Zebedee was allowed to go back to her friends, on entering into her own recognisance to appear again if called upon. Articles in the newspapers began to inquire how many more murderers would succeed in baffling the police. The authorities at the Treasury offered a reward of a hundred pounds for the necessary information. And the weeks passed, and nobody claimed the reward.

Our Inspector was not a man to be easily beaten. More inquiries and examinations followed. It is needless to say anything about them. We were defeated—and there, so far as the police and the public were concerned, was an end of it.

The assassination of the poor young husband soon passed out of notice, like other undiscovered murders. One obscure person only was foolish enough, in his leisure hours, to persist in trying to solve the problem of Who Killed Zebedee? He felt that he might rise to the highest position in the police-force if he succeeded where his elders and betters had failed—and he held to his own little ambition, though everybody laughed at him. In plain English, I was the man.

V

Without meaning it, I have told my story ungratefully.

There were two persons who saw nothing ridiculous in my resolution to continue the investigation, single-handed. One of them was Miss Mybus; and the other was the cook, Priscilla Thurlby.

Mentioning the lady first, Miss Mybus was indignant at the resigned manner in which the police accepted their defeat. She was a little bright-eyed wiry woman; and she spoke her mind freely.

'This comes home to me,' she said. 'Just look back for a year or two. I can call to mind two cases of persons found murdered in London—and the assassins have never been traced. I am a person too; and I ask myself if my turn is not coming next. You're a nice-looking fellow—and I like your pluck and perseverance. Come here as often as you think right; and say you are my visitor, if they make any difficulty about letting you in. One thing more! I have nothing particular to do, and I am no fool. Here, in the parlours, I see everybody who comes into the house or goes out of the house. Leave me your address—I may get some information for you yet.'

With the best intentions, Miss Mybus found no opportunity of helping me. Of the two, Priscilla Thurlby seemed more likely to be of use.

In the first place, she was sharp and active, and (not having succeeded in getting another situation as yet) was mistress of her own movements.

In the second place, she was a woman I could trust. Before she left home to try domestic service in London, the parson of her native parish gave her a written testimonial, of which I append a copy. Thus it ran:

I gladly recommend Priscilla Thurlby for any respectable employment which she may be competent to undertake. Her father and mother are infirm old people, who have lately suffered a diminution of their income; and they have a younger daughter to maintain. Rather than be a burden on her parents, Priscilla goes to London to find domestic employment, and to devote her earnings to the assistance of her father and mother. This circumstance speaks for itself. I have known the family many years; and I only regret that I have no vacant place in my own household which I can offer to this good girl.

(Signed)

HENRY DERRINGTON, Rector of Roth.

After reading those words, I could safely ask Priscilla to help me in reopening the mysterious murder case to some good purpose.

My notion was that the proceedings of the persons in Mrs Crosscapel's house, had not been closely enough inquired into yet. By way of continuing the investigation, I asked Priscilla if she could tell me anything which associated the housemaid with Mr Deluc. She was unwilling to answer. 'I may be casting suspicion on an innocent person,' she said. 'Besides, I was for so short a time the housemaid's fellow servant——'

'You slept in the same room with her,' I remarked; 'and you had opportunities of observing her conduct towards the lodgers. If they had asked you, at the examination, what I now ask, you would have answered as an honest woman.'

To this argument she yielded. I heard from her certain particulars which threw a new light on Mr Deluc, and on the case generally. On that information I acted. It was slow work, owing to the claims on me of my regular duties; but with Priscilla's help, I steadily advanced towards the end I had in view.

Besides this, I owed another obligation to Mrs Crosscapel's nice-looking cook. The confession must be made sooner or later—and I may as well make it now. I first knew what love was, thanks to Priscilla. I had delicious kisses, thanks to Priscilla. And, when I asked if she would marry me, she didn't say No. She looked, I must own, a little sadly, and she said: 'How can two such poor people as we are ever hope to marry?' To this I answered: 'It won't be long before I lay my hand on the clue which my Inspector has failed to find. I shall be in a position to marry you, my dear, when that time comes.'

At our next meeting we spoke of her parents. I was now her promised husband. Judging by what I had heard of the proceedings of other people in my position, it seemed to be only right that I should be made known to her father and mother. She entirely agreed with me; and she wrote home that day, to tell them to expect us at the end of the week.

I took my turn of night-duty, and so gained my liberty for the greater part of the next day. I dressed myself in plain clothes, and we took our tickets on the railway for Yateland, being the nearest station to the village in which Priscilla's parents lived.

VI

The train stopped, as usual, at the big town of Waterbank. Supporting herself by her needle, while she was still unprovided with a situation, Priscilla had been at work late in the night—she was tired and thirsty. I left the carriage to get her some soda-water. The stupid girl in the refreshment room failed to pull the cork out of the bottle, and refused to let me help her. She took a corkscrew, and used it crookedly. I lost all patience, and snatched the bottle out of her hand. Just as I drew the cork, the bell rang on the platform. I only waited to pour the soda-water into a glass—but the train was moving as I left the refreshment-room. The porters stopped me when I tried to jump on to the step of the carriage. I was left behind.

As soon as I had recovered my temper, I looked at the time-table. We had reached Waterbank at five minutes past one. By good-luck, the next train was due at forty-four minutes past one, and arrived at Yateland (the next station) ten minutes afterwards. I could only hope that Priscilla would look at the time-table too, and wait for me. If I had attempted to walk the distance between the two places, I should have lost time instead of saving it. The interval before me was not very long; I occupied it in looking over the town.

Speaking with all due respect to the inhabitants, Waterbank (to other people) is a dull place. I went up one street and down another—and stopped to look at a shop which struck me; not from anything in itself, but because it was the only shop in the street with the shutters closed.

A bill was posted on the shutters, announcing that the place was to let. The out-going tradesman's name and business, announced in the customary painted letters, ran thus:—*James Wycomb, Cutler, etc.*

For the first time, it occurred to me that we had forgotten an obstacle in our way, when we distributed our photographs of the knife. We had none of us remembered that a certain proportion of cutlers might be placed, by circumstances, out of our reach—either by retiring from business or by becoming bankrupt. I always carried a copy of the photograph about me; and I thought to myself, 'Here is the ghost of a chance of tracing the knife to Mr Deluc!'

The shop door was opened, after I had twice rung the bell, by an old man, very dirty and very deaf. He said: 'You had better go upstairs, and speak to Mr Scorrier—top of the house.'

I put my lips to the old fellow's ear-trumpet, and asked who Mr Scorrier was.

'Brother-in-law to Mr Wycomb. Mr Wycomb's dead. If you want to buy the business apply to Mr Scorrier.'

Receiving that reply, I went upstairs, and found Mr Scorrier engaged in engraving a brass door-plate. He was a middle-aged man, with a cadaverous face and dim eyes. After the necessary apologies, I produced my photograph.

'May I ask, sir, if you know anything of the inscription on that knife?' I said.

He took his magnifying glass to look at it.

'This is curious,' he remarked quietly. 'I remember the queer name—Zebedee. Yes, sir; I did the engraving, as far as it goes. I wonder what prevented me from finishing it?'

The name of Zebedee, and the unfinished inscription on the knife, had appeared in every English newspaper. He took the matter so coolly, that I was doubtful how to interpret his answer. Was it possible that he had not seen the account of the murder? Or was he an accomplice with prodigious powers of self-control?

'Excuse me,' I said, 'do you read the newspapers?'

'Never! My eyesight is failing me. I abstain from reading, in the interests of my occupation.'

'Have you not heard the name of Zebedee mentioned—particularly by people who do read the newspapers?'

'Very likely; but I didn't attend to it. When the day's work is done, I take my walk. Then I have my supper, my drop of grog, and my pipe. Then I go to bed. A dull existence you think, I dare say! I had a miserable life, sir, when I was young. A bare subsistence, and a little rest, before the last perfect rest in the grave— that is all I want. The world has gone by me long ago. So much the better.'

The poor man spoke honestly. I was ashamed of having doubted him. I returned to the subject of the knife.

'Do you know where it was purchased, and by whom?' I asked.

'My memory is not so good as it was,' he said; 'but I have got something by me that helps it.'

He took from a cupboard a dirty old scrap-book. Strips of paper, with writing on them, were pasted on the pages, as well as I could see. He turned to an index, or table of contents, and opened a page. Something like a flash of life showed itself on his dismal face.

'Ha! now I remember,' he said. 'The knife was bought of my late brother-in-law, in the shop downstairs. It all comes back to me, sir. A person in a state of frenzy burst into this very room, and snatched the knife away from me, when I was only half way through the inscription!'

I felt that I was now close on discovery. 'May I see what it is that has assisted your memory?' I asked.

'Oh yes. You must know, sir, I live by engraving inscriptions and addresses, and I paste in this book the manuscript instructions which I receive, with marks of my own on the margin. For one thing, they serve as a reference to new customers. And for another thing, they do certainly help my memory.'

He turned the book towards me, and pointed to a slip of paper which occupied the lower half of a page.

I read the complete inscription, intended for the knife that killed Zebedee, and written as follows:

'To John Zebedee. From Priscilla Thurlby.'

VII

I declare that it is impossible for me to describe what I felt, when Priscilla's name confronted me like a written confession of guilt. How long it was before I recovered myself in some degree, I cannot say. The only thing I can clearly call to mind is, that I frightened the poor engraver.

My first desire was to get possession of the manuscript inscription. I told him I was a policeman, and summoned him to assist me in the discovery of a crime. I even offered him money. He drew back from my hand. 'You shall have it for nothing,' he said, 'if you will only go away and never come here again.' He tried to cut it out of the page—but his trembling hands were helpless. I cut it out myself, and attempted to thank him. He wouldn't hear me. 'Go away!' he said, 'I don't like the look of you.'

It may be here objected that I ought not to have felt so sure as I did of the woman's guilt, until I had got more evidence against her. The knife might have been stolen from her, supposing she was the person who had snatched it out of the engraver's hands, and might have been afterwards used by the thief to commit the murder. All very true. But I never had a moment's doubt in my own mind, from the time when I read the damnable line in the engraver's book.

I went back to the railway without any plan in my head. The train by which I had proposed to follow her had left Waterbank. The next train that arrived was for London. I took my place in it—still without any plan in my head.

At Charing Cross a friend met me. He said, 'You're looking miserably ill. Come and have a drink.'

I went with him. The liquor was what I really wanted; it strung me up, and cleared my head. He went his way, and I went mine. In a little while more, I determined what I would do.

In the first place, I decided to resign my situation in the police, from a motive which will presently appear. In the second place, I took a bed at a public-house. She would no doubt return to London, and she would go to my lodgings to find out why I had broken my appointment. To bring to justice the one woman whom I had dearly loved was too cruel a duty for a poor creature like me. I preferred leaving the police force. On the other hand, if she and I met before time had helped me to control myself, I had a horrid fear that I might turn murderer next, and kill her then and there. The wretch had not only all but misled me into marrying her, but also into charging the innocent housemaid with being concerned in the murder.

The same night I hit on a way of clearing up such doubts as still harassed my mind. I wrote to the rector of Roth, informing him that I was engaged to marry her, and asking if he would tell me (in consideration of my position) what her former relations might have been with the person named John Zebedee.

By return of post I got this reply:—

SIR,—Under the circumstances, I think I am bound to tell you confidentially what the friends and well-wishers of Priscilla have kept secret, for her sake.

Zebedee was in service in this neighbourhood. I am sorry to say it, of a man who has come to such a miserable end—but his behaviour to Priscilla proves him to have been a vicious and heartless wretch. They were engaged—and, I add with indignation, he tried to seduce her under a promise of marriage. Her virtue resisted him, and he pretended to be ashamed of himself. The banns were published in my church. On the next day Zebedee disappeared, and cruelly deserted her. He was a capable servant; and I believe he got another place. I leave you to imagine what the poor girl suffered under the outrage inflicted on her. Going to London, with my recommendation, she answered the first advertisement that she saw, and was unfortunate enough to begin her career in domestic service in the very lodging house, to which (as I gather from the newspaper report of the murder) the man Zebedee took the person whom he married, after deserting Priscilla. Be assured that you are about to unite yourself to an excellent girl, and accept my best wishes for your happiness.

It was plain from this that neither the rector nor the parents and friends knew anything of the purchase of the knife. The one miserable man who knew the truth, was the man who had asked her to be his wife.

I owed it to myself—at least so it seemed to me—not to let it be supposed that I, too, had meanly deserted her. Dreadful as the prospect was, I felt that I must see her once more, and for the last time.

She was at work when I went into her room. As I opened the door she started to her feet. Her cheeks reddened, and her eyes flashed with anger. I stepped forward—and she saw my face. My face silenced her.

I spoke in the fewest words I could find.

'I have been to the cutler's shop at Waterbank,' I said. 'There is the unfinished inscription on the knife, completed in your handwriting. I could hang you by a word. God forgive me—I can't say the word.'

Her bright complexion turned to a dreadful clay-colour. Her eyes were fixed and staring, like the eyes of a person in a fit. She stood before me, still and silent. Without saying more, I dropped the inscription into the fire. Without saying more, I left her.

I never saw her again.

VIII

But I heard from her a few days later.

The letter has been long since burnt. I wish I could have forgotten it as well. It sticks to my memory. If I die with my senses about me, Priscilla's letter will be my last recollection on earth.

In substance it repeated what the rector had already told me. Further, it informed me that she had bought the knife as a keepsake for Zebedee, in place of a similar knife which he had lost. On the Saturday, she made the purchase, and left it to be engraved. On the Sunday, the banns were put up. On the Monday, she was deserted; and she snatched the knife from the table while the engraver was at work.

She only knew that Zebedee had added a new sting to the insult inflicted on her, when he arrived at the lodgings with his wife. Her duties as cook kept her in the kitchen—and Zebedee never discovered that she was in the house. I still remember the last lines of her confession:

The devil entered into me when I tried their door, on my way up to bed, and found it unlocked, and listened a while, and peeped in. I saw them by the dying light of the candle—one asleep on the bed, the other asleep by the fireside. I had the knife in my hand, and the thought came to me to do it, so that they might hang *her* for the murder. I couldn't take the knife out again, when I had done it.

Mind this! I did really like you——I didn't say Yes, because you could hardly hang your own wife, if you found out who killed Zebedee.

Since that past time I have never heard again of Priscilla Thurlby; I don't know whether she is living or dead. Many people may think I deserve to be hanged myself for not having given her up to the gallows. They may, perhaps, be disappointed when they see this confession, and hear that I have died decently in my bed. I don't blame them. I am a penitent sinner. I wish all merciful Christians good-bye for ever.

EXPLANATORY NOTES

Abbreviations

AD   *After Dark* (1856): two-volume collection containing six stories with a linking narrative.

FD   *The Frozen Deep and Other Tales* (1874): two-volume collection containing three stories.

HW   *Household Words* (1850–9): weekly journal edited by Dickens.

LN   *Little Novels* (1887): three-volume collection containing fourteen stories.

QH   *The Queen of Hearts* (1859): three-volume collection containing eleven stories with a linking narrative.

A Terribly Strange Bed

First published in *HW* 109 (24 Apr. 1852) and the first of Collins's many contributions to that magazine; collected in *AD*.

5   *Rouge et Noir*: card game in which the stakes are placed on any of two red and two black diamond-shaped spots marked on the table.

7   *Austerlitz*: battle in which Napoleon defeated the Russians and Austrians in 1805.

11   *'Voyage autour de Ma Chambre'*: popular work, published in 1794, by Xavier de Maistre (1763–1852), French soldier, artist, and novelist.

12   *Guido Fawkes*: Guy Fawkes (1570–1606), the best-known of the conspirators involved in the Gunpowder Plot, his forename here being facetiously Italianized.

13   *Childe Harold*: Byron's celebrated poem, *Childe Harold's Pilgrimage*, published between 1812 and 1818.

16   *entresol*: mezzanine floor.

17   *posse comitatus*: the Latin phrase, usually abbreviated to 'posse', signifies a group of citizens who can be called on to assist the authorities in pursuing a criminal or preserving law and order.

A Stolen Letter

Originally published as 'The Fourth Poor Traveller' in 'The Seven Poor Travellers', a jointly-authored group of linked stories that formed the 1854 Extra Christmas Number of *HW*, published on 14 December 1854. The other contributors were Dickens, G. A. Sala, Adelaide Anne Procter, and Eliza Lynn. Collins's contribution, for which he received ten pounds, is the second longest story in the group, exceeded only by Dickens's opening story. Reprinted in *AD*.

21 *hearth-stoned*: cleaned with a hearthstone, a soft stone used on floors.

38 *jockeyed*: cheated.

Mad Monkton

Originally published in two instalments in *Fraser's Magazine*, November–December 1855, under the title 'The Monktons of Wincot Abbey' and described as 'edited by Wilkie Collins'; reprinted in *QH* as 'Mad Monkton'.

47 *hartshorn*: sal volatile (ammonium carbonate), used as smelling salts.

97 *'breached to'*: possibly an error for 'broached to' – i.e., veered suddenly so as to turn the ship's side to windward.
   on her beam ends: having keeled over through an angle of ninety degrees.

The Ostler

Originally published as the second story in 'The Holly-Tree Inn', a jointly-authored group of linked stories that formed the 1855 Extra Christmas Number of *HW*, published on 15 December 1855. The other contributors were Dickens, William Howitt, Adelaide Anne Procter, and Harriet Parr. Collins received sixteen guineas for his contribution, the longest in the group. Dickens had written to him on 30 September: 'Of course the H.W. stories are at your disposition. At the office I will tell you the idea of the Christmas number, which would put you in train, I hope, for a story.' Reprinted in *QH* under the new title of 'Brother Morgan's Story of the Dream-Woman'; expanded and adapted (as 'The Dream-Woman') for Collins's American reading tour; further expanded for inclusion in *FD*.

The Diary of Anne Rodway

Originally published in two instalments in *HW* 330–1, pp. 1–7, 30–8 (19 and 26 July 1856). Reprinted as 'Brother Owen's Story of Anne Rodway' in *QH*.

144 the first of the two instalments for the original magazine publication ends here.

147 *knock up*: fall ill (slang).

148 *clue*: thread, especially one used to provide guidance into or out of a maze or labyrinth.
   Rosamond's Bower: various early texts, including a ballad collected in Percy's *Reliques of Ancient English Poetry*, tell the story of Rosamond Clifford, who lived in the twelfth century and was probably a mistress of Henry II. According to the legend, the king kept her in a kind of maze, but his queen discovered her whereabouts by following a thread and brought about her death.

153 *cribbed*: stole or pilfered (slang).

The Lady of Glenwith Grange

First published in *AD*, where it is the only item not to have appeared previously in a magazine.

166 *Izaak Walton*: Walton (1593–1683) published *The Compleat Angler* in 1653.

169 *Angola cat*: a long-haired variety of cat ('Angola' is a corruption of 'Angora', the former name of Ankara).

180 *'Mounseer'*: vulgar corruption of 'Monsieur'.

185 *scouted*: exposed.

187 *Travaux Forcés*: transportation with hard labour.

The Dead Hand

Originally published in *HW* 394 (10 Oct. 1857), as part of the second of the five chapters of 'The Lazy Tour of Two Idle Apprentices', written jointly by Collins and Dickens. Serialization of 'The Lazy Tour' had begun the previous week. 'Chapter the Second' opens with an introductory section by Dickens, Collins's story occupying pp. 340–9 of the magazine. Reprinted in *QH* as 'Brother Morgan's Story of the Dead Hand'.

195 *Doncaster*: Collins and Dickens had been 'in the town of
      Doncaster . . . in the middle of the month of September'
      some three weeks before the story was published, and had
      stayed at the Angel Hotel. Ellen Ternan was then appearing
      at the Theatre Royal.

The Biter Bit

Originally published as 'Who is the Thief?', with the subtitle
'(Extracted from the Correspondence of the London Police)', in
the *Atlantic Monthly* (Apr. 1858); reprinted as 'Brother Griffiths'
Story of the Biter Bit' in *QH*.

234 *cigar-divan*: room in a coffee-shop or similar establishment
      set aside for smoking.

John Jago's Ghost

Serialized under this title in the British magazine *The Home Journal*
from 27 December 1873 to February 1874, and almost simultaneously, but under the title 'The Dead Alive', in *The New York
Fireside Companion* from 29 December 1873 to 19 January 1874.
Reprinted in *FD* under the former title.

252 *Dumas the elder*: Alexandre Dumas (1802–70), prolific
      French novelist and dramatist.

The Clergyman's Confession

First published in two instalments in the *Canadian Monthly* (Aug.–
Sept. 1875), where it appears with the above title. Retitled 'Miss
Jéromette and the Clergyman' for its republication in *LN*.

308 *Temple*: this legal quarter near the Strand housed two of
      London's four inns of court, the Inner Temple and Middle
      Temple.
      Cremorne: by the time the story was written, the Cremorne
      Gardens in Chelsea had become notorious as a haunt of
      prostitutes, and many readers would have been aware of this.
      The Gardens were closed in 1877, not long after the story's
      first appearance.

The Captain's Last Love

Published with the above title in *The Spirit of the Times* (23 Dec. 1876); retitled 'Mr Captain and the Nymph' for its republication in *LN*. It may possibly use material from *Iolani*, Collins's first novel — set in Tahiti, written in 1884, and never published. The manuscript, lost for nearly a century and a half, recently (1991) turned up and is in the hands of a private collector; preparations for its publication are in hand.

352   *park*: area in which military equipment is placed.

Who Killed Zebedee?

Published with the above title in *The Seaside Library* (26 Jan. 1881); retitled 'Mr Policeman and the Cook' for its republication in *LN*.

364   *character*: written reference.

ANTHONY TROLLOPE

An Autobiography

Ayala's Angel

Barchester Towers

The Belton Estate

The Bertrams

Can You Forgive Her?

The Claverings

Cousin Henry

Doctor Thorne

Doctor Wortle's School

The Duke's Children

Early Short Stories

The Eustace Diamonds

An Eye for an Eye

Framley Parsonage

He Knew He Was Right

Lady Anna

The Last Chronicle of Barset

Later Short Stories

Miss Mackenzie

Mr Scarborough's Family

Orley Farm

Phineas Finn

Phineas Redux

The Prime Minister

Rachel Ray

The Small House at Allington

La Vendée

The Warden

The Way We Live Now

A SELECTION OF **OXFORD WORLD'S CLASSICS**

HANS CHRISTIAN ANDERSEN	**Fairy Tales**
J. M. BARRIE	**Peter Pan in Kensington Gardens** and **Peter and Wendy**
L. FRANK BAUM	**The Wonderful Wizard of Oz**
FRANCES HODGSON BURNETT	**The Secret Garden**
LEWIS CARROLL	**Alice's Adventures in Wonderland** and **Through the Looking-Glass**
CARLO COLLODI	**The Adventures of Pinocchio**
KENNETH GRAHAME	**The Wind in the Willows**
THOMAS HUGHES	**Tom Brown's Schooldays**
CHARLES KINGSLEY	**The Water-Babies**
GEORGE MACDONALD	**The Princess and the Goblin** and **The Princess and Curdie**
EDITH NESBIT	**Five Children and It** **The Railway Children**
ANNA SEWELL	**Black Beauty**
JOHANN DAVID WYSS	**The Swiss Family Robinson**

THE OXFORD SHERLOCK HOLMES

Arthur Conan Doyle

The Adventures of Sherlock Holmes
The Case-Book of Sherlock Holmes
His Last Bow
The Hound of the Baskervilles
The Memoirs of Sherlock Holmes
The Return of Sherlock Holmes
The Valley of Fear
Sherlock Holmes Stories
The Sign of the Four
A Study in Scarlet

The
Oxford
World's
Classics
Website

www.worldsclassics.co.uk

- Information about new titles
- Explore the full range of Oxford World's Classics
- Links to other literary sites and the main OUP webpage
- Imaginative competitions, with bookish prizes
- Peruse *Compass*, the Oxford World's Classics magazine
- Articles by editors
- Extracts from Introductions
- A forum for discussion and feedback on the series
- Special information for teachers and lecturers

www.worldsclassics.co.uk

American Literature

British and Irish Literature

Children's Literature

Classics and Ancient Literature

Colonial Literature

Eastern Literature

European Literature

History

Medieval Literature

Oxford English Drama

Poetry

Philosophy

Politics

Religion

The Oxford Shakespeare

A complete list of Oxford Paperbacks, including Oxford World's Classics, OPUS, Past Masters, Oxford Authors, Oxford Shakespeare, Oxford Drama, and Oxford Paperback Reference, is available in the UK from the Academic Division Publicity Department, Oxford University Press, Great Clarendon Street, Oxford OX2 6DP.

In the USA, complete lists are available from the Paperbacks Marketing Manager, Oxford University Press, 198 Madison Avenue, New York, NY 10016.

Oxford Paperbacks are available from all good bookshops. In case of difficulty, customers in the UK can order direct from Oxford University Press Bookshop, Freepost, 116 High Street, Oxford OX1 4BR, enclosing full payment. Please add 10 per cent of published price for postage and packing.